All This Time

Praise for the Walker Family Series

"Tagg gets better and better with each new book. Beckett and Kit's story is more than just their story; it expands to the entire Walker and Danby families as well as the community of Maple Valley in a way that will cement Tagg as a go-to author in this genre. Told poignantly and with a good deal of toe-curling swoon-worthiness, the reunion of these childhood best friends is sweet and funny and sincere.

—*Romantic Times Book Reviews* on *Keep Holding On*

"Melissa Tagg writes with humor, depth and sincerity. The story of Beckett and Kit will keep you 'holding on' until the very last swoon-worthy page. Tagg is one of romance's finest authors."

—*Rachel Hauck*, New York Times *& USA Today* Bestselling Author, on *Keep Holding On*

"Tagg captures the familiar cadence of life in a rural Midwest community while bringing gentle compassion to such sensitive topics as grief over the death of a spouse. A thread of historical drama adds an entertaining element of tension to the book's quintessentially American plot, and its inspirational themes are prominent yet seamlessly woven into the dialogue and relationships. An engaging sequel and satisfying read, especially for fans of small-town romances."

—*Booklist* on *Like Never Before*

"*Like Never Before*, second in Tagg's Walker Family series, follows a close-knit, loving family as they struggle with life's uncertainties and losses. Endearing characters, deft writing, and an interesting historical mystery will intrigue readers, but the real gem is Tagg's well-handled theme of the need to trust in a loving, sovereign God."

—*CBA Retailers + Resources* on *Like Never Before*

"*From the Start* embodies Tagg's best! Delightful. Endearing. And full of engaging characters and tingling moments reminiscent of our favorite films and stories. I'm thrilled this is the beginning of our journey with the Walkers and eagerly anticipate this wonderful family's next chapter."

—*Katherine Reay*, bestselling, award-winning author, on
From the Start

"*From the Start* is guaranteed to win the heart of readers with this delightful story of a retired football player looking for his future, and a writer trying to figure out how to pen his story—while rewriting her own. Colton is downright swoon-worthy, and this first book in this hometown series about the charming town of Maple Valley, Iowa, scores a resounding touchdown! Tagg just gets better and better."

—*Susan May Warren*, bestselling, award-winning
author, on *From the Start*

Books by Melissa Tagg

Walker Family Series
Three Little Words (prequel e-novella)
From the Start
Like Never Before
Keep Holding On

Where Love Begins Series
Made to Last
Here to Stay

Enchanted Christmas Novella Collection
One Enchanted Christmas
One Enchanted Eve
One Enchanted Noel (coming November 2017)

"A Maple Valley Romance"
in the *Right Where We Belong* collection

All This Time

A Walker Family Novel

Melissa Tagg

LARKSPUR
PRESS

To the writing friends who helped me brainstorm this series years ago while we lounged on the bank of the Mississippi River:

Alena Tauriainen
Gabrielle Meyer
Lindsay Harrel

I'm so grateful for your friendship, and I love you lots!

1

A single, strained scan of the church's hollowed interior was all it took for the whispers of Bear McKinley's past to turn to bellows.

The shards of glass from broken windows. The Portuguese slurs in scribbled neon graffiti on the walls. The scuffs on the pastel clay-tile floor where the furniture must have been dragged away.

Worse, the look on John's face. The one that told Bear, even this many years later, he'd never leave behind the label—*criminal.*

"You can't seriously think I had anything to do with this." Bear forced down the last dregs of the lukewarm coffee John's wife, Elizabeth, had handed him before he'd left their shared, cramped apartment this morning. Another failed attempt to fit in with the people here in Brazil—he could never quite hide his distaste for the stuff.

And yet, he kept trying. Maybe that was his problem.

"Of course I don't think you did this." John's eyes, gray as his hair, were weary and worn, revealing so much more than mere disappointment with this latest round of vandalism.

It was the fourth incident since Bear had landed in

South America ten months ago. More than one person had pointed out that the fledgling church had never encountered so much as a speck of resistance within the community before Bear's arrival. John—the well-respected missionary who'd helped start the church—had always stood beside him, waved off the thinly veiled remarks. But now . . .

Resignation weighed heavy in John's slumped shoulders.

"I know about the rumors, John. I know what people are saying about me."

That helping build a church was one thing, but what was a guy with no training, no seminary degree, and a decidedly lacking Portuguese vocabulary going to do once the new building was finished? Worse, that maybe he was only here because those felony convictions made it too hard to get a job in the States.

The faint call of an illegal street vendor, offering his key-cutting services from the bustling sidewalk outside, jarred Bear's already taut nerves. He kicked at a Brahma beer can, probably left by the vandals, sending it clanking across the vacant room that should've been filled with new teakwood chairs. Who stole *chairs*?

And here he'd thought the unopened letter in his pocket would turn out to be the worst part of this day.

John dabbed a handkerchief over his forehead. The morning had already turned sweltering, Amazon humidity clawing through gaping windows, unusual for fall in Sao Paulo. It was still hard to think of the end of May as autumn. Back in Iowa, spring showers and mild temperatures likely still held summer at bay.

Iowa. Such a faraway place—another hemisphere, another lifetime—but it lingered at the borders of his heart. Happy memories for a soul that wasn't supposed to be this parched. He'd lived there only for five years—

waiting out his probation until he could join John and Elizabeth in South America—but it'd become more of a home than his birthplace, Atlanta, had ever been.

More than, it seemed, Brazil might ever be.

"Bear—"

"They want me to leave, don't they?" He wasn't even sure which *they* he meant. Church members who'd learned one too many details about Bear's background? Leaders with the international outreach mission John represented? They'd only reluctantly allowed Bear to help with the church construction in the first place.

He'd been hopeful his temporary position might grow into something permanent. Once completed, the new building would include an attached community center where they planned to host an afterschool program for kids and a free clinic a couple days a week. He'd counted on being the one to run the place down the road. Might even allow him to finally make use of his paramedic background and—

But no. He could see reality etched into every crease in John's face. "I've had two calls from the mission board already this morning," John admitted.

Bear paced to a broken window. The cloud-veiled Jaragua Peak, Sao Paulo's highest mountain, rose in the distance. So much beauty overlooking so much disparity. From its glass-gilded high-rises to the sprawling favelas—slums, they'd have called them in the States—this city had beckoned to him once upon a time. He'd thought the things so far out of reach for so long—purpose, passion, belonging—might catch up to him here. Had been so certain that serving alongside John and Elizabeth was his answer, the fulfillment of the promise he'd made in that dank prison cell:

I'll go. I'll finish what Annie started. I'll do what she couldn't.

Brazil was supposed to be his fresh start, his second chance.

Instead, this now-sullied cement structure seemed to stand as a monument to his own huddled childhood memories—the litter, the glass, the loud street outside.

And the writing was, quite literally, on the wall: *Vaza! Go Away.*

Some people simply didn't get second chances.

"Bear, you have to know how much Elizabeth and I have loved having you here."

John's past-tense wording was enough to eradicate any lingering remnant of hope. Bear toed a jagged piece of glass away and dropped to perch on an overturned bucket.

"We look at you and we think of our Annie."

Her name squeezed the air from his lungs. "Please don't—"

John strode to his side and clamped one palm on his shoulder. "We love you like our own. You know that."

He should return the sentiment. Tell John all that his and Elizabeth's support had meant to him over the years. Even from afar, they'd gotten him through the darkest days of his life back in Atlanta and then continued to buoy him through those in-between years in small-town Iowa. By inviting Bear to join them in Brazil, Annie's parents had given his life meaning, made it possible to believe a man really could erase all that was behind him.

He should tell John that the man's constant belief in him meant the world. But he couldn't get past the anger, or maybe hurt, tightening his throat now. "Go ahead and say the *but*."

"The *but*?"

Bear stood, his movement so swift the bucket knocked over behind him. "But even you are starting to wonder if there's something to the accusations."

John blinked, the lines in his face deepening under sunburned blotches.

"You, more than anyone, know where I come from." Bear hated the hard bite in his own tone, hated his inability to turn it off. "You, more than anyone, have reason to doubt."

"I don't doubt *you*, Bear, but you once used the term 'far-reaching' to describe your family's . . . activities. The thought has crossed my mind—"

"Far-reaching as in Atlanta's outskirts, not another continent."

"You told me how much they resented you leaving."

Resented wasn't nearly strong enough a word. "This has nothing to do with them." He wouldn't even entertain the thought. It was too ridiculous. "I left Georgia six years ago." Mere hours after the last prison cell buzz he ever hoped to hear. "I haven't even talked to any of them since."

John righted a tipped-over garbage can and started picking up the trash strewn about the empty space. "That's not true, though. What about those letters from your sister-in-law?"

Bear swiped a can from the floor, crunched it with one palm, and chucked it into the bin. He'd rather not talk about Rosa. Or her repeated letters—including the one in his pocket now. The one that probably said the same thing as all the rest: *Rio's in trouble again. I don't know what to do. The kids . . .*

"You can't just keep ignoring it, Bear."

He tossed another can. It hit the rim and clanged against the floor. "Ignoring what?" His family? He'd been doing that just fine for years now. He sent Rosa money when he could, but that was it.

"The fact that this isn't solely about the vandalism or the rumors or the accusations of a few misguided people."

"That's exactly what it's about."

John stepped around the garbage bin to face Bear. "You forget how well I know you. You were torn up inside even before the vandalism began. Between your family, Annie, those letters . . . you're hiding."

"You have no idea what you're talking about." The words ripped from him, harsh and punishing, echoing in the cavernous building. "I came here to help people—to help *you.*" Because he owed John and Elizabeth. Owed them more than he could ever possibly hope to repay. And because of that promise. "I'm not hiding."

The storm inside him hit a fever pitch, too many thundering emotions all clambering for precedence. It wasn't supposed to be like this. The shambles of his past were never supposed to have a place here.

He was supposed to build a church. He was supposed to serve people in need. He was supposed to change lives the way John and Elizabeth—and yes, their Annie—had changed his so many years ago.

Instead, here he was once again—living with the shame of a branding he didn't deserve.

"The mission board has decided to take applications for the community center position."

The news dropped with a thud.

"You're welcome to apply, of course, but the board won't be hiring until October or November. In the meantime . . ." John's posture drooped. "They feel you should return to the States for now." A ripped piece of tarp waved in the breeze from the door-less opening behind him. He waited one labored beat. "It's not only the mission board that's asking you to leave."

Bear forced himself to meet John's eyes. "What are you saying?"

"I'm saying I care too much about you to see you like

this—so tightly wound. How can you effectively serve others with so much still gnawing at you? This doesn't have to be forever. But for now . . . I think you need to go back. You need to go home."

Bear lowered his head into his hands, his fingers rubbing his temples before scraping down his cheeks. With his back against the cement wall behind him—somehow cold despite the day's heat—he slid down to sit on the floor, knees bent, Rosa's letter crinkling in his pocket.

Home? He didn't even know where that was anymore.

2

*R*aegan Walker's siblings were unbelievable. All of them—the two sitting across from her in the rattan chairs and the one whose pixelated face watched her from the computer screen. Darn technology.

"An *intervention*?" The porch swing creaked as she shifted to cross her arms in front of her denim overalls. At least her gardening gloves hid the fact that her hands had balled into fists. "You've got to be kidding me."

A late-May breeze hummed through the wind chimes dangling above, and sunshine gushed over the rambling lawn in front of Dad's house. Mom and Dad had picked the perfect place to build their home, nestled into a clearing a few miles outside Maple Valley.

Rural Iowa outdid itself today—rested and revived after a long winter, hints of summer present in fully clad trees and so much vibrant green. The cobalt, cloudless sky, the tingle of warmth, the damp, earthy scent in the air—it had all seemed so promising an hour ago. She'd pulled on the faded overalls she found at the back of her closet and tucked her hair under one of Mom's old straw hats, intent on a peaceful Sunday afternoon of yard work.

But then Kate and Beckett had rolled down the gravel

lane in Beckett's classic convertible, toting along Logan all the way from Chicago thanks to a laptop and the internet. *Unbelievable!*

"It's not an intervention, Rae." Even fuzzy from straining wi-fi, Logan's eyes radiated concern. Up until today, she might've considered it impossible to ever get all that annoyed at her oldest brother. He was the quiet one, the gentle one.

Turned out it didn't matter how gently a person told you your life was a wreck. It stung all the same.

"You showed up here out of the blue. You took turns telling me all the things I'm doing wrong in my life." She pulled off Mom's hat and plunked it on the seat beside her. "Sounds like an intervention to me."

"Raegan, you're not listening." This from Kate. Kate the newlywed with the handsome husband and the flourishing writing career. Easy for her to talk about the importance of "having direction in life."

"Oh, I'm listening. So far, we've covered my lack of college degree. How I can't possibly be satisfied working multiple part-time jobs. How I'm too old to still be sleeping in my daybed." Because apparently being a couple months from twenty-seven and still living in her childhood bedroom spelled *pathetic.*

Kate leaned forward, elbows on her knees. "We did not say those things."

Raegan's feet flattened on the porch floor. The swing stilled. "You implied. I inferred."

"We just want you to be happy." Logan again. "We couldn't care less if you have a degree. I only mentioned college because I thought you might want to take some art classes."

Kate jumped in again. "And there's nothing wrong with living at Dad's. But you've never had a chance to experience life outside Maple Valley. We want to make sure there's nothing holding you back. If it's Dad's health you're worried about—"

Raegan jerked to her feet, yanked off both gardening gloves. "Has it ever occurred to you guys that maybe I *like* living in Maple Valley? That big cities and big careers have never held the allure for me they do you all?" She chucked one glove at Kate, then the other at Beckett. "If I had a third it'd be hitting the computer screen right now, Logan."

His chuckle only added to her exasperation. This wasn't funny. It was an ambush.

Couldn't they see she was doing just fine? She enjoyed her life. She cycled through jobs often enough to give her variety, and she had plenty of friends and outside activities to keep her busy.

And then there was the apartment. The one where she stored her secrets. A treasured hideaway right in the midst of a town where most people knew most things about most everyone. Her own private joy.

Maybe she should just tell Logan and Kate and Beck about the apartment, the makeshift art studio she'd set up there. But then she'd have to tell them *whose* apartment it really was and that'd set off a whole new round of uncomfortable indictments. But it might be worth it if it convinced them she wasn't just wasting away here at Dad's, that she was . . . happy.

She was, wasn't she?

I am. Of course I am.

As long as she didn't think too long about Mom. Or too hard about Bear.

She shoved past her siblings before either image—the mother she'd lost or the man she missed—could take root in her mind. She marched down the porch steps, squinting in the bright sun. She heard Kate say her name, then Beckett's resolute, "Let me."

By the time Beckett caught up to her, she'd already rounded the house to where she'd balanced her ladder earlier. Made sense that he'd be the one to follow her. They were the closest in age and, most of the time, in temperament. They understood each other.

At least, she'd thought they did. But someone who understood her wouldn't bombard her like this. She stared at her shadow against the rustic wood exterior of Dad's house. Did Dad agree with his three oldest offspring? Did *he* wonder when or if she'd ever move out?

She'd ask him if he wasn't on his way to Chicago right now to see Logan and his family. He'd left right after church. It was his first solo trip since the brain tumor last year, the subsequent surgery and long recovery over the winter.

"Can you at least appreciate that I brought Twizzlers?"

Raegan whirled. "A bribe's not going to work, Beck."

She expected a smirk but received instead a consoling chuckle. "Not a bribe. A peace offering."

Hard to believe, sometimes, that this settled, bearded man in the plaid flannel shirt and grass-stained jeans had still been a corporate lawyer back in Boston this time last year. He looked thoroughly the part of the orchard co-manager he'd become.

"Hasn't Kit tired of all that hair on your face yet?" She grabbed the bag of licorice from his hands and tore it open.

"She likes the beard. She says I look like a lumberjack."

"She's blinded by love."

Beckett practically beamed. One of these days he'd up and marry Kit Danby, his childhood best friend turned girlfriend, and then it'd be just Raegan and Dad once again, living in this house with too many empty bedrooms.

Which was why she hadn't been able to use Beckett as an excuse when her siblings brought up her own living situation. He might be sleeping in his old bedroom just like her, but they all knew he wouldn't be there long. He already spent more time at Kit's orchard than he did here.

In other words, Beckett had direction. Plans. A trajectory for his life.

All the things it seemed a person was supposed to have if they wished to avoid interventions from well-meaning but pushy siblings. She'd known she was slower than the others at figuring out what came next after young adulthood. She just hadn't realized there was a deadline.

"You know what my first thought was when Kate and I pulled into Dad's driveway and saw you up on this ladder?"

She chomped on a Twizzler. "That this was a horrible idea and you should let your little sister live her life the way she wants?"

Beckett's lone dimple appeared. "No. I thought, 'Man, she looks like Mom.'"

Raegan swallowed, tension easing just the slightest, just enough to let in a wistful longing. "I was wearing her hat."

"Wasn't just that. You look like her. Always have. The blue eyes, the blond hair, especially now that it's grown out a little."

She was the only one of her siblings to have inherited their mom's lighter coloring. The rest all had Dad's chestnut eyes and dark hair. She'd felt so much more like she fit in back when Mom was alive.

Ten years, and sometimes it still hurt as if it were yesterday.

"Of course, Mom never had pink streaks in hers," Beckett added.

The pale pink strands threading through Raegan's hair were a far cry from the bold blues and purples she'd experimented with in the past. But she liked the softer look. It felt somehow fitting for the relatively subdued feel of this year so far. She welcomed the change, the calm. Last year had been hard—Dad's illness, Bear's leaving.

Maybe, too, watching her siblings settle so fully into lives that suited them so wholly. Both Kate and Beckett had moved back to Maple Valley, entering new stages in their careers—or in Beckett's case, finding a new career altogether. Logan had discovered a fresh joy after the pain of his first wife's death. And in the past couple of years, all three had fallen deeply in love. She was happy for each of them, she really was. But it was hard not to feel . . . behind. No matter how much she said otherwise.

"We didn't mean to offend you, you know. If you tell me you're perfectly content with life as it is, living here and working as a librarian and lifeguard and dogwalker—"

She rolled her eyes and shoved the licorice bag at Beckett. "I haven't walked a dog in two years."

"Well, I forget what gigs you've got going at the moment."

She stepped onto the ladder's first rung. "Library, community center pool, and I'm helping Dad at the depot." Although after going stir-crazy all winter, Dad was taking on more and more hours at their town's little tourist stop—the Maple Valley Scenic Railway and Museum. He probably wouldn't need her help much longer.

"Okay. You tell me that your life looks the way you want it to look, and I won't say another word."

She twisted to face Beckett. "You'll call off the others, too?"

"Yes. As long as you can honestly say you're happy just as you are, that you aren't hiding any hurt or regret, that I'm just imagining the fact that you might still be pining—"

"Don't even say it, Beck. You're so far off base."

"Am I?"

"I'll prove it." She hopped off the ladder, her purple canvas shoes thudding in the grass. She reached into the pocket of her overalls and produced the paper she'd been meaning to give back to Beckett for weeks. Months, really. She kept carrying it around with her, waiting for the perfect time.

A swift glance was enough to make Beckett's jaw tighten. "The airline voucher. Rae, I gave you this for a reason."

Oh, she knew why he'd given it to her. He'd presented it to her the day of Kate's wedding, way back in December. He'd expected her to go running down to South America, chase stupid Bear McKinley across the equator.

Bear McKinley with the handsome face and the mesmerizing eyes and the noble need to go play missionary thousands of miles away. He might've spent five years living in Maple Valley, but he'd always been clear about his eventual move—a move that had finally happened last summer. And Beckett had been around to witness the aftermath. He called it pining. She called it adjusting.

"I just don't want my little sister hurting over a situation that could change—change for the better—if she was only brave enough to do something about it."

That was what he'd said when he'd given her the

airline voucher. They were the words of a brother who cared.

But one who simply had no idea what he'd asked of her. Travel down to Brazil? It was impossible . . . for reasons that had nothing to do with Bear.

"It was never going to work, Beck. We were only ever friends." Though she was pretty sure she'd worn her hopeless crush on her sleeve since the day she'd met him. Embarrassing, really, but this was *Bear* they were talking about. Who could blame her?

Beckett let out a sigh and reached for the voucher. "I guess, considering how long it's been, I kinda knew you weren't going to use it. Suppose I can take Kit somewhere fun before it expires. I just thought—"

"I know what you thought and it was incredibly sweet of you. I only held on to it this long because I hated the thought of disappointing you." She met her brother's eyes. "But I'm fine, Beckett."

His quick blink couldn't hide his doubt. "You want some help cleaning the rain gutters?"

She shook her head and moved to the ladder once more. "No, but thanks anyway."

"I'm leaving the Twizzlers." By the look on Beckett's face, there was more he wanted to say, but he had the grace to leave it at that. Seconds later, he angled out of sight, and within minutes, she heard his car pulling out of the driveway.

Well, that was that. She could finally get to work. The ladder jostled under her moving hands and feet, each step like a climb to freedom. Freedom from the tension, the strain of her siblings' visit.

From the lie she might've just told Beckett.

I'm fine.

No, not a lie. She *was* fine. She enjoyed her jobs. She was over Bear. She was delving back into her art.

And it'd been exactly one year, seven months, and thirteen days since her last attack.

At the top of the ladder now, Raegan pulled a crumpled garbage bag from her pocket, shook it free, and then reached into the hunter-green gutters. She wrinkled her nose at the damp mess—soggy leaves, twigs. She should've held on to her gardening gloves.

She went to work clearing the gutter as far as she could reach, only pausing when her fingers closed around something hard. A baseball? She pulled it free from a tangle of dead foliage. One of Beckett's?

She readied to toss the ball over her shoulder at the same instant that an unexpected voice came from behind her. "Ah, Raegan Walker." She jerked in surprise, lobbing the ball.

And then nearly fell off the ladder at the sound of a thump, followed immediately by a man's moan. *Oh no . . .*

She rotated to see the bent-over form—bushy white hair, sweater vest, both hands now covering one eye.

Oh brother. She'd just clocked the mayor.

She scurried down her ladder. "Mayor Milt, I am so, so, *soooo* sorry."

He peered at her from his one good eye. "And here I came to offer you the opportunity of a lifetime." He spoke in his usual dramatic fashion. "But you'd better get me an ice pack first."

This couldn't be where Bear's brother and sister-in-law and their kids lived—this dilapidated apartment complex with the dingy brick and the rows of rusted metal doors.

Then again, why was he surprised? He and Rio had

spent the bulk of their childhood only a few blocks away, living in a pit just like this right down to the thrumming bass coming from one of the units, the yelling from another.

"You just had to come back, didn't you?" His whispered words were carried away on a sticky breeze. That was Atlanta for you—hot and suffocating, even on the brink of twilight.

Who was he speaking to, anyway? The younger brother who'd apparently decided to return to the squalor of his youth?

Or himself?

Well, he wouldn't be here long. John had insisted it was time for Bear to face his past. But what did that even mean? No, what was done was done. It was time to think about his future—which was what he'd been doing for the past five days as he packed his belongings, booked his plane ticket back to the States, and said his goodbyes.

He'd mistakenly assumed the mission board would simply hand him the community center position. But if that wasn't to be, fine. He'd pour his efforts into proving himself the best man for the job. Though his paramedic certification had lapsed years ago, he'd re-train as an EMT—that should be useful in running the free clinic. He'd get letters of recommendation from former employers. He'd study Portuguese.

And if he wasn't invited back to Brazil, he'd find some other nonprofit or church organization or mission group that wanted him. He could dig wells in Africa or build homes or roads in a developing country somewhere.

Because he'd made a promise. And he intended to keep it.

He just had to do this one thing first.

Bear closed the door of the rental car he'd picked up at the airport. He hadn't slept a wink on the nine-hour flight from Brazil. Instead, he'd spent the entire, wearying ride ping-ponging between pained replays of his last hours in Sao Paulo—the tears in Elizabeth's eyes, the regret in John's—and rereads of Rosa's letter.

Bear,

I'm writing you one more time, but only because I'm desperate. Not because I think you actually care. If you did, you'd have come by now. You'd at least have given me a phone number to call.

It's been three weeks since I've seen Rio. This isn't normal, even for him. There have been threats. You know the world we live in.

I can't hide this from the kids much longer. I don't know what to do.

Come home. Please.

Rosa

He'd read it so many times it'd engrained itself in his brain. *Come home.* Didn't Rosa realize this city and all it represented to him had stopped being *home* long ago?

He rubbed his palms on his unshaven cheeks, trying to massage away his exhaustion as he walked the uneven sidewalk toward Building B. Identical buildings rose up on either side against the backdrop of a burning dusk. So familiar, this hemmed-in, caged feeling.

Everything in him had wanted to ignore Rosa's plea. Send money like every time before and let that be enough. He'd walked away from this world—twice. He had exactly zero desire to return.

And he wouldn't have except for one thing. Well, two. The nephew he'd seen but once and the niece he'd never met.

Rio and Rosa might've chosen to stay in this place—with its unbending family loyalties and crime-as-a-lifestyle ways—but those two kids hadn't. And thirty-two wasn't so old an age he didn't remember what it was like, wishing he'd been born to any other family on any other street.

He'd stay a few days, a week at most. Make sure the refrigerator was full, the kids healthy. He'd play uncle for a bit—maybe take them out for ice cream or catch a ballgame. Maybe that would be enough to convince John he wasn't *hiding*.

As for Rio's alleged disappearance, more than likely his brother was sitting in a jail cell or off on a drug run. He couldn't help Rosa there. He'd tried that already. It'd cost him—cost Annie—too much.

No. There'd be no playing hero this time. He'd check in on Rosa and the kids, do what little he could to improve their situation. But then he had to find some way to press a restart button on his own life.

Bear climbed clanging metal stairs to reach the second floor, then trekked the walkway until he reached Unit 232. He could feel the beads of sweat on his forehead, his too-long, black hair damp at the tips where it brushed over his ears. He knocked, waited. The smell of rotten fruit wafted in from somewhere, probably that overflowing dumpster he'd seen near the bottom of the stairs. Another knock.

The door inched open, its sliding chain lock in place.

"Rosa?"

The shadowed eyes visible in the darkened sliver of space blinked. "Bear?"

"Yeah. You gonna let me in?"

The door swung open, and the next thing he knew, the slight woman was tugging him through the doorway. He tumbled over the threshold and she slammed the door behind him, hastily sliding the chain lock back into place. She whirled. "I thought you'd never come."

"Nice to see you, too. Why's it so dark in here?" Only the reddish light of sunset squeezed through the angled blinds, painting garish stripes on the opposite wall. He sidestepped a doll missing an arm to turn on a lamp on an end table. Nothing. No electricity?

He expelled a sigh rife with all the angst and frustration of the past week.

Past week? Try the past decade.

"How long, Rosa?"

"Electricity was turned off yesterday. We've still got water."

His brother's wife was even shorter than he remembered, barely coming up to his chest. But she seemed to be pulling herself up to her full height now, such as it was, shoulders stiffening under a dress that hung on her gaunt frame. The smell of stale fried food permeated the living room, if it could be called that, with its spare furnishings that even in the dark he could tell were on their last legs.

"I'm doing the best I can. No thanks to you."

"Rosa—"

"Over and over I wrote to you. I begged you." Her faint Puerto Rican accent was so similar to his mother's. Did Mom ever think of him now? Wonder what had become of him? For all he knew, she and his stepdad still lived only a mile or two from here.

"I'm here now. If Rio still isn't home—"

"He isn't. He's in jail. I found out after I'd already sent you my last letter. Good old Atlanta P.D."

Well, at least it was the safer of the two options Bear had pictured. "All right, then we just need a plan to get your electricity back on and—"

Rosa thumped one finger into his chest. "I *have* a

plan. You will make it easier for me to follow through. Come." She started down a dim hallway.

"Follow through with what?"

She ignored him as she entered the kitchen. This room was lighter at least, thanks to the window over the sink and a flickering streetlamp outside. But that meant it was easier to see the disarray of this space—the empty takeout containers littering the counter, the stained tile on the floor, the pile of dishes in the sink.

And the duffel bag on the table, bulging and unzipped. Rosa immediately went to work, stuffing in a pile of clothes. "Rosa, talk to me. What is this?"

"This is everything you need to take the kids. We're being evicted. I just received a thirty-day notice today. So I'd appreciate it if you'd take the kids for two or three weeks while I sort everything out. Perhaps a month. Get them out of Atlanta. Out of the state, if you can."

Shock froze his thoughts, his words. She wanted him to do *what?*

"Even if we weren't being evicted, it's too dangerous for them here. Someone threw a brick in their bedroom window two days ago. There was a note tied to it—only one word: *Rio*. My husband may be in jail, but his *activities* still affect us."

Bear's mind spun. She'd mentioned threats in her letter. He hadn't realized—"Rosa, if things are that bad, we need to go to the police."

"The police don't help people like us."

How many times had he heard that exact sentiment? From his father, his mother, his stepdad. From the relatives and friends who made up the tight-knit world he'd grown up in where there was always something to hide and someone else to blame.

"They'll help if we go to them. We'll give them all the facts we can. You'll have to be honest about anything you know of Rio's actions. Drugs, stealing, whatever he's been up to." Had Rio gotten in the middle of a turf war? Sold on someone else's beat? Cheated a buyer?

Rosa yanked on the bag's zipper. It caught and snagged. "I'm not going to the police. I'm going to work extra hours and find a new place to live. And maybe I can find out what Rio has done, try to fix it. But I can't do that when I'm constantly concerned about the kids."

His aggravation finally spilled over, and he yanked the bag from Rosa's grasp. "You've got to listen to reason. I know you're worried about Rio—"

"Aren't you? Do you even care about him?" Anger flashed in her eyes.

And he simply couldn't help it—the crack in his voice, the bitter pain in his words. "That's not fair, Rosa. You know all I gave up for him. And for you. You *know*."

An eerie calm settled over her. "I'm thankful for the price you paid, Bear, but it is no good to me now if you walk away again."

How could she say that? "I'm trying to help you. If you'd only listen—"

"There's no more time for that. Come see Jamie and Erin."

Jamie and Erin. Why did hearing their names make this all worse somehow? *How could you do it, Rio? Endanger your kids, send your wife into a crazed panic?*

But Rosa didn't seem panicked now. She walked evenly, albeit briskly, across the apartment to an open door. Muted lamplight blurred through the blanket taped over the room's broken window. In a quilt-less twin bed, the kids lay together, spindly limbs sprawling. They both had Rio's thick, black hair—well, and Bear's.

"Jamie and Erin." An unexpected sheen of regret tinted his whisper. His nephew and his niece. *Family.* He tasted the word, and for once, it wasn't sour.

"Rio has tried to be a good father, Bear," Rosa said softly. "He's had a good job as a truck driver for almost three years. We don't see him much, but he's done his best to provide."

Oh, Rosa. She knew as well as anyone that in their circles, *truck driver* generally translated to *drug runner.* She'd grown up with it just like him.

"It's only been in the past six months that something has changed again. I don't know what he's doing, but it's different this time. I need to find out why we're receiving these threats. My father will help."

"Your father is this neighborhood's equivalent of a mob boss." And last Bear knew, the man hated Rio. Hated Bear, too. Hated anyone with the last name McKinley, really. Probably why Rio had been drawn to Rosa in the first place. Any chance at defiance, he'd take it.

"Which is why I need his help. He knows everything that goes on. But I will not risk Jamie and Erin's safety. Whatever Rio has done—or is somehow doing still—it's hitting too close to home." A churlish gust of wind blew against the window, loosening one corner of the blanket. Rosa crossed the room. "I was going to take them to a friend, but this is better. You're family."

"I just got back to the States, Rosa. I don't even know where I'm going to live." Although instinct kept suggesting he return to Iowa. To Maple Valley, where everyone seemed to think the best of him. He'd landed there originally thanks to a prison chaplain's connections—a cousin's spouse's friend who owned a construction company. There'd been a job waiting for him as soon as he was released from prison.

For a time, he'd made a life for himself in that peculiar little town, made friends. Seth Walker, who'd become his best friend. Seth's cousin, Raegan, who . . .

Who probably could have been more than a friend if the timing hadn't been so off. If he hadn't been . . . well, who he was.

But the point was, no matter what the future held, he needed a job for now, and it shouldn't be hard to find one in Maple Valley. Plus, he still had his apartment there. He'd had it on the market a full year before moving away without a single bite.

Rosa's sharp inhale sliced into the room, cutting off his thoughts.

"What is it?"

He covered the room in two long strides to stand beside her at the window. Black sedan in the back parking lot, two figures emerging.

Rosa rushed past him. "Jamie, wake up." She rustled the larger of the two kids in the bed.

Bear turned from the window. "What's happening? Do you know those men?"

Jamie rose groggily from under a stained sheet. Rosa reached for the girl, thrusting her at Bear. "Take Erin."

The child—was Erin four or five by now?—tucked immediately against his chest. "Who are they, Rosa?"

But she was already hustling from the room, pulling Jamie with her. "You need to go, Bear. Out the front."

"Mama?" Erin stirred in his arms.

Rosa swiped the duffel bag from the floor in the kitchen and shoved that, too, at Bear. "Please do not go to the police. Give me some time." She practically dragged Jamie through the living room, her every movement frenzied. "Just leave Atlanta. They'll find my kids if you stay here. If they could find you in South America—"

Every muscle tightened from so much more than the weight in his arms. "Wait, what? They found me?

Who—?" He forced himself to breathe as he stepped outside the door Rosa now held open. "Come with us."

She shook her head. "I'll call you when I know more. You need to go. *Now.*"

She slammed the door in his face. And for a moment, he couldn't move. Couldn't think. What was happening?

And then he felt the tug on his shirtsleeve. He met the frightened eyes of his nephew, Rosa's *now* still ringing in his ears. If there was even an ounce of validity to her fear . . .

He grabbed Jamie's hand. "Let's go."

3

"How could you say no?"

Raegan froze at the sound of the voice that belonged to the man she'd done her best to avoid for nearly ten years now. If she stayed down here, crouched behind the circulation desk in the public library, would Mr. Hill go away?

"The mayor offered you a wonderful chance to put your talent on display and you turned him down flat." Mr. Hill actually tsked. He tsked! Wasn't that kind of thing supposed to be reserved for little old ladies with knitting needles?

Maybe she deserved it, though. She *had* given the mayor a black eye, after all. And yes, she'd turned him down flat. He'd asked for a favor, framed it as "the opportunity of a lifetime," and had seemed more upset about her no than his bruising eye.

"You can stay down there as long as you want, Raegan Walker. I'm not going away."

Raegan suppressed a sigh and forced herself to her feet, pasting on a smile for her former high school art teacher. "Hi, Mr. Hill."

Thin, wire-rimmed glasses sat low on the man's nose. His face was a maze of lines, all tugging downward as he looked at her now. All because she'd dared to politely refuse Mayor Milt's request for a painting—an original piece of artwork, meant to be the centerpiece in Maple Valley's upcoming art show.

Not just any art show. The Heritage Arts Council sponsored a regionally renowned event once a year in cities throughout the Midwest. It drew critics from around the country and at least three or four of its best-in-show winners had gone on to earn national acclaim over the years. Scoring the show had been a feat never accomplished by Maple Valley. And, in fact, Maple Valley hadn't technically been chosen to host this year's show—not originally. That honor had gone to Dixon, a larger city to the north.

But just a week back, a major sewer line had burst along Dixon's main street. It flooded downtown businesses, tore up sidewalks, and wreaked such havoc that the town had been forced to pull out, even though the show—slated for late July—was still nearly two months away.

Mayor Milt had tried so hard to hide his delight when relaying the whole thing to Raegan. But he was beside himself with excitement. And he couldn't understand why Raegan wasn't.

"It's tradition, Raegan. A local artist from the hosting city always produces an original piece to be revealed during the show. Something grand that captures the spirit of the community. It could be a painting, a sculpture, a mural, you name it. You are the first and only name on my list. You have to say yes."

Except that she didn't. Couldn't.

"Why in the world would you say no?" Mr. Hill's glasses slid lower on his nose. He nudged them up with his shoulder, something she'd seen him do a dozen times every art period in high school.

Wasn't the better question why in the world Mayor Milt had approached Raegan in the first place? Yes, she'd been something of a standout amateur artist in her teenage years, but that was forever ago.

And yet, Mr. Hill looked at her now as if it was only yesterday he'd spent numerous hours after class working with her, nurturing her love of oils and canvas, teaching her advanced techniques. He'd entered her paintings in area shows, had written letters of recommendation to art programs around the country.

Two of which had offered Raegan full-ride scholarships. And she was pretty sure Mr. Hill had never stopped being disappointed in her for turning them down.

"Mr. Hill, I'm honored that Mayor Milt asked me. Really, I am. But I haven't kept up with my art and—"

"Oh, come now. I know you ordered a new set of brushes at the craft store a few months ago. And Sunny Klassen saw you load an easel into your car a while back."

This town—one big merry-go-round of spinning gossip. She loved the place, but a girl didn't have a hope of keeping a secret around here. Although why she'd felt the need to hide the fact that she was dabbling in painting again, she had no idea. It just felt . . . personal. Somehow significant in a way she didn't quite understand. Private.

But apparently not that private if people in town had picked up on it. So wait, did that mean everyone in Maple Valley knew about the apartment? Surely not. They would've asked. They would've pried. And somehow word would've reached Bear . . .

Her neck warmed just thinking about it.

"I'm really sorry, but the library closes in fifteen minutes and I've still got books to shelve. Maybe we could talk about this another time?" Or not at all.

She turned to the loaded cart full of alphabetized books. Since the library had nearly emptied of patrons, she might have time to get them all put away before closing up. She veered the cart around the circulation desk and started for the Mystery section.

"We're not finished here, my girl."

My girl. He'd called her that back in high school, as if she were his granddaughter and not his student. She'd eaten it up, the attention he'd shown her, his belief in her art. Which was probably why it pained her to see him now. He must feel so let down.

"I can't commit to a painting," she said as she wedged the cart into the narrow aisle between shelves. "I know this whole event is a huge honor for Maple Valley. It'll be great for all the businesses in town with all the extra foot traffic. But trust me, I'm not the artist who should be representing the community."

Mostly because she was pretty sure she didn't have the right to call herself an artist in the first place. She'd gone almost an entire decade without picking up a brush.

Until this past New Year's Day, when sentiment or curiosity or yearning or *something* had caught her in its grip long enough to send her to the hobby store for supplies. But she'd barely been able to bring herself to do anything with said supplies. She'd swirled colors over a couple canvases, but she didn't have a single finished piece to show for these past five months of dabbling.

No, she wasn't an artist. She was just a twenty-six-year-old adult wondering if there was anything left to a long-dormant talent. Who snuck away to paint in someone else's apartment.

"I know it's a tight timeframe. Two months doesn't give your creative muse much space to percolate." Mr. Hill gripped the opposite end of the book cart. "But you love this town. I know you do. Unlike so many young people who can't wait to get away from their hometown, you've chosen to stay."

Raegan pulled a book from her cart, letting her hair fall over her eyes, an attempt to hide all the doubt Mr. Hill might see residing there.

Or rather, the truth. She hadn't chosen to stay in Maple Valley. Not really.

She *had* to stay. There was a difference.

"It would mean so much to so many people here," he went on. "It'd mean so much to *me*. And I think, perhaps, it'd mean more to you than anyone."

She stared at the line of Agatha Christie spines on the shelf. There'd been a time when she would've jumped at a chance like this. When Mr. Hill's words of praise had filled her mind with ambitious hopes, when those scholarship offers had lured her into imagining a life beyond the borders of this quaint Iowa town.

But then Mom had gotten sick for the final time. Life had turned inside out. And the attacks had begun in earnest, squeezing Raegan's lungs and stealing her breath, inescapable and . . .

She shoved a book into place, closed her eyes, inhaled.

One year. Seven months. Fifteen days.

"Raegan, are you all right?"

She nodded too quickly. "I'm fine."

"You put *The Mystery on the Blue Train* before *Murder on the Orient Express*."

She swapped the books, then slid a piece of hair behind her ear.

"You have a gift, my girl. I wish I knew why you were so scared to use it."

Silence hung thick in the air around her—air that smelled of books and lemon Pine-Sol, the same mingling scent that greeted her every time she walked into the library. She loved this place, she did. So why, tonight, did it feel so confining?

"Mr. Hill—" she began, but when she looked up, he no longer stood in the aisle with her.

"Miss Walker?"

Raegan turned in the opposite direction to see her favorite library patron—Elise Linder, with her mother standing close by. She shook her hair out of her face and Mr. Hill's visit from her mind—tried to, at least. "Hey, I was hoping you'd get here before closing."

The nine-year-old's hazel-eyed gaze was fixed on a spot over Raegan's shoulder. Ever unseeing, this adorable bookworm. And yet, somehow, Elise was one of the most observant people Raegan had ever met.

Raegan reached into the bottom shelf of her cart. She came up with a stack of books. "As requested: one Percy Jackson, one Boxcar Children, and two Nancy Drew mysteries." She bent in front of the girl. "Brand new, unabridged, in braille—just like you like them."

Elise's bobbed hair bounced around her pert chin as she inclined her head toward the sound of Raegan's voice. Raegan placed the books in Elise's outstretched hands, then watched as she roved her fingers over the cover of the top one. *"The Mystery of Crocodile Island."*

"It's a good one. Nancy, Bess, and George go to Florida. Ned Nickerson shows up, of course. There's a dangerous submarine, snakes—"

"Don't give it all away," Elise said with a laugh. Propping the books under one arm, she reached with her other for an embrace—finding first Raegan's cheek and then winding her arm around Raegan's neck. "You're my favorite library lady."

Raegan grinned up at Elise's mom as she hugged the girl. "I like the sound of *library lady* so much more than librarian's assistant."

A mother's love gleamed in Mrs. Linder's eyes. "I'm pretty sure Elise would live here if she could."

Raegan just wished Elise could see the beauty of the library she loved so much—the domed ceiling, the marble stairway, the rich cherrywood archways and pillars. One of Maple Valley's most eccentric and wealthiest residents had donated the mansion to the community back in the seventies. It'd housed the public library ever since.

Raegan pulled back and donned her best librarian's tone. "Now, you just make sure you return those books by the time they're due."

"As if she won't have all four finished by the end of this week." Mrs. Linder patted her daughter's back. "Elise, can you go sit on the bench and get your books loaded into your backpack? I want to talk to Miss Walker for a second."

Raegan straightened as she watched Elise make her way to the bench a few feet away. The child knew exactly how many steps to take, when to stop, feel, sit.

She turned to Mrs. Linder. "Does she have another surgery coming up?"

"Beginning of July." The woman's eyes were on her daughter, a mix of pain and hope and caution swirled together. "We've decided it's to be the last one. We can't get her hopes up any longer."

Three failed surgeries in the past five years. And somehow Elise continued to thrive in the midst of it all. "Well, if there's anything I can do to help—in addition to making sure our braille selection continues to grow, of course—just say the word."

Mrs. Linder's gaze moved to Raegan. "That's what I wanted to talk to you about. I know what you've been doing—buying the books with your own money, donating them to the library. That is beyond sweet of you. And far too generous."

Shoot, had the head librarian said something? "You weren't supposed to know that."

"Well, I do, and I'm more grateful than I can say."

"I just know how much Elise prefers braille to audio. She can race through them faster that way. A bookworm after my own heart."

Mrs. Linder leaned in for a hug. "You're just like your mother."

Just like your mother. Raegan had been hearing it her whole life—could never quite bring herself to believe it. Mom had traveled the world, started a foundation that to this day still changed lives. And that wasn't the only dream she'd chased. She'd poured just as much of her heart into her marriage and her kids as her career.

And when the cancer had invaded—not once, not twice, but three times—Mom had planted her feet in the soil of her faith, rooted and strong.

No. If Mom was the sun, then Raegan was the moon—merely reflecting another's brilliance.

Raegan stepped back from Mrs. Linder's embrace. "I'll see you at the Summer Carnival?" The town had been gearing up for its annual carnival, always the first weekend in June, for weeks.

Mrs. Linder nodded. "Wouldn't dare miss it."

Minutes later, Raegan watched as Elise's mom led her down the marble stairs and out the front entrance, then glanced at the clock. Just enough time to finish her shelving.

Soon she had all the library lights off, the doors locked. She found her bike resting where she'd left it on the rack in the parking lot and then began the ride across town, Mr. Hill's voice plying her the whole way.

"You have a gift, my girl. I wish I knew why you were so scared to use it."

She wished she knew, too. But how could she agree to the mayor's request when she couldn't manage to finish any one of the half-begun pieces currently cluttering the apartment she rode toward now?

It took her nearly twenty minutes to arrive at her destination—the second-floor apartment above Coffee Coffee, Maple Valley's lone coffee shop overlooking the riverfront. She perched her bike against the building and then climbed the wooden stairway at the side of the building. Raegan let herself in with a key and traipsed through the kitchen, into the living room.

Her easel, canvas, paints, brushes . . . all of it awaited her. Maybe tonight she'd do more than underpainting. Maybe . . . maybe she'd settle on an image—a landscape or portrait or a bowl of fruit if nothing else—and bring it alive in color.

But first, a shower. She was sweaty from the ride across town and her hair still smelled like chlorine from her shift at the pool earlier today. She'd have to put her same jeans back on, but at least she had a clean shirt here—one big enough to pull double duty as a painting smock.

Her hair was still dripping, the bathroom still fogged with steam, when she heard the first thump. And then a door closing.

Raegan froze.

Footsteps. A soft voice.

Her heartbeat skipped. *Who* . . . ?

The bathroom door swung open and her shriek collided with a gasp. A man's gasp.

"What the—Raegan?"

And now her heart just plain stopped, she was sure of it. Bear McKinley stared at her in shocked silence, wide-eyed and so broad-chested he nearly filled the whole doorway. Even more ruggedly handsome than she remembered. Ridiculously, annoyingly so.

And then, in one deft move, he invaded her space, butting into the room and closing the door behind him. She took a step back, nearly tripped over the towel behind her. Had Bear always been this big? A person shouldn't be so tall. It was intimidating and overwhelming and . . .

He was supposed to be in South America!

"What in the world are you doing here?" He spoke slowly, his gaze sliding down her frame and up again. "And why are you wearing my shirt?"

Clearly the turmoil of the past week had finally gone to Bear's brain. That was the only possible explanation for what he was seeing now—Raegan Walker, wet hair straggling over her shoulders and matted to her cheeks, in *his* bathroom in *his* apartment.

Wearing *his* T-shirt. One that hadn't been nearly as paint-splattered the last time he'd seen it.

Raegan backed into the sink, her *oomph* followed immediately by a panicked, "Why'd you close the door?"

He took a step closer to her, not that all that much space had separated them anyway. He'd forgotten how tiny this apartment really was, especially the closet-sized bathroom. Did he honestly think Jamie and Erin would be more comfortable here than a hotel suite somewhere?

Might not be big, but it's free. It's away from Atlanta, which is what Rosa wanted.

And it'd been the only place he could think to go.

He owned the apartment mortgage-free. It'd felt like a gift straight from God back when he'd first come to Maple Valley. The coffee shop owner below had first rented it to him and later offered to sell it to him for a ridiculously cheap price. Had said *he* was doing *her* a favor by taking it off her hands—and her insurance policy.

He missed that feeling—that sense that God was guiding his steps. Lately life felt too much like grappling in the dark.

"I asked a question first, Rae. Two, I believe, and I've got plenty more where they came from. Like, why does my living room look like an art studio? And since when do you take showers in *my* bathroom?" And was it too much to ask that he get just a moment's peace after the insanity of the past week?

Somehow in the span of days, he'd gone from wannabe missionary to caretaker of two kids who were probably even more bewildered about their situation than he was.

Raegan gripped the counter behind her, those sky blue eyes of hers clouded with confusion. Maybe, too, embarrassment. "You're supposed to be in Brazil."

She moved as if to flee the room, but he was too quick for her. He planted both palms on the counter on either side of her. He wanted answers, and he wanted them now. In the meantime, he'd choose to ignore the fact that she smelled like a dang tropical island. And looked . . . even better than he recalled. Which was as far as he'd let that thought go.

"Glare at me all you want, Raegan, but I think you're forgetting a wee conversation we had, you and I, before I left. The one where I said I wished I could've found someone to buy or at least rent this place and you said, and I quote"—his voice notched to a falsetto—"'Oh, Bear, let me work on it. I've never played real estate agent before. I'll email you when I find a buyer.'"

"I do not talk that high-pitched."

"I catch you trespassing and that's all you have to say?" His gaze wandered over her face, eventually landing on the faintest scar peeking from her eyebrow. "Where's your eyebrow ring?"

She folded her arms, elbows jutting into his chest. "You ask too many questions, Bear McKinley."

He'd forgotten the way Raegan had of saying his full name. Too, how much he'd once liked it. He'd probably grin right now and keep goading her if he wasn't entirely baffled and light years past bushed.

Two full days behind the wheel after mostly sleepless nights in a series of hotels would do that to a person. And poor Jamie and Erin were more worn-out than he was. Erin hadn't even awakened when he'd carried her up the stairs to the apartment he thought he'd find empty. Jamie had crashed on the couch almost immediately, oblivious to Bear's puzzlement over the state of the place or the light peeking from under the bathroom door.

At least he'd heard from Rosa. Whatever she'd feared when she'd seen those two men outside her apartment hadn't materialized—not yet, anyway. But she was still insistent on Bear keeping charge of the kids for the next few weeks. *This will be good for them. They should get to know their uncle.*

So far, there hadn't been much getting to know each other, though. The kids were clearly and understandably uncomfortable, having been whisked away from their home. Erin had finally started loosening up during today's drive, but Jamie had yet to speak in more than monosyllables.

Bear pushed away from the counter, scrutiny straying to the mirror behind Raegan. Man, he looked as tattered as he felt—circles under his eyes, days' worth of whiskers shadowing his cheeks. Even his skin, however bronzed by the beady South American sun, seemed pallid. "Fine. I'll go first. I closed the door because I've got two exhausted kids out in the living room, and they've been through enough this week. If they're sleeping soundly out there, then I don't want to disturb them."

"Kids?"

"And I haven't heard a word from you since last fall—nothing about any buyers or renters—so I assumed I'd find this place empty."

She just stared at him, so many questions flickering through her eyes. The same eyes that had taunted him night after night his first few weeks in Brazil. Always begging the same question: Had he made a mistake, never giving things a chance to develop with Raegan Walker?

He'd met Raegan not long after moving to Maple Valley nearly six years ago. They'd formed an easy, nearly instant friendship. But he'd always been careful to make sure it stopped there. No dinners or movies, just the two of them. Nothing that could be mistaken for a date.

Because that was the way it had to be. Because he knew he'd leave eventually and, more importantly, because never again would he put himself in the position of having to choose . . .

He let out a breath he hadn't realized he'd been holding and said the first thing that came to mind solely to escape any thought of Annie, of Rio, of the one choice he regretted above all. "You know, for being about three sizes too large, my shirt's an okay look on you."

He shouldn't have said it. But it was true. Sometimes Raegan Walker was too cute for her own good. Or his good. But he'd managed to skirt around his attraction to her before. He could do it again. Not as if he'd be in Maple Valley nearly as long this time.

"It's a versatile piece of clothing." Raegan reached

for the extra fabric that gaped below her waist. "Sometimes I wear it like this." She pulled at the bottom of the shirt and tied a knot at the side. "See?"

"That's very nineties of you."

"Well, someone once told me there's nothing boring about my fashion sense."

Yeah, he'd been that someone. Not that he was one to put a lot of thought into most people's choice of attire, but Raegan wasn't most people. Between the streaks in her hair, the dozen bracelets that usually crowded both wrists, the eyebrow ring, the clothes that always seemed to pop with color . . . she tended to stand out.

The undeniable truth washed over him now, as heady as the steamy warmth of the bathroom. He'd missed Raegan more than he'd thought possible. Plain and simple and jarring as that. His sudden desire to hug her was drowned out only by his need to back away from her.

Raegan seemed to read his warring thoughts. She moved in for the barest of hugs—so slight and quick it could hardly be called an embrace—and then she immediately opened the door and padded from the room.

He took his first full breath since catching her here, and followed her into the living room. Raegan had stopped a few feet from the couch, gaze on the huddled forms of Jamie and Erin nestled into the couch he'd bought years ago.

"My eleven-year-old nephew and five-year-old niece," he whispered.

"I didn't realize . . ."

What? That he had family? Unsurprising considering he'd made a concentrated effort *not* to mention them when he first arrived here. And then, after a few months, a year, it'd been easy to forget they even existed—other than the occasional check sent to Rosa. For a short while, he'd been almost as happy in Maple Valley as he had back when Annie and her parents had taken him under their wing.

The thought caused a prickled inhale, enough to draw Raegan's gaze. He nudged his head toward the kitchen. "Please tell me there's food here. I'm starved." Maybe if he ate, the headache lingering around the edges of his brain might dissolve.

She nodded and they crossed the small space to the kitchen right off the apartment's entrance. "I keep a few snacks around."

And yet, it didn't seem like she'd moved in. The only furnishings were those he'd left behind. There were no pictures on the fridge, no dishes in the sink. Other than art supplies, he hadn't seen anything to indicate she actually lived here.

Raegan opened a cupboard, and when she turned around, she held a bag of licorice in one hand and a granola bar in the other. "Take your pick."

He reached for the bar. "Still addicted to Twizzlers, I see." He downed the granola bar in three oversized bites. Raegan held out a second before he'd even finished. "And you still remember my appetite, too."

"Nobody could forget your appetite, Bear. Seth still kicks himself for not getting a picture of you to hang on the wall of his restaurant in honor of eating the most burgers in one sitting."

Man, it'd be good to see Seth Walker again. Raegan's cousin owned The Red Door, Maple Valley's most popular restaurant. He'd spent a few Friday nights playing live music there before he'd moved to Brazil. Seth had been as close as a brother.

Closer.

A smattering of guilt prowled around the edges of his mind—for the excitement he felt at seeing Seth again compared to the concern he couldn't seem to make himself feel for Rio.

Rio, who was in jail. Rio, who had turned his back on the second chance Bear had tried so hard to give him.

"Not sure my eating habits are what I want to be remembered by," he said around another bite.

"Trust me, you're remembered for more than that. Everyone will be happy you're back. Speaking of which, how long are you back for, anyway?"

"I don't know."

"How long are your niece and nephew staying with you?"

"I don't know." *Please. Not now, Rae.* Not now when his nerves were shot and his energy gone.

"Well, you should bring them to the Summer Carnival this weekend. Are their parents—"

"Rae." He choked out her name, swallowing his last bite with a painful gulp. "I can't do this now."

She stared at him for a moment that stretched until he thought it might snap. Or *he* might snap. Maybe he already had by the look in Raegan's eyes. Had he yelled just now or only whispered? He didn't even know. He dropped to a chair, fingers moving to his temples.

"I'm sorry. I'm just . . . I'm so tired. I can't even tell you all I've been through this week. Between the flying and the driving, Brazil and Atlanta and . . . I need to sleep. Is there still a bed in the bedroom?"

She only nodded.

"Good. I'll put the kids in there and take the couch. That is, assuming you're not—"

She shook her head quickly. "I'm not living here. I've only been hiding out here to paint. That's all. I planned to pay you rent all along. I'll write you a check—"

He held up his hand. "Not tonight, all right? Would you mind, um, leaving?"

She gave a resigned shrug and turned to the door. Hand on the knob, she cast him one more look of concern. "Are you okay, Bear?"

He couldn't answer that. Not without lying. "Goodnight, Rae."

4

*R*eturning to Bear's apartment felt a little too much like returning to the scene of a crime.

Which, Raegan supposed, it sort of was, considering she'd been squatting for months.

She truly had tried to find someone to buy or rent the space, but it was small and crowded and the noise from the coffee shop below made it a tough sell. She should've emailed Bear the day she'd gotten the crazy idea to use it as her makeshift studio. The place just had such good lighting, such a pretty view of the river, and she already had a key and . . .

Enough excuses. She owed the man five months' worth of rent and an explanation.

But that was not what drew her to Bear's doorstep this morning. No, it was the thought of those two kids waking up to mostly bare cupboards and an empty fridge. In other words, no breakfast. Save for the bag of Twizzlers. Unless Bear had scarfed that down, too.

Regardless, he'd obviously been in no shape to think ahead last night.

Whereas she hadn't been able to stop thinking. Wondering. So here she was, standing on his second-floor doorstep and knocking, white paper bag in hand and eyes cast to the gray sky where lolling clouds hovered thick and threatening.

Her gaze strayed down the block while she waited to be let in. The line of buildings, pastel siding and colorful awnings, ended in a smudge of brown at the far end of the block. The vacant building with its ruddy, weather-worn brick and faded white letters—*Hay & Feed Store*—had long been the riverfront's sole eyesore.

But it never failed to evoke a poignant mix of gooey happiness and heartfelt longing in Raegan. Mom had loved that old, abandoned building, never tired of telling the story of her and Dad's first date there.

"Never have two trespassers had such a wonderful, romantic time as we did that night."

Thunder rumbled overhead. If Bear didn't let her in soon, she might end up ducking raindrops on the way back to her bike. She probably should've opted to drive into town this morning.

But anytime she could avoid getting behind the wheel, she did. Even if it *had* been one year, seven months, and sixteen days. Maybe one of these days she'd allow herself to stop counting. Maybe eventually she'd be able to stop remembering . . .

Just as she lifted her hand to knock again, the door creaked open. But it wasn't Bear standing on the other side. It was the little boy—Jamie, right? His brown-almost-black hair, same shade as Bear's, poked out every which way, and it appeared he'd slept in the wrinkled red T-shirt and jeans he'd clearly grown out of months ago, considering his ankles and bare feet poking out underneath.

His shoulders drooped as he let out a breath. "You're not my mom."

Enough disappointment churned in those four sighed words to wrench rather than tug at her heart. And all the questions that'd kept her awake last night flooded in all over again. Why was Bear here? Why were the kids with him? Where were their parents?

And how could he have gone five years without mentioning them? Erin would've been born during the years Bear lived in Maple Valley. He'd never said a word.

The first raindrops plopped on the wood landing around her feet. "Your name's Jamie, right? My name's Raegan. Can I come in?"

"You're a stranger."

The sky growled above. "I'm your Uncle Bear's friend. Can you get him?"

"He's still sleeping." The voice came from behind Jamie. Erin peeked around her brother, her thick, dark hair mashed to her head in waves. She wore a long cotton shirt. No pants. "He snores."

"Erin," Jamie hissed, "go back to the bedroom. She's a stranger."

Raegan couldn't help a charmed grin. These kids were so cute they could almost give her own niece a run for her money. Not that she'd ever dare say so to Logan.

A raindrop tapped her cheek. "Jamie, you're a good older brother for looking out for your sister, but I promise I'm a friend. I even brought breakfast."

Erin clapped her hands behind him. "Yay, I'm hungry."

Raegan pulled out her phone. "Look, I'll even prove that I know Bear." She scrolled through her photos. "Here's a picture of me and him."

It was the only one she hadn't deleted in the weeks following his move. Call her sentimental.

Or just plain pathetic.

Whatever. So she'd had a crush on Bear back then. What was so wrong with that? The man had a heart-melting smile and strong arms and he played guitar and *sang.* What normal, red-blooded, unattached girl wouldn't form a few romantic notions about a guy like that?

Plus, he'd somehow managed to live in Maple Valley for years without spilling a slew of personal details. In other words, he was the closest thing this gossipy little town had to a man with a mysterious past. It only added to his appeal.

But she'd had more than enough time to get over him. The photo on her phone? Just a happy memory. Nothing more.

Jamie looked from her phone to her face and back to the phone. Finally, with an overly mature, wary resolve, he backed up to let her in. "You really brought breakfast?"

"Yep. Donuts, muffins, the works." Plus a breakfast burrito from The Red Door for Bear and a half-gallon of milk instead of coffee. Because the man had warped taste buds and didn't like the stuff.

She dropped the paper bag on the counter and moved into the living room. Sure enough, Bear's sprawling form crowded the couch. The thing was way too small for him. How sore would he be when he woke up?

A tiny hand tucked into hers. "He doesn't wear a shirt when he sleeps."

Erin's whispered words drew another grin. And a blush. And the instant need to look away from Bear's bare chest. "I see that." Her attention strayed to his face instead—all sharp angles, from his broad forehead to his high cheekbones and his sloping nose, all except the curve of his overly long lashes. She squeezed Erin's hand. "Come on, let's go back to the kitchen and let him keep sleeping."

Although how Bear could sleep with the ruckus drifting into the apartment from the coffee shop below or the roar of thunder outside, she hadn't a clue. Apparently he could sleep through anything.

But what about these kids? Coffee Coffee opened at five-thirty every morning and was often bustling until ten at night. The apartment was about as sound-proof as a plastic tent. Bear couldn't keep them here long-term.

Long-term? She didn't even know if he was staying another day.

In the kitchen, she pulled a pile of napkins from the sack and then started unloading her breakfast loot on the table. "Hope you guys like chocolate-covered donuts. Or banana nut muffins. Because those are your choices."

"We love them." Erin climbed into one of the vinyl-cushioned chairs at the table. Raegan gave the back of the chair a scoot to move her closer to the table.

She turned to the cupboard, opening the one in which she knew she'd find a few glasses Bear had never boxed up.

Even if she hadn't spent half her evenings over the past few months hiding away in this apartment, she'd have known her way around Bear's kitchen with her eyes closed. Years ago, she'd helped him settle into the space. She'd coaxed him into painting the walls a buoyant red, picked out matching towels and curtains and even coerced him into purchasing a red-faced coffeepot.

"*But I'll never use it,*" he'd argued in the middle of the department store aisle.

"*Do you ever plan to have friends over? Don't you at least want to be able to offer coffee to your guests?*"

"*I live above a coffee shop, Rae. I think my guests will be fine.*"

"*It's the principle of the thing. It's a mark of adult-hood. You need a coffeepot.*"

He'd given her one of his usual longsuffering nods, probably only humoring her to shut her up and get out of the store. But nevertheless, there sat the coffeepot on his counter.

It was a little embarrassing now, remembering how pleased she'd been when he'd bought this place, thinking it was a sign that he might decide to settle in Maple Valley, after all.

Jamie slid into the chair beside Erin and reached immediately for a donut. He tore into it with relish.

"You eat like your uncle, you know that?" After pouring two small glasses of milk, she lowered into the remaining chair.

Jamie spared her a brief glance before taking another oversized bite. "How do you know Uncle Bear?"

"Don't talk with your mouth full, Jamie."

Raegan chuckled at Erin's scolding. Jamie only scowled.

"To answer your question, I met Bear when he first moved to Iowa."

"Is that where we are? Iowa?" Jamie took a drink of milk and swiped the back of his hand over his mouth.

"Bear didn't tell you?"

The milk in Jamie's glass sloshed as he set it down. "He just came and got us one night. Mom told us to go with him. We had to hurry."

Curiosity faded into something closer to alarm. They'd hurried?

"He carried me." Erin said it with delight, chocolate smeared over her lips.

"Where were you when Bear came for you?"

Jamie shrugged and reached for a second donut. "At home."

"And where's home—"

A displeased grunt interrupted her before she could finish the question. "I might've known."

Raegan rotated in her seat. Bear filled the space of

the doorframe separating the living room and kitchen, irritation plainly spelled out in his stormy black irises, in the stern set to his jaw. Why did he look so grouchy? Hadn't he always boasted about being a morning person?

At least he wore a shirt now. One that did very little to hide the stretch of muscle behind his crossed arms. The tattoo wrapping around one bicep was visible under his sleeve. "Raegan." He hissed her name.

"I brought breakfast."

"Can I talk to you for a second?" He nudged his head backward.

She turned to the kids. "Save me a donut, guys, okay? One with sprinkles." She pushed away from the table, mouthing a *What's wrong?* to Bear as she ducked past him.

He faced her in the living room. "What's with the inquisition in there?" He poked one thumb over his shoulder. "Cross-examining the kids? Really?"

"I brought breakfast—"

"This is my apartment, and those kids are in my care. Why we're here is not any of your business." He loomed over her. "I asked you to leave last night, Rae, and I didn't say anything about coming back."

She couldn't stop her flinch. Never, in her years of knowing this man, had she seen him like this. Last night she'd witnessed shades of shock and anxiety and exhaustion in Bear. But not this . . . this anger. Pure, frightening frustration. Directed entirely at her.

"Bear—"

The sound of breaking glass cut in and then a squeal from Erin. A crash.

Bear whirled, flying into the kitchen before she could blink. And only a second later, his yell reached her ears. "Call 9-1-1, Rae."

At the sight of Jamie's slumped form, his swollen eyes and lips and throat, Bear's every movement jolted into autopilot. He raced across the kitchen, Jamie's wheezing beckoning his panic.

But the panic didn't come. Only a rush of uncanny calm. He reached Jamie's chair, his nephew's name slipping from his lips and his hands gripping Jamie's arms. "Jamie, keep breathing." One palm slid to Jamie's wrist. Erratic pulse.

Somewhere in his periphery, he was aware of Erin's tears, the spilled milk pooling on the floor around his feet. Raegan's voice on the phone.

"Let's get you out of this chair. I need you to lay on the floor."

If his voice registered with Jamie, the boy didn't show it. His wheezing only worsened, and it didn't take more than a glance to tell his swelling throat was constricting his airway. He dragged Jamie from his chair, lowering him to the floor. "Erin, has this happened before?"

He spared a glance at Erin's frightened features, took in her nod.

"Ambulance is on the way, Bear." Raegan knelt over him. "What can I do?"

"I think it's an allergic reaction." A severe one. He slid one finger into Jamie's mouth, felt his tongue. No swelling there, at least. "There's a duffel in the bedroom. See if there's an EpiPen. If this has happened before—"

Raegan had already raced from the room.

Jamie's eyes were so swollen now, he likely couldn't see a thing. Anaphylactic shock—Bear knew the signs. *How could you not tell me, Rosa?*

"It's going to be okay, Jamie. I'm right here." He

crouched on his knees, Erin's whimpers still coming from behind. He squeezed Jamie's clammy hand, then went to work on the boy's shirt, using both hands to stretch and loosen the collar.

"I think I found it."

Raegan had barely reappeared in the room before he was on his feet again and reaching for the object in her hands. "Good."

"Do you know what to do with it?"

He didn't bother answering, only lowered to his knees again, fist closed around the pen. With his free hand, he pulled the safety cap from the pen. He placed the pen against the boy's thigh and in a quick motion, pushed the auto-injector into his leg through his jeans. He could feel the spring-loaded needle releasing, and he held the pen in place, counting through gritted teeth. "One. Two. Three."

He released the pen. Stilled. Waited.

"Did it work?" Raegan's soft voice asked from above. She held Erin now, one palm rubbing the little girl's back.

He reached for Jamie's wrist, felt his pulse once more. And prayed.

Bear stood beside the hospital bed, staring at the boy he barely knew. The swelling around Jamie's eyes and mouth had already begun to subside, thanks not only to the epinephrine, but also the oral antihistamine the doctor had administered. His skin was still blotchy, but that too would go away soon.

Jamie opened one puffy eye. "I don't want to stay here."

Bear brushed his fingers over the unruly waves of hair tangled over Jamie's forehead, but Jamie flinched and pulled away. Bear let his hand drop. "It's only for a few hours. The doctor just wants to make sure none of the symptoms return or get worse."

"Can I at least watch TV?"

"Of course."

He handed Jamie the remote and then simply watched while the boy flipped through channels, finally landing on a cartoon. Bear couldn't take his eyes away from Jamie, couldn't settle his own nerves, as if he were just waiting for another attack, ready to spring into action all over again.

His stomach growled, and it hit him that he'd not had a thing to eat this morning. But the pungent smell of disinfectant, the steady beeping from a room next door, the leftover fear—it all stole his appetite.

Why, now, couldn't he summon the calm he'd felt a couple hours ago when his training had kicked in on that kitchen floor? Even in the ambulance, a composed familiarity had sustained him. He'd always been good in the heat of a crisis.

It was when the dust settled and the waiting began that he buckled under pressure.

Bear smothered a sigh now. Any confidence he might've felt in that ambulance had wilted the moment the ER doctor asked him about Jamie's allergies, his past reactions, his medical history and Bear was forced to admit his cluelessness. The doubt on the doctor's face had only expanded when Bear had tried to explain in stilted starts and stops why he knew so little about the child in his care.

And then there were the forms, the health insurance paperwork to deal with.

I can't do this, God. It wasn't a prayer so much as a

plea for intervention. It was one thing to make a mess of his own life. It was another to take responsibility for two others.

Jamie's eyes were fluttering closed now. The poor kid was probably more wrung out than ever with what he'd just been through.

Bear stayed by Jamie's bed until he was sure the boy was asleep, and only then did he trudge from the hospital room. He nodded at a woman as he passed the nurses' station and followed the signs to the waiting room. He lifted his hand to the back of his neck, kneading the muscle that was just as tight there as every other part of his body.

Raegan looked up the second he slogged into the waiting room. "Hey," she said as he approached. Erin sat on her lap, flipping through a picture book, content as could be.

He dropped into the chair next to her. "Hey."

"Is he—"

"He's fine. Definitely an allergic reaction. Were there nuts on those donuts?"

Guilt seeped into Raegan's eyes. "Not the donuts, but there were banana nut muffins. I don't think he ate one, though. But I guess if some of the nuts got onto one of the donuts . . ."

"If it's a severe enough allergy, just being in the same bag could do it." Bear reached over the wood armrest to squeeze Raegan's hand. "You didn't know. Not your fault. I could've just as easily given him something in the past couple days."

Raegan lifted Erin and settled her in the chair next to her. "I feel so bad, though."

He wanted to reassure her. Apologize for earlier, for towering over her and accusing her of interrogating the kids. But he couldn't manage anything other than to lean over, elbows on his knees. "They gave me all these hospital forms to fill out, and I don't know anything. Not his medical history, not his medications. I don't even know Jamie's middle name."

"It's Matthew," Erin piped in, looking up from her book.

Matthew. Like his own middle name. He sank his forehead into his hands.

Rosa. He needed to call Rosa. Tell her what had happened. And while he was at it, he could ask her what she was thinking—not telling him about Jamie's allergy. Worse—sending her kids off with a man so horribly inadequate. He might've known what to do on the kitchen floor. But now?

In the past few days, he hadn't been able to think ahead more than an hour at a time. But here, in the taut silence of the waiting room, reality crashed in on him. He was in charge of two kids—two *lives.* He didn't have a job. He didn't have a plan.

"Bear, you knew exactly what to do back at the apartment. You knew what was happening, you knew to look for an EpiPen, you knew how to use it. You were amazing."

"Used to be a paramedic. That's all."

"You were a paramedic? What? When?"

"Like a decade ago. Back in Atlanta." His other life. The life that chased him wherever he went. He shook his head, dropping his hands and staring at the blank blue wall across the room. "How could Rosa do this? Pack up her kids and send them off with a guy who has no clue what he's doing? And fail to mention that one of them has a life-threatening allergy? What kind of mom—"

"Bear." Raegan's voice was soft with gentle warning. She tipped her head toward Erin, still occupied by her book.

54

He rose, moved down a few seats, waited until Raegan followed suit and settled next to him. "This is such a mess, Rae."

"Their mom. Your sister?"

He shook his head. "Sister-in-law, married to my brother."

"You've never mentioned a brother. Or any family, really."

Not an oversight, which Raegan had probably guessed by now. He looked up, gaze flitting to the TV hanging overhead, the droning news, then over to Raegan. Patient, kind Raegan with the kind of family he'd grown up dreaming about. The kind with the loving, upstanding parents and the nice house and the family traditions—like big breakfasts and classic movies and games of basketball in the driveway.

Was it any wonder why he'd gravitated to Raegan, to Seth, all the Walkers? Just like with Annie and John and Elizabeth. Would there always be that piece of him looking for a stand-in family?

"This morning the kids mentioned that you left in a hurry. I'm assuming they meant left Atlanta?" There was a hesitant tint to Raegan's words, as if she was worried he'd overreact the way he had this morning.

"I'm sorry for being a jerk earlier, Rae."

"You weren't a jerk."

"I was. You were trying to do something nice."

"I was barging in."

"But in your usual thoughtful way." He mustered the closest thing he had to a smile.

It dissolved too quickly, lost in a puddle of need. On any other day he would have brushed off her question about Atlanta. But today, in this moment, he needed something more than the comfort of his own privacy. "We did leave Atlanta in a hurry. My brother's in jail, but apparently whatever he's been involved with has been spilling over to Rosa and the kids. My guess is, he's got himself in the middle of a drug war again." The explanation came fast, ferocious. "Rosa's family has always been big on the meth circuit. The McKinleys deal mostly in heroine, crack. Either one intrudes on the other's territory and things go sour fast."

He glanced away so he wouldn't have to see whatever form of shock Raegan might exhibit—disdain, disgust, maybe just pure disbelief. "That's my background, Rae. Can't count the number of times my dad came home and told my mom to take me and Rio to the park or the pool or something just to get us out of the way so he could conduct the 'family business' right in our apartment."

"Oh, Bear."

"Violence, vandalism, stealing, all part and parcel. I tried to get Rio out of that world. Can't even tell you the lengths I went to." Or what it'd cost him. What it'd cost John and Elizabeth's daughter. *Annie.* He couldn't tell Raegan that part because he might just lose it entirely, fall apart right in front of her, if the words passed his lips.

No second chances.

Raegan touched his arm. "So the kids are with you because . . ."

He shrugged, looked to Erin, who'd climbed down from her chair and now hopped around the room. "Rosa said something about threats, but honestly, I don't know what to believe at this point. She wouldn't let me call the police. If you ask me, it's because she's scared of child protective services. She just begged me to take the kids. Their apartment is a wreck. Utilities shut off. Rosa got a thirty-day eviction. I'm starting to think there's a lot more she didn't tell me."

"So you came here," Raegan finished for him.

"Because I didn't know where else to go. Or what to do. I still don't." He finally let himself meet her eyes. And oh, a man could live on what he saw there. Not pity or aversion or even surprise. Just pure, unadulterated respect.

But *how* . . . how could she look at him like that, so much esteem in her gaze, after all he'd just told her?

"You got those kids out of a bad environment. You probably saved Jamie's life this morning. I'd say you're doing just fine so far. And now you're not alone."

It was as if she knew the very words his soul needed to hear. He had to look away lest she see the grateful, tired tears pooling behind his eyelids.

"There's just one thing, Bear."

He blinked. "What's that?"

"You can't keep Jamie and Erin in the apartment, nor can you keep sleeping on that couch. Not if you're going to be here for any length of time."

"It's that obvious how sore I am?"

"There's that, yes." Her laugh was an antidote he hadn't known he needed. "And also, I kinda want my art room back."

How many ways could a person say a kind but firm *no*?

Raegan pocketed her phone, choosing to disregard Mayor Milt's latest message as she bounded toward the front door. He'd texted her three times today already, the gist of every message the same—he wanted her to reconsider the art show, his request for an original painting.

"Raegan, I really don't think this is a good idea."

And then there was Beckett and his silly concern

about the car pulling into the driveway this very moment. Or rather, the occupants of the car. One occupant in particular.

"I said I really don't think—"

"This is a good idea." Raegan interrupted her brother as she pulled open the door and stepped onto Dad's front porch. "I know. I heard you the first seventeen times you said it."

The rain from earlier in the day had finally let up, leaving behind a lingering cool and that loamy, muddy scent she loved so. Why did anyone ever want to move away from Iowa? Every season had its beauty. Every landscape had its gorgeous layers of color. Even the black soil of freshly tilled fields was pretty in its promise of new life waiting to push through in leaves and stalks of green and gold.

Beckett let out an aggravated snort behind her. "And yet, there's the guy now, all ready to move in."

"You say 'move in' as if he just pulled up in a U-Haul. They've got all of a duffel bag and one suitcase between them, Beck. Bear's not moving in. He's just staying here with the kids for a week or two. It's not as if we don't have enough bedrooms. Dad always says his house is open to anyone and everyone."

Besides, Bear was clearly miles past exhausted. He needed help. Bear McKinley, who'd never seemed to need anything in the past, needed help.

It was as if he were a completely different man than the one she'd known before. That Bear had been calm, purposeful, peaceful. He'd always had a sage word of advice, always offered a gentle listening ear.

This Bear? He seemed almost . . . broken.

"I know hospitality is rule of law around here." Beckett marched onto the porch beside her. "But this is *Bear*."

"Who you've never even met." Which meant his qualms were entirely illogical.

Beckett crossed his arms as Bear stepped out of the rental car. "Don't have to meet the guy to know I'm not his biggest fan. You moped about the dude for months. Don't forget, I was here."

Strands of hair fluttered around her cheeks in the breeze as she watched Bear open the back driver's side door so Jamie and Erin could spill out. "Yes, you were here, and if you'll remember, you bought me a plane ticket and told me to run after him."

Beckett rolled his eyes. "If you *had* run after him and the two of you had gone all happily-ever-after on us, then I'd obviously like him. But as it stands now, he's just the guy who waltzed in to town years ago, played around with my little sister's heart, and then ditched her. For all I know, now he's back to do the same. Right under our own roof."

"He didn't play around with my heart and he didn't ditch me." If only she hadn't texted Beckett. Then he'd most likely be off somewhere flirting with Kit instead of here. "You should talk to Logan or Kate. Better yet, Seth. Or even Dad. They all know Bear. They all like him."

Did Seth even know Bear was back yet? Her cousin and Bear had been practically attached at the hip. Before Seth had gotten married, he'd lived here in the basement for a few years, which meant Bear had spent plenty of time at the Walker house. Seth said all the time that he never would've gotten his restaurant built without Bear's constant help and encouragement.

That was the kind of guy Bear was—all strength and soft edges. If Beckett would quit with the overprotective big brother act for a second, he might see it for himself in the way Bear swung Erin up onto his back for a piggy-

59

back ride, placed his palm on Jamie's shoulder, guiding him toward the house.

His nephew didn't seem to appreciate the gesture, though. Jamie pulled away to walk ahead of Bear.

"Be nice," she hissed to Beckett before their guests reached the porch steps. "Hey, guys. Welcome to the Walker B&B."

"B&B?" Jamie's forehead wrinkled. Hardly any of this morning's swelling was apparent now.

"Bed and breakfast. My dad always jokes that he feels like he's running one. If it's not his adult children hanging around, it's his nephew living in the basement or Colton Greene camping out in one of the bedrooms."

"Colton Greene?" Jamie gasped. "Like the football player?"

"The very one. He's married to my sister. They live in town now."

Bear climbed the steps, Erin still on his back. "You're sure your dad doesn't mind this?"

"Are you kidding? He loves having a full house. He won't be home from Chicago until later this weekend, but trust me, he'll love having you here."

Bear turned to Beckett. "You must be Beckett." He shifted Erin in order to free one hand.

Beckett took his offered handshake. "The only Walker you haven't met, apparently. But I've heard a lot."

Raegan glowered at Beckett over Bear's shoulder until her brother forced a grin. Fake, but at least it was an effort.

"Let's get you all inside and I'll show you where you'll be sleeping. Bear, is the car unlocked? Beckett can get your bags, if so." She ushered Jamie inside. "Feel free to explore."

"I kinda get the feeling Beckett's not feeling as good about this arrangement as you, Rae," Bear said as he followed her into the house. He toed off his shoes just inside the door, then set Erin down. She went running off after Jamie, up the staircase to the second floor.

"Ignore Beck. It's been like forty-five whole minutes since he last saw his girlfriend. He's probably just in withdrawal."

Bear trailed her up the few steps into the split-level home's living room. It couldn't look much different than the last time he was here—brown leather furniture, throw pillows and blankets in greens and blues, fireplace mantel crammed with photos.

And the framed family portrait over by the picture window, the one in which Raegan still had braces and teenage acne. But then why would anybody ever look at her in the picture when they could look at Mom? She'd still been healthy when that portrait was taken, years into her first remission. Her skin had a luminous glow, her blond hair had finally grown out, and her smile . . .

It was comfort and safety and faith and home.

"You look even more like her now than you did back when I first met you. Especially with your hair long."

Her gaze shot to Bear. "Beckett said the same thing the other day."

"Beckett who clearly doesn't like me."

"Don't pay any attention to him. He's just protective. He thinks . . . or assumes . . . that is, he's under the impression that the two of us, that there might be more . . ." Great, now her cheeks were warming.

Understanding unfolded in Bear's dark eyes. "Ah. Gotcha."

"But I set him straight, don't worry."

"I wasn't worried."

"I mean, I have no thought that we, that you and I . . ." She waved her finger back and forth between them. "What I'm trying to say is, I didn't offer to let you stay here because—" Bear was grinning. Why was he grinning? "What?"

An amused gleam took over his expression. "Just thinking about how funny it'd be if Beckett walked in the front door and saw us—"

"Uncle Bear, can we have the room with the bunk beds?" Erin's voice bounded in, along with her footsteps on the carpeted stairway.

Raegan placed her hands on her hips. "If Beckett walked in and saw us what?"

Bear shrugged. "I can think of any number of things to set his suspicious imagination running wild."

"Things like *what*?"

He only patted her head. "Never you mind. I don't want to get you in trouble. Or myself. I'd hate for Big Brother out there to call me out." He moved past her toward the stairway.

"Don't pat my head like I'm five, Bear McKinley."

"I'm five!" Erin called from the stairs.

Bear threw her a wink over his shoulder.

She didn't know whether to laugh or glare, so she just stood there flummoxed and probably—definitely— blushing. Caught between delight and the disconcerting thought that maybe Beckett had a point. This might be a bad idea. All those months she'd spent trying to get over Bear and now . . .

"Where do the bags go?"

She hadn't even heard the front door open, but there stood Beckett, suitcase under one arm and duffel over his shoulder. "Upstairs."

They found her guests on the second floor, peering in the doorway to Beckett's room. Jamie reached for her arm. "Please can we stay in here? I've always wanted bunk beds."

"We've got two extra rooms up here, so you don't

have to share—"

"We want to share," Jamie cut in, a sudden tension tightening the boy's features.

For at least the tenth time since all Bear had told her in the hospital about these kids and their background, her heart lurched. "Whatever you want. Of course, this is Beckett's room, but I'm sure he won't mind temporarily relocating." She shot her brother a cajoling look.

"You sleep in a bunk bed?" Bear turned from the doorway.

Beckett grimaced. "Yeah, so? Raegan sleeps in a daybed."

"I know, but—"

Beckett released the bags and they thumped to the floor. "Wait, you *know*? Why do you know what kind of *bed* my *sister* sleeps in?"

Oh, for Pete's sake. "Because he's been to our house before, Beck, like a hundred times."

There was that impish grin on Bear's face again. "Yeah, I've hung out in Raegan's room lots."

Was that scowl of Beckett's supposed to look menacing? And what did Bear think he was doing?

"All right, I'm calling it. Jamie and Erin, you can have Beckett's room. Bear, you can have the basement where Seth used to sleep. That way, you can have some privacy. Both of you men, stop being idiots."

Erin giggled at that, and Jamie was already climbing the ladder to the top bunk. Beckett took off down the hallway.

"You know, if you're trying to get my brother to like you, you're doing an awfully lousy job."

But Bear wasn't looking at her. His eyes were on the kids, the look on his face somewhere between worry and wonder. "Jamie telling you he's always wanted bunk beds—that's about the most I've heard him say at once."

He swallowed. "I've been wondering if he's just not talkative in general or if it's me he's . . ." He didn't finish the sentence.

"He's had a lot of change in a short amount of time, Bear. He's adjusting. What can I do to help?"

He turned to face her. "You're already helping. You're putting us up."

"Technically my dad's the one doing that. Even if he isn't here at the moment." But she'd called him this afternoon and he'd said he was okay with it . . . as long as *she* was okay with it.

Dad hadn't been overt as Beckett, but his underlying concern was there, all the same. She'd assured him she was more than okay with it. She'd keep a firm hold on her heart this time around. No whimsical emotions. No too-tight attachments. Just common sense and sisterly friendship.

"I'm really grateful, Rae," Bear said now. "More than I can say."

She could practically feel it, the depth of his gratitude. From the day she'd met Bear, he'd seemed a pillar of strength. And yet, he'd never talked of family, of friendships other than those formed while in Maple Valley. Who did Bear have to depend on?

"What else can I do, Bear? What do you need?"

He rubbed his hands over his cheeks—something she *had* seen before, his thinking move. "A shave, for one thing. And a job."

"I can help with that. The job, not the shave. I know basically everybody in town and have worked for half of them. What kind of job do you want?"

He only peered at her, the soft polish in his opaque gaze nearly impossible to look away from. It'd always been like this with Bear—one look and she could swear he could read her every thought.

While she couldn't begin to decipher his.

"I can't believe you never told me you were an artist."

Case in point. Where had that remark come from? "*Were* is the key word. I haven't painted in years."

"The current state of my apartment might suggest otherwise."

A sheepish tickle crept through her. "About that—"

"But it fits. I should've seen it. You've got artist written all over you, even down to the way you decorated that basket with flowers on that turquoise bike you're always riding around. Your bedroom is basically one big art project—not that Beckett would like me knowing that. And I remember when Seth was building The Red Door and you constantly had ideas for colors and furniture. I think you might be the most creative person I've ever met."

She couldn't find a single word to say in response. Not one word.

Finally, Bear leaned forward to press a gentle kiss on her forehead. "I missed you, Rae." He lingered only for a moment. Long enough for his warmth and the musky scent of his nearness to invade her senses. Long enough for her flighty heart to somersault.

Okay, fine, definitely a bad idea.

But it was too late now.

5

Raegan blamed Bear's smile. His voice. The look in his eyes when he'd called her the most creative person he'd ever met.

"There. That's where I think the mural should go." Raegan pointed to the old Hay & Feed Store, its reddish blend of brick and stone colliding with a sapphire sky. Mayor Milt's head tipped beside her.

"You've got artist written all over you." Bear's words had done what Mayor Milt's, even Mr. Hill's, hadn't been able to—they'd gotten her to ask, *What if?* A dusting of scattered possibilities, drifting in like wind-blown lilac petals—fragrant and enticing—had kept her awake past midnight last night. Pondering, considering, imagining, until . . .

The idea had taken root. *A mural.* A mural painted over the aged exterior of the building Mom used to love so. Now that would be a centerpiece for an art show.

Raegan had called Mayor Milt first thing this morning, before she could change her mind.

"I don't understand." Mayor Milt traced his white mustache with one finger, gazing at the building with a perplexed slant to his features. "I was thinking something more along the lines of that landscape painting you did in high school. The one that took first place in that show down in Des Moines."

He remembered that? "You said you wanted something grand. You specifically mentioned a mural."

"But—"

"And what better place for a mural than a vacant building that's been in need of a facelift for years?"

"What if a business wants to move in someday?"

"And the likelihood of that is . . ."

Mayor Milt shrugged. "Fair enough. It's a pit inside. But we've got less than two months until the show. You really think you can paint an entire mural in that time?"

Raegan's fingers curled around the Americano she'd picked up at Coffee Coffee just down the block. The one mugful she'd downed at home this morning hadn't cut it—not after such a short night. After finally falling asleep around one in the morning, she'd awoken not much later to the sound of Erin's cries. She'd padded down the hallway to find the little girl still shaking from a nightmare.

Erin had reached for her the moment she'd entered the room. She'd ended up spending the rest of the night curled beside Bear's niece in the bottom bunk.

She stifled a yawn, dew-tipped grass tickling her bare toes and cool air feathering over her cheeks. By this time tomorrow, this riverfront sidewalk and the rambling stretch of green over in the town square would begin filling up with booths and tables and lights for the Summer Carnival. Just the first in a slew of events packed into Maple Valley's annual calendar—with the art show on July 22 being this year's crowning achievement.

Could she get a mural done in seven weeks?

Maybe the more important question was, did she actually *want* to carry out this crazy idea? Or was it just the rash result of being way too swayed by Bear McKinley?

She could've sworn that was admiration in his eyes yesterday. But she couldn't take on a project this huge just to impress the man who'd taken up residence in Dad's basement.

Pink-tinted hair fluttered in front of Raegan's face. "It's not a lot of time, I'll grant you that. I'll need to come up with a design. We'll need to clean and prime the brick before I can even get started painting. It could be tight."

But it could also be . . . fun. Maybe even thrilling. The chance to explore an old dream and see what might be left of it. And it'd be an act of love for her hometown.

Of course, if she failed, she'd be failing in front of the whole community. It'd be a far cry from playing around with paints in the privacy of Bear's apartment. Hence, her initial *no* when Mayor Milt first asked.

"I'd need to talk to the council, probably the Chamber of Commerce, certainly the town beautification committee." Mayor Milt scratched his chin. "But . . . perhaps." He turned to her. "Mind if I ask what changed your mind? You seemed pretty set against this whole thing earlier in the week."

"I suppose maybe . . ." She took a breath as the truth glided through her. *Maybe deep down I just want to live up to the Walker name.*

Logan had written speeches for presidential candidates. Kate had published books and seen her screenplays turned into movies. Beckett had gone from being a successful lawyer to helping Kit Danby save the local orchard.

Somewhere along the way, every one of her siblings had found their ambition, their purpose. Oh, they'd each had a wandering season. They'd faced difficulties—

outright tragedies, in some cases. Logan had lost his first wife. Kate and Beckett had nursed deep hurts. And they'd all had to find a way to deal with Mom's death.

But hardship, struggles, pain . . . somehow it had all served to sharpen her sister's and brothers' passions, deepen their vision. They were all moving toward something.

Whereas Raegan couldn't seem to see past her next shift at her latest part-time gig. But this project was an open door she hadn't seen coming, and yeah, maybe at first she hadn't been brave enough to even consider walking through it.

But this morning, in the breeze and the sun, with the whisper of Bear's words still tucked in her mind, something deep in her soul spoke a hushed, *Go. Try. You never know.*

"You suppose what?" Mayor Milt prodded.

But the jingling of the bells over Coffee Coffee's front door stopped her from answering—and then the sight of a woman emerging into the sunlight. She wore a purple scarf like a headband, and her teal-rimmed glasses matched the long skirt that billowed around her legs. Why did she look the faintest bit familiar?

And why was she staring at Raegan so intently?

The woman's lips stretched into a smile of recognition and she started toward Raegan. But Raegan's brain couldn't come up with a name or any other details to signify how she might know her.

Seconds later, the woman stopped in front of her. There was just enough white teasing her copper hair— creases lining her face, too—to indicate she was likely closer to Dad's age than Raegan's.

But it was the tears in her eyes that stood out most. And then the shaking of her voice. "You look so much like her. It's like seeing a ghost."

Before Raegan could comprehend what was happening, she found herself wrapped in a hug, enveloped in the scent of lavender. She met Mayor Milt's startled eyes over the woman's shoulder even as something in her heart warmed.

How could a hug from a stranger feel so . . . meaningful?

The woman laughed over Raegan's shoulder before eventually stepping back. "I'm sorry. You must think I'm ridiculous."

Raegan ran one palm over her arm, then repeated the gesture with the opposite arm. "No, not ridiculous, though I am wondering who you are." And where she'd seen her before.

The woman used the end of her scarf to dry her eyes and said simply, "I'm Sara."

"You waited thirty-six hours to tell me you're back in town?"

Seth Walker wadded an apron and chucked it at Bear from across the sprawling stainless steel counter that filled the middle of the The Red Door's gleaming commercial kitchen.

Bear caught the apron before it could land on Erin's head where she sat in front of him on a waist-high stool. Jamie stood by Bear's side, apparently not as eager as Erin to dig into the cinnamon rolls that Shan, Seth's head chef, had dished out for them.

"I'm here now, aren't I?" Bear had already given his friend—Raegan's cousin—a boisterous embrace the minute he'd arrived at The Red Door and found Seth filling in for an absentee waiter. With every table in the restaurant packed, Seth had insisted Bear bring the kids to the kitchen.

At which point Bear had made the mistake of mentioning they'd arrived in town a day and a half ago.

"That's two whole nights I went to bed thinking my best friend was thousands of miles away when really he was just down the road."

The sugary-sweet scent of the rolls pulled a gurgle from Bear's stomach. Man, it was good to see Seth again. "I feel bad for your wife if it was really me you were thinking about those two nights when you got in bed."

His friend pitched a towel next. The man could pass for Beckett Walker's twin—same dark hair and eyes, though Beckett had more height and Seth more brawn. "You know what I meant. And put on the apron. We're bursting at the seams this morning and I had two employees call in. I could use an extra hand. I bet Shan won't mind if the kids keep her company for a little while. Will you?"

Shan glanced over from the oven, fanning herself with her hat. "Of course not. Better than having you two yacking away and taking up space in my kitchen."

Seth grinned. "Hurry up, put on the apron."

"Really? Because believe it or not, I came here this morning to ask about a job." Which made this a case of awfully good timing, even if it was a tad humiliating to ask his friend for work.

But for all the uncertainty staring him in the face, one thing was certain: He needed a job, an income. He had two children to take care of in the immediate future, and in the distant future—he hoped, he prayed—he'd need at least somewhat of a financial cushion when he returned to Brazil. Even if the mission board did offer him the community center/clinic position, it probably wouldn't come with a full-time salary.

Plus, he planned to check with local community colleges about EMT training as soon as he could. With any luck, he'd find a summer course. But that, too, would require a boost to his current dwindling bank account.

Seth pulled a plastic tub from atop an industrial dishwasher. "You came here to ask for a job? Here I thought it was to apologize for taking so long to let me know you're back."

"You're not going to let that go, are you?"

He thrust the tub at Bear. "Bus a few tables for me and I might."

Bear glanced down at the kids. "Will you guys be all right in here for a bit while I help Seth?"

Jamie climbed onto a stool next to Erin but didn't answer. "Who's Seth?" Erin asked.

Seth rounded the counter and held out his hand to Erin. "I'm your uncle's friend."

Erin stuck her little palm in his. "Like Raegan?"

Seth lifted his eyebrows as he looked to Bear. "Possibly not exactly like Raegan. Never been entirely sure on that point."

Bear let the suggestive quip pass. "Jamie, don't you want to try one of Shan's rolls? They're pretty amazing."

Jamie shook his head. "Can I play a game on your phone?"

It was all Jamie had wanted to do last night, too. While Raegan had entertained Erin with a coloring book, Bear had tried his hardest to engage Jamie. He'd been hopeful the boy's apparent excitement over the bunk beds meant some kind of breakthrough. But Jamie had slipped right back into the same reticent silence that had kept Bear company all the way from Atlanta to Iowa.

He muffled a sigh and handed over his phone before following Seth out the kitchen's swinging door.

Chatter, laughter, and the sound of clinking dishes

packed the spacious restaurant, and awe filled Bear all over again, just like it had so many times in past years when he'd stepped into Seth's place.

This building used to house the First National Bank—as evidenced by the lettering still etched above its front door. Seth had taken out a loan years ago to purchase and renovate the abandoned building. From the rich wood beams crisscrossing overhead to the amber lighting and brick accents, the space was the perfect blend of rustic and urban. A stone fireplace ornamented one corner, where Bear used to provide live music back when The Red Door first opened.

Seth had harbored a dream for this restaurant even when it was still a worn-down, empty shell of a building with dust-covered floors and rusted vaults at the back. Sort of gave a man hope—that what started as a vision sometimes really could turn into a reality.

If only Bear could put some kind of definition to his own vision—draw a border around his desperate, unyielding desire to make his life count. To make a difference the way Annie had wanted to. The way they might have together if . . .

If he'd chosen differently.

Bear spent the next forty-five minutes winding from table to table, clearing dishes and delivering meals to customers, in between checking on Jamie and Erin.

Only when the breakfast crowd thinned and business slowed did he have a chance to give Seth the bare-bones recap of how and why he'd ended up back in Maple Valley.

"You have a brother?" Seth wiped down a table next to the one Bear was currently clearing. "Five years and you never thought to mention him?"

Bear dropped a glass in his tub. "Not my favorite topic of conversation."

"And he's in jail? You don't seem all that concerned."

There wasn't a speck of accusation in Seth's tone, only curiosity, confusion. "This isn't anything new, Seth. Any mess Rio's in is of his own making."

"Kind of harsh, don't you think?"

Harsh? If Seth had any idea . . .

Silverware clinked as he jostled the tub.

"What about the kids? They're probably a little confused, aren't they? I mean, if this trip was as impromptu as you said."

No *probably* about it. Even from down in the basement, he'd heard Erin's cries last night. By the time he'd reached the second-floor bedroom, Raegan was already in the room, comforting his niece. Bad dream, she'd said, and Erin wanted to talk to her mom.

Yeah, well, so did Bear. But each time Rosa called, she seemed in a hurry. She'd thank him repeatedly for helping with the kids, assure him all was well, and then spend the remainder of her call talking to Jamie and Erin.

He kept trying to tell himself this was perfectly normal. Kids visited relatives all the time. This visit was just a little more spur-of-the-moment than most. Rosa needed a break and he was helping out. Everything was fine.

Maybe if he repeated it long enough, he'd start to believe it.

"So, what're you going to do, Bear? How long will Jamie and Erin be with you? After the kids go home, are you staying in town? Are you staying at Case's indefinitely?"

What am I going to do? The question had harassed him constantly since leaving Brazil. "Do we have to play twenty questions?"

"Well, if I'm going to give you a job, it'd be nice to know how long you're planning to stick around. Surely you've already fielded these questions from Rae. Is being here a short-term thing again? Long-term?"

What am I going to do?

Bear plunked the plastic tub onto the table, clattering plates and glasses and drawing attention from around the room, bringing the restaurant to a momentary hush.

"Ooo-kay." Seth paused with his rag mid-swipe. "Message received."

Slowly, voices cluttered the quiet once more. Head hanging, Bear dropped into the chair in front of him. "Sorry."

Seth took a seat across from him. "You're a lot more tightly wound than I remember, Bear."

Tightly wound. Same words John had used before asking him to leave. "I'm . . . it's just . . ." He rubbed his grizzled cheeks and forced a breath of calm. "This whole week—leaving Brazil, going to Atlanta, winding up here—it happened faster than I could blink and I . . . I think I'm still in shock."

"I'm sorry, man. For the questions. For Brazil not working out. For all of it."

"I really thought Brazil was *it*, you know? Maybe it still is, I don't know. It just feels like my life is suddenly on hold." Again. He'd already spent five years in Maple Valley, waiting to join John and Elizabeth in Brazil. He'd have gone the day he walked out of that state prison if he could've. But there'd been a whole slew of parole requirements that made it impossible, including a probationary period before he was eligible for a passport again.

If he hadn't been as "tightly wound" the last time he was in town, it was because back then he'd known what was coming. He'd had his future mapped out.

Seth studied him in that searching way he had. Reminded Bear of Raegan's dad—patient, perceptive. "Is this really such a bad thing, though, Bear? So God pressed pause. So you take a breather for a couple months. You're only thirty-two. You don't have to set the course for your whole life today."

"Easy for you to say. You opened your own restaurant by the time you were thirty."

"Ever think of just staying here? It's not a bad place to land."

Think of it? Sure. But seriously consider it? How could he? It'd be like betraying Annie all over again.

"Long as I've known you, Bear, you've talked about helping people. Serving. Making a difference. You could do all that here. You've already done it, in fact. When I thought I might never get this restaurant built, you were the friend always encouraging me."

And it'd felt good at the time. But all along, he'd known he couldn't stay. Not if he wanted to fulfill the vow he'd made. "I made a promise once." To God. To himself. To Annie.

Only she hadn't been alive to hear it.

John and Elizabeth's daughter had been so young when she died—only days past her twenty-first birthday. She'd planned to follow in her parents' missionary footsteps, had dreams of leaving her mark on the world. *"One life at a time, Bear. That's how we change the world. One life at a time."*

Commotion cut the troubling memory short. That was Erin's voice screeching through the noise of the restaurant. Bear bolted from the table, hurrying into the kitchen. Jamie and Erin were both out of their seats, Erin near tears as Jamie held Bear's phone up high.

"Guys, what's going on?"

A tear slipped down Erin's cheek. "He won't let me have the phone. I just want to call Mom."

"Fine, take it," Jamie huffed. "But I already told you

there's no point. She doesn't want us."

There was anger in Jamie's voice.

There was hurt.

Bear's pounding heart slowed, emotion clogging his throat where words should've formed. *Say something.*

Shan entered from the pantry, arms full of baking supplies. "I'm sorry, Bear. I only left for a second."

"It's okay." It was his fault. He shouldn't have left them for so long. The poor kids had been dragged across multiple state lines, had slept in a different bed every night for the past four nights. And he deserted them at a counter in a restaurant kitchen by themselves?

He crouched in front of them, lifting one hand to rub Erin's back but training his eyes on Jamie. "Your mom doesn't *not* want you. She loves you."

Jamie's brown eyes blinked, his long, curling lashes lending a trace of youthfulness to a face that otherwise seemed far too world-wise for his age.

Please, God, show me how to reach him.

"Do you want to call your mom, Jamie? Because we can do that. Right now."

But Jamie only turned away as Erin buried her face against Bear's shoulder.

And there was that nagging question again. What was Bear going to do?

If meeting Sara Jaminski this morning had been a surprise gift, then tonight was Christmas morning. It was laughter and food and family . . .

And so very many memories of Mom, wrapped up as stories—most of which Raegan had never heard before— all told in Sara's dulcet, reminiscent tone.

Sara. Mom's best friend while growing up. That was what Sara had told her earlier today. What had started as a chance conversation by the riverfront had ended with an invitation to dinner tonight.

Raegan relaxed into the cushioned chair on the second-floor deck at the back of Dad's house. Kate and Beck and Seth and their significant others were all crowded around the patio table, fireflies and laughter dancing under the strands of white globe lights strung together overhead. They'd long since emptied every takeout container on the table. Cool evening air and a dawdling sun painted the sky in pastel wisps.

"I can't picture it. Not in a million years." Kate sat with both elbows propped atop the table, her husband's arm draped casually around her. "You're telling me my mother, the woman who for years insisted she couldn't carry a tune, once got up in front of her entire high school and serenaded my dad?"

Sara tucked a flyaway strand of hair into the same purple silk scarf she'd worn this morning gypsy-style over her head. "Oh, she wasn't lying about not being able to carry a tune. Flora used to mouth the National Anthem at basketball games because she was convinced actually attempting to sing the thing out loud was an affront to her country."

Raegan pulled her knees up to her chest, wrapped her arms around her bare legs. Too chilly, really, for the cotton shorts and peasant blouse she wore. Goosebumps trailed her skin, but she didn't care. Tonight, with its sliver of a moon, felt perfect. Her hungry heart couldn't get enough of Sara's recollections about Mom. She could stay out here all night.

Unlike Bear—who'd gone inside a good hour ago, carrying a sleeping Erin with Jamie straggling behind.

"But yes, your mom did serenade your dad," Sara

went on. "I'm surprised none of you have heard the story before now. I thought it'd go down in Maple Valley High lore."

What was really surprising was the fact that none of them had ever heard Mom or Dad even mention Sara. Had there been some falling out? Maybe Raegan would ask Dad when he came home from Chicago on Saturday.

"So you're moving back to Maple Valley for good?" Beckett asked now.

Sara nodded. "Yep. Denver's been good to me for thirty years now, but the moment my father told me he might sell the ranch, I had this twinge. I knew it was time."

J.J.'s Stables—Raegan rode her bike past the sign for the sprawling ranch all the time. J.J., who had to be well into his eighties if not closing in on ninety, always drove an old horse-pulled carriage in Maple Valley parades, offered horseback rides during town events, sleigh rides in the winter. She'd never realized he had a daughter. A daughter who, at age fifty-nine, had decided to leave Colorado, return to her hometown, and embark on a brand-new life. As Sara had explained earlier, she'd decided to bring her counseling career with her and meld her two loves by reviving her family's rural property and offering animal therapy, horse camps, and other programs.

"Of course, now that I'm here and realizing how much work I have to do, I'm starting to question that twinge," Sara said with a light laugh. "The house and stables are fine, but the cabins are practically falling down. They haven't been used in decades."

Raegan's attention perked up. "Wait, do you need help? Do you need to hire somebody?"

Beckett gave Raegan a crooked smirk. "Do you really need a fourth job, Rae?"

"Not for me. For Bear."

"Hey, I already said he could have a job at the restaurant." Seth leaned forward to look toward Raegan.

"Yeah, but how many hours can you realistically give him?" Ava, Seth's wife, piped in. "Without taking hours away from your other employees, I mean."

"And besides, Bear's an outdoor guy," Raegan added. "He'd probably way rather work on restoring a few cabins than wait tables." She glanced to Sara. "I mean, if you're looking for someone." Was she being too forward with a woman she'd just met today?

But Sara gave an appreciative nod. "There's certainly more to do than I can handle on my own. Originally, I'd hoped to run a day camp later this summer, but when I realized how much work needs to be done, I sort of gave up on the idea, figured I'd have to wait until next summer. But if I had the right kind of help, maybe it could happen."

"Bear is definitely the right kind of help." Raegan straightened. "He's the hardest worker I know."

Beckett harrumphed. "Sort of feel like I should resent that."

Kate lifted her nearly empty glass of iced tea, ice cubes clinking. "Me too. Writing books is super hard." She flashed Raegan a knowing, playful look over the top of her glass. "But then, this is *Bear* she's talking about. None of us could hope to compete."

Raegan resisted the urge to narrow her eyes. Was this how it was going to be for the next two weeks, or three, or however many Bear stuck around? She really should have been better about concealing her hopeless infatuation with Bear years ago. She might have talked herself into getting over it, but clearly her siblings weren't about to let it go.

Not that she minded the teasing—not really.

What bothered her was that constant, niggling sense that her siblings only saw her as the little sister with the silly crush and the part-time jobs usually held by high schoolers. The little sister who couldn't quite grow up.

Maybe if they knew, if they understood . . .

Why she stayed. Why she couldn't go. What had happened that time she tried.

She stood too abruptly. "I'm going to go find Bear. That is, if you'd really be interested in talking with him."

Sara glanced around the table, as if picking up on more than the siblings' jokey exchange. "Of course."

Raegan escaped into the house and traipsed through the first floor, listening for footsteps overhead. Was Bear still tucking in the kids?

But the deep, drifting voice she heard didn't come from the second floor. She stopped on the top step of the carpeted staircase that led down to the basement den.

"Rosa, I'm serious, this isn't working. Jamie doesn't want to be here. Erin's having nightmares."

Bear—apparently on the phone with his sister-in-law. She crept halfway down the stairs. Bear had seemed distracted all evening. But between mulling over her meeting with the mayor and trying to figure out where she'd seen Sara before, she'd had a crowded mind of her own.

But the frustration in Bear's voice tugged at her now. "You're not listening, Rosa. I don't think—"

He cut off, apparently interrupted, the sound of his pacing reaching up to her.

Raegan chewed on her bottom lip. She probably shouldn't stand here eavesdropping. She started to turn, but her foot caught on an abandoned shoe she hadn't noticed on the step. She hobbled, grabbed for the stairway railing.

Too late. She thumped to the carpet, arms flailing,

and half skidded, half rolled down the remaining stairs, landing in a heap on the floor, barely managing to hold in a groan.

Until she looked up. Saw Bear staring down at her, phone still at his ear. "Going to have to call you back, Rosa. Someone just dropped in."

The groan escaped.

Bear crouched down in front of her. "Well, hey there."

Were his eyes actually twinkling or had she hit her head too hard on the stairway wall? She shifted, wincing when she straightened her right leg. "Are you going to help me up or what?"

"Or what." His gaze roved over her limbs, stopping at the rug burn on one bare knee. "Are you hurt?"

Try mortified. "I'm fine."

"You landed on your ankle kind of weird."

"I'm really okay."

He ignored her, warm fingers brushing over her skin as he studied her ankle. "You might've sprained it."

She pressed both hands to the carpeted stair behind her and started to stand, but the second she rose, the stab of pain in her ankle told her Bear might be right. Great, she was humiliated *and* injured.

"See? You should listen to the former paramedic. I might know what I'm talking about."

She balanced her weight on her left foot, one hand clamped onto the railing. Shoot, her ankle really did throb. "That's not very gentlemanly. Laughing at a girl when she's hurt."

"So you admit you're hurt? And I'm not laughing."

"You are. You're just not showing it."

"Well, I'm about to make up for it by being a perfect gentleman now."

"What do you mean by—"

Before she could finish the question, he'd swept her off the floor with one arm under her legs and the other around her back. "Bear!"

"What? I'm not about to make you hop up the stairs on a sprained ankle. We need to get some ice."

"You don't even know if it's . . . I could've . . . you . . ." She couldn't finish a single spinning thought. Not pressed this close to the man. Not when he smelled like mint and spice and felt as rock solid as a cement wall.

Bear started up the steps, and at the jostling movement, she instinctively clasped her hands around his neck. *Mistake.* Because it made him smile. Didn't even matter that it was a smug smile. The effect was the same.

She looked away, training her attention anywhere—everywhere—but his face. The framed family photos on the wall. That stupid shoe she'd tripped over. The front door leading in from the porch up at the top of the stairs.

"This is so completely unnecessary."

"Maybe. Maybe not."

"I think you might just be showing off."

His chest rumbled with his laughter. "Yes, Raegan. I'm carrying you up the stairs solely because I want you to see how strong I am. Next, I will fell a tree and then lift it over my head." He stopped at the top of the steps. "Why were you coming down here, anyway?"

She made the blunder of looking at him again—right into those marble eyes with the dark lashes and the crinkles at the corners.

And in an instant, the quickening of her pulse eradicated every lie she'd ever told herself about being over Bear McKinley. She wasn't over him. Probably never had been. She'd simply grown adept at ignoring her stubborn heart.

"I found you a job," she finally managed to sputter.

"I already found myself a job. At Seth's."

"This is a better one. Working for Sara, fixing up some cabins. Right up your alley."

"Really? I wouldn't have to wear an apron. That's a plus." He stopped short of the landing. "I don't know, though. With the kids, how can I think of taking a job—any job? Jamie wouldn't even say goodnight to me when I put them to bed. I'm just waiting for Erin to wake up with another bad dream. Seriously, there's a piece of me that wonders if I should be taking them back to Atlanta."

Dread barged in. He'd just returned. He couldn't leave again.

Get ahold of yourself, Walker. He didn't come back for you.

"Bear—"

He shook his head. "I'm sorry. I've got to stop dumping my problems on you."

The man had no idea—did he?—how much she cared about him. If he did, he'd know she'd never resent having his problems dumped on her. She welcomed it, in fact. Probably too eagerly.

"Let's talk about something else." Bear climbed the last step. "Tell me about your morning with the mayor. What did he think of your mural idea?"

She'd spilled the idea to Bear over breakfast this morning while he'd wolfed down two bowls of cereal before she'd even finished her first cup of coffee. He'd seemed entirely at home in Dad's kitchen—barefoot, clad in track pants and a plain tee. He'd been clear-eyed and the closest to peaceful she'd seen him since his arrival in town.

Footsteps thumped on the front porch now, keeping her from answering Bear's question, and the front door swung open. "Honey, I'm home!"

"Dad?" Raegan's attention jerked away from Bear.

Dad stopped on the welcome mat, garment bag slung over one arm, boisterous greeting fading as he looked from Raegan to Bear and back to Raegan again. "Huh. Am I intruding on something?"

Raegan squirmed in Bear's arms until he set her down. "I fell—"

"I think her ankle—" Bear began at the same time.

"Dad's home?" Kate's squeal came from the living room. "I thought you weren't returning 'til Saturday."

"Had to come back early," Dad explained, eyes still on Raegan and Bear. "There's a last-day-of-school field trip at the depot tomorrow and Gary's sick, so I'm covering."

The sound of patio doors sliding, more footsteps, drifted in as they all turned to the activity now filling the first floor.

Until Dad's sharp inhale sliced into the clatter. "Sara?"

Sara stood at the edge of the living room, eyes fastened on Dad. "Case. It's so nice to—"

Dad's bag thumped on the floor. "You shouldn't be here."

6

According to Raegan, last night Sara Jaminski had said the old cabins on her family's ranch property needed a little TLC. But looking at them now, Bear had to think burning them down and starting from scratch might be the more expedient option.

He resisted the urge to pinch his nose, opting instead to hold his breath as he stepped into the fourth and final cabin.

He'd come out to the Jaminski ranch this morning mainly at Raegan's urging. He had a feeling at this point she was less concerned with him landing a job with Sara and more hopeful he'd play detective and figure out why in the world her father had all but ordered the woman from his house last night.

Sara had taken the hint, leaving not five minutes after Case arrived.

"This one's not quite as bad as the others," Sara said as she followed him inside the cabin now. "No dead mice."

Bear allowed himself a full inhale through his nose. *What do you know? She's right.* No stench. No holes in the windows or busted ceiling beams.

But like the other three cabins he'd looked at in the

past few minutes, this space was cluttered with trash—old mattresses piled along one wall, boxes strewn about the floor, blankets, dishes, metal cots rusted and broken. Sunlight streamed through dirty glass. It could take a week just to clear the cabins of junk. And then they'd need cleaning, painting, window and roof repairs . . .

"So what do you think?" Sara toed a ripped pillow, its feathers scattered about their feet. "Could we have the cabins ready by mid-July?"

Bear rubbed the back of his neck, the stuffy heat of the cabin causing him to sweat. Mid-July. A month and a half. Could he even commit to being in Iowa that long?

Where else do I have to go?

Besides, dirty as this work might be, it was preferable to bussing tables at The Red Door. There was something gratifying, even soothing, about manual labor. Much as he sometimes missed his short-lived paramedic career, working with his hands, putting his muscle to work had never failed him. His first job working roadside construction had allowed him to escape his parents' dysfunctional home and move out on his own at age seventeen. It'd helped him pay his way through EMT training and then the paramedic program at a community college in Atlanta.

Then years later, after Atlanta, after incarceration, desperate to escape all over again, his willingness to sweat had served him well once more. Thanks to that prison chaplain's Iowa connections, he'd had the opportunity to work his way up a building construction crew.

Bear gave the run-down cabin a second once-over. "I think I could make middle of July happen."

"Really?"

"Have to be honest, though. I can't work long hours right away. I've got my niece and nephew to look after.

But after they go back to Atlanta . . ."

He couldn't even finish the thought. Already the thought of returning Jamie and Erin to Atlanta grated on him. Those kids were laying claim to his heart—and fast.

And yet, the same frustration filled him now that had prompted him to call Rosa last night. Jamie was angry and hurting, and Bear didn't know how to reach him. He'd tried all day yesterday—tried talking to him, tried coaxing him into shooting hoops or playing catch. No luck. And what Jamie had said at the restaurant that morning—about his mom not wanting him—Bear couldn't stop replaying it.

Because he could've said those same words himself at that age. About his own mom, his dad, eventually his stepdad.

"Tell you what," Sara said now, yanking his attention to the present. "I'd like to host a one-week horse camp in late summer *if* the cabins are ready in time. Sort of a test run before going all out next year. I'll pay you the same hourly wage I'm paying my full-time stable hand to get them in shape by July 15." Sara started for the door. "You get them turned around by July 1, I'll tack on a three-thousand-dollar bonus."

Bear stopped in the cabin doorway. "Seriously?"

"I really want the work done." Sara turned, smiling. "And I really don't want to be the one to do it. Not when I'm trying to set up my counseling office at the same time."

Three thousand dollars . . . *above* his regular wages. After the way he'd torn through his savings in Brazil, the amount sounded like a fortune. It'd more than pay for his EMT training and give him a nice head start on being able to support himself when he returned to Brazil.

If he returned to Brazil. He'd heard from John just this morning, a quick email assuring Bear that John hadn't forgotten about him, that he still planned to recommend him for the community center position.

Bear followed Sara outside, thankful for the fresh air curling around him. The vibrant landscape spreading before them was a swell of green and gold—prairie grass and wildflowers swaying under the breath of the breeze, the land beneath stretching in an endless rise and fall of hilly plains.

No wonder Sara had said she missed this place. Between the rolling fields and the unending blue sky, she owned a piece of rustic paradise. If he were Sara, he would've come home to this place years ago.

Then again, maybe she'd had reasons for staying away. Heaven knew, Bear could understand that. Maybe Case Walker's opposite-of-welcoming reaction upon seeing her had something to do with it.

At least there'd been one good thing about Case and Sara's uncomfortable reunion last night. It'd taken Case's attention off Bear, the fact that he'd been traipsing around the man's house carrying his daughter.

And possibly having too good a time doing so.

He didn't know what to do about that. Only knew Raegan better be icing that ankle again this morning, especially if she planned to amble around on it at that carnival tonight.

Sara sifted her fingers through the tall pampas grass as they walked toward the main ranch grounds now. She looked so different today than she had yesterday. No flowy skirt or colored scarf. This morning she wore Levis and a simple white tee. Her fiery hair was tucked under a blue bandana.

"You know, I've been praying about how in the world I was going to fix this place up while also setting up my therapy practice. I think you might be my answer to prayer, young man."

The answer to someone else's prayer. Wasn't the first time he'd heard it. Annie used to say that the day he walked into her life was the culmination of all her prayers. If only they'd known . . .

In the distance, over the long field and through a line of bordering trees, he caught sight of the roomy red barn that marked the main ranch property. He knew from the tour Sara had given him earlier that several other outbuildings dotted the land, along with at least two outdoor training rings. And farther back was the white farmhouse with forest green shutters where Sara now lived.

When he was a kid, he'd dreamed of living in a place like this, of trading in his family's cramped apartment for space and freedom and miles and miles of land ripe for exploring. That'd been his and Rio's favorite game—playing explorers.

He glanced over his shoulder at the weatherworn cabins. For once, a mess he knew how to fix.

"I'm grateful you're willing to hire me so quickly. And that you didn't even make me write a résumé or cover letter. Does this count as our interview?"

Sara laughed. "Raegan Walker vouched for you. Good enough for me."

"Didn't you just meet Raegan for the first time yesterday?"

"Yes, but my history with the Walkers goes way back." She glanced over at him. "And now you're wondering about said history and asking yourself why Case Walker snubbed me the way he did last night, am I right?"

"Nosy Parker isn't really my style." No matter how much Raegan might be hoping he'd come back with answers. She'd certainly fished last night. But Case had been tight-lipped, turning in for the night less than an hour after arriving home.

"I think I like you, Bear McKinley," Sara said, hooking her thumbs through her belt loops. "Now, to make this official, I'll need to have you fill out a W-4. Probably better do a background check, too."

Bear's throat dried up, his steps slowing. His hand found the back of his neck once more. Sweaty again.

"Not that I'm worried you've got some sordid criminal record lurking in your past." There was teasing in her voice.

One Bear couldn't bring himself to latch on to.

"But I've got a financial advisor helping me with all the business aspects of setting up the ranch," Sara continued. "He insists background checks are part of the hiring process. Along with too many tax forms to count. Seriously, it's painful."

Bear came to a full halt, kneeling down under the pretense of freeing a thistle from one of his shoelaces. All the while those two words clogged his brain: *criminal record.*

He had to tell her. Didn't he?

"Bear?" Sara stopped ahead of him.

He'd told the church leaders in Brazil—about the felonies, the prison sentence, even Annie—and look where that had gotten him. He ignored the scratchy sting of the thistle, tossed it aside, and stood. "The thing is . . . that is . . . I—"

He stopped, attention snagging on the winding dirt road in the distance that bordered the field where they walked. An old blue Taurus idled at the top of the ditch, the shadowed figure inside turned their way.

"Something wrong?" Sara followed Bear's gaze.

"Do you know whose car that is?"

"No. Probably just someone looking for wild asparagus. Or rhubarb. I always see people stopping along these rural backroads."

Possibly. But why was the driver just sitting there? Staring?

And why the unease limping through Bear? It wasn't as if he recognized the car.

"Bear?"

Probably nothing. Probably just the thought of Rio and their unstable childhood a few minutes ago that had resurrected the wary suspicion that used to cloud his everyday life.

Don't be silly. You're in Iowa. Not Atlanta. He lifted his hand and waved.

Immediately the car's engine rumbled to life and it sped down the lane.

Sara shrugged. "Midwestern friendliness lets us down. Could've at least waved back." She started walking again. "Now, what were we talking about?"

More like what they weren't talking about—or what he wasn't going to admit to, anyway. His record. His conscience told him to tell Sara now, not to wait for a background check to reveal the truth. But his common sense reminded him about what had happened in Brazil.

What he wouldn't give for those felony convictions to disappear the way that car just had. He stared at the fog of dust left behind.

Maybe he'd get lucky. Maybe Sara would forget about the background check.

A man could hope.

The rumble of the train engine drew Raegan to the depot's boardwalk. Dad was back from giving his last ride of the day.

Which meant he couldn't avoid her any longer. *About time.*

Hazy steam billowed around the train as its wheels came to a screeching halt in front of the oblong depot building. The 2-8-2 Mikado steam locomotive, with its black body and red wheels, was Dad's favorite of the Maple Valley Scenic Railway's trains. And after helping at the depot off and on throughout high school—and again these past months—she probably knew its specs almost as well as Dad did. It was a 229,280-pound beast that could take almost six hours to start when the engine was cold. Each run of the heritage railway's fourteen-mile track consumed around 1,500 gallons of water and nearly a ton of coal.

Raegan hefted the wooden box-stairs across the boardwalk, careful not to put too much weight on her right ankle as she moved, and lined it up to the car door where the school kids would spill out any second now. Her gaze drifted to the waves of green extending from the depot grounds that eventually blended into a hillside packed with copses of dogwood and pine. Metal and wood track disappeared into the thicket.

Such a unique little tourist spot, this heritage railroad. Maybe she'd somehow portray it on the mural. That is, if Mayor Milt and the council and all his various committees approved the project.

And if she didn't lose her nerve.

"Raegan!"

The squeal of a woman's voice came from the now-open train door. *Oh dear.* Diana Pratt bounded down the steps to the boardwalk, her platinum hair piled into an updo way too fancy for an afternoon train ride with her gaggle of second graders.

"Hey, Diana." Raegan knew what was to come before the teacher several years her senior even opened her mouth.

"I've been hearing the whispers for *days*." Diana drawled the word, eyes growing wide as her students hopped off the train around her. "But your father just confirmed it. Bear. McKinley's. Back."

"I know and—"

Diana rolled her eyes and planted her fists on her waist. "I know you know. Already got the man staying in your house and everything. Something wrong with his apartment?"

"Uh—"

"Never mind. Do you know his favorite kind of pie?"

"Not sure." Kids' footsteps and laughter clattered over the boardwalk. "Don't you need to get your students on the school bus?" Raegan's ankle throbbed. She'd iced it for a couple hours again this morning—Bear's orders—and the swelling wasn't nearly as bad as it'd been last night.

Still. Bear would probably have her head if he'd seen how much she was on her feet today.

"You really don't know? Figured you would what with the way you used to follow him and your cousin around like a little puppy."

There went this conversation, zipping straight from awkward to unpleasant with impressive speed. "Actually, Diana, maybe you should worry about pies later. Tommy Jenkins is peeing in our hydrangea bush at the moment."

Diana gasped and spun. "Tommy!" Her high heels clattered as she hurried away.

Dad's chuckle came from behind.

Raegan turned, all her weight on her left foot. "That Jenkins kid has nice timing."

"Let me guess, she was plying you with questions about Bear, too?" Dad closed the train door and pushed the wooden stairs against the depot's pale yellow siding.

"Wanted to know his favorite kind of pie."

"Not an unmarried man in this town who hasn't been the recipient of one of her pies." Dad tugged off his conductor's hat. Poor man. He loved his gig at the depot, but the costume-like garb—the blue overalls and matching hat—drove him bonkers. Far cry from the military uniform he'd worn back in his young adult years.

Crazy, sometimes, to think the same Dad who spent his days giving train rides and operating a small-town railroad museum had once served his country in Vietnam and had gone on to a prestigious diplomatic career. She'd heard him say time and again that he'd never once regretted leaving all that behind, moving the whole family home when Mom got sick the first time.

But did he ever wonder what life might look like now if things had turned out differently? If circumstances hadn't intruded on his own dreams and ambitions?

She knew what he'd say if she asked him, though. Mom *was* his dream. Raising his children *was* his ambition. As for any other unfulfilled aspirations, his faith gave him peace that God had him right where He wanted him.

It was a line she'd echoed often through the years when wondering if she'd made a major mistake—turning down those scholarships, never pursuing her art. The difference between Raegan and Dad, though, was that he meant it. He really did feel at peace.

Whereas Raegan . . . half the time she didn't know what she felt. Other than a numb acceptance that this was her life. This was what she'd chosen. And it was a fine life. A good life. It was enough.

Or at least, it should be.

As for her faith, it felt at times as dim as twilight. As if, after too many unanswered prayers, the sun had set on her days of wholly entrusting her heart to God.

The voices and laughter of the kids faded as they loaded into the bus in the parking lot. "Listen, Dad, about last night—"

"Feel free to take off early tonight, Rae. I know you've got a booth to man at the Summer Carnival." Dad combed his fingers through his silver hair as he strode into the depot.

Raegan followed him in, half hopping, trying to remember when she'd last swallowed a couple Tylenol. Freshly polished woodwork gleamed around walls painted in rich hues of blue and gold. Glass display cases held salvaged railroad relics, and framed town photos adorned the walls.

"I don't have to be in town until five. I've been waiting all afternoon to talk."

"Rae—"

"I've never seen you like that, Dad." Like he'd been the moment he'd spotted Sara. So . . . hardened. The creases etched into his face stiff and unyielding. Shoulders set and his every feature seemingly on edge.

He started down the narrow hallway that led to his office. "I was tired. I'd had a long drive. I didn't expect to see her."

"I met Sara in town. She said I looked like Mom. She told us all these stories—"

"I'm sure she did."

She didn't have to see Dad's face to catch his grimace. "I'm sorry if I shouldn't have invited her for dinner."

"Nothing for you to be sorry about. You didn't know." He entered his closet of an office, barely large enough to fit a small desk in the corner. The space smelled like Dad, like coffee and Old Spice.

"And I still don't. I don't know . . . what it is I don't

know. She said she was best friends with Mom." And finally last night, just before falling asleep, Raegan had remembered where she'd seen Sara before. "She was at Mom's funeral—at the graveside service. I saw her standing up the hill, watching from a distance."

"I know she was there." Dad glanced at her ankle. "If you're going to be here for a while, sit down."

She obeyed, plopping into the chair at his desk. "I just want to understand. Sara's moving back to town. She's taking over J.J.'s Stables. Bear talked to her just this morning about a job. We'll see her around all the time, I'm sure."

"We won't. 'Least, *I* won't."

"And you won't tell me why?"

Dad's only answer was to hang his hat on a hook beside a slim window.

"This isn't like you."

"I've got some paperwork to finish up."

"But—"

"Enough."

There was a silencing bite to his tone she'd never heard before. Worse, an anguish idling in the background, blunt and undeniable and so very familiar.

And suddenly she was seventeen again, standing unseen behind a tree in a cemetery filled with too much sunlight. Watching Dad fall apart at Mom's grave. Convinced nothing in the world would ever feel right again.

"Dad."

He turned just slightly to look down at her. His face was an ashen gray—like it'd been last year when the symptoms took hold. Before the tumor, the surgery. Days of worry when her ever-strong, ever-present father just didn't seem okay.

"When's your next checkup?"

He shook his head as he lowered to perch on the edge of his desk. "That's not what this is, Rae."

"You had an operation on your *brain* last fall. And now you're not acting like yourself. I read the list of surgery risks. 'Personality changes' was right at the top. So you can't blame me for wondering—"

He reached out to squeeze her shoulder. "Believe me, I would've had the same reaction to that woman showing up at any time, before or after my tumor. I am absolutely fine, and I will continue to be fine as long as . . ."

As long as he didn't have to see Sara. "But—"

"Please just let it go. As a favor to me, let it go. Can you do that?"

Raegan nodded, willing away the unsettling feeling that came from the realization that Dad had secrets. Locked-away pieces of his past, of himself. The wind flapped against the building, rattling a loose pane in the window. This wasn't how their family was supposed to operate. They weren't supposed to hide.

But then, who was she to talk? She had a secret art studio.

And she could name the date of every panic attack she'd ever had that no one in her family knew about.

One year. Seven months. Nineteen days.

"So tell me about Bear." Dad's voice cut in—a rescue, a relief. Protecting her from another tussle with the same old unanswerable questions: Why couldn't she talk about it—the panic attacks? What was she so scared of?

And why, in a family of dreamers and achievers, did she have to be the one broken one?

She swallowed. "What about Bear?"

"Never fails to amuse me the way all my children feel the need to play coy when I do my snooping-because-I-care father routine." Gone, just like that, was the angst in Dad's expression from only moments ago. "For once

I'd love to hear one of you say, 'Wow, Dad. You're really astute when it comes to things of the romantical nature. Yes, I am in fact tangled up in knots about So-and-So.' And in case it's not clear, for you, So-and-So translates to the guy currently camping out in my basement. The one I saw carrying you up the stairs last night."

Raegan resisted the urge to roll her eyes. But at least this was the Dad she was used to—teasing, prying, affectionate. "Romantical? Is that even a word?"

"You could do worse than Bear. He's not a bad guy."

If Dad thought he had to convince her of that fact, he wasn't as astute as he claimed to be.

Dad tapped his chin. "Then again, he does have that tattoo. And I've never been all that keen on tattoos."

"Well, you weren't that keen on my eyebrow ring either. But you adjusted."

"So you're saying I should make it a point to adjust to the tattoo? In case of any future developments of the relationship variety?"

"Dad."

Dad held up his hands. "Fine. I'm only ribbing you. Just know that Beckett's got an eagle-eye watch on Bear."

"Believe me, I do. And I realize that as a little sister I'm supposed to appreciate his protectiveness, but as an intelligent, twenty-first-century woman I'm itching to remind him I can look out for myself."

Jamie laughed.

Jamie *laughed*.

And Bear felt his insides melt.

Raegan bent in front of the boy atop a stool, paint-brush in her hand, as a lightning bug swooped past her ear. She attempted a scold. "If you don't sit still, Jamie, you're going to end up with paint all over your face."

"It tickles." Jamie kicked his heels against the stool beneath him.

"Yes, but you see, I've got a reputation to maintain as the best face painter in town. And your uncle paid a whole dollar for this. I'd hate to mess it up." Raegan met Bear's eyes over Jamie's shoulder, her dimpled grin enough to prompt a laugh of his own. A blazing sunset cast a halo of color over her hair, and the string of lights around her carnival booth glimmered in her eyes.

"A whole dollar indeed. Extortion." Especially considering the sign behind her advertised only fifty cents. But he'd have paid fifty dollars to hear that laugh from Jamie, just as he'd already gladly forked over quarters at booths from one end of the lit-up square to the other.

A warm breeze folded around them, carrying the sugary-sweet smell of cotton candy. Erin's little hands were clasped around Bear's neck from her perch on his shoulders.

Tonight it really was possible to believe everything would turn out okay. Background check or no, the job at Sara's ranch would work out. Jamie would keep laughing, finally start opening up, and both kids would thrive during this break from their everyday lives. Rosa would get their living situation sorted and Rio . . .

Bear's optimism faded. Probably best not to think about it.

So he wouldn't—not tonight. Tonight was about the kids. It was about making up for lost time.

"We've been over this, Bear McKinley," Raegan said now. "My booth was supposed to shut down fifteen minutes ago. I deserve the extra fifty cents for working overtime."

Around them, the square was a swarming hive of carnival activity, lines of people extending from food trucks and cheers flaring from booths where contestants attempted to toss rings onto bowling pins or knock over piles of soup cans. Rainbow-colored lights traced the white arch of the bandshell, where a bluesy quartet warbled to the clusters of townspeople gathered on blankets and lawn chairs.

"I think I like carnivals, Uncle Bear," Erin whispered into his ear, squeezing his neck.

"Then I brought you to the right town, kid." Maple Valley was its own idyllic Norman Rockwell painting of a world. Although, this weekend's carnival was downright run-of-the-mill compared to some of the things Raegan dragged him to over the years—rubber duck river races, parades on obscure holidays, historical reenactments.

Bear rounded to the front of Jamie's stool to observe Raegan's handiwork. "Captain America shield. Nice."

Raegan leaned forward to blow on Jamie's cheek, then held up a mirror for him to see the finished product. "Pretty snazzy, Jamie."

Seth? When had he crept up on them?

At the sound of Seth's voice, Erin immediately started kicking Bear's sides. "Let me down, Uncle Bear."

He complied, letting her slide down his back until her sandals plopped in the grass. She ran to Seth, the purple flower Raegan had painted on her cheek just minutes ago already smudged. "See my flower?"

Bear lifted his hand for a high-five-turned-hug from Seth. "Have to say, I'm kind of jealous of how much my niece loves you." Erin had taken to Seth almost immediately at the restaurant yesterday. Then last night at the outdoor dinner with Sara and the Walkers, Erin had insisted on sitting by him.

Seth grinned and crouched. "Hey, you. I was just about to go buy myself a funnel cake. I might be willing to share."

At his side, Ava made a gagging noise. "Gross."

Seth glanced up at his wife. "If by gross you mean delicious, then yes."

"We've already had corndogs and ice cream tonight," Bear warned. "Funnel cakes might send us over the edge."

"What's a funnel cake?"

It was Jamie who asked the question, drawing everyone's surprised attention.

"Heaven on a plate," Seth answered. "Pure sugar. A carnival staple. Don't tell me you've never had one before."

Erin replied before Jamie could. "We've never even been to a carnival before."

Maybe a simple statement shouldn't be so affecting. Maybe plenty of kids grew up without going to carnivals or trying deep-fat-fried batter covered in powdered sugar. Look at his own childhood . . .

Of course, there had been that one school fair once. Some kind of fundraiser thing. He and Rio had ridden their bikes, snuck past the ticket booth, used the change he'd dug from beneath couch cushions to buy cotton candy.

Rio had been all of five or six at the time. Hadn't been able to get over the way the cotton candy dissolved on his tongue. Kept laughing . . .

Jamie's laugh—that's why it'd coiled itself around Bear's heart. It was Rio's—the tone, the rhythm, the merry glint in his chocolate eyes. Ten years Bear had spent training his brain to forget. Hard to do with his brother's spitting image in his care.

"Can we try funnel cake, Uncle Bear?" Jamie asked now.

Uncle Bear.

He blinked. Hard. If the kids wanted funnel cake, they'd have funnel cake. And cotton candy. And nachos. And they'd play every single game in this square tonight. Come back tomorrow and do it all over again.

"Absolutely. Coming with, Rae?"

She shook her head. "I'll meet up with you after I get the booth closed up."

Erin was already reaching for Seth's hand.

"We'll wait for you," Bear said. "We can help."

"There's no need, really. All I have to do is bring the money box to the center booth, take down the sign, clean up my brushes, and cover the table with tarp."

"All on that twisted ankle? I don't think so." At least she'd been seated for most of the evening. Still irked him, though, that she hadn't gotten her ankle X-rayed.

"I'm not going to let you carry me around the town square, Bear McKinley, if that's what you're thinking."

"Did I say anything about that?"

"How about a compromise?" Seth placed his free hand on Jamie's shoulder. "We'll get a head start while you two finish your bickering and you can meet up with us when you're done." He started to steer Jamie and Erin away.

"Jamie has a nut allergy," Bear called after him. "Check on the frying oil."

Ava nodded back at him. Assured, Bear turned back to Raegan. "Now, where's the money box go?"

But instead of moving from her stool, Raegan simply peered at Bear. Man, her eyes were blue. *Blue*-blue. There was probably some other word for the color. Azure, maybe?

"Change of plans." Raegan tapped the stool across

from her. "Sit."

"Why?"

"I overcharged you for Jamie. I'm going to make sure you get your money's worth."

She wanted to paint *his* face? "Unnecessary."

"Just sit, Bear."

He sat.

Raegan reached for her paint palette, then hovered in front of him, studying his face. "You know, this would be easier if you bothered to shave once in a while."

"I shaved this morning."

"And you're already this . . . stubbly? Is that a word?" She dabbed her brush into a smudge of brown paint and leaned closer. Close enough he could feel the warmth of her skin, the tickle of her hair against his forehead. She smelled of vanilla and sweetness.

Did she know she had a streak of yellow paint on her right ear? "Raegan, you don't have to—"

"Yes, I do." She touched her brush to his cheek.

Jamie was right. It tickled. "Why?"

"Because for a second there, after Erin said she'd never been to a carnival, you got the most forlorn look on your face." She met his eyes.

Cerulean. Maybe that's the word. "I just . . ." He looked down at his hands, folded in his lap where his knees almost met hers. "I suddenly realized how much I've missed out on. By staying away from Atlanta, I mean. I've missed Jamie and Erin's entire lives. I had a reason for leaving Atlanta, for staying away. But when I look at those kids . . ."

A firefly circled in front of him, catching his gaze and leading it into the distance, where the lazy lull of the quartet's latest ballad drifted and the sun was a mere sliver in the sky.

There had to be so much Raegan wanted to ask him.

Why he'd left Atlanta. Why he'd left Brazil. Why he'd kept his past hidden away like a confined specter—allowed to haunt Bear and no one else.

But when she spoke again, there were no questions. No prodding queries. "You might have missed a lot, but you're with them now. Why not focus on that?" She swirled her brush in red paint. "Just focus on right now."

"Not sure if I even know how to do that." Most of the time, he felt like he was in a tug-of-war between the past and the future. If he wasn't running from his regrets, he was chasing some kind of redemption.

Never quite finding it.

Sure, he believed in a God who forgave his sins; forgot them, even. But the world didn't forget. Bear didn't.

"Bear, you could make this the best summer vacation Jamie and Erin have ever had. You've been given a gift—this time with them. Don't miss out on that because you're too busy thinking about all you didn't do in days gone by or all you need to do in days to come."

She caught her lip between her teeth then, a look of concentration in her eyes as bristles brushed his cheek.

Maybe just blue. A rich, swirling blue with layers as deep as the Atlantic. "Scares me a little, Rae, how well you seem to know me."

"Funny. Half the time I'm not sure I know you at all. I didn't know you used to be a paramedic." Raegan's fingers were on his chin, holding his face in place.

"I didn't know you used to paint."

"Touché. Actually, speaking of that, Mayor Milt stopped at my booth a while ago. Only took him a day to run the mural project past all the powers-that-be."

"It's a go?"

"It's a go."

"And how do you feel about that?"

Her brush stilled against his cheek. "Excited. Nervous. Could possibly throw up if I think about it too much. It's been a long time since . . ."

Her voice trailed. Her brush moved again.

His curiosity swelled. "Why'd you stop painting, Rae?"

"Not sure it was ever a conscious decision."

But there had to have been a reason—he could see the hint of it now, something like sorrow—or maybe fear—wavering in her eyes. *You have secrets, too, don't you, Raegan?* Things she held close.

How had he never sensed that about her? She'd always just been Raegan Walker—Seth's carefree cousin with the funky hair and the happy family. And, yeah, the pretty eyes and pretty smile and pretty, well, everything else. But he realized now there was a depth to her he hadn't allowed himself to notice before.

Probably because he'd been trying so hard *not* to notice too much, to keep at least some degree of distance between them. How many times had he repeated the same thing over and over throughout the years? *You can be attracted to her, but you can't act on it. Because you're leaving. Because she's staying. Because . . . Annie.*

But Annie seemed far away tonight. And if he did what Raegan said, focused on right now—no past, no future . . .

He stilled in an instant when he felt Raegan's breath against his face. She'd bent forward to blow on his cheek, just like she had Jamie's.

He sat frozen on the stool, trying to pretend every nerve in his body hadn't immediately come alive. "What, uh . . . what did you paint?" His voice came out a rasp.

She leaned back. He let out a breath. She held up her mirror.

"A bear? Really?"

Her dimples appeared. "Not just a bear. Smokey the

Bear. Don't you recognize him? Just a sec, don't move yet. Smokey's hat is a little crooked." She touched her finger to his cheek and rubbed, biting her lip again.

"I'm probably going back to Brazil." The rushed words skidded off his lips. "There's a community center connected to the church I helped build. We're going to do children's programming, a free clinic. I'm hoping to help run it."

Raegan looked away. "Okay."

"So I'm not really sure how long I'll be in Iowa."

She set the mirror down, folded her arms. "Are you trying to tell me something, Bear?"

No, he was trying to tell himself something. And it wasn't working. "I just thought you should know."

"Well, now I know." She picked up the metal money box and thrust it at him. "Here, you can deliver it to the center booth."

He opened his mouth to say . . . what? There was nothing *to* say. He'd made one too many bad calls in his life, the worst of which had cost him Annie.

He wouldn't risk it again.

7

"Did half the town really need to come out and watch this?"

Raegan stood in the middle of the street that traced the Blaine River, clumps of people gathered along with her, watching as the scaffolding went up around the old Hay & Feed building. Members of the Maple Valley High School varsity football team waited close by with buckets and scrub brushes, ready to give the brick a wash down once the city crew had the scaffolding in place.

"They're excited, sis. We all are." Kate lingered at Raegan's side, the smell of her half-eaten scone pulling a growl from Raegan's stomach.

She hadn't even bothered with breakfast this morning. Too much to do. She needed to stop by the hardware store to order paint supplies, finalize her design, get started on priming the brick as soon as Coach Leo's team finished its work.

And force herself to ignore the distraction that was one Bear McKinley. She was convinced that abrupt little announcement Friday night about his plans to return to Brazil had been a signal of sorts—just like his first stint in Iowa. *"Don't get too close. I'm leaving."*

So, why, then, in the four days since, had he kept

pulling her into each day's activities? As if perfectly synced to her thoughts, her phone dinged for the third time in the past ten minutes.

We're going horseback riding later today. Come with.

She should be flattered that Bear had so thoroughly taken her advice to heart. Ever since the carnival, he'd gone all out to bond with Jamie and Erin. Jamie seemed slower to respond but Erin had eaten it up. After those first few nights, the bad dreams had subsided. Her adoration for her uncle was obvious.

I know how you feel, kid.

Which was why it was important that today she stay focused on her many errands, on her real life. Not the pretend one in her head where Bear settled down in Maple Valley and stopped pushing her away.

Can't join you, but have fun. I've got a mural project to work on.

"Let me guess—Bear?" Kate elbowed her. "That man is spoiling those kids rotten—fishing and swimming and that sleeping bag fort he built in their bedroom last night. I think he's taken them to the ice cream shop every day this week."

"Keeping tabs on him?"

"This is Maple Valley, Rae." Kate said it as if it explained everything. Which it did. "Dad's the one who told me about the fort, though. I think he's getting attached to them."

Dad wasn't alone. Raegan was already dreading the day Bear had to take Jamie and Erin back to Atlanta. If she was feeling that way, what must Bear be thinking about his eventual separation from his niece and nephew?

Rattling metal pulsed in as one of the city guys rounded the scaffolding, shaking its supports and testing its steadiness. Gosh, she was going to have to climb that thing. Probably should have factored that in before taking on this project. At least her ankle no longer bothered her.

"This one." Mr. Hill spoke up from her other side. She'd almost forgotten he was there. Her old art teacher held Raegan's iPad open in one hand, having swiped through every one of the designs she'd spent nearly the entire weekend and the first couple days this week working on. "This is it. The one with the sunflowers."

Kate leaned over to check out the screen. "Ooh, I like it, too."

Each of Raegan's mural concepts was a collage of community scenery—the train station, the riverfront, the square, the old church bell tower she and probably every current and former teen in Maple Valley had climbed on a dare at some point in high school.

But the sunflower design was unique, including a tangle of stems and petals that wove through the medley of images, tying them together.

"I like that sunflower heads are actually made up of a bunch of tiny flowers," she explained. "It's the coolest, most intricate spiral design. Each tiny flower is part of a whole picture. Feels like a good metaphor for Maple Valley."

Still, she couldn't get over the feeling that her design was missing something. But she'd stared at the digital sketch endlessly without knowing what.

Mr. Hill grinned and handed over her iPad. "Have I told you yet how glad I am you finally said yes to this thing?"

Only about fifteen times since she'd arrived to see the crowd gathered in front of the Hay & Feed building.

Raegan slipped her tablet in the canvas bag slung over her shoulder. "I'm honestly not sure why I did say yes." Except that she couldn't deny her budding desire to nurture the seed of a dream planted so long ago. One long-abandoned, thirsty, and yellowed—but maybe not entirely rootless.

She was doing it for her town. She was doing it for herself.

The building rose up in front of her, sunlight skating over its burgundy brick. What had been a shadowed structure, empty and forgotten, suddenly teemed with life and potential.

I'm doing it for Mom.

Mom, who had seen possibilities everywhere she looked. Who'd loved this old riverbank eyesore. Who'd once called Raegan her favorite artist.

"When you paint, daughter, you put your heart on display. You give shape and color to your emotions. And you challenge the rest of us to see in a different way, to feel what we might not otherwise. Your art isn't for you and you alone, Raegan. It's meant to be shared."

A tender breeze feathered over her cheeks, the scent of cherry blossoms and the frothy river tugging at her senses. Raegan could do this. Despite her nerves, despite her tight timeline, despite her fear of the whole town watching her fail . . . she could do this.

She could, couldn't she?

"Raegan Walker!"

Her eyes snapped open. She hadn't realized she'd closed them. The call came from atop the scaffolding. T.J. Waring, captain of the varsity team, had both arms propped on the railing, his sandy hair flopping over his forehead. The metal structure clattered as more team members climbed up to the platform behind him.

"Decided whether to go out with me yet?"

Beside her, Kate snorted. "That Waring kid doesn't give up."

Raegan cupped her hands around her mouth. "I thought I told you I don't go on dates with minors."

The guys around T.J. jostled his sides, but the kid was entirely unfazed. "Turned eighteen last week."

She glanced at Mr. Hill. "I used to babysit him. He proposed to me once when he was seven."

"Is that how you got the whole football team to clean the brick for you?"

She shook her head. "No, that was all Mayor Milt's doing. He told Coach Leo it'd make for good team bonding."

But cleaning the brick was just the first step. It'd need primed next, and then would come the chalk or pastel outlining. All this before she could even start painting.

And once the painting was complete, the whole thing would need at least two coats of sealant to protect it from the elements—either a gel gloss or matte seal and then a removable acrylic varnish.

Plus, she somehow had to fit this major project around her other jobs. And since it was all outdoor work, weather would always be a factor. Too many rainy days like that summer a couple years ago when the river had flooded the town, and she could find herself sorely behind.

"Tell me it's not T.J.'s goofiness that has you suddenly white as a sheet, Raegan."

She turned to her old teacher. "This is crazy, isn't it? Real artists would never commit to this huge of a project on this short of a timeframe."

"Don't do that, my girl."

"Do what?"

"Shortchange yourself. You *are* a real artist. You've been commissioned for a painting. This is meaningful and significant. Take it seriously." He grinned then—the same wide grin he used to give her in high school when pleased with her work. "But not so seriously that you don't have fun."

He patted her shoulder before turning to leave. But he paused a few feet away. "Go with the sunflower design."

"It's not too Van Gogh-y?"

"It's bright and whimsical and perfect."

The sound of water sloshing against the brick building, the scratching of scrub brushes, drifted over the street. Somewhere behind her, an approaching car honked, prompting the crowd to scoot aside.

And there went her phone dinging again.

Work on the mural later. Hang out with me and the kids today!

The man was relentless.

STOP TEMPTING ME, BEAR MCKINLEY. Too much to do. Errands to run. Afternoon shift at the library.

She paused. Grinned. Then added,

Plus, at the moment, I've got an amorous teenager to deal with who has just asked me out for the hundredth time.

Might not hurt for Bear to know *some people* didn't hold her at arm's length. But he didn't miss a beat.

Cradle robber. ☺

"Mr. Hill's right, you know." Kate.

Raegan pocketed her phone. "About the sunflower concept? It's my favorite, too. Except I feel like it's missing a little something. Just don't have any idea what."

"Not that. I mean, about not shortchanging yourself. I used to do the same thing with my writing. Didn't think I'd be a real writer until I was published. And then I was published and still didn't feel adequate. So I started thinking I'd be a real writer when I got an award or scored the right reviews. After those things happened, I thought, well, I'll be a real writer when I write something more serious than romantic screenplays." Kate finished off her scone. "But Colton loves to remind me that being a writer isn't about the work I produce or what everyone else says about that work—it's about the way I see the world. He says I process life and faith and emotion in writing—that stories help me connect with myself, with God, with other people."

"You know, you kinda hit the jackpot with that guy."

Kate's grin reached to her eyes. "Trust me, I know. But I think it's probably the same for you and art. And that's what makes you an artist. Not how many paintings you've completed or how many people see them or how perfect they are."

Raegan turned away from the scaffolding to face Kate. "I think I might've hit the jackpot with you as a sister, too."

Kate pulled her into a hug. "You definitely did."

"Isn't this the point where you're supposed to return the sentiment?"

Kate leaned back, her laughter floating on the breeze. "You're the best sister a girl could ask for, and I'm ridiculously proud of you. I hope you know that. This mural is going to be amazing."

"I don't know about that."

"I do. Now, as long as we're being all sisterly and such, tell me about Bear."

Raegan groaned and started down the sidewalk. "Not you too."

"You've been spending a lot of time together."

"Can't help it. He's living in Dad's house." A flash of color emerging from Coffee Coffee caught Raegan's eye. Sara? She moved with a natural grace, copper curls swaying over her shoulders. Raegan paused mid-step, indecision knotting through her. She'd been half-hoping to run into the woman for days. *But Dad* . . .

"I'm just saying, the two of you would have awfully cute kids."

"Can it, Kate, or I'll take back that jackpot comment."

Kate only smirked.

Sara spotted them then, hesitance slowing her steps. She carried a Coffee Coffee cup. Raegan lifted her palm in a wave and called, "We've got to stop meeting like this." Sara smiled and started toward them.

"What about Dad?" Kate whispered.

Raegan ignored the question—mostly because she didn't have an answer for it. She loved Dad; she respected him. In no way did she want to make him upset.

But talking to Sara last week, listening to her memories of Mom, it'd been a balm for that pain-chapped piece of her heart that never seemed to heal, no matter how many years passed since Mom's death. Of course she could talk to Dad and her siblings, but Sara had new stories, had known Mom for years before Dad ever came into the picture.

Something about Sara was just . . . different.

And besides, she had something to give her. Raegan reached into her messenger bag, coming up with a small, slim photo album, its cover creased and one plastic page leaning out its side. She'd gone searching for it the same night Sara had come to dinner.

"Hi, Raegan, Kate." Sara stopped in front of them. "How are you both?"

Raegan's stomach growled. She laughed. "Hungry, I guess."

Kate said something about being busy but eager for summer. Sara said she understood the feeling.

"Although with opening my office—setting out the shingle, as it were—and trying to get the ranch up and going at the same time, I don't foresee too many relaxing summer days." She sipped her coffee before glancing at Raegan. "Have to say, that Bear is something else. In just two mornings of work, he already has the first cabin cleared out. Thanks for recommending him."

What, no teasing comment from Kate? No reply that Raegan, more than anybody, already knew Bear was something else?

"I'm glad it's working out," Raegan said. "And I'm glad we ran into each other. I found this the other night." She opened to the photo tilted out just slightly—two teenage girls. Even in its sepia tone, the curly hair on the woman on the right gave her away as a younger Sara. And on the left, Mom—bobbed hair, lanky teenage figure, a face so very familiar to the one that stared back at Raegan every morning when she looked in the mirror.

Sara's inhale was quick, sharp, her expression shifting into one of such pure longing it erased any doubt Raegan might have had about this sidewalk meeting. *Sorry, Dad . . .*

"I loved your mom like a sister. If I could go back . . ." Sara shook her head as if to dislodge whatever regret she'd been about to spill. "Your father took this picture, you know."

"Really?"

"We'd gone down to the bridge to snap a picture of Case and Flora. Case had just received his letter from the

draft board. He wanted a nice photo to take with him."
A hint of sadness laced Sara's tone. "Flora insisted the
two of us get a picture, too."

Oh, how Raegan wanted to ask about the rift between Dad and Sara. But even more, she just wanted to
talk about Mom. To hear more of Sara's stories.

Sara must have read the desire in her eyes. "I know I
just came from Coffee Coffee but if you girls have time,
we could . . . I was going to say 'hang out,' but I'm
nearly sixty and those words just feel ridiculous coming
out of my mouth."

Raegan grinned. "I could use some extra caffeine.
And breakfast."

Kate made an apologetic excuse—Colton was waiting
for her. The truth or was Kate simply better at respecting
Dad's wishes than Raegan?

Sara turned to Raegan. "So it's just you and me."

Sorry again, Dad. "It's just you and me."

"Erin, you're a regular cowgirl."

Erin beamed from atop the back of a russet pony
with knobby legs and a docile manner. Harley, Sara
Jaminski's full-time stable hand, walked alongside the
pair, leading Penelope in a circle around the dusty arena.

Bear had already taken a dozen pictures of Erin and
the pony from his seated post on the wood fence that
enclosed the ring. He'd text them to Rosa later today.

Now, if he could just get Jamie interested.

"All right, Jamie, tell me the truth: Do you think
Penelope is as funny a name for a pony as I do?"

The boy sat beside Bear on the fence—quiet, unen-
gaged. Bear didn't get it. He'd thought he'd turned some

kind of corner with his nephew at the carnival last Friday. Jamie had laughed, he'd chattered. *He called me Uncle Bear.*

But since then, Jamie had reverted to his former overcast state, only allowing the briefest glimpses of enjoyment in their activities during the past few days. And though he'd made no protest about coming to the ranch this afternoon, he'd barely said a word since they stepped onto the property. When Harley offered him a ride, Jamie had only shaken his head.

"I mean, they could at least nickname her Penny, couldn't they?"

Jamie's shrug said too little and too much all at once.

"Son, if you don't—"

Jamie's whole body seemed to shudder as he slid off the fence, dirt billowing around his feet when he landed. "I'm not your son." He tramped to the arena's entrance and marched off toward the barn without a backward glance.

Son. Bear had hit a sore spot. Should he follow Jamie right away or give him some space first?

His phone answered for him, blaring from his pocket. He answered without glancing at the screen, mentally kicking himself for hoping it was Raegan on the other end. "Hello?"

He *should* be hoping it was Rosa. His sister-in-law hadn't called in three days. Maybe that accounted for Jamie's mood today.

But neither Raegan nor Rosa answered his greeting— no one did. He tried again. "This is Bear."

Only silence and the unnerving sound of someone's breathing in reply. Maybe the reception was bad out here in the country.

Last try. "Hello?"

Nothing.

He lowered the phone, tapped out of the call, searched his screen for the caller I.D. No luck. *Unidentified Number.*

Huh. Could it have been John calling from Brazil? He'd promised to send the mission board's application for the community center position as soon as it was available. Maybe he had news.

Or it was nothing—just a misdialed number or prank call.

Bear stuffed his phone in his back pocket and glanced back and forth between Erin, still having a blast on her pony ride, and the barn Jamie had disappeared into. "Erin, you okay if I go find your brother?"

Erin squealed as Penelope flicked her mane.

Harley shot Bear a squinted grin. "I think that's a yes."

Bear had gotten to chat with Harley several times over the past days as he worked out at the cabins. Well, cabin. He'd only managed to clear one of them so far, working a couple hours on both Monday and Tuesday morning while Jamie and Erin played nearby. But Sara didn't seem to mind his slow progress. After all, he'd promised to pick up his pace once he returned the kids to Atlanta.

He banished the thought as he trooped toward the barn, just as he had every time it entered his mind in recent days. His niece and nephew had been in his care for a week and two, almost three, days now. What had started as a niggle of affection when he'd seen them sleeping in that shabby apartment had, with every day that passed, deepened into a hard-and-fast, intense love.

The gaze of the afternoon sun shuttered as Bear stepped into the barn. He blinked to adjust to the dim, scouring the row of stalls on each side of the expansive space for Jamie. A rustle of movement overhead captured his attention. He moved toward the ladder leading into the haymow.

"Jamie?"

Just like that phone call, no reply.

But he found his nephew easily as soon as he emerged into the barn's upper level. His feet found the wood-planked floor, the sweet, musty scent of hay encasing him. Bales of it—some strung solidly, others half undone and strewn about the mow—covered nearly every inch of the floor.

Jamie sat atop the highest of the stacked bundles.

"More in the mood for climbing than horseback riding?" Bear hiked his way over hay that slid like sand until he reached his nephew. He settled beside him with a satisfied exhale. "You know what's missing from this haymow?"

Jamie shook his head. That was something, at least.

"A swinging rope. I assumed every haymow in the world had one."

Jamie's brown eyes journeyed the room before he finally answered. "I didn't know it was called a haymow."

"Learn something every day, don't you?"

Quiet slanted in, like the sunlight through the cracks between boards in the barn's roof. Bear let the hush land and stretch, searching for the right words, trying on one trite remark after another. Discarding each one before it could pass his lips.

Maybe Jamie didn't need comfort from an uncle he barely knew. He certainly didn't seem to want it.

But he needed something.

He needs everything.

A stable home life. Clothes that fit. A dad who cared more about his kids than his career of crime.

A mom who remembered to call. *Why* hadn't Rosa

checked in since Sunday? Bear had tried calling her—twice, even three times each day this week. Had her phone plan been cut off like her utilities? Even if so, there were still such things as pay phones. Or she could borrow a friend's.

Maybe she was truly that busy finding a new place to live, working extra hours, fixing whatever had gone wrong with Rio's latest activities . . .

As if that were even possible.

Should he be worried about her? She'd mentioned going to her father. But Luis Inez was the last person Bear could ever imagine asking for help. For as long as he could remember, the Inez and McKinley families had been on opposite sides of ceaseless turf fights. Things had only gotten worse when Rio and Rosa took up together as teens.

And then there'd been the raid. Bear's interference. The arrests and the short trial and Inez watching from the back of the courtroom . . .

"At least this is better than the other times."

Jamie's soft voice surprised Bear so much he jerked, kicking a wad of hay and sending it scattering. "What?"

"It's better than the other times we were taken away."

Bear's breath caught, all thoughts of Luis Inez fading. Taken away? "By who?" But even as he asked, he knew. He'd guessed correctly—hadn't he?—about why Rosa had been so insistent he not call the police.

Child Protective Services. How many times? And for how long? And why? Had Rio been dealing right from home—like Dad used to? Worse, had he started cooking?

Why hadn't Rosa just left him? Unless—was she dealing, too? Using?

God, it's such a mess. And it's not fair. Jamie and Erin don't deserve this.

If it was a prayer, it was one fueled by frustration. Anger. Wasn't it enough that Bear and Rio had a crappy childhood? Did history have to repeat itself so stubbornly?

Shouldn't God step in and do something? Isn't that what He was there for?

Or was it up to Bear? An appalling thought, considering what had happened when he tried to help Rio.

Maybe if you'd been quicker to help him in the first place . . .

Shame, like clockwork, like always, ticked its way in. But this wasn't about Bear and Rio. It was about Jamie and Erin.

"Jamie—"

"I don't want to talk about it."

"Okay." Bear waited, hesitated, then reached out his palm to settle on Jamie's knee. For once, Jamie didn't grimace, didn't recoil. In fact, he seemed to ease just the slightest.

Maybe, for right now, it was enough.

But he'd call Rosa again as soon as he was alone. He'd get the answers he needed. And he'd make one thing very, *very* clear: No chance on earth or anywhere else was he returning these kids to the life they'd known before.

It was Sara's advice that drew Raegan back to the mural site at the end of the day, to the building soon to become her canvas.

The three-story building loomed large and overwhelming in front of her, its newly burnished brick rough underneath her fingertips. Swollen clouds and the scaffolding's platform overhead muted any light of dusk.

"So far, everyone I've shown my designs to likes the sunflower concept the best," Raegan had told Sara this morning as they'd sipped iced mochas at Coffee Coffee. *"I feel like something's missing, though."*

"Does the design have to be perfect before you can start painting?" Sara had asked.

"Not necessarily. But considering I've got such a tight deadline, I'd be a lot more comfortable diving in if it was."

"Well, I'm no art critic, that's for sure. But I like to think the best art in some way tells the truth. What's the truth you're trying to tell with this mural, Rae?" Sara had laced her fingers atop the coffee shop table.

Raegan hadn't had an answer.

Sara had suggested she spend some time alone at the building. After all, she'd noted, it was the building itself—Mom's memories attached to it—that had inspired Raegan's project in the first place.

Raegan stepped out from under the cover of the scaffolding. Should she attempt to climb it now? Heaven knew she'd rather make her first ascent alone rather than under the watchful eyes of everyone in town. It'd be the peak of embarrassment to discover an unforeseen fear of heights with an audience.

A driving wind rattled the scaffolding and churned the river across the way into currents. As usual, she'd biked here tonight. She should probably head home before those grumbling clouds let loose.

But it wouldn't take that long to scale the metal structure. Besides, she needed to get a feel for what working from the platform might feel like.

She rounded to where a built-in ladder led up the side scaffolding. One of the city crew who'd helped erect the scaffolding today had told her she'd need to work in a harness. Something about the city's insurance policy. But she'd be fine tonight without it. After all, those high schoolers who'd cleaned the brick hadn't been attached to anything—the safety of the guardrail had been enough for them.

She was halfway up the scaffolding when she felt the first raindrop. *Hurry up.* She moved her hands and feet faster, eventually heaving herself over the edge and onto the platform. She rose to her feet slowly, uncertain of the structure's steadiness. Though metal clanked with her movement, it seemed stable enough.

She padded over the raised stand, the prickly breeze raising the hair on her bare arms as she looked out at the riverfront. Lamplight fogged the street below. She was only about fifteen feet off the ground, but it was enough to send her pulse hammering.

She wasn't scared exactly. Just . . . cautious.

She turned toward the building, inching as close to the edge of the platform as she dared, only minimally reassured by the guardrail. Yes, a harness was a good idea.

She reached out to the touch the brick. It wasn't anything like her usual smooth canvas. It curved and dipped under her fingertips, course and uneven.

Okay, this was silly. She didn't suddenly feel inspired standing up here. She felt overwhelmed and intimidated, more uncertain than ever. And chilled—she felt chilled from the wind and the raindrops now pattering against the metal underneath her feet.

A jagged band of lightning chose that moment to flash in the sky.

Great, surrounded by metal rails while there's lightning. Real smart, Rae.

She needed to get out of here before this turned into a full-fledged storm. But as she crossed to the edge of the platform, an explosion of thunder boomed with enough force to freeze her in place. Not a full second later, the sky let loose. The torrent crashed in, smacking against Raegan, against the platform underneath her, the clatter loud enough to drown out her shriek.

Another flare of lightning lit her surroundings in a garish clash of light and shadows.

And the first flicker of dread jolted through Raegan. *No. Not now.*

She forced her feet to move toward the ladder but halted when she realized it was slick with rain. Was it even safe to climb down now? If she slipped . . .

Yeah, but if lightning strikes . . .

The far-off memory of another frightening blend of isolation and indecision lurked at the borders of her awareness. It only ever swooped in on her in moments like these. As if it laid in wait. As if she hadn't spent years tamping it down.

The storm. The ice. The sheet of white outside her car and the swelling of her panic inside.

Her lungs squeezed as the fear—always the fear—twisted around her now just as it had then.

She squeezed her eyes closed against the ringing in her ears, the racket of the rain. Listened for Mom's voice. *"One deep breath. And then another."*

The whispered echoes seemed to grow fainter all the time. The pitch of Mom's tone, the rhythm of her words—she was losing the memory.

It's okay. I'm not lost this time. Just breathe.

But the next breath wouldn't come. Only trembling. And numbing. And falling.

It might have thundered then. Or maybe that was the sound of an engine. But she couldn't make out the sounds over the thudding of her heart.

Not again. Please not again.

"Raegan?"

Her vision blurred as her knees hit the metal floor.

8

Not even a long, hot shower had been enough to scorch from Bear's mind the image of Raegan in a heap atop the scaffolding stage, trembling and as white as winter.

He stood outside her bedroom door now, fist raised and ready to knock. But he hesitated. She might be asleep. She *should* be asleep. *He* should be asleep. It was after midnight.

But when he'd tried lying down on that futon down in the basement, when he closed his eyes, he kept seeing her shaking hands and nearly blue lips, kept watching her gasp for breath.

It played out all over again in front of him, even as he stared at her bedroom door.

He'd just turned the light out in Jamie and Erin's room when he'd heard Case and Beckett talking down the hall. Apparently Raegan had taken off an hour earlier—on her bike.

Because Raegan went everywhere on her bike. She had a car. Why did she so rarely drive it?

Both father and son had been concerned about the upcoming storm. Bear had jumped in, offering to run into town and pick her up. But when he'd arrived at the

Hay & Feed building, he'd seen Raegan's bike, but not the woman herself.

Until glaring lightning had shined a spotlight up above. His focus sprinted up just in time to see Raegan fall to her knees.

He was soaked through by the time he reached the top of the scaffolding's ladder. He'd crouched next to her, saying her name, brushing her wet hair away from her face. But it was as if she couldn't see him or hear him, could only pant for breath.

His mind had grappled for explanation. Was she suddenly sick? This seemed like an attack. Asthma? But she wasn't wheezing . . . more like hyperventilating.

A panic attack?

It was another growl of the thunder that finally seemed to snatch her from the trance. With his arms around her, he'd felt it—the slow easing of her breathing, her loosening muscles. "Raegan?"

She'd tilted her head as if only then sensing his presence. "Bear?" She'd blinked, pulled away, stood. And then, "Please don't tell my dad."

It was the last thing she'd said to him all night. After he'd helped her down the scaffolding, stuffed her bike in the trunk, he'd finally asked, "Are you okay now?"

But she'd only turned to the window, shivering.

He'd flicked off the car's A/C.

Bear lifted his fist once more. Raegan clearly hadn't wanted to talk earlier, and she'd escaped to the second floor the minute they'd walked into the house. He'd respected that. Figured they'd talk tomorrow.

But that was before he'd spent an hour tossing and turning. Besides, technically it *was* tomorrow.

"Uncle Bear?"

He whirled before he could knock. Jamie stood just behind him, wrinkled white tee and tousled hair, sleepiness heavy in his eyes. "Hey. What're you doing up?" *Uncle Bear.* It was the second time Jamie had called him that. Maybe those few minutes up in the haymow had done more good than he realized.

Even if they had left Bear as unsettled about the kids and their future as he was about Raegan now.

"I had a dream about my dad."

Bear rubbed his cheeks, stubble like sandpaper under his palms. "A good dream or a bad dream?"

Jamie only shrugged.

"Do you need a drink of water? A snack?"

Jamie's head tipped, and even in the dim of the darkened hallway, Bear could see the reservation in his nephew's eyes. The anxiety. "What's jail like?"

Bear's track pants rustled as he knelt, his mind whirling with the wish that Jamie didn't have the details on his dad's whereabouts. Then again, there'd been plenty of times growing up when Bear had spent multiple nights in a row wondering where his own parents were. Not knowing didn't feel any better than knowing.

"Bear?"

His gaze met his nephew's. Jail. Jamie wanted to know what jail was like.

A picture of Rio flashed in his mind. Rio in an orange jumpsuit in a hovel of a cell, stark gray walls and a lumpy mattress. Except, no. He wasn't picturing his brother. The face in the image was his own.

"It's a little lonely, Jamie. And the food probably isn't that good."

Memories trampled in: The isolation even in crowded quarters. The smells—metal and sweat and worse. The rattle of cuffs and bars. Days bleeding into one another too slowly to distinguish.

His desperate attempt to keep believing his choice was worth it.

The anguished letter that told him it wasn't.

Annie.

"Do you think my dad is scared?"

He closed his palms over Jamie's skinny arms, did his best to level his tone into something close to reassuring. "I think your dad is just fine. And maybe it's best to try not to think about him for a little while. Think about that game of basketball Seth and Beckett promised for tomorrow—just us guys. You need to rest up so we can win."

Jamie nodded, not entirely relieved, clearly. But at least he didn't ask anything further about Rio. And once again, he'd let Bear near enough to comfort him without pushing him away. Bear squeezed his hands lightly over Jamie's arms before steering him toward Beckett's bedroom. He tucked the boy into the top bunk, leaned over the bottom bunk to kiss Erin's cheek, and quietly closed the door as he left the room.

Raegan's door stared at him from across the hallway.

"So, should I be concerned about this?"

He spun for the second time that night, heart leaping into his throat at the sound of Case Walker's voice.

Raegan's dad stood just feet away, shadowed by the doorframe of the master bedroom. Strange that he'd barely run into the man since that first night Case arrived home, what with the carnival over the weekend, all his activities with the kids the past couple days.

"Uh, hey, Mr. Walker. Sorry, concerned about . . . ?"

"Finding a young man hovering outside my daughter's bedroom door in the middle of the night. Doesn't that seem like the kind of thing a father might not appreciate?"

If there wasn't the faintest trace of a smile tugging at the corner of Case's mouth, Bear might feel the need to flee to the basement. There weren't many people he found intimidating. But Case Walker exuded strength and authority, even if he was generally one of the most mild-mannered men Bear had ever encountered.

"Sir, I was only . . . that is . . . I just wanted to make sure she's . . ."

"Lighten up, son. I was only badgering you for my own enjoyment. I think I know you well enough to know there's not any funny business going on here." Case crossed the narrow hallway to stand in front of Bear, one eyebrow raised. "There's *not* any funny business going on, is there?"

"No, sir. Of course not."

That was a full-on grin breaking across Case's face now. He patted Bear's shoulder, then waved his hand toward the stairway. "What do you say you and I have a midnight chat?"

Didn't exactly sound like a request.

"And enough with the *sirs*," Case added as he started down the steps.

The stairs creaked into the quiet of the night, the rest of the house nestled into sleep. No, it definitely hadn't been the best idea to tiptoe his way up to the second floor earlier. He should've stayed down in the basement.

What were you going to do, anyway? Wake Rae up for a middle-of-the-night heart-to-heart?

When they entered the kitchen, Case pulled out a stool from the massive island counter that spanned the middle of the room. "Sit."

A flashback toddled in—of Raegan at the carnival, the exact same tone in her voice when she'd commanded him to sit so she could paint his cheek. People were always telling Raegan she was exactly like her mother. But she had plenty of her father in her, too.

Bear sat and proceeded to watch as Case went about filling his coffeepot with water, dumping in heaping spoonfuls of decaf coffee. Within minutes, the pot groaned as the coffee began percolating.

Case turned from his roost at the counter. "Now then. Let's talk."

Was it pathetic—the slight twinge of fear that rattled through Bear? "Listen, sir, about Rae—"

"I didn't mean let's talk about Raegan and I thought I told you to drop the *sir*."

"Sorry." And he *didn't* want to talk about Raegan? "I just assumed—"

"That you were about to receive a lecture on dating my daughter?"

"I'm not dating your daughter."

"You would be if you had any sense at all."

Bear didn't know whether to laugh or go hide under the dining room table. "You're very forthright, Mr. Walker." At Case's amplified glower, he tacked on, "Case."

"Well, I hope you'll return the favor by shooting straight with me." He folded his arms. "About Sara."

Sara? That's what he wanted to talk about? "I don't understand."

"How much has she filled you in on?"

"Sir—Case," he stumbled. "She hired me to clean out and repair the cabins on her property. That's all. She hasn't filled me in on anything other than the details of the job." She hadn't even approached him with a W-4 or that dreaded background check yet. With each day that passed, he grew more hopeful he might be able to avoid that awkwardness altogether.

Could be a lot worse than awkward. If Sara knew the full scope of his criminal record, he could find himself out a job. Unless she proved more gracious than some of the church leaders down in Brazil.

And you really want to return?

Wasn't so much a matter of want. With everything in him, he *needed* to return. How else was he supposed to repay John and Elizabeth for all his choice had cost them? How else was he supposed to keep his vow to Annie?

He'd promised to go with her back when she was alive. He'd promised to go for her after her death.

"Bear?" Case was looking at him now as if trying to read the jumble of thoughts crowding his over-tired brain.

"Whatever the deal is with you and Sara, I'm in the dark. If you're worried I'm going to spill some sordid story to Raegan, don't be. 'Cause I've got nothing." He spoke too rigidly, almost harshly.

But between his worries about Jamie and Erin, his concern for Raegan, his fear of Sara finding out about his criminal record, the desperation that seized him the moment any thought of Rio or Annie hurdled in, he was at the end of his patience.

Case's eyes narrowed. "Nobody said anything about sordid."

"I shouldn't have phrased it like that."

The coffeepot grumbled and Case turned, freeing Bear from the weight of his scrutiny. He waited mutely while the man pulled a couple mugs from a row of hooks underneath the cupboard.

"Coffeepots that pause automatically are one of the best inventions of the last century," Case said as he poured both cups, the overbearing aroma of the brew filling the kitchen. His tone had gone lighter. A conscious shift or solely the relieved result of realizing Bear didn't know his and Sara's story? "Kate always tells me to get one of those fancy Keurigs, but as long as I don't have to wait for a full pot to perc, I'm happy enough with my Mr. Coffee." He set one cup in front of Bear. "Drink up."

Bear stuffed down his distaste and lifted the mug, taking a long swallow. He gasped at the strength of the drink.

"I know. My kids say I like it way too muddy. I say all their taste buds just need to man up."

Then no way was Bear going to tell Case he avoided the stuff whenever he could. He forced another gulp.

"Listen, son, you ever want to talk, I'm here."

Bear's gaze snapped upward. Case's expression was neutral, his attention on his coffee mug. He'd said it casually enough, but the offer was rife with significance, whether Case knew it or not. Bear could talk to Seth. Sometimes he could talk to Raegan, if he could keep himself from making too much of their familiarity.

But ever since leaving Brazil, he'd sorely missed having a father figure on hand. Time and again while living in Maple Valley, he'd seen Case Walker take one of his offspring under his wing—offer just the right words or support at just the right time.

What must it have been like for Raegan and her siblings—even Seth, who'd spent so much time at his uncle's house—growing up with a dad like Case?

"I appreciate that . . . Case. Truth is, I have a lot of uncertainty in my life right now. I don't know why Jamie and Erin's mother hasn't called in a few days. I'm concerned about what's going to happen to them when they have to go back. I'm worried about my own future." *I'm worried about your daughter.*

"And your brother?"

Bear's throat dried, the bitter taste of the coffee clinging. "He's the least of my concerns right now." *Not even close to true.*

Nor had it been true in any of the past five, six, seven years when he'd told himself Rio didn't deserve any more of his care or compassion. But it'd grown so much easier simply to not think about him.

"Well, he's one of Jamie's concerns, that's for sure."

Case had heard that hallway conversation?

"He might need to talk about his father, even if you don't."

Bear bristled. "And what am I supposed to tell him? Make up some excuse for why Rio apparently cares more about his chancy lifestyle than his own kids? Pretend he hasn't made one horrible choice after another?"

Case didn't appear affected by Bear's rising vexation. "I've never known avoidance to convert into healing, Bear. That's all I'm saying." He sipped his drink. "All it does is stretch out the hurt. That boy is hurting."

"But anything I have to say about Rio . . . I'm not sure it'd help."

"You don't have to recite a homily in his honor, son. Just talk. Let Jamie in. Search your heart for a happy memory to share with him."

Bear swallowed. "And if I can't find one?"

"Then you probably aren't trying hard enough." Case closed his fingers around his mug. "In which case, you might want to ask yourself who you're really trying to protect. That boy or yourself?"

Seventeen hours since the last attack. So this was what square-one felt like.

Raegan pushed her way through the red metal door leading into the men's locker room. The sound of splashing and echoing voices drifted in from the indoor pool, and the smell of chlorine clung to the air.

There were days when having multiple jobs was a

blessing. Between her shift at the library this morning, the depot this afternoon, and now the pool this evening, she hadn't had to see Bear once.

Which meant she didn't have to deal with the litany of questions she knew he'd only barely held back last night—probably wouldn't have if he hadn't been interrupted before knocking on her bedroom door.

Yeah, she'd heard him out in the hallway. Had held her breath until Dad had pulled him away.

She dragged a rolling yellow mop bucket into the locker room, its creaking hinges echoing off the cement walls. This was her least favorite task, but it came with the territory. Usually she could make a good time of it—stick in her earbuds, let Frank Sinatra's crooning convince her she was dancing across a ballroom rather than lugging a heavy, wet mop over a slippery floor.

But today all she could think about was last night. She hefted the mop from its bucket and plopped it against the floor.

Was it the storm or the height that had caused the attack? Or both? Or neither? She'd had plenty of panic attacks in the past that seemed to bruise their way in without cause. But they usually hit the fastest and hardest when she was already feeling fearful. Or lost. Or hurt.

Or any barrage of unwanted emotion.

It was why she worked so hard to stay upbeat. Secure. Surrounded by familiarity and comfort. Why she stayed in Maple Valley. Why she avoided travel. Why . . . so many things.

"Rae?"

She stilled, standing stiff beside a row of rusted old lockers as the red door clanked to a close. Bear? "What are you doing here?"

He stepped farther into the room, his dirt-stained

jeans and tee evidence of the work he must've done out at the ranch today. His sun-kissed skin couldn't hide the pale circles under his eyes. Had his night been as sleepless as hers?

"Shouldn't I be the one asking you that, this being a men's locker room and all?"

"Cleaning duty." She tapped the mop bucket with one foot. "Every employee has to take a turn each week. Today's my unlucky day."

"You ever worry you're going to walk in on some guy taking a shower?"

She dunked the mop into the bucket, then squeezed its water free. "I always wait 'til public hours are over. There's an all-female senior citizen water aerobics class in the pool now. I'm safe." She plopped the mop onto the concrete floor. "But I did once accidentally walk in on Lenny Klassen in only a towel."

"You didn't."

"I did. He hasn't been able to talk to me without turning fire-engine red since." She swished her mop over the floor in a figure-eight pattern, her hair flopping over her face. This was good—light conversation. Maybe Bear hadn't sought her out to ply her with questions.

"Speaking of . . ."

She sloshed the mop into her bucket again. "Of fire engines?"

"Of people not being able to talk to people."

So much for that.

She brushed her hair over her shoulder and for the first time all day, met his eyes. But only for an instant. "What about it?" She moved backward, angling around the row of lockers until she lost sight of Bear.

But he grabbed hold of her rolling bucket and followed her to the other side of the room. "You're avoiding me."

Concrete turned to tile where the men's showers began. "No, I'm working." She mopped harder, faster.

"You're feeling awkward or embarrassed or *something* about what happened last night." He stepped over her wet floor to reach for the mop's handle, his fingers closing just above hers.

"Don't tell me how I feel, Bear McKinley."

"I just think we should talk about it. Rae, seeing you like that, it scared me half to death. You were as white as a ghost. You went from barely breathing to hyperventilating." She tried to jerk the mop away, but he held too tight. "I thought you were going to pass out."

"Well, I didn't. And it's over now. I don't see why we have to talk about it. You didn't need to come find me for some big curative conversation. You should be with Jamie and Erin." She glanced at his dirty, rumpled clothing. "Or maybe taking a shower. Just not here."

"Jamie and Erin are having a grand time with Beckett and Kit at the orchard. They're fine. You're the one who's not."

Her glare was enough to make him loosen his hold on the mop. She yanked it away, retreating into the one private shower stall at the end of the room. The pungent scent of the mop bucket's bleach rose up as she heard Bear let out a frustrated exhale. She heard his heavy footfalls rattling the lone, long bleacher that lined the aisle in between the lockers.

Good, he was leaving.

So why did she feel even worse than before? Why the tears pricking her eyes? She stood with both arms curling around the mop's handle, shoulders slumped. One tear escaped and then another and with the third, a sob she couldn't hold back.

"Rae?"

She sensed Bear's presence the moment he ducked

into the shower stall behind her. He didn't even hesitate to gently pull the mop free and turn her to face him. She wilted against him without argument.

"I . . . I kept hoping it wouldn't happen again. I counted the days and then the months and the years." She clung to his shirt as his arms closed around her. "I th-thought I might make it two years. I thought I was b-better . . ."

There was no stopping her tears now. She let them fall, felt them soaking Bear's shirt as she shook against him, quiet cries expelling the noisy tumult of her heart. Hushed minutes passed, the tick of the clock hanging on one wall, the faint voices from the pool, all fading into the background as Bear breathed into her hair.

Until, finally, slowly, she began to still. Her trembling dwindled, along with her tears. She clasped Bear's shirt and used it to dry her eyes. She sniffled again, freed a raspy laugh. "I-if your shirt wasn't ruined before, I think I just finished the job."

"They're only tears, Rae."

She glanced up at him. "Clearly you don't wear mascara."

He lowered his gaze to his shirt. Smudges of black stained his front. He smiled. "Never liked this shirt all that much anyway."

It was the smile that made her tense just for a moment. Of course she'd needed to cry, but had she had to do it like this? In front of him? But just as quickly, she released her breath and leaned into him once more. This was no worse than last night, after all. "Sorry to fall apart on you. Again."

He lifted one hand to brush through her hair. "I really don't mind."

"I guess you're probably wondering . . ."

"You don't have to explain, Raegan. But if you want

to, if it'd help, I'm here. I'm your . . . friend."

She tipped her head toward his. "My friend."

The word had never felt more inadequate. She took a fortifying breath, along with a step backward, knocking into the mop bucket. His hands slid to her arms to steady her before dropping to his sides.

"It was a panic attack."

"I figured out that much."

"I get them sometimes. They started when I was a teenager." The words seemed to scurry from her lips, as if she might not get them out if she didn't hurry through the explanation. "The worst was the time after . . . after Mom. I—I was upset. I got in my car and started driving, and by the time I realized I was lost . . ." She turned away.

"Why didn't you want me to tell your dad? If this is something that happens regularly—"

"It doesn't. At least, it hadn't for a long time."

"But you've been dealing with this on your own? All this time?"

She didn't answer.

"Raegan, that's not good. You need to talk to somebody."

She shook her head, backing away and bumping into the wall of the shower stall behind her. "No."

"But—"

"I'm fine, Bear." *I'm fine. I'm fine. I'm fine.* Why did no one ever believe her?

Because they're not idiots. Because you don't even believe yourself.

"You're not fine."

"Well, I don't need fixing."

"I'm not trying to fix you. But there are therapists or counselors or—"

"Please, just stop."

"I care about you, Rae. I hate the thought of you dealing with this all alone. I could talk to your dad with you and—"

In a flash, she lifted her hand to jerk the shower knob and an instant shower of icy water sloshed from overhead. Bear sputtered as Raegan held herself flat against the wall of the stall, avoiding the onslaught.

"Why you—" Bear reached for her with both arms, pulling her into the stream of water.

Her shriek bounced off the cement walls. "Bear!" Her squeal turned into laughter as she didn't even try to get away, and just that fast, her tension washed away. "I can't believe you," she stammered through giggles.

"You started it." His shirt was matted to his chest.

"Only to get you to stop."

"You couldn't have picked the hot water knob?" Bear fumbled for the faucet and turned the water off, his laughter still mingling with Raegan's. He shook the water from his hair, only to earn another squeal from Raegan as the water hit her. "Serves you right, Walker." He pulled his shirt free from his chest, ringing it out.

"I think my shoes are ruined." She pushed the hair out of her eyes, shivering. And then stilled as Bear's attention dropped to her soaking canvas shoes before slowly traveling upward to where her shorts and tee were now plastered to her. And in an instant, all the strain from minutes before was back in full force.

Only different now.

"I just want to help, Rae. What can I do to help?"

Her breathing was still heavy, her hair dripping around her cheeks, and the question in Bear's eyes went so much deeper than his words. His gaze strayed to her lips and stayed there even as she grasped for a reply.

"I . . . you . . ."

The locker room door slammed.

The smart thing to have done back in that locker room would've been to hold Bear at arm's length—just like he'd done for so many years with her.

When that door had banged to a close and the community center manager had gasped at finding the two of them huddled together, soaking wet in a shower stall, Raegan should've taken it for the escape it was.

Bear had already seen her in the throes of a panic attack. He'd held her while she emotionally broke down. Wasn't that enough?

"We don't have to do this tonight, Rae."

The man was a mind reader. His hand encased her own as she stood facing the scaffolding of the Hay & Feed Store. They'd gone home to change into dry clothes before driving back into town, somehow managing to avoid Dad or Beckett and any uncomfortable questions their drenched appearance might induce in the process.

Too, they'd successfully evaded any conversation about what had happened back in that shower stall. Or, well, hadn't happened. Had maybe almost happened?

Raegan honestly wasn't sure. Except the way Bear had looked at her . . .

"Did you hear me?" He squeezed her hand now. "We can wait until tomorrow."

No, she wanted to do this now. Get it over with. If she had any hope of moving forward with this mural project, she needed to know whether the height was going to be an issue. Whether she could climb the scaffolding without falling apart this time.

If she couldn't . . .

Well, better to know now. Let down Mayor Milt early enough that he had time to find another artist.

The thought tasted bitter and went down hard. When had she begun to want this so badly? It'd taken her days to agree in the first place and ever since, sagging confidence had filled her with all kinds of doubt. The final thing she remembered from last night, just before falling asleep, was the sobering conviction that she needed to call Mayor Milt first thing in the morning.

Because she couldn't do this. Not if it meant a constant fear of a repeat performance of Wednesday night.

But when she and Bear had emerged from the community center into the summer night air, with chalk-like clouds lit by soft evening colors above, when Bear had turned to her and asked again what he could do to help, she'd been struck by a desire so vigorous there'd been no denying it.

"I need to climb up the scaffolding again."

"That's not what I meant, Rae."

"But that's how you can help me. I want to do this mural. I want to make the mayor and the town and my family proud. But I can't do it if I can't handle working from the scaffolding."

He'd opened his mouth as if to argue again but had apparently thought twice. He'd freed a long, patient exhale instead. *"I don't think the kids will mind an extra hour at the orchard. Last I checked in, Beck was giving them rides on a four-wheeler. If you're sure . . ."*

"I'm sure," she said now. "I want to do it."

"Okay, then." Bear released her hand and started toward the ladder. "Do you want me to go first or you?"

"You can."

He clasped a rung at shoulder height and stepped one foot onto the lowest rail. He twisted around before pulling himself up. "Are you sure you shouldn't go first?"

"Bear, it wasn't the ladder that gave me trouble last

time."

"But when you do this on your own, when you're painting, you're going to use a harness, yeah?"

"Yep."

"Promise?"

Despite all the pummeling emotion of the past twenty-four hours, a whisper of amusement tickled inside. "Yes, Bear, I promise I'll use a harness. Does that make you feel better?"

He didn't even crack a smile. "A little." He started climbing.

The structure jostled with his movement and she waited until he was halfway up before starting her own ascent. Like last night, the climb took no more than a minute. Only this time, Bear waited at the top, his palm outstretched to help her over the edge.

He had her on her feet in seconds, but he kept hold of her hand.

She didn't pull away.

"No storm tonight," he said.

"No storm." Instead, just enough sun peeked over the horizon to breathe warmth into the evening. It rippled over the river in shades of orange and cast an amber glow over the street below. A soft calm settled over her like a cotton blanket.

"Bear."

"What?"

"You don't have to stare at me the whole time we're up here." She slid her hand free.

"What if I want to?"

She spun her gaze to his face—his crooked grin, those crinkles at the corners of his eyes. He had to pick *now* to be charming? After he'd seen her at her worst? Twice in the past twenty-four hours?

Then again, when was Bear McKinley ever *not*

charming?

"I think we're good. Let's go home."

His smile drooped. "We just got here."

"And I made the climb and I'm fine. Clearly I'm okay with heights." What she wasn't okay with was the flurry of attraction currently pushing her stomach toward blizzard conditions. "So we can go. Mission accomplished."

He crossed his arms. Stubborn man.

Handsome man.

She shouldn't have come here with him—alone. And she never should've turned on the water in that shower stall. She should've pulled away from Bear the moment her tears ceased. Heck, she probably never should've invited him to stay at Dad's. She should've—

"Well, *my* mission isn't accomplished," he said. "Instead of moving to the ladder, Bear padded to the edge of the platform and lowered to sit. He gripped the lowest guardrail as he dangled his legs over the edge.

"Your mission is to loiter up here?"

"My mission is to watch the sunset." He tipped his head so she could see his wink. "Preferably with a pretty girl at my side."

"I should groan and roll my eyes at that."

"And yet, you aren't."

No, in fact, she was doing another thing she shouldn't—crossing the platform and plopping down beside Bear. Although, unlike him, she couldn't bring herself to suspend her legs over the edge. Instead, she crossed her legs, keeping a good half a foot between herself and the rim of the platform. "You shouldn't flirt with me, Bear McKinley."

"I'm not flirting."

"You called me pretty."

"Stating a fact."

"Well . . . thank you." She folded her clammy hands in her lap.

"You're welcome." He kept his gaze slanted toward the horizon, the light of sunset bobbing in his dark eyes.

Jamie's eyes. Did Bear realize how many features he shared with his nephew? Same mop of dark hair over ears that bent outward ever so slightly. Same shape of their chins. Jamie's face wasn't yet as contoured as Bear's, but she had a feeling that, come adulthood, their profiles might be identical.

"Rae?"

Her "Hmm?" came out a murmur.

"Back in the locker room, you started to say something about your worst panic attack. After your mom . . ."

Somehow she'd known he'd ask. Even as she'd allowed herself to relax for a few seconds there, she'd been waiting for it. Maybe that was why she'd been so eager to call it a night, head home. "I'm not sure I'm ready to talk about it."

He turned to her. "That's okay."

"It's not that I don't trust you. I hope you know that."

"I do." Bear still held on to the railing with one arm.

"No one even knows about the panic attacks. I've never told anyone." Except that wasn't quite true. "Other than my mom. They started when her cancer came back the third time. She found me in my room the first time. I was terrified—didn't know what was happening."

When it happened a second time—and then a third—Mom had wanted to take her to a doctor.

But Raegan had resisted, ashamed at the thought of causing more trouble for her family than they were already facing. When Mom had protested her protest,

Raegan had assured her that if it happened a fourth time, she'd agree to an appointment.

From then on, any time she'd felt the slightest tremor, she'd stolen away to her bedroom—or the nearest isolated location. She'd learned to spot the signs early, to make excuses for sudden absences. To return as if nothing had ever gone amiss.

And Mom, sick as she was, had bought it.

"I don't understand why you'd keep this from your family, Rae. You have the most supportive father in the world. Your siblings would do anything for you."

"I know all that." She twisted her hands together. "At first I didn't say anything because I was embarrassed. I felt horrible about adding one more thing to everyone's already overflowing plate. Bear, we knew Mom was dying. That last bout with cancer, we knew it."

She could still picture each sibling's face when Dad and Mom had sat them down in the living room to talk. Logan's silent stillness. Kate's tears. Beckett's balled fists.

"And then after she died, after the accident—"

"The accident?"

Her focus swooped to her lap. "That attack I mentioned—the worst one. I was . . . I was in the car." It was as much as she could get out now. If she let herself replay any more, she might come undone.

And she was just too . . . tired. Exhausted from the emotional tumult of the past day.

Bear—kind, patient Bear—seemed to instantly understand. For the third time that night, he reached for her hand.

"I just couldn't tell Dad. Not after everything he'd been through. And then later . . . you don't understand how it is with my family, Bear. I know they're wonderful and supportive and all the things you said. But they're all so . . . successful. Do you have any idea how long I've been the odd one out? I don't look like the rest of them. I don't have big ambitions like the rest of them. Now they're all getting married left and right and settling down and they think it's odd that I've never been . . . I guess, unsettled."

"Except that you are unsettled, Rae. I know because I've been there—in that place where you're supposed to be happy, the place you thought you wanted to be. But inside, everything's off, no matter how much you deny it."

"Brazil?"

He only nodded.

"And that's why you left? Because you were unsettled? So why do you want to go back?

"Why do you stay?"

She didn't answer and he didn't force it. Instead, after a hushed pause, he laced his fingers through hers. "There are other people you could talk to. You could talk to Sara. She's a therapist."

"Bear—"

"Will you just consider it? I promise I won't say another word about it if you'll just think about it."

The breeze lifted his hair from his forehead. He traced her thumb with his own. "I'll think about it." Because she couldn't say no to him. Not when he looked at her like that—as if unwilling to take another breath until he was certain she was going to be okay.

His sigh of relief was accompanied by the easing of his grip on her hand. But he didn't release it. Minutes faded into each other as the last remnant of the sun sank low in the west. Only when it disappeared entirely did Bear turn to her again. "Ready to go?"

At her nod, he pulled her to her feet. But before she could angle toward the ladder, Bear's forehead wrinkled as he looked over her shoulder.

"What?" She turned to the street.

"That car."

Not hard to tell which one he meant. Only one besides her own rested at the curb—a long, blue Taurus spotlighted by the flush of the streetlamp. Was that a man or a woman sitting inside it? Hard to tell from up here.

"That's the second time I've seen it, just idling with someone inside."

"It's not exactly an unusual car, Bear."

"Yeah, but it's after eight. Every business on the waterfront is closed." Unease hovered in his voice.

"Bear—"

The screech of tires interrupted her as the Taurus lurched into motion and disappeared down the road.

The apprehension in Bear's eyes only deepened.

9

*T*his didn't make any sense at all.

"You're telling me there's no record of a Rio McKinley in any jail in the greater Atlanta area."

Bear held his phone to his ear, the tiny interior of Raegan's car stifling despite the huffing A/C. The idling engine rumbled. Outside the windshield and across a blacktopped parking lot sat the Maple Valley Community Hospital, a mix of beige brick, glass, and gleaming chrome.

The man on the other end of the phone, a Sergeant Something-or-other with the Atlanta Police Department Zone 4, spoke again. "Not only is there no record of him in jail at present, but I don't show any arrests in the past eighteen months."

Bear leaned his head against the headrest and closed his eyes. Why had he even bothered with this call? Anytime he meddled in Rio's life, it only caused trouble.

But in the twelve hours since that conversation atop the scaffolding with Raegan, he'd begun to feel like a hypocrite. He'd urged her to talk to her family while he'd spent years avoiding his own. Plus, it'd been slowly sinking in for days now—especially after talking to Case Walker a couple nights ago—that the cavern of distance between Rio and himself didn't only affect Bear. It'd impacted Jamie, too.

Jamie needed more than the dodging reply Bear had given him the other night when he'd asked about Rio. And yet, Bear didn't want to fill his nephew's head with thoughts of some grand family reunification if there was no chance of healing between Bear and Rio.

So earlier this morning he'd tried texting Rosa to find out what jail currently housed Rio. *One conversation. Just call him to say hi. Make sure Rosa has filled him in on the kids.*

But Rosa had never replied. So he'd moved on to Plan B: On the way to the hospital for his meeting with the EMS director, he'd made the long-distance call to the Atlanta P.D.

Only to find out that, if Rio was, in fact, in jail—and why would Rosa lie about that?—it wasn't in Atlanta. *Doesn't make sense at all.*

"Can I help you with anything else, sir?"

"No, uh, thanks anyway." Bear turned off the car as he ended the fruitless call. So much for that.

Just five minutes ago, he'd been laughing to himself as he pulled into the hospital parking lot, thinking about how funny it'd be next time Raegan dropped into her Honda and couldn't reach the steering wheel. They'd switched cars for the morning since she was taking the kids out to the train depot and his rental had more room. He'd had to adjust her driver's-side seat as far back as it could go in order to fit in her compact car. He'd pictured her scrunching her nose, muttering his full name.

Now confusion wiggled through him. It was certainly possible Rio had been arrested and jailed elsewhere—different city, maybe even a different state. But he distinctly remembered Rosa mentioning the Atlanta P.D.

Maybe it was better this way, though. What was he

going to say, anyway? *"I can't get ahold of your wife, so I might as well tell you: Your kids are in Iowa and they're doing fine. And oh yeah, I'm thinking they should just stay here. With me."*

Right. He'd sound like a child abductor.

Although, if he were honest, perhaps that was the real reason he'd wanted to talk to Rio. He couldn't stand the thought of returning Jamie and Erin to Atlanta. Sunday—three days from now—would mark two weeks since Rosa had thrust her children into his care. He could feel the time ticking by too quickly, raising his hackles with every move of its hands.

He was a mess of warring desires. Explore the possibility of reconciliation with his brother? Or let the cavern grow even wider by insisting . . . what? That if Rio and Rosa couldn't get their act together, he'd refuse to return their kids?

As if he really needed to add kidnapper to his rap sheet. Besides, did he really think the kids would be better off with him? It wasn't like his life was any more stable than anyone else's at the moment.

He wasn't even planning to stay in the States. What was he going to do? Cart the kids down to Brazil?

Then again, John still hadn't sent him the application for the community center position. Bear had sent an email to the mission board yesterday. No reply yet.

Still, he had to keep trying, doing whatever he could to improve his standing with the mission. Which was why he was here now. He'd stayed up half the night last night Googling for information on local EMT programs, trying to figure out if any of his former training might carry over. But the internet's answers had proved convoluted and unhelpful. Thus, his morning phone call to the local emergency response director.

Bear pushed open the car door, moisture-tinged air

rushing over him as he stepped out. The morning's humidity this ninth day of June sagged the spindly young trees dotting the hospital grounds.

Think about Rio and Rosa later.

Limp clouds rolled overhead in a colorless sky, smudged shadows shifting over the sidewalk in front of him that lead to the hospital. Inside, he stopped at the front desk, asked to speak to the EMS department director, and within minutes found himself seated across from a man who probably had little more than a decade on Bear. The cramped office barely had room for the small metal desk it contained. A whiteboard spanned the wall behind the desk and contained a list of names and what looked like a.m. and p.m. on-call schedules.

"You're lucky you caught me when you called earlier this morning," the director—Gage Whitaker, according to the placard on his desk—said after shaking Bear's hand and motioning for him to sit in the metal folding chair opposite him. "Don't spend much time at my desk."

The chair creaked as Bear lowered onto it. "Thanks for seeing me on such short notice. I appreciate it."

"So you're here about a job?"

"Not exactly." He leaned forward in the worn chair.

"Really? Heard through the grapevine you're a paramedic. Even got an application ready for you." He held up a stapled clump of papers.

"*Former* paramedic."

"Shame. We've got a small paid staff—four paramedics and myself—with a larger crew of volunteer EMTs on the side." Gage leaned back in his vinyl chair, balancing against the wall behind him. "I'm advertising for an additional full-time paramedic right now and am always on the scout for volunteers. I was all prepared to do a job interview after you called."

"I wish. Thing is, I do want to get recertified. That's why I called."

"How long's it been?" Gage tapped his pencil on the desktop.

"About ten years."

Gage dropped his pencil with a scant "Oh."

"And it was a Georgia certification, at that. I realize it's not as simple as taking a quick refresher course, and considering I may not be in the country that long, I'm probably going to have to settle for EMT training—"

"Why'd you let it lapse in the first place?"

All the air seemed to seep from the room. "It, uh, wasn't entirely my choice. My life got . . . complicated. I had to turn my attention elsewhere."

To an arrest and a court case and the hardest decision he'd ever made. To a sentencing that stole so much more than his freedom.

"I guess what I'm wondering is, considering my past training, is it possible to skip ahead some? Is there some kind of reinstatement process I can go through?"

"You'd have to get approval from the Bureau of Emergency and Trauma Services to pursue reinstatement and you're looking at a couple months, at least, on that. To be honest, with it being an out-of-state certification and lapsed so long, I have a feeling they'd send you straight back to basic EMT training anyway."

Bear swallowed his disappointment. "I had a feeling you'd say that. In which case, do you have any advice on best programs? I looked up a bunch of information last night. I saw there's a program at Des Moines Area Community College that starts on the fifteenth—"

Gage leaned forward, the front legs of his chair thumping to the floor. "Look, Bear, you realize there's no chance you can get into a program that quickly, right? You'll have to retake a prerequisite CPR class, for one thing. Not to mention, you'll need to get accepted into DMAAC first."

"You're saying I'm too late for the summer course?"

"I'm saying at this point you'll be lucky if you can get in on the fall program. You can apply for late acceptance, but . . ." Gage shrugged.

Not get into the fall program? He could handle staying in Iowa through the end of the year if it meant being recertified and therefore upping his chances with the mission board. But if he couldn't even start training until next year, well, surely the mission would hire someone else.

And a college application? How could Bear not have factored that in? Had he really thought he'd just call the school and land a spot in the program? College applications required time, sometimes interviews, even physicals or immunizations.

Which brought up another complication he hadn't considered. "Do you know, um . . . do you think a background check is part of the process?" Had it been when he'd gone through the training in Atlanta? He didn't remember.

Gage's scrutiny turned even more skeptical. "Yep. In Iowa, once you go through the training, it's the Bureau that makes the final call on whether to certify. That's the point at which the background check comes into play."

So Bear could go through the entire twelve-week program and *still* not walk away a certified EMT?

"Why?" Gage slid the application he'd held up earlier into an open drawer. "Is that a problem?" He closed the drawer.

This meeting had turned as pointless as that phone call to the Atlanta P.D.

Raegan couldn't shake the feeling that she was betraying her father.

But she also couldn't deny the sense of tranquility that had blanketed her the moment she'd settled into the cushioned wicker rocker in Sara Jaminski's sunroom. It smelled of lavender, the scent she'd come to associate with the older woman.

After spending the morning at the train depot, Raegan had originally planned to spend her afternoon off fiddling around with her mural design. After all, the masonry primer she'd ordered wouldn't arrive until tomorrow—which meant there was nothing she could do at the site itself until then.

She'd holed up in Bear's apartment with a blown-up photo of the Hay & Feed building spread out on his kitchen table. The idea was to come up with some sort of grid system for the actual painting of the mural.

But after an hour of attempting to focus, she'd finally given up. Twenty minutes later, she'd found herself here.

"This was my favorite room in the house even as a kid," Sara said as she set a cup and saucer on the lace-covered end table beside Raegan. She lowered onto the dainty loveseat that sat against one honey-colored wall. "My mother joked until the day she passed away about how she used to find me curled up right here on this loveseat many mornings. Apparently I had a habit of sleepwalking my way out here."

"Beckett used to sleepwalk as a kid. We'd find him on the porch steps using his basketball as a pillow." Soft sunlight cascaded through the open windows that rounded three sides of the room. An array of plants in stands and hanging in baskets ornamented the room, along with a small bookshelf and French sliding doors that led into the main house.

Raegan hadn't called before showing up at Sara's house. Hadn't even known if she'd go through with the haphazard notion even as she sat in her car facing the old farmhouse on the ranch property, watching a rusted metal windmill spin in the wind.

But then Sara had emerged from the barn in dusty jeans and an old tee, work gloves and boots. Raegan had slid from her car as Sara approached, coercing what little bravery she might possess to the surface. *Bear's right. If I keep holding this in, nothing will ever change.*

She could go on counting the days between panic attacks, taking false comfort the higher the number grew, riding her bike everywhere, refusing to travel alone.

Or she could stop hiding.

Sara had stopped in front of her. "You look like you need to talk."

Raegan had only nodded.

Ten minutes later, here she was, sitting across from the woman who'd managed to transform from cowgirl to counselor with just a change of clothes. She wore tan linen pants now and a thin oversized white sweater, another one of her colorful scarves tied around her hair.

If Dad knew, he'd want me to talk to someone, too, wouldn't he?

Raegan lifted her teacup, the soothing aroma of Earl Grey wafting over her. "I'm sorry to show up so out of the blue."

"Trust me, after thirty years of living from appointment to appointment, constantly answering to a calendar controlled by my assistant, I love the freedom of being a little more impromptu here in the country." Sara tucked her legs underneath her on the loveseat, then quieted. Waiting, most likely, for Raegan to explain why she'd come.

Just start talking. She's a counselor. She's not going to judge you.

But the thought of repeating all she'd told Bear—going even deeper—petrified her. It might have felt freeing to spill her tears to Bear, but she'd begun to wonder since if that comfort had been less about finally liberating her secret and more about the man whose arms she'd fallen apart inside?

She'd felt terrifyingly vulnerable, but also closer to him than ever before. Figuratively *and* literally. If that locker room door hadn't slammed when it did . . .

Her teacup clattered against the saucer.

"Raegan." It was a gentle prodding.

She placed her cup and saucer on the end table. "I get panic attacks. I don't know why. I just know I hate them. I thought I'd learned how to curb them—I was closing in on two years—but . . ."

"But you had one recently?"

"Two days ago."

"And before that?"

"I was with Kate in Chicago. She'd been injured in a car accident, so I stayed with her for a couple weeks to help her out. I went to the store for her one day. It was only a half-mile away, so I walked, but I took a wrong turn on the way back and . . ." She'd eventually shown back up at Kate's without the groceries. "It really wasn't that bad, though. Not even close to the worst I remember."

Sara was still a picture of calm and relaxation. None of the doctoral curiosity Raegan might have expected. "Can you tell me about the worst?"

Raegan slid her palms over her khaki shorts until they reached her bare knees. This was what she hadn't been able to tell Bear.

You have to try. Just say the words.

"It was about a month after Mom died."

A month that had felt like a year.

A month that had felt like a day.

In her grief, time had turned to elastic, stretching and then constricting, minutes and hours all mixed up and muddled. But then there'd come a day when it seemed somehow life was supposed to simply go on again. Logan and Kate had returned to their jobs. Beckett had resumed college classes, and even Dad had started dressing for work again.

Everyone had someplace to go.

Except Raegan. After being homeschooled the past year—other than art classes and a few other extracurriculars at the public school—she'd spent most of her days at home with Mom. Her decision after the cancer came back.

But now there was no Mom and the house had emptied and her hollow heart couldn't handle the loneliness.

She could still feel the gnawing despondency that had propelled her to the garage, into her car, onto the road . . .

Raegan pulled onto the gravel lane that separated home from a still-snow-covered field. Dad always said there was nothing quite so head-clearing as a country drive. Maybe if she just got out of the house for an hour or two, listened to the radio and enjoyed the wintry scenery, she could figure out how to resume regular life the way the rest of the family had. Get back to the last classes of her senior year and learn how to function again.

It wasn't until an hour later that she realized she'd left her phone sitting on the kitchen counter. No matter. She knew where she was. Light snowflakes fluttered outside her windshield, but she'd been driving in rascally Iowa weather for almost two years. She could handle a gentle snowfall.

Raegan let her mind wander, memories of Mom mingling with images from the past month. The funeral—beautiful despite the clinging sorrow. Day after day of family and caring friends crowding Dad's house. The tears and embraces and attempts at smiles and laughter and hope.

And the casseroles. So many casseroles.

Raegan's stomach growled and she glanced at the clock on her dash. 4:06? It would start getting dark soon. She'd been gone over two hours. Time to turn around, especially considering the way the snow had picked up.

Except . . . her gaze traveled the landscape around her, attention suddenly sharpening. Where exactly was she?

The first twinge of consternation gurgled to life.

Half an hour later, concern had warped into distress. What had been a pretty snowfall was now nearing blizzard proportions. She'd gotten turned around in a maze of rural backroads. She didn't have her phone, hadn't passed a sign for a nearby town in miles— probably wouldn't have been able to read it if she had, considering the sheets of white against a now-dark sky.

The panic rushed in, alarm darting through her limbs and squeezing her lungs and . . .

The car began to swerve. Ice or gravel or simply her own rattled condition jerking her tires. A shriek flew from her lips as she lost control of the vehicle. And then . . . nothing.

Other than the glare of headlights.

And a voice. "Oh good, you're waking up, Miss Walker."

"W-Where . . . ?"

"You're at St. Luke's Hospital in Omaha."

Hospital. Alone.

By the time she'd opened her eyes, the panic was beginning all over again . . .

Raegan's knuckles were white, fingers clenched in her lap from the pang of the memory. "Apparently I was half out of my mind when the ambulance came. And then I had another attack in the hospital." She could only remember it in snatches. The racing heart, the retching. The thrashing and the hands of hospital staff holding her down. "The worst is, I injured someone in that car accident. This nice old man. He broke his leg in two places."

She'd been so guilt-ridden she'd barely heard the ER doctor's assessment of her own injuries—nothing more than a few bruises. But he'd tossed around words like *therapy* and *anxiety* and *medication.*

Hot tears trailed down her cheeks now.

"They wanted to keep me overnight, call Dad. But I was over eighteen. I got out as soon as I could, found a hotel in Omaha to park in until the blizzard was over. And I had plenty of time to think that night. I played every panic attack I'd ever had over in my head. I made a list of the signs."

"You tried to pinpoint your triggers."

Raegan nodded, using the tissue Sara had handed her at some point to wipe her eyes. "Except sometimes there aren't triggers. Sometimes it just . . . happens. So I made another list—all the things I need to avoid."

"Things like?"

"Being alone in a new place. Getting lost. I bought a bike after that. Doesn't help much in the winter, but at least in the spring and summer and fall, I can bike as much as possible. I don't have to worry as much that I might . . . hurt someone again." She blew her nose. "I thought it was working just fine. Life, I mean. I knew what to avoid. I knew what I needed to do. Until the other night . . . I was okay."

Sara leaned forward. "But here's the thing, Raegan. Life can be so much more than okay." She took both of Raegan's hands in her own.

More than okay. It sounded wonderful. But getting there . . . "How?" Her voice came out tinny and uncertain and . . . and hopeful.

Sara squeezed her hands. "You've already taken the first step. You're here right now."

One good thing about this short-term job working for Sara Jaminski—it gave Bear an ideal opportunity to take out his frustrations on an endless number of inanimate objects.

Bear tossed a lumpy cushion from an old bench onto the growing mountain behind the cabins. The late-morning sun cast golden beams through cotton clouds in a picture-perfect sky. The mowed pasture behind the cabins gave way to prairieland—wildflowers, tall grass, knots of dogwood and hickory nut trees. The sky was a blue-gray swirl draping the horizon.

Erin's singsong voice carried on the breeze, along with the squeaking of the tire swing he'd rigged in a nearby tree. Jamie was spending the afternoon with Beckett, having taken a liking to that four-wheeler Beckett rode around the orchard.

This was Bear's fourth day of work at the ranch, and if he could put in a few good hours lugging junk and debris today, a full day tomorrow, he could start on the actual cabin repairs by next week.

And if he kept busy enough, he might be able to tune out the unsettled choir warbling in his head. The one continually and needlessly reminding him of all the messes in his life . . . and his helplessness to sort out any of them. After that hospital meeting this morning—the email from John he'd received not much later—Brazil felt further out of reach than ever before. He still hadn't gotten ahold of Rosa. He had no idea where Rio was. He'd seen that blue Taurus again—this time waiting in the hospital parking lot when he'd emerged.

And then there was Raegan. She filled every leftover nook in his too-full mind—and much more of his heart than he wanted to admit.

The lilt of Erin's singing reached his ears once more. At least someone was enjoying this day. Bear had made sure to check on her every ten minutes or so, but so far, she hadn't come close to tiring of the swing.

Bear wiped a bead of sweat from his brow and dragged himself into the third cabin. Its musty smell assaulted him the second he stepped over the threshold. At least there was no sloping ceiling beam hanging loose in here like in the one remaining cabin. He was saving the worst for last, half worried the roof might up and cave in on him the second he stepped inside. He'd warned Erin to stay out.

He gripped the edge of a busted table now, hefting it with a grunt. A muscle pulled in his shoulder, but he ignored the pain and inched his way backward toward the cabin door.

"Bear?"

He dropped the table and a second leg splintered. He glanced over his shoulder to see Raegan in the doorway, her pale hair tangling about her shoulders and the light from outside silhouetting her figure. He swiped the back of his palm over his forehead and turned. "What are you . . . ?" He breathed in too much dust and coughed before he could finish the question.

"What am I doing here? I was at Sara's house. I saw your car out here. Well, that is, my car."

They hadn't traded back yet.

She eyed his broken load. "Can I help you move that table?"

He took in her white cotton top and spotless jeans. "Everything in here is covered in an inch of dirt. You'd ruin your clothes."

She stepped into the room, pulling a band from around her wrist and then lifting her hair into a haphazard ponytail. "If you'll recall, my mascara destroyed one of your shirts yesterday. I owe you."

"I've got it, Rae. Honestly. You could give Erin a push on the swing, though. I've been lax."

"Erin is content as can be." She stepped over the table's broken leg and scanned the room. "If you don't need help with the table, I'll move this."

The queen mattress in the corner with so many stains it was impossible to tell what color it'd been originally? Even he'd been avoiding that gross monstrosity. "Rae—"

She ignored him, bending over to grasp one corner of the mattress. She gave a futile tug. When it didn't budge an inch, she backed away, hands on her hips. After a moment, she moved to another corner and tried again.

This time when it didn't move, she gave it a kick, sending a plume of dirt into the air around her feet.

Despite this day's frustrations, he couldn't help a grin—one he didn't hide nearly quick enough when she tossed a look back at him. "Don't you dare make fun of me, Bear McKinley."

"Did I say a word?"

"Here I am trying to do a nice thing for you." She

gripped the mattress.

But before she could give it a third yank, he side-stepped the table and crossed to the opposite side of the mattress. He lifted it easily.

"Thank you." Raegan cocked one eyebrow. "And for the record, this is what graciously accepting help when it's offered looks like. You should take note." She scooted backward.

"Are you kidding? I've been accepting help from you and your family for almost two weeks, Walker. You do remember that I'm staying in your dad's house, right?"

"How could I forget? I can hear you snoring in the basement all the way upstairs."

He could see the muscles straining in her arms even though he'd taken on the bulk of the mattress's weight. "I do not snore that loudly."

"There's never any cereal left in the cupboards."

Yes, and he'd left cash on the counter twice now in an effort to help pay for groceries. Each time, he'd come back later to find it sitting on the futon in the basement. "I'm sorry, I just really like my cold cereal."

"Clearly you haven't been around my family long enough. *We* know how to do breakfast right. And it *doesn't* include Lucky Charms."

They'd nearly made it to the doorway. "You Walkers and your rules and traditions. I've never considered you as snobs, but when it comes to breakfast—" Wait a second. Something had just registered. "You said you were at Sara's?"

She paused, backed up against the table he'd abandoned. "Yeah. I, uh . . . took your advice. We had a good talk. Set up a regular appointment and—" She paused. "Stop wobbling the mattress, Bear."

"I'm not—" He stopped. The mattress definitely was wobbling. Shaking. As if something was inside . . .

He dropped the mattress in time with Raegan's

squeal.

"Do not tell me that's a mouse in there." She backed away. "Do not."

"Might not be a mouse. Might be a rat."

She shrieked again. "Do something!"

A shudder skated through him as a lump in the middle of the mattress moved again. "Do what?"

"I don't know. Jump on it?"

"That's your solution? Jump on the bed? You want me to kill it by—" His own yelp escaped when the whole mattress jerked. "Let's just get out of here." He scrambled around the mattress, grabbing Raegan's arm as he passed and tugging her through the cabin door.

Raegan had burst out laughing before they even spilled outside. "Bear McKinley is scared of mice."

"Me? You were the one screeching in there like a banshee."

"Fine, we're both pathetic. We literally just ran away from a rodent."

He swiped the back of his hand over his forehead, probably leaving a trail of dirt. "I was only rescuing you. If you really want me to go back in there and mercilessly kill whatever animal is living in that mattress, I will. I saw an old badminton racquet in one of the cabins. I can use that."

She clasped her hands together. "My hero."

"But you'll have to live with it on your conscience."

She stepped toward him. "Bear—"

"I'm serious. I'll do it. I'll march right back in there and—"

She interrupted him by closing the space between them and lifting up to her tiptoes to plant a kiss on his cheek. It happened so fast he was still mid-blink when she stepped away.

But not so quickly the touch of her lips didn't stir his awareness. "What was that for?"

"For hounding me to talk to someone. For suggesting Sara. It wasn't easy talking to her and I have a feeling it's only going to get harder. But I need to do it. I realize that now. It's not so much that the weight is off my shoulders, but I'm not shouldering it alone now."

There was something soft and fragile in the way she looked at him now. Her eyes seemed bluer than ever and the smattering of freckles over her cheeks and nose alone were enough to distract a man.

"A few minutes ago, you mentioned accepting help from me and my family. But you've helped *me*, Bear McKinley. More than you know."

Even if he'd known what words to say in reply, he couldn't make his voice work. Not with the clamor of desire rising inside him. To finally give in, throw caution to the wind and admit the magnetic pull he felt toward this woman . . .

But also to free his every care and concern, let them all fall at her feet, come what may. It consumed him—the need to tell her about Rio and prison and Brazil and why he'd left. To tell her about this morning's discouraging meeting with the EMS director and then about the application John had just sent over this afternoon. The one with the question he'd dreaded:

Have you ever been convicted of a felony? Circle YES or NO. If yes, explain.

Maybe even to tell her about Annie.

"Bear?"

Could she see it on his face? The anguish he couldn't stand much longer? "Raegan, I—"

He was cut off by the sound of crashing wood, a shriek. *Erin!* Oh Lord, he'd forgotten . . . he'd completely forgotten. Hadn't even looked to the swing—the empty swing.

He whirled and bolted for the cabin, the one he'd told her not to enter. A thick haze of dust and debris blasted him inside. That loose ceiling beam lay crooked over broken chairs and a bunk bed and . . .

And Erin.

His chest constricted at the sight of her, skinny arms and legs sprawled on the dirt-covered floor, her little body shaking as she coughed. "Erin, honey, I'm here." He clambered over a mess of wood and metal, thrusting the jagged beam out of the way and kicking aside the chair blocking his path to Erin.

Her cough morphed into a wail. "Uncle B-Bear!"

He pushed away a damp mattress and stooped to Erin's side. "I'm right here. Try not to move for a second, okay?" His attention swept over her, hooking on her scraped up forehead, the blood on one knee. If she'd taken the brunt of the beam's fall instead of those chairs, if she'd been a foot or two to the right . . .

She was trying to sit up now, trying to reach for him. A good sign. Satisfied that she hadn't broken any bones, he gathered her to him. "It's all right, Erin. I've got you." His legs burned in his crouched position.

"C-Couldn't breathe." Erin buried her face against him, her scratched up arms winding around his neck.

"You must've had the wind knocked out of you. Tell me what hurts."

"E-Everything!"

Only as his pulse steadied was he able to muster the barest smile. Oh, he loved this dramatic little girl. He caught Raegan's gaze from the doorway, nodded to assure her Erin was more scared than hurt.

"Am I going to die?"

He patted his niece's mussed hair and stood, lifting her with him. "I think you're probably going to survive. My heart might be another story. You might've just shaved off a few years of my life." He carried her out into the sunlight where he could get a better look at her injuries. Amazingly, nothing that some disinfectant and

Band-Aids couldn't handle, although she might end up with a nice-sized goose egg on her forehead.

Still, considering what could've happened . . .

He shuddered.

"Are you cold, Uncle Bear?" She still gripped his neck.

"Not cold. Relieved." And angry at himself. He'd been so caught up with Raegan he'd not so much as glanced at the swing when they'd come outside. What had he been thinking, even having Erin out here with him when he'd known how dangerous that loose beam was? "Let's get you home, Erin."

His phone rang just as he bent to lower her to the ground, but she clamped her legs around him, refusing to let go. "I want to stay with you, Uncle Bear."

He pulled a leaf from her hair, ignoring his phone. "I just need to grab a few things from the other cabin."

Erin touched his cheeks with both hands, her large brown eyes still rimmed in red from her tears. "No, I want to stay with you forever."

He just looked at her, this child who'd so thoroughly stolen his heart with her infectious laugh and easy affections. The sun had browned her skin after so much time playing outside, no matter how much lotion he slathered over her. "I want you to stay with me, too, Erin."

She grinned and kissed his nose. "Forever?"

He could only nod and kiss her back and swallow his choking angst. His phone called out again—a text message this time.

But only after he'd settled Erin in the car, told Raegan they'd meet her back at the house, did he read the message. Beckett?

You need to get down to the police dept. It's Jamie.

168

10

"Look, Chief Roberts—"

"That'd be Ross. But like I said, you can call me Sam."

Bear stood with flattened palms on the waist-high counter in the Maple Valley Police Department. The man on the other side looked far too laidback considering he'd just accused Jamie of vandalizing the outside of Baker's Antiques. Something about tipped-over flower boxes and eggs thrown against the front window.

"Chief Ross." He spoke slowly. "If Jamie says he didn't have anything to do with the vandalism, he didn't have anything to do with the vandalism."

Jamie sat behind Bear on a vinyl bench edged up to the wall. A mirror on the opposite wall captured his slumped posture, his crossed arms, an expression likely meant to portray defiance.

But all Bear could see was the distress hovering in his nephew's dark irises. It was enough to make him want to pound his fist on the counter. "You might not believe him, but I do. And I won't stand for Jamie being falsely accused."

Chief Ross straightened, the faint streaks of distinguished gray at his temples a contrast to the rest of his relatively youthful appearance. At least compared to the only other police officers Bear had ever known.

The ones who'd arrested him in Atlanta.

Who'd booked him that first night in jail.

Escorted him to and from the courtroom.

It was all he could do not to ball his fists now. "Jamie will *not* be taking the fall for something he didn't do."

Chief Ross folded his arms. "I've not accused your nephew of anything. There's no 'taking the fall.' Let's not get overly dramatic. I've simply questioned him."

"Without a lawyer."

"Actually, Beckett Walker, who happens to be a lawyer, was here the whole time. I asked Jamie all of three or four questions."

The way the man said Beckett's name hinted at a personal history between the two. But Bear didn't have patience for that now.

Nor had he had patience for Beckett when he'd first arrived at the station. He'd been too intent on seeing Jamie to pay attention to Beckett's explanation then, but it replayed in his mind now.

Apparently Beckett had needed to run into town for something at Klassen's Hardware. He'd brought Jamie along, had gotten distracted looking for whatever it was he needed in the store, and the next thing he knew, Jamie had disappeared.

He'd found him less than five minutes later, just down the block outside Baker's Antiques, enduring a tongue-lashing from the store's owner. The police chief had arrived on the scene right after.

"Why didn't you just let Beckett take him home?"

Chief Ross—Sam—rolled his eyes. "Because a very disgruntled Mr. Baker was standing there outside his store expecting me to do something. And for all I knew,

Jamie was lying. Thought it best to bring him here and wait for you."

Now Bear's fists did ball. "He wasn't lying."

"I can appreciate that you believe the best of your nephew—"

"He *wasn't* lying."

"Do you know how rare vandalism is in this town? Other than the annual TP-ing of the head basketball coach's house, we don't get so much as a peep of trouble. We're as Mayberry as it gets." Sam shook his head. "So I'm sorry, but when a local, well-loved business gets vandalized and the new kid in town is seen outside the store, can you really blame Mr. Baker for jumping to conclusions?"

Yes, Bear could blame him. He had half a mind to march right over to the antique store and give Mr. Baker an earful of his own.

"I didn't do it." Jamie jerked to his feet.

"I know you didn't." Bear clamped his palm on Jamie's shoulder, looking to the police chief once more. The man did look genuinely apologetic. Had to give him that. "Are we done here?"

Sam nodded.

Without another word, Bear steered Jamie toward the doorway. Afternoon had given way to evening, but the day's warmth held on. A mosquito landed on Bear's arm. He slapped it away.

"Are you hungry, Jamie? We can stop over at The Red Door for a burger if you want." Raegan had taken Erin home. He could text her not to wait on dinner.

But Jamie shook his head.

"All right, then."

They settled in the car where he'd parked it at the curb just outside the station. As soon as he'd flipped the ignition, Bear reached for the A/C knob. But he didn't shift out of Park. Not yet.

"Jamie—"

"I didn't do it." Jamie shoved his seatbelt into its latch. "And I didn't see who did."

"You don't have to convince me, so—" He stopped himself before using the endearment. *Son.* Last time, it'd only irritated the boy.

But if Jamie had noticed his near-slip, he didn't let on. Only turned to the window.

"That boy is hurting." Case Walker's voice drifted in as the A/C puffed from the vent. *"He might need to talk about his father, even if you don't."*

Case had said to search his heart for a happy memory to share. But they were so few and far between. Buried underneath craggy failures, relentless regrets. When he tried to think of Rio, all he could conjure were the bad memories.

The morning he'd found the money in Rio's bedroom.

The afternoon he'd followed his brother to the warehouse.

The evening they'd spent in the back of a cop car.

Outside his windshield, a *V* of birds pointed through the sky overhead. The whooshing air conditioning fanned Jamie's thick hair and flapped his T-shirt against his reedy torso.

A happy memory, a happy memory . . .

Bear's gaze roamed the gray pavement stretching in front of them—a dead end street that eventually reached the Blaine River, right at the foot of the Archway Bridge.

There it is.

He cleared his throat. "You know, Jamie, when we were kids, your dad and I used to play under this bridge in our neighborhood. There was a creek." One filled with litter, water russet and sullied. Graffiti had covered the cement bridge, and what little grass cleaved to the eroded landscape was trampled and brown.

"I don't know why, but it was our favorite place to play. Only your dad was constantly wading in the water and I was constantly telling him not to 'cause the water was so gross and there was always scrap metal lying about the riverbank." He could still hear his own boyish, bossy voice warning Rio about tetanus and rashes. And Rio, who used to set his jaw just as Jamie had back in the station, ignoring every word and wading in.

The memory almost made him smile. Did Rio ever think of those days? Despite the struggles of their childhood—the absentee parents, the Goodwill clothes that earned them the other students' scorn in school, the streetwise way of life at far too young an age—they *had* had happy moments. Brotherly moments.

Bear should have held on to that. When he'd graduated high school and moved into his own place the very same day, he should've taken Rio with him. He never should've left him behind. By the time he'd realized how much trouble his younger brother was in, it was too late.

And his last-ditch, drastic effort hadn't done any good.

If he could go back . . .

But I can't. There was no reversing time. No second chances.

His knuckles turned white over the gearshift.

"I thought I saw him. That's why I left the hardware store." Jamie's voice was a mere whisper above the rasping A/C.

"What?"

Jamie turned to him, a tentative confession in his inky eyes. "I thought I saw Dad."

"Oh my word, what's happening in here?"

At Dad's voice, Raegan looked up from her cross-legged position on her bed, her hair fanned all around her face and Erin standing behind her. "Oh, we're just playing beauty salon."

Dad stepped into the room. "With markers?"

Erin's bare feet bounced on the bed beside her. "I'm giving Raegan rainbow hair."

Dad's laugh lines deepened. "I see that."

"Don't worry. They're washable markers." Might take an extra shampooing but it was worth it for Erin's delight. Now if only Bear would get home soon, or at least text or call. Let them all know things were okay with Jamie. Surely it was just a mix-up.

Still, out at the cabins, he'd already been so churned up before he even received the text from Beckett. There was a storm brewing inside that man—a man who'd done so much for so many. If only she could find some way to encourage him. She'd been racking her brain for the past hour.

"Can I color your hair, too, Mister Case?"

Raegan exchanged a grin with Dad at the term of endearment Erin had given him the day she met him. Dad had suggested "Uncle Case" but Erin had declared that would be too confusing, what with Bear being Uncle Bear and all.

"Oh, I'm not sure the markers would work as well on silver hair."

"I bet the dark colors would, Dad." Raegan gave him a teasing wink.

"All the same, I think I'll leave the beauty salon-ing to the women of the house."

Erin capped a red marker. "I'm not a woman. I'm a little girl."

"Quite right. Forgive me." Dad leaned over to ruffle Erin's hair, then returned Raegan's wink before leaving the room.

Raegan watched his retreating form, torn between the lightness of just now and the guilt that had refused to budge from her conscience ever since going to see Sara this afternoon. Dad had been so clear last week about his feelings regarding the woman, if not the reason behind them.

But he hadn't specifically told Raegan not to interact with her. And even if he had, Raegan was a grown adult, capable of deciding who to spend time with.

But I live under his roof. The least I can do is respect his wishes.

This was *Dad*, after all. There was no one in the world she admired more.

Except, well, Bear came awfully close. More than close, really. Was she a horrible daughter if she admitted it might be a tie?

You have to tell him sometime.

She knew she did. Especially since she'd set up a standing weekly appointment with Sara. They'd only skimmed the surface this afternoon, but already Raegan could feel the slow turn of a key in a long-locked chamber of her heart.

"*We're going to talk about more than the panic attacks,*" Sara had said. "*You understand that, yes? We need to talk about why you've hidden them. Why you haven't spoken to your family about it. We'll probably talk about painting, too—why you stopped.*"

"*And if we talk about all that, you'll be able to figure out what's wrong with me?*"

"*Raegan, you're not a broken toy. You're a woman*

with hurts and struggles just like everyone else."

"I Googled, Sara. I read about panic disorders. I might have a mental illness."

"Which puts you in the company of about twenty percent of the population. Except unlike many people who walk around each day struggling with things like depression and anxiety, who choose to numb their emotions however they can, you're here. You're owning your story."

Sara made it sound so . . . triumphant. Courageous. But if Raegan was so brave, why didn't she go downstairs and sit down across the dining room table from Dad and tell him where she'd been this afternoon? Why could she tell Bear, a man who drifted in and out of her life, and Sara, a woman she'd just met recently, about the panic attacks, but not her own family?

Raegan's gaze traveled her bedroom as Erin kept coloring her hair. Bear had called the room artsy, and she supposed it was. From the colorful hill of throw pillows on her bed to her violet walls, one ornamented with vintage frames she'd found years ago in a collection of thrift stores in Ames and Des Moines—back when she'd not been nearly as nervous about driving longer distances. She'd removed their glass panes, spray-painted them white, and hung them in a perfect collage. They complemented her white vanity and matching headboard.

Erin jumped on the bed beside her. "Look in the mirror, Raegan. I used every color."

"You're done already?" Raegan rose from the bed and reached her vanity in two steps. Oh. Boy. "You really did use every color."

Beckett's reflection appeared in the mirror beside her. When had he come home? "You look like Rainbow Brite."

"You don't know your eighties cartoons, Beck. Rainbow Brite didn't actually have rainbow hair. Just a multicolored dress."

"Now you should color *my* hair, Raegan." Erin still jumped on the bed, markers bouncing at her feet.

"I'm afraid like Mister Case, your hair is just a little too dark. We'd have to dye it blond first, and I'm thinking your Uncle Bear might get a little upset with me if I do that."

"No, he wouldn't. He loves you."

Raegan could only sputter in reply. Obviously Erin didn't mean anything by the words. But that didn't stop an unwieldy blush from creeping over her cheeks.

Or Beckett from folding his arms and pinning her with a glare. Really? Nearly two weeks and he *still* hadn't warmed to Bear?

"Listen, Rae, can I talk to you for a sec?"

"About Jamie? What exactly happened? Is everything okay?"

"Everything's fine, but . . ." He glanced at Erin. "Hey, Erin, I saw Mister Case down in the kitchen with a package of Oreos. I bet you could talk him into sharing."

She scrambled off the bed and out of the room before Raegan could blink.

"Wow, that was impressive. I mean, I've been known to run for cookies, too, but she might've just bested any of my personal records."

No chuckle from her brother. Not even a smirk.

"Look, Beck, if this is about what Erin said—"

"It's about Bear."

Her hands found her hips. "What about him?" And why did she have a feeling she wasn't going to like the direction of this conversation?

"How much do you know about his life before Maple Valley?"

"This stint or the last one?" Not that she knew that much about either. Anytime the topic of Brazil came up, he'd either turned vague or dodged the subject entirely, segueing with the finesse of a dance master.

She did, however, know a little more about his childhood now than she had before. Not much, but it was enough to break her heart. She'd taken her own family, her relatively stable growing-up years for granted far too often.

"The last one," Beckett said.

"I know he lived in Atlanta as a kid. I know at some point he was a paramedic." She returned to the bed, picking up Erin's markers and replacing them in the Crayola box. Would her colored hair stain her pillowcase tonight? "I know his home life wasn't a cake walk."

"So you don't know . . ." Beckett took a breath, as if wavering on whether or not to say what he'd obviously come to say. "You don't know about the prison sentence?"

She dropped the box of markers. "What?"

"Multiple felonies, Raegan. Car theft. At least one drug count."

"I don't . . . *what*?" Not Bear. He didn't have a lawless bone in his body. "How do you even know?"

"Google. It's a thing." He leaned against her vanity. "I'm a little surprised you never looked him up online yourself."

"I don't pry, Beckett. I don't feel the need to research my friends. Why would you even think to do that?" Her mind dizzied. Bear had said his *parents* dealt drugs. He'd insinuated his *brother* was in and out of jails and prisons. He hadn't said anything about himself.

"Jamie's spent time at the orchard. He's said some things. Just offhand comments, but they made me wonder."

"So instead of asking Bear, you went and Googled him? And now you're coming to me with this? What do you want me to do? Have some big confrontation with him?" Heat spread through her. She strode across the room, pushed lacy curtains aside, and flung open the window.

But the only air to seep into the room was thick with humidity.

"The A/C's on. Dad hates it when we open windows when—"

"I don't need a lecture on Dad's rules, Beck." She dropped to her bed.

Beckett pushed away from the vanity. "Look, I'm not trying to be the villainous bearer of bad news. I care about you. Bear's living in our house. He's got secrets, baggage."

"You're a fine one to talk. You, who stayed away from Maple Valley for six years because of an arrest warrant waiting back at home."

Beckett's gaze darkened. "Not the same thing and you know it."

"Wait. That's what this is, isn't it?" She looked up at him, realization skimming over her like the clammy air pushing into the room. "You're feeling guilty. You weren't around for years. You didn't get to play big brother last time."

"Raegan—"

"Kate and Logan both had their chance to tease me and advise me and do all the older sibling stuff where Bear is concerned the first time around. But you only got in on the aftermath. You're making up for it." She rose to her feet once more. "You guys always do this. If it's not sitting me down on the front porch to tell me to get my life together, it's going behind my back to do an amateur background check. You know what I'd love? I'd love it if for once somebody in this family saw me as more than 'the little sister.' If you trusted me to make my own choices, use my own judgment."

Beckett just stared at her from the middle of the bedroom. He ran his fingers through hair that could've used a trim ages ago. "Raegan." He clamped his lips together, clearly not yet grasping the words he wanted to say. He turned away from her.

It'd been a mistake to open the window. Now the room was hot and muggy.

Finally, Beckett faced her again. "Maybe it was the wrong move, digging into Bear's past."

"Not maybe. It was."

"But all of the rest of that stuff you said . . ." Something flickered in his eyes. Not anger. Not even frustration. Hurt? "This whole family teases each other. This whole family doles out advice. Has nothing to do with birth order. If *Dad* was dating somebody who was keeping an entire criminal history from him and I happened to know, I'd tell him."

"Bear doesn't have—"

"We're not perfect, Rae. Lord knows I'm not. But I wasn't trying to demean you." He pierced her with a look, then reached into the back pocket of his jeans, pulled out a rolled-up piece of paper. "It's an article I printed out from an Atlanta paper. About Bear's sentencing. Read it or don't."

He dropped it on the bed beside her, then started for the door. But he turned before leaving the room. "We only see you as 'the little sister'? That might say more about how you see yourself than how we do, Rae."

He closed the door behind him.

Bear hadn't moved from the car. He'd parked in Case Walker's driveway, cut the engine, watched as Jamie slid out the passenger door and jogged to the house. And then he'd simply . . . stayed.

Sticky air clogged the car's interior, his open window letting in the evening's heat and mosquitos.

Still, he didn't budge from his seat.

"I thought I saw Dad."

Impossible.

He'd mentally muttered the word at least a hundred times on the drive out of town. Rio couldn't be in Iowa. Even Jamie, by the time he was done explaining, had talked himself out of what he'd thought he'd seen.

"I was waiting for Beckett in the store and I saw this man walk past the window and it looked like Dad. So I ran out after him." But by the time Jamie made it out the door of Klassen's Hardware and down the block, the man he'd seen had already turned a corner. And by then, Mr. Baker had discovered the vandalism. Jamie had found himself in the wrong place at the wrong time. *"It probably wasn't even him. I'm so stupid."*

"You're not stupid, Jamie. I don't want to hear you talk like that about yourself."

"Aren't you mad that you had to come to the police station?"

"No."

Annoyed at Mr. Baker for instantly accusing Jamie, sure. Trying not to be irked at Beckett for letting Jamie out of his sight, maybe.

But if he was mad at anyone, it was Rio for putting Jamie in this situation in the first place. For doing whatever he'd done to wind up in jail, leaving a confused, hurting son behind.

Rio can't be in Iowa.

But then, where was he? In some other jail *not* in

Atlanta? Why hadn't Rosa ever replied to his text yesterday? Why was she letting two, three days lapse between calls to the kids? What was with that blue Taurus he'd seen so many times? And the hang-up calls—there'd been at least three of them.

Was Bear turning paranoid or did all of this add up to . . . something?

Helpless confusion spilling over, he banged on the steering wheel with one hand and sprang for his phone in the cup holder with his other. He speed-dialed Rosa, knowing before the first ring even sounded in his ear he'd be speaking to her voicemail rather than her.

Probably better this way. He could say what he had to say uninterrupted.

He didn't bother with a greeting. "I've had it, Rosa. I can't get ahold of you. Rio's MIA. And every day with Jamie and Erin convinces me the only thing waiting for them back in Atlanta is a mess they don't deserve. If you know where Rio is, *tell me*. And while you're at it, maybe you can tell me what you meant that night in your apartment—about *them*, whoever they are, finding me in South America." Because if *they* had somehow found Bear here, too, if he was only bringing trouble to more people he cared about, then . . . then he didn't know what.

He didn't know anything. And it was suffocating him.

"You asked me to keep the kids for two or three weeks. It'll be two weeks on Sunday, but at this point, I'm done counting days. I won't do it, Rosa. I won't bring them back if all it means is they return to a shoddy apartment and crappy meals and clothes that don't fit. I won't do it."

He ended the call and tossed his phone to the passenger seat. Breathing heavily, he leaned his head over the steering wheel. Had he really just done that? Threatened Rosa?

At the sound of the passenger door opening, he lifted his head. "Rae? Hey. What are you—"

"Want to go for a drive, Bear?" She dropped into the seat beside him.

"But—" He thought better of arguing when he noticed the red rims of her eyes. She'd been crying? And what in the world had she done to her hair? With a nod, he pressed the button to close his window and returned the key to the ignition. "A drive. Good idea."

11

Raegan didn't regret refusing to read the article Beckett had printed out. Nor did she regret not asking Bear about it last night during that quiet country road drive, barely a word spoken between them.

She was, however, beginning to regret telling Kate about it.

"You seriously didn't read it?"

"I seriously didn't." Raegan pulled her plastic-covered sleeping bag from the shelf in Dad's garage, her arms and neck and back griping at her. She'd spent nearly six hours today working at the mural site, using a roller brush to cover her brick canvas with primer. T.J. Waring and Webster Hawks from the football team had stopped by to help for a couple hours. Raegan guessed she had Kate's husband—who'd been assistant coaching the team for a couple seasons now—to thank for that.

But she'd done much of the work herself, and her sore muscles were none too pleased with her for it.

It was progress, though, and that was gratifying. The primer should be dry by morning, which meant with enough harnessed determination, tomorrow—Saturday—she could finally get started on the mural for real. She'd start with a light chalk outline on the brick, then would come underpainting in bold swatches of color before she got around to any detail work.

Kate stood on the patio, coating her arms with bug spray, the sickly-sweet smell fogging the air around them. "If it's a newspaper article, it's public record. It's not like you'd be stealing Bear's private journal and reading it."

"If Bear wanted to tell me about . . . about whatever was in that article, he would've." Raegan swiped the back of her palm over her forehead, the late-afternoon sun beating down on her. Maybe suggesting a camping trip on the hottest day in June so far hadn't been the best idea. Then again, their campsite was a little clearing just down the ravine behind Dad's house, less than a five-minute walk back to civilization and air conditioning. And at least yesterday's humidity had gone into hiding today.

Besides, she and Bear had decided last night—they needed this. Each in their own way had found their lives turned upside down in the past two weeks. Each was desperate for a mental and emotional reprieve. Nothing like a night under the stars, s'mores, and a campfire to hush their anxieties—even if only temporarily. Might even cool off once the sun bedded down.

Plus, it'd be a treat for the kids.

Kate finished with the bug spray. "Well, all I can say is, that's some awfully good self-control. I'd have been too curious to ignore it. Hey, I could read it for you."

"Hardly my point in telling you."

"Then what is your point?"

"Beckett. Can you believe he had the nerve?" Raegan hauled another sleeping bag from the shelf.

Kate picked up a box loaded with camping supplies—bags of marshmallows, paper plates, campfire roasting sticks. "Gonna have to call you on that, sis. Don't you remember when we first met Colton? *You* did the online research then. Presented me with his entire backstory in Google form."

"That's different. You were writing a book about him. He'd hired you to complete his memoir and then refused to open up to you." She started walking across the backyard and toward the ravine.

"And you were attempting to help me, just like, I'm sure, Beckett was trying to help you."

She should never have brought this up. The whole point of this little camping escapade was to get away from it all. Even if "away" was more mental than physical. Just didn't make sense to go stake out a campground when they had such a pretty piece of nature just down the ravine.

But cajoling Kate into helping her dig out all the camping gear in Dad's messy garage, complaining to her about Beckett's actions last night—probably not the best idea. Still. Her sister had made two previous treks to the campsite with her, saving Raegan double the solo trips. Bear was already down at the site, setting up tents, watching the kids.

"By the way, thanks for helping with this, Kate."

"There was a subtle 'drop it' hidden somewhere in there, yeah?"

The grass rustled under her sandals. "No point in talking about it. You guys don't understand Bear the way I do. In our family we're all over each other's business. It's normal to us. Bear's not used to that. He holds stuff close to the chest and he doesn't like being poked and prodded."

She stepped under the leafy cover of the ravine. She could hear Jamie and Erin's laughter drifting through the trees. Walnuts and twigs, old gnarled leaves crunched under her feet as she started down the hillside.

"Don't poke the bear," Kate said. "Got it."

"Kate."

"Fine. No joking *or* poking. I do get it, Rae. But don't hold it against Beckett forever, okay? And maybe as long as you're at it, fix whatever's up with you and Dad."

Raegan barely avoided tripping over a fallen branch. "Me and Dad?"

"Something's off and it's been off for days and I'd bet my next book advance it has something to do with you and that Jaminski woman grabbing coffee the other day."

Her sister should win some kind of award for her gift of perception. She didn't even live in the same house as them. "Kate—"

"You don't have to tell me what's up. I don't want to be in the middle of anything."

"There's nothing to be in the middle of." Not yet anyway. But after she told Dad about therapy with Sara . . . *if* she told Dad . . .

Of course, she'd tell him. Just not tonight. *Just one night away from it all. That's what Bear and I decided.*

Which would upset Dad more? That she'd found a confidante in the one person he didn't like? Or that she'd kept her panic attacks from him all these years?

Not tonight.

"Also, for the record," Kate said, "while I'm happy to help you get set up for this little camping spree, you'll forgive me if I insist on going home to sleep tonight. I've never really understood the allure of sleeping under the stars." She pushed a low-hanging branch out of the way. "Plus, there's a decided lack of mosquitos in my bedroom that I quite appreciate *and* it has one very wonderful thing your campsite does not—"

"Let me guess—"

"My ridiculously handsome husband."

Raegan groaned, shifting the load in her arms.

"Groan all you want, little sister. Isn't going to stop me. I fully intend to gush about that man for the rest of my life."

"Well, you are a romance writer." The sound of the creek's trickle grew closer.

"Hey, Rae?"

She stopped at the shift in Kate's tone. "Huh?"

Kate set her box of supplies at her feet. "I'm pregnant."

Raegan's sleeping bags hit the grass. "*What?*"

"Due around Christmas."

"Are you . . . I can't believe . . . oh my gosh, give a girl some warning before you give her the best news ever!" She pulled Kate into a boisterous hug. "A baby, you and Colton, I'm so happy!"

And Kate was clearly overjoyed—her smile shining with an unabashed glow. She picked up her box and started walking again. "Dad's the only one that knows so far."

"Dad knows? And he's kept it a secret?" Raegan followed, shaking her head. "I wonder how many secrets he's kept for all four of us over the—"

She stopped mid-step as a *thwack* rent the air. Raegan peered past the tents toward the sound.

Bear stood over a stump of a tree, a thick log standing upright and an ax in his hand. That tattoo around one arm peeked out from under a damp shirt that stretched over taut muscle. He lifted the ax high and brought it down again.

Raegan turned to Kate with her jaw gaping, her voice low. "He's like a mountain man."

Kate didn't look nearly as impressed. "He's really sweaty."

"He's . . ." She glanced over once more. *Amazing.*

"Shouldn't we tell him Dad has a whole pile of fire-wood under a tarp by the garage?"

"Don't you dare." Raegan's laughter trailed as she turned and started for the tents once more. But when she didn't hear the shuffle of Kate's footsteps beside her, she looked over her shoulder. "Coming?"

"What happens when Bear has to return the kids to Atlanta? Is he coming back here? I know he's got that job at the ranch but after that . . . what then?"

"Dunno." Her voice was flat.

"What do you hope he does?"

Raegan couldn't bring herself to answer. Something told her she didn't need to, anyway.

For once, there wasn't even a hint of a tease in her sister's gaze. "A close friend once told me that it's okay to admit what I want."

Raegan's arms tightened around the sleeping bag. "Bear's future isn't about what I want."

"Maybe not, but what you want matters. What you care about matters. Not just to the people who love you, but to God. And if you care about Bear, if you care *for* him—"

"Kate, please, can we not do this now?" Not when the man himself wasn't all that far away and for all she knew had perfectly decent hearing.

Not when she'd been trying so hard to smother the willful voice of her heart. She'd been half in love with Bear McKinley for *five years*. And it'd gotten her exactly nowhere. If the things she cared about mattered so much to God, why didn't He ever seem to do anything about them?

Bear. The panic attacks. *Mom . . .*

Her attention drifted to where Jamie and Erin stood on the little wooden walkway over the creek, tossing rocks into shallow water. The very spot where Dad had proposed and then decades later, they'd posed as a family for that portrait hanging in the living room.

"Rae—"

"I just want to enjoy right now, Kate. That's all." She just wanted to enjoy this time with Bear and the kids.

And forget all the rest of it. Even if only for a night.

Bear plunged his head into the ice-cold water of the creek, knees sinking into the soggy bank beside the damp shirt he'd peeled off a second ago. He let the water slick over his face and through his hair before lifting his head and shaking it from side to side.

Erin's squeals rang out from behind him. "You got me wet, Uncle Bear."

"Oh, you think you're wet now, just wait." He snaked his arm out and tucked his palm around her waist, pulling her toward the shallow water, her laughter accompanying the splash of Jamie's footsteps. "Ah, your big brother doesn't want to be left out, I see."

He lugged Erin into water that barely would've reached past his knees were he standing, her shrieks and giggles—Jamie's matching laughter—the best sounds he'd heard all day.

So much better than the clanging worries pulsing in his brain. He'd taken his frustrations out on piles of broken tree branches and all he'd gotten for the effort was sweat-glistened skin and more firewood than they could possibly need for tonight.

He should've left his phone back at the house. Then Rosa's text wouldn't have been able to disrupt what was supposed to be a one-night break from the mess hovering outside the bubble of this campsite.

Fine. They're better off with you right now anyway.
Check in again in a couple weeks.

A response to his angry voicemail from last night. But she couldn't mean it. She couldn't be as cold and unfeeling as her words tried to sound. He'd seen her that night in her apartment. Behind the angst, behind the frenzy, there'd been a mother's love. A desperate love.

And if this was her reaction to his refusal to return the kids, it only proved right his growing conviction that there was so much more going on than merely an apartment eviction. He just wished he had any idea what to do about it.

I can't solve anything tonight.

What he could do was make sure his niece and nephew had the best first camping trip of their lives. So he held tight to Erin as he crawled into the creek, dragging her legs in the water beneath him. She clasped her hands around his neck, couldn't stop laughing, and then, despite himself, neither could he. Especially when Jamie jumped onto his back.

The next minutes were filled with splashing and more laughter, more squeals. Erin and Jamie teamed up, pouncing all over him until they'd successfully landed him on his backside on the creek bed below him.

"Do you surrender, Uncle Bear?" Erin's clothes clung to her skin, her hair in straggles around her cheeks.

"Never," he said through panting breath.

Jamie splashed a wave of water in his face. "Now do you surrender?"

Bear shook his hair again, spraying them both with water. "Nope."

"Try tickling him."

Raegan. He looked over his shoulder to see her standing a few feet from the edge of the creek, hands on her waist and eyes so blue they put this dirty creek water to shame. "What if I'm not ticklish?"

Jamie lunged at him. "Let's find out."

Both kids attacked his stomach with their fingers, giggling, sending more water flying in every direction. He didn't even flinch.

He poured every speck of smug delight he could into the smile he cast at Raegan.

"It's not working." Erin plopped her fists on her waist, just like Raegan, her pout ridiculously endearing.

He pulled himself to his feet, reaching for both kids, lifting one under each arm.

"Hey!" Jamie yelped.

He carried them out of the water and plunked them on wet grass in front of Raegan. Good thing Case's house was a mere run up the hill away. All three of them were soaked through.

"You're not ticklish?" Raegan asked as he straightened in front of her.

"Try it yourself if you're not convinced." He got way too much enjoyment out of her flicker of a glance at his bare chest and the blush that crawled up her cheeks. He leaned in. "Go ahead."

"You're ridiculous." But she didn't back away.

"What's stopping you?"

"Propriety." There went her hands on her waist again.

"Not a word I generally associate with you."

"I feel like I should be insulted by that."

"On the contrary." He leaned down to pick up his discarded shirt and the phone he'd thankfully remembered to yank from his pocket before wading into the creek. He pulled the shirt over his head in time to see Jamie wringing out his own shirt over Erin's head, her bubbling giggles unceasing. "I'm glad you had this camping idea, Rae."

"Me too. Even if it is so hot I'm regretting not chopping my hair weeks ago."

She pulled a band from around her wrist and reached up behind her head to tug her hair into a ponytail. He'd seen her do the same about a hundred times, but the sun must be getting to him because right now that one little routine proved entirely too . . . mesmerizing.

Somewhere in the back of his head, that old mantra tried to resurrect itself. *You can be attracted to her, but . . .*

What was the *but*? He couldn't remember it. And the nagging voice had been steadily fading since a few nights ago out on that scaffolding. Since that afternoon in the men's locker room shower stall.

Fine, since the day he'd returned to Maple Valley to find Raegan Walker in his apartment.

Nonetheless, he pulled his gaze away. "Hey, kids, what do you say we go find dry clothes?"

They started for the ravine.

He turned back to Raegan. Great, now with her hair up, it was too easy to notice the freckles on her bare shoulders. He should probably just go throw himself in the creek again already.

"I don't even know why I grew it out in the first place," she was saying. "It's so annoying. I never know whether it's going to be straight or wavy, it's always falling out of ponytails. It takes longer to dry in the morning."

"Is there a reason we're talking so much about your hair?" He moved to follow the kids.

Raegan two-stepped to keep up with him. "Because we promised not to talk about any of our problems. The serious ones, that is. I figure my hair woes don't count as serious."

He stopped at the edge of the ravine, watching as the kids scrambled over the lawn. "Actually, speaking of that . . ." He opened Rosa's text and handed his phone to Raegan.

Took her less than a millisecond to press her lips together. "That's . . . unbelievable."

"I think it's a cover. When she told me two weeks ago that it was safer for the kids to be with me, I honestly thought she was exaggerating. Now I can't help but wonder . . . well, all kinds of things. My imagination's going wild." He combed his fingers through his wet hair. "Sorry. We weren't going to talk about this."

"But if you need to . . ."

"What I need to do is talk to the kids. Let them know they'll be staying here a while longer. I mean, if your family's okay with it." He said it like a question.

A silly question, according to the expression on Raegan's face. "Of course it's okay."

"Think I should talk to them now?"

"Might be good. Get it over with so they can come back down here and enjoy roasting hot dogs and having a campfire."

He nodded and stepped out of the cover of the trees.

"Bear?"

He glanced over his shoulder.

"Leave your phone at the house this time."

He lifted his hand to salute her, then crossed the lawn. Ten minutes later he'd shed his wet jeans and changed into clean clothes. He emerged from the basement. Jamie and Erin's voices reached him from the second floor as he climbed the stairs.

"I think he's twenty."

"He can't be twenty." Jamie's tone was pure older brother knowing. "That's too young. I think he's forty."

"That's too old."

"No, it's not. Dad's thirty, I think. And Bear's older than Dad."

Bear leaned against their doorway until they noticed him, Erin's wet clothes strewn about the room. He'd seen Jamie's abandoned in the bathroom when he passed. "I'm thirty-two, guys. I'll be thirty-three in August."

Jamie puffed his chest. "I was closer to being right."

He ruffled his nephew's still-damp hair as he strode into the room. He dropped onto the bottom bunk and Erin immediately went for his lap. "We can have a birthday party for you. Raegan will help us."

At his sister's declaration, Jamie's focus shot to Bear, his question spelled out so plainly on his face. He wanted to know where they'd be in August. Wanted to know if they'd be together.

Bear wasn't going to get a better opening.

"Actually, as long as we're on the topic, how would the two of you feel about staying here a little longer?"

Jamie lowered onto the bed beside him. "How much longer?"

"I'm not sure. But probably, uh, maybe a couple more weeks?" Maybe he shouldn't have brought this up without a more concrete plan.

But it wasn't fair to the kids to be left in the dark. Erin might be fine going with the flow, but Jamie was old enough to know this arrangement wasn't normal.

"We get to stay with you?" Erin's eyes lit up. "And Raegan?"

"Yeah. For now."

"What about Mom?" Jamie asked it quietly.

Bear reached his arm around the boy's back and tugged him to his side. "She misses you." He assumed. "But she's heard about all the fun stuff we've been doing so far this summer." Through texts she hadn't bothered to answer. "She doesn't want to cut it short."

"Maybe she could come here and do more fun stuff with us." Erin jumped off his lap. "Let's go back down to the tents."

Jamie hadn't moved.

Bear squeezed Jamie's shoulder. "You all right with this, son? Because if you're not—"

From under the shelter of Bear's arm, Jamie glanced up.

You called him son.

But Jamie didn't look angry. He didn't lash out as he had last time. Instead, he simply nodded. "I'm okay with it." Then he surprised Bear with a full-fledged embrace, his head against his chest and his wiry arms circling as far as he could reach.

Bear had to blink to hide his sudden rise of emotion. Not just at Jamie's surprise show of affection. But at the conviction that this wasn't normal. Two kids shouldn't be so happy to be away from their home, so accepting of their parents' absence. It was completely wrong.

But he hugged his nephew anyway, welcomed Erin into the circle when she jumped onto the bed beside them.

So completely wrong.

Then why did this feel so right?

The buzz of cicadas filled the darkened hillside, a frog's croaking downstream, the whir of a midnight breeze pushing through the trees. The smoky smell of the campfire's lingering embers swathed the night air.

Raegan turned over atop her sleeping bag, eyes to the flap at the top of her tent that opened to the moonlit sky. She grinned. From the moment Bear and the kids had returned from the house, tonight had been near perfect. They'd roasted hot dogs, taught the kids how to make s'mores, laughed when Erin ended up with sticky marshmallow in her hair and Jamie's burnt to such a crisp it fell off his roasting stick.

Kate had stuck around for a couple hours, and Dad, too, stopped down for a bit. But eventually, it'd just been Bear and Raegan and the kids, sitting on old lawn chairs around the fire.

Until Jamie and Erin had both fallen asleep.

And then it'd been just Bear and Raegan. Talking about everything and nothing.

It's okay to admit what I want.

Kate's words rolled around in her mind. Well, if Raegan admitted it right now, *this* is what she wanted. She wanted tonight again and again. And even if that's all she ever got—Bear's presence and his friendship—it might be good enough.

Muted light through the tent's mesh screen snagged her gaze. She rose to her knees and pulled a T-shirt over her camisole, then unzipped the tent. Bear?

She caught sight of his shadowed form with flashlight extended turning a slow half-circle as he surveyed the trees bordering their campsite. He must not have awakened the kids when he slipped from his tent.

Raegan had assumed Erin would sleep in her tent, but when the time had come to turn in, she'd refused to let go of Bear. Raegan had seen their huddled outline through the tent's screen flap before she'd hunkered down in her own tent—one kid tucked on either side of Bear.

The sight had warmed her and made her want to cry, all at the same time.

Grass scratched her bare feet and ankles now as she padded toward Bear. He turned before she reached him.

"Rae?"

"Can't sleep?"

"Thought I heard something." He glanced to the trees once more. "But I think maybe I'm just becoming paranoid."

He said it lightly, but he wasn't joking, was he? He'd told her in sparse words and a dull tone last night about Jamie thinking he'd seen his dad. He'd mentioned the hang-up calls, the multiple sightings of that blue car.

"It's after midnight."

He flicked off the flashlight. "Right. We should be sleeping."

"No, I mean, it's technically tomorrow. That agreement not to talk about stuff is now null and void. So . . ."

Even in the dark, she could make out his light smile. "Are you seriously never going to get tired of me spilling my problems to you?"

"Something tells me, Bear, you've never spilled to me half of what's on your mind."

"Maybe I've just never wanted to burden you with all of it."

"Except friends are supposed to help carry each other's burdens. At least, that's what the best kinds of friends do. And I know I'm not Seth, but—"

"No, you're not. You're definitely not."

The husky timbre of his voice chased away whatever else she'd planned to say. And for a moment thick with significance, his moonlight-tinted eyes, often so unreadable, were an open window into a heart she'd longed to explore. *Please tell me I'm not the only one, Bear. Tell me it's different this time and you feel the same as I do and maybe somehow . . .*

He cleared his throat. And the cicadas' sharp hum infiltrated once more.

She let out a breath and her head tipped down. "I was in prison."

She looked up. The shades were drawn once more, his gaze hooded, only the faintest hint of uncertainty peeking through, as if he wasn't at all sure he should've said it. And yet, he went on.

"Multiple felonies. I confessed, so there wasn't even much of a trial. Just a swift sentencing." He chewed over his next words, the unbearable pause stretching so long Raegan was sure he could hear her hammering heart. Finally, he met her eyes. "The thing is, I was . . . lying. I didn't do any of what they said I did. Of what *I* said I did."

Goosebumps climbed over her skin, but she couldn't make her arms move to fold together and ward off the cool. Shock held her frozen. "I don't . . . I don't understand."

"It's just . . . I felt so guilty for leaving Rio, and if I hadn't been so focused on myself . . . he was just doing what he saw everyone else around him doing . . . and Rosa was pregnant and . . ."

"Bear."

Hearing his name was enough to halt his frenzied explanation. And saying it was enough to unfreeze her limbs. Raegan reached out to touch his arm. "Slow down. Start at the beginning."

He swallowed. Nodded. "I moved out the day I graduated high school. Got my own place, got a job. Just couldn't wait to get away from my parents and all the crap Rio and I had to put up with growing up." His jaw flexed. "I didn't even think about Rio. Just figured he'd do the same when he graduated. I tried to spend time with him now and then, but I got busy with paramedic training and Annie."

Annie? She tried to cover her inhale, the pang of

dread-laced curiosity. But he had to have seen it.

He looked to the ground. "Met her outside a church of all places. I was just passing by, she was just leaving a Sunday service."

Of course, there'd been a girl in his past. Maybe more than one. It's not like it'd never occurred to her before. Stung all the same.

"I'd never met someone like her, Rae—or her family. Close-knit, kind—not just to their own, but everybody. I'd never seen faith like what she had."

Had?

"Her parents are John and Elizabeth, the missionaries I was with down in Brazil."

Wait, did that mean . . . had Annie been in Brazil, too? Was that why he'd gone? The sting sharpened.

But Bear was already moving on.

"Anyway, I had this whole new life and I loved it. But it was Annie who brought Rio up one day. She asked me how he was doing and I realized I didn't have any idea. So one morning I went back to the old neighborhood to see him." He stopped, pain twisting through every corner of his expression. "No one was home, but I still had a key. Don't know why I did it, but I stopped in Rio's bedroom. I saw a floorboard sticking out. Knew I was prying, but it'd always been his hiding place and I suddenly had this horrible feeling. I thought I'd find drugs, but instead it was piles of cash."

He rubbed his palms over his cheeks, the pace of his words picking up again. "I came back in the afternoon and he was pulling out of the parking lot when I arrived. Ignored me when I honked. I ended up following him to this warehouse. And from there, it was just a huge mess."

"Bear, you don't have to tell me—"

"He was in charge of all of it, Rae. I thought he was

just mixed up in something bad, but no. In the two years since I'd moved out, he'd gone from troublemaker at fifteen to practically a ringleader at seventeen. He'd actually poached men from Luis Inez—Rosa's father, possibly one of the most dangerous men in Atlanta."

"What were they doing at the warehouse?"

"The usual—stealing cars, stripping them, selling parts. They weren't manufacturing drugs, at least, but there was plenty of dealing going on."

That still didn't explain how Bear had ended up the one in prison. Or why in the world he would've confessed. Unless . . .

Understanding flooded in, drenching her with disbelief. "Bear, you didn't."

"I was in the wrong place at the wrong time. I'd gone in to confront Rio, but the cops raided. We somehow ended up in the back of the same police car. That's when Rio told me his girlfriend was pregnant."

His tone had gone numb as the memory glazed his eyes.

"What was I supposed to do, Rae? He'd already been arrested twice and he was less than a month from eighteen. They would've tried him as an adult."

"Bear—"

"He was going to be a father. He would've missed Jamie's birth. I didn't have so much as a speck on my record. I figured a judge would go easier on me. If I hadn't left him behind in the first place, practically forgotten about him . . ."

The pieces fit together, forming a picture she couldn't handle. Bear had confessed out of guilt. Out of love. But the thought of him locked away in a prison cell, punished for someone else's crime . . .

It was all she could do to blink back tears. "But it wasn't your fault, Bear. Rio was old enough to make his own choices."

"Didn't end up mattering anyway. I did it because I thought I was giving him a second chance at a better life. A fresh start like what I'd had. But it didn't change anything." He shook his head. "Except, no, that's not the truth. It made everything worse."

His anguish ripped at her heart, and it was the most natural thing in the world to reach for him. He let her fill the space between them, didn't move so much as a muscle save his ragged inhale as she lifted both hands to his cheeks. "Bear McKinley, you are the very best person I know." Not a single qualifier, and she meant it with everything in her.

"Rae—" His breath was warm on her face.

"You are kind and noble and brave. Everything you just told me might be shocking, but it's also not really that surprising. I already knew you were amazing. I've known it forever."

He opened his mouth as if to argue once more, but she spoke again first.

"What I didn't know was that it was possible to admire you even more than I did before. But it is and I do and—"

And now he was the one to cut her off. Not with words, but with movement so swift she didn't have time to so much as gasp before he clasped both her arms and lowered his lips to hers. For one astonished moment, she couldn't move or even think.

But then he softened his grasp on her arms and his first kiss turned into a second.

And all the desire she'd pushed and pushed and *pushed* away finally broke free. She twined her arms around his neck and relaxed into him, every nerve alive and warmth making its way through her, puddling in her heart.

"Raegan." He whispered her name against her lips. "I . . . we . . ."

She didn't let him finish. Couldn't. Not when she'd waited so long for this. She kissed him now, years of longing poured into the embrace.

No, she hadn't been honest earlier. Bear's presence, his friendship—not enough.

She wanted *this*, too. Again and again.

"Uncle Bear?"

So instantly did Bear let her go that she would've stumbled if not for his steadying hand even as he turned.

"Erin?" Bear's voice was a mere rasp. "Did you have a nightmare?"

She shook her head, her sleep-tousled hair a mess of tangles around her face. "But I woke up and you weren't there."

"I was just getting some fresh air. Come on, kid, I'll tuck you back into your sleeping bag." With a quick, indiscernible look at Raegan, Bear disappeared with Erin into his tent.

Raegan touched her fingers to her lips as she listened to Bear's hushed tone settling Erin. Jamie must've woken up, because his voice, too, drifted from the tent.

After a couple minutes, Bear finally emerged from the tent. He zipped the flapping door, then whispered through the mesh. "Be back in a sec."

A whisper of disappointment wriggled in.

Raegan hadn't moved from the spot where he'd left her. Probably still looked as dazed as she felt.

But Bear . . . all the emotion that had filled his voice earlier—and then filled that kiss—had begun to visibly seep away. "I'm not sure how much Erin saw . . . of that. But she was still half asleep. She'll probably forget by morning."

Did that mean they, too, were supposed to forget it?

Like that's possible. "Bear, that kiss—"

"Raegan."

"Don't apologize for it. Please don't apologize."

"I wasn't going to apologize. I was just going to say . . ." He rubbed the back of his neck, offered her a sheepish smile. "I don't know what I was going to say."

Gosh, she wanted him to kiss her again. But the moment, it seemed, had been broken. "Earlier . . . you said that everything got worse." She had to ask. "How could it get worse than you going to jail?"

"I'd rather not . . . I can't . . ." The shades fell into place over his eyes once more. But just before he slipped into the tent, he gave her the barest answer. "Annie died."

12

*B*ear had pressed *Send* on two applications today—one to the mission board in Brazil, one to Des Moines Area Community College. He'd signed up for a CPR class at the local hospital. And he'd started caulking holes in Sara Jaminski's cabins.

Didn't matter how many tasks filled his Monday, though. They couldn't drive Raegan from his mind. Or those kisses. Or the fear that he'd somehow gone and made everything worse.

Until the phone call. The fourth one like it. No greeting, no voice. Just heavy breathing.

And that was it. He'd waffled long enough. Bear pulled open the door of the Maple Valley Police Department.

At least his course of action was certain in this one thing. If only he felt as sure of what to do about Raegan. He couldn't stand the awkwardness that now hovered like a low-slung cloud between them. On Saturday when he'd woken up in his tent, a kid on either side of him, Raegan had already left the campsite. He'd barely seen her that day.

They'd wound up next to each other in church on Sunday. But after a couple stilted tries at small talk out in the church lobby and then again as they sat around two pushed-together tables at The Red Door, all the local Walkers crowded around, she'd disappeared with Kate and hadn't returned until evening.

Avoiding him. Obviously.

She'd been the one Friday night to order him not to apologize for kissing her. Had she switched stances, though? Was *she* sorry it'd happened?

"Can I help you?"

Bear blinked, the details around him flashing into focus. The smell of fresh coffee. Voices and a phone ringing. A cop in uniform twirling a set of car keys in his hand while he read a newspaper. A pool of desks sat behind the counter, lined at the back by a row of offices. Details he'd been too livid to see last week when he was here for Jamie.

A woman with brown skin and sleek black hair waited for him to speak. How long had he been standing here?

The phone calls. Rio and Rosa.

He was a mess of battling worries today. Raegan. The kids. Raegan. The kids.

He knew the kids were his most immediate concern, he just couldn't get over the feeling that with a few kisses—maybe even more, with all he'd told Rae—everything had changed Friday night.

Or maybe nothing had changed at all. Maybe he'd simply finally accepted what had been there all along—the truth that he was over-the-moon crazy about Raegan Walker. He loved her laughter and her friendship. He loved all the amusing quirks that made her who she was. He loved the vulnerable glimpses she'd given him into her heart. And he loved the strength and bravery he wasn't sure she knew she had.

Yet he'd still sent off that application to Brazil.

God, I don't know what I'm doing or why anymore.

"Sir?" The woman in front of him prodded him.

You do know one thing—you know what you're doing here.

Was that hushed reminder his own thoughts or God replying? Either way . . .

"Is Chief Ross around?"

Too perfectly timed, a door marked "Police Chief" swung open near the back of the department.

"Claudia, you're going to think I'm a dolt, but I broke my printer again and—" The man Bear had met last week cut off as he came out of his office. "Oh. You. You here to ream me out some more?"

"I don't know, you bring any more eleven-year-old kids in for questioning?"

The chief approached the counter. Deep-set eyes and an imposing height—even to Bear—loaned an appropriately firm stature to the chief, though an amused smile played about his mouth. "I would've thought with enough time to simmer down you would've realized by now I did Jamie a favor. Saved him from Mr. Baker's yelling before a crowd could form."

"If you're waiting for me to thank you—" He stopped himself. *He'd* come here. For help. Not getting off to the best start. "Sorry. And, sure, thanks for sparing Jamie further embarrassment. I guess."

Now Chief Ross—Sam—was fully grinning. "Real convincing, McKinley, but I'll take what I can get. Do you need something?"

Bear glanced from Sam to Claudia and back to Sam again. "I've got an odd situation. Honestly don't know if you can help me or not. But I thought I could at least, I don't know, maybe bend your ear for a few minutes."

"An odd situation, huh? I once responded to a 9-1-1 call from a ninety-year-old woman who'd trapped a mouse in her purse. She didn't want to kill the thing. Asked me to drive it out to the country, free the mouse, and then return her purse."

An image of that jostling mattress in Sara's cabin found the surface of his thoughts. He could still hear Raegan's squeals, her teasing voice accusing him of being scared of whatever creature lived in the thing.

She wasn't entirely wrong. "Did you do it? Free the mouse?"

Claudia nodded her head, looking to Bear. "And Odette Hays still thanks him every time she sees him."

"Still carries that purse, too." Sam waved his hand toward his office. "Come on back. You can tell me about your odd situation."

Bear followed the chief around the counter, past the collection of desks, and into a simple office. Sunlight streamed in a narrow window. A framed photo of a young girl and a couple of coffee mugs sat on the windowsill.

"Take a seat."

Bear dropped onto the lone black chair that faced Sam's desk. "I don't really know where to start."

Sam turned to the mini-fridge in the corner and pulled out two bottles of water. He set one on his desk in front of Bear. "Beginning's usually a good spot."

Problem was, Bear didn't know where the beginning began. All he knew was that Rio wasn't in a single Atlanta jail. Rosa hadn't called or texted again since Friday night.

And he couldn't shake the goading sense that something was wrong.

"Well, you met Jamie the other day. He and his younger sister are staying with me at the moment. It was only supposed to be for two or three weeks, but . . ."

The story spilled from him in spurted starts and

stops. Rio's history of criminal activity—what little Bear knew of it, anyway. Rosa's urgent request that Bear take the kids away from Atlanta. His current anxiety about not being able to reach either of them.

Just for good measure, he threw in the details of his own history. Prison. Brazil. The vandalism that had driven him away and then that cryptic comment Rosa had made about "they" being able to find Bear in South America.

He finished with the phone calls, the blue Taurus, and Rosa's final text Friday night.

By the time he ran out of words, Sam sat transfixed, palms flat on his desk and water bottle unopened in front of him. Whereas Bear had downed his entire bottle throughout the telling.

"Wow." Sam rubbed his chin. "This is, um, not the kind of thing I hear every day." He reached for his water, twisted its cap, and proceeded to guzzle half the bottle.

Bear traced the seam of his chair's armrest. "Not of the same caliber as a mouse in a purse, I suppose."

"To be sure." Sam emptied his bottle with his next drink. "The fact that we're talking about two individuals in another state whose whereabouts may or may not be in question—"

"They're certainly in question to me."

"Yes, but you said prior to last month, you've hardly had any contact with your brother and sister-in-law in a decade. Just because you don't know where they are doesn't mean anyone else doesn't know where they are." Sam launched his empty bottle toward a recycling bin in the corner. "But regardless, because we're talking about another state, it's kind of tricky. Even trickier, the kids."

"Jamie and Erin seem to be handling everything fine. As far as they know, they're just spending some time getting to know their uncle." He hoped, anyway. But

Jamie was perceptive. He might suspect more than Bear had let on. "Still, I'm getting more and more unsettled about the whole thing."

Sam's face was unreadable. "Don't blame you. And the phone calls—under normal circumstances, I'd chalk it up to a prank. But considering . . ." He leaned forward, lacing his fingers atop his desk. "I'd like to have one of my officers look at your phone, just in case there's anything we can do to trace the call. And I'd like you to write down some details for me: your brother and sister-in-law's names, their address. Social security numbers would be great, if you have them."

"I don't."

"That's all right. In any case, write down as much as you can. Then I'll start making calls, see if there's someone on the Atlanta force who can help us out."

"Do I need to file a missing person's report or anything?"

"Like I said, I don't think we can really consider your brother missing at this point. If it were your sister-in-law sitting in here, that'd be different. But you said yourself you haven't had contact with him in years. For all you know, he's hanging out on a buddy's couch and your sister-in-law is simply enjoying a break from motherhood." He shook his head. "Besides, most P.D.s won't let you file over the phone anyway. So for now, let's focus on gathering contact info. You noted your sister-in-law said something about going to her father's house. I'll want his name, and any other names of family members or friends we might be able to make inquiries with. If we're lucky, we'll find both of them easily."

"And the blue Taurus?"

"Common car. Not much we can do on that one. Not without a license plate number."

He'd tried to catch the number the fourth time he'd

seen the car—out at the ranch on Saturday afternoon, sitting in that same spot on the same gravel road where he'd first seen it. But the driver had spotted Bear's attention too quickly, sped off in a cloud of dust before Bear could focus on the plate.

"As for the rest of it, we're simply not going to know anything until we start looking." Sam stood. "I'll get some paper and we'll review it all."

Bear let out a slow exhale. He might not have answers yet. But he had help. It was a start.

Moving around the scaffolding with the extra weight of the harness had almost started to feel normal.

And the chalk markings over the brick were almost detailed enough to be a work of art on their own. They should be. Raegan had spent half of Saturday and—she glanced at her watch—five hours today outlining after her morning shift at the library.

"You ever going to be ready to start painting, my girl?"

At the sound of Mr. Hill's voice, she spun and crossed to the edge of the platform, leaning over the guardrail "Hey, I'm working as fast as I can. I do have three other jobs, you know." Though, Dad had cut her hours at the railroad down to nearly nothing.

Mr. Hill shielded his eyes as he looked up at her. "You mind company up there?"

"Of course not."

A moment later, the metal structure rattled as he began his climb.

It'd been a good idea to limit her mural to the building's second floor, bordered by cement above and below.

If she would've tried to incorporate the first or third floors, it would've required a more complicated scaffolding setup, and the chances of completing the thing by the art festival would diminish drastically.

She had enough doubts about finishing in time as it was—less than six weeks to go. But Mayor Milt was counting on her. Heck, the whole town was counting on her. How many times in the past week had someone stopped her on the sidewalk or at church or Seth's restaurant just to tell her good luck? Jenessa Belville, who had run the local newspaper ever since Logan had sold it to her, had even come by the site on Saturday. She'd taken pictures of Raegan working, asked her a few questions. Apparently the article would run in the digital publication later this week.

She turned back to the pastel outline taking shape over the painted brick. A cluster of shadows passed over the wall—clouds gathering overhead. Another summer storm was on its way in tonight, according to the forecast. Which was why she'd opted for her car rather than her bike when she'd left the house today.

Not that she had any intention of being on the road—in a bike or car or otherwise—in a storm. Not when both her most recent attack and her worst had taken place during storms.

Even a decade later, she could still hear the crash of metal from the accident pushing through her panic. Sara would make her describe it, wouldn't she? The unembellished explanation she'd given last week was only the beginning, she knew. She'd have to relive the whole thing—what little she could remember of it, anyway.

If it really helped, maybe it'd be worth it. If she could learn to cope, build a mental arsenal of tools not just for avoiding panic attacks but managing them when they happened, if she could figure out how to handle the embarrassment and stop hiding, stop living in denial . . .

Maybe one day there wouldn't be that niggle of dread every time she got behind the wheel. Maybe she'd be able to drive farther than Ames or Des Moines or Omaha without fearing the worst.

Maybe, for once, she'd be able to picture herself in a new place with new people doing new things.

Not just picture it. Live it.

And if Bear insisted on going back to Brazil, maybe this time . . .

She almost snorted out loud. What? She'd go with him? A few impromptu kisses and she was already imagining a future beyond Maple Valley?

Granted, they'd been perfect kisses. Worthy of one of Kate's stories. No, maybe too good, because there couldn't possibly be words to adequately describe them.

Maybe God *did* care about her desires.

"That smile on your face makes me want to throw out a few dozen 'I told you so's.'" Mr. Hill's footsteps stopped beside her. "You're enjoying yourself."

She wasn't about to tell her old teacher the real reason for whatever foolish expression covered her face. But he did have something of a point. She *had* enjoyed herself today. More than she'd expected to, especially considering the confusing emotions flurrying like a tempest inside her ever since Friday night.

Try ever since Bear came back. No, ever since you met him.

Especially since Friday night, though.

But for a while on Saturday and again today, she'd been able to lose herself in her art. Creativity had whooshed in like a gale too long held at bay. She'd let it carry her along. And she'd felt almost as exhilarated as she had when Bear kissed her.

Almost.

"You're smiling again. You're happy."

No, I'm ridiculous. After all, she'd hardly spoken to Bear since Friday. For all she knew, he regretted the whole thing. It was why she'd done her best to avoid him ever since. She wouldn't be able to handle it if he made some big speech about how it shouldn't have happened. Or worse, if he tried to pretend it hadn't happened at all.

"Happy *and* pensive," Mr. Hill said.

"Sorry. I've spent a ton of time alone today. Having trouble getting out of my own head."

"Well, you're gonna want to escape your thoughts long enough to hear this." Mr. Hill turned to face her, enthusiasm brightening his already pleased expression. "I've persuaded Forrester Carlisle Young to attend the festival."

Raegan wiped her chalky hands on her apron. "Forrester Carlisle Young? I don't know the name."

Mr. Hill gaped. "You've been away from the art world for far too long, my girl."

"Was I ever really in the art world, though?"

"He's the Dean of Arts at Rhode Island School of Design. We go way back. I knew him when his name was still Phil Leech. He changed it before his first showing at a gallery in NYC. A pretentious-sounding nom de plume, if you ask me—three last names? Come on. But I can forgive him because he's an artistic genius."

And he was coming to little old Maple Valley for a regional art festival?

Mr. Hill must've read her question. "We've been saying we were going to catch up for years. The festival gives us an excuse. Want to know the best part?" He leaned forward, a gleam in his eyes. "He remembers you."

Raegan felt her forehead scrunch. "What? I never met him."

"I told him about you, of course. Raegan Walker, I knew from that first watercolor you ever did in Intro to Art as a freshman that you were something special. I'd been telling Phil about you for years. He couldn't personally offer you a scholarship back then because he was still new at the school. But today he could open so many doors for you."

Mr. Hill's meaning sunk in. This Forrester Carlisle Young, aka Phil Leech, wasn't just coming to Maple Valley to visit his old friend or stop by the festival. He was coming to see *her*. "Oh, Mr. Hill, no—"

"Don't even say it, my girl. There's no point. He's already accepted my invitation *and* I spoke to Mayor Milt and the festival committee. They're adding him to the judging pool. That part doesn't matter to you—your piece won't be judged. But it'll be great publicity for the event, that's for sure."

"I'm not ready for this, Mr. Hill. What if the mural doesn't turn out well? What if I can't even finish it?"

"What if it does and what if you do and what if it's a masterpiece?"

She looked back to her brick-canvas. Primer, chalk outline . . . didn't feel like nearly enough progress now. Her pulse quickened.

"Take a deep breath, Raegan."

Not Mom's voice this time. Sara's. She'd been just about to leave the woman's house last week when Sara had stopped her on the doorstep.

"Before you go, let's try something—a breathing exercise. Inhale four seconds, hold four seconds, exhale four seconds."

Four seconds in. Four seconds hold. Four seconds out.

Mr. Hill didn't understand. It wasn't the thought of a famous artist critiquing her work that sent shoots of dread from her shoulders to her toes. It was that last question. *What if it's a masterpiece?*

That last question and what it could mean. Open doors were one thing. But the space on the other side? It might be too big and she might be too small. She wasn't ready.

I'm not Mom.

Mom, who'd chased a passion all the way to the East Coast, cast her vision and reeled in a dream. Raegan wasn't Dad or Logan or Kate or Beckett, for that matter, either. She wasn't Seth.

She was Raegan the homebody with the part-time jobs and the same bed she'd slept in since she was nine.

And here, not five minutes ago, she'd let her imagination wander halfway down the globe because a man named Bear McKinley had kissed her.

They might've been magical kisses but they weren't *that* magical. They couldn't change who she was. She was finally acknowledging her panic attacks, yes. Finally reaching out for help.

But she was still a woman with too many fears and too many faults.

"Now, the thing you'll really want to think about, is what other work you can show Phil."

Mr. Hill was still talking?

"I know you won't have much time, but even if you can eke out one landscape—"

"Mr. Hill—"

"Don't do it again, Raegan, please. Don't walk away from your gift. Don't let this opportunity pass you by. Find a few hours some evening and get out your oils. See what you come up with. If nothing else, maybe we can pull out some of your old work to show Phil. Just think about it, Rae. Think about what it could mean."

Four seconds in. Four seconds hold. Four seconds

out.

A canopy of gray shrouded the landscape. "I'll think about it." If only to urge Mr. Hill away. Reclaim the solace she'd found on this second-story platform earlier today.

But even when he'd gone, the peace didn't return.

"You can never, ever tell any of the Walkers about this."

Bear sat on a stool at the counter in Coffee Coffee, Jamie and Erin on either side of him. Both kids had seemed restless back at the house after supper tonight. He'd finally decided on a little jaunt into town. Thought maybe he might get lucky and run into Raegan, too.

But when he'd glanced at her mural building as he drove past, there was no sign of her.

"Are you talking to me or the kids?"

Coffee Coffee's young, ever-sarcastic owner, Megan Harrow, stood on the other side of the counter with a towel over her shoulder and her jet-black hair tied in a knot atop her head. He'd always had a feeling she wasn't nearly as caustic as she generally tried to appear. Megan could dress in black and rim her eyes with as much eyeliner as she wanted—wasn't enough to entirely disguise her soft side.

Bear had become a regular at the coffee shop below his apartment back when he'd actually lived in his apartment. The eclectic atmosphere of the place more than made up for his coffee distaste—a boho mix of bright furniture and tables of varying colors, lanky windows that peered into the picturesque riverfront, the fact that he never could guess what kind of music would be playing over the speakers.

This evening it was some languid indie rock band.

"Both," he answered Megan. "You know how the Walkers feel about their breakfast foods. Like they're the only people capable of pulling off the perfect morning feast. If they knew how I often I bring the kids in here for donuts, I'd never hear the end of it." At least three mornings last week.

And apparently the habit had expanded into an evening ritual as well. Though, he had every intention of purchasing extra donuts to-go once Jamie and Erin finished tonight's treat. That'd take care of breakfast tomorrow. Raegan wouldn't even be able to make fun of his cereal consumption.

If she was around, that is. How much longer could she keep avoiding him?

Megan pulled the towel from her shoulder and wiped down the counter. "Your niece and nephew might agree to keep your secret, but you forget—I'm tight with that family."

Yes, he'd seen firsthand a couple of years ago the way Kate Walker had taken Megan under her wing. When a flood had pummeled the coffee shop right around the same time as an unexpected pregnancy had knocked Megan off her feet, Raegan's sister had become the younger woman's support system.

It was a Walker thing—gently towing in anyone in need of a lifeline. When he'd first moved to Maple Valley after his prison release, he'd been so intent on appearing put together. Admirable. Unwavering in his faith and untiring in his work ethic. But deep inside, loss had scraped him hollow—Annie, Rio, the life he used to hope for. He'd needed what the Walkers had offered—kindness and a sense of belonging, of family.

And they were doing it all over again now. Not just with him, but Jamie and Erin, too.

Beside him, Erin dunked her donut into a glass of chocolate milk. Jamie had barely touched his own, so intent was he on whatever book he'd brought home from the library this morning. The kids had gone with Raegan for her morning shift. And Jamie had come home talking about a girl he'd met—Elise something or other.

"She can't see, Uncle Bear. She reads braille. It's cool."

If he wasn't mistaken, Jamie might have his first crush.

Megan pulled another donut from the glass case nearby and slid it in front of Bear. His second.

"I still look hungry?" He'd wolfed down his first in four bites.

"No, but since you won't buy a specialty drink, I have to make sure your patronage is worth my financial while."

"I was already going to buy extras for tomorrow."

"You should really consider giving coffee another chance. I've actually had some success lately converting a former coffee-hater. The other day, he didn't even wince when he tried a drink of my latte."

"He?" Was Megan actually blushing right now? Megan, the sarcastic barista, blushing. It was worthy of a newspaper article. "Clearly, I've missed some things while I've been away. Who's the *he*?"

"When did you get so nosy, Bear?"

"When did you get so blushy, Meg?"

His phone's ringtone kept him from anymore teasing. Somehow he knew, even before he pulled it from his pocket, what he'd see on the screen. *Unidentified Number.* He bit back an aggravated grumble. Fifth call.

But Chief Ross had told him to keep answering. So he did, lurching his phone to his ear and giving only a gruff, "What?"

Megan's eyebrows rose.

He waited for the familiar breathing on the other end. Instead . . .

"Bear?"

A punch in his stomach couldn't have surprised him so thoroughly. After a quick glance at Megan, her understanding nod, he spun on his heels and strode from the shop. Sultry air hastened to envelop him as he stepped into the sun. "Rio?"

That had been his brother's voice, hadn't it? He may not have heard it in a decade, but he knew it.

But the voice didn't answer.

"Rio, if it's you, talk to me. Why do you keep calling like this?"

There was the breathing again.

"Could you at least tell me where you are? Or what's up with Rosa? This is so far past ridiculous, I can't even—"

Click.

He closed his eyes, a defeated sigh slogging through him. *It was Rio. It had to be.*

Bear should've been calmer. Nicer. Patient. He should've . . . he should've not blown it, that's what. Because a swift and surprise longing suddenly filled in all the gaps of his unanswered questions—to talk to his brother. Not just fire off bulleted questions like he'd done.

But just . . . to talk.

He opened his eyes. Across the road and down a sloping green, the Blaine River tussled against the day's gusting, damp air, coming rain heavy on the horizon. He'd been here in Maple Valley during the flood almost two years ago. Had spent hours sandbagging in the wind and the rain with the rest of the town. He'd felt like he was defending his own home.

But that phone call—his certainty of Rio's voice on the other end—it was an inexplicable inner tug. A pull in a direction that made no sense. Atlanta wasn't his home. It couldn't be.

Why, then, did one measly syllable—his name—uttered on a call that lasted less than thirty seconds, seem to reach inside him now? Was that really all it took to charge the fortress—anger, resentment, endless frustration—he'd built around his heart where Rio was concerned?

He turned from the river and looked through the windows of Coffee Coffee. Up at the counter, Jamie had finally closed his book and now sat on the stool next to Erin. He was attempting to balance a half-full glass of milk on his head while Erin looked on, clapping with glee.

It was getting late and the sky would break open any minute. He needed to get them home.

But he couldn't help one more glance at his phone. *God, if that was Rio—or even if it wasn't—be with him wherever he is. Please.*

It was the first prayer his heart had murmured for his brother in so many years. Too many. And it kept replaying, becoming a jumbled, wordless refrain, as he gathered the kids and paid Megan for their donuts and drove back to the Walkers' house.

By the time he pulled into the driveway, his windshield wipers were moving at full speed. No thunder, but lightning glazed the underbellies of the clouds. Where was Raegan's car?

It was the first question he asked when he found Beckett in the living room.

"She's working on the mural this evening," Beckett said as he padded through the room, oblivious to Bear's instant concern.

Bear followed him into the kitchen. "Have you looked outside? It's shaping up to be a monsoon." Just the dash from the car to the house had turned him into a wet mess. Jamie and Erin had already gone upstairs to change.

Beckett opened the fridge. "Well, then, let's hope she has an umbrella."

"Has she checked in with you? Or Case?"

"Uh, pretty sure Dad stopped tracking her whereabouts around age eighteen, McKinley."

Beckett had barely pulled the pitcher of OJ from the refrigerator when Bear slammed it closed.

"Hey, careful. You about took off my hand."

"She doesn't like storms. I don't get you. Last time it stormed, both you and Case were concerned. Remember? I ended up going into town to pick her up. Now suddenly you don't care?"

Beckett took a swig of OJ straight from the pitcher. "She'd taken her bike into town that time. She's got her car tonight. I don't know why she insists on riding her bike all the time. She's a funny girl sometimes."

"She's not a girl, Beckett. She's a fully-grown woman."

Beckett set the pitcher on the counter with a thud. "I don't need you to tell me my little sister is a woman."

Bear glared at him from across the island. "Did you ever stop to ask yourself *why* she does what she does? Why she hates storms so much?"

"Why don't you tell me? You clearly know her so much better than I do." Sarcasm ran rampant in his voice.

"I'll tell you this, riding her bike is about more than riding her bike." He was saying too much. He knew it. But how could nobody in this family have figured out there was more going on inside Raegan than she ever let on?

"So now you're her psychiatrist in addition to being her hero?"

Bear slammed his fist into the counter.

Beckett froze, his scowl slowly dissolving into a jumble of shock and comprehension. "You're serious."

"What's all the racket? Sounds like . . ." Case's voice drifted as he came upon the scene of the two men facing off.

"Yes, I'm serious, but I don't have time for this," Bear finally said. "I'm going to find her." He turned from the kitchen.

"Bear," Beckett called after him.

But he kept walking. Past Jamie and Erin now sitting wide-eyed behind a coffee table strewn with puzzle pieces. Out the front door and into the rain.

13

Crinkled tarp whipped against the side of the building—against Raegan—as she struggled to secure it in place.

"Raegan!"

The scaffolding shook as Bear bolted up it.

"What are you doing here?" She had to shout to be heard over the racket of the rain on the metal platform. Her clothes were plastered to her body, the unwieldy plastic refusing to cooperate. Oh, why hadn't she listened to her instinct and covered her work forty-five minutes ago when the clouds had first rolled in?

"You shouldn't be out in this."

"It's just rain. I won't melt." A sharp gust of wind jerked the tarp free and slapped it against Raegan. It covered her face and arms and nearly knocked her off her feet.

She heard Bear's pounding footsteps as he hurried to her, his hands snatching the plastic away from her as laughter burst from her lips. She swiped dripping hair from her face, allowing herself to see the stern set of Bear's jaw as he thrust the tarp away.

"That was funny, Bear. I just got attacked by a tarp. You're allowed to laugh."

Exasperation fueled his voice. "I was worried about you."

"As you can see, I'm fine. Wet, but fine. Losing a wrestling match with the tarp, but fine." Except after pulling the tarp away from her, Bear hadn't held on to it. The pummeling wind blew it against the guardrail. Raegan lunged for it.

Too late. The maelstrom carried it away as if it were nothing more than a kite.

"Great."

"Let's go, Rae."

"But the mural—" Her attention darted to the wall. Pastel streaks ran down its side. "I almost had it covered, Bear. That's an entire day's worth of work—ruined."

Rain streamed down his cheeks. "I'm sorry, but I thought I was going to find you up here having a panic attack. Do you have any idea how worried I was? I flipped out on your family back at the house, didn't just break the speed limit on the way into town—shattered it."

"What did you say to my family?"

He ignored the question, reaching for her, pulling her to him. "All I could think about was the last time."

The last time. When he'd found her on her knees hyperventilating, coming undone. She squeezed her eyes shut against his chest. That was how he saw her now.

Maybe she should love that he cared enough to race into town and find her. Maybe she should relish his arms around her. This was what she'd wanted, wasn't it?

No. Not like this.

She pulled away, hugging her arms to herself. Rain fell in slanted sheets, but even through the deluge she could see the confusion in Bear's expression.

"Is this about Friday night, Rae? Are you . . . should I not have . . . ?"

She shook her head before he could form a full question.

"I really am sorry about letting the tarp fly away."

She turned away. What was wrong with her? The man was drenched because of her. He'd come looking for her in a storm for the second time in as many weeks. He'd demonstrated his friendship, his kindness, his dependability over and over and over. He'd entrusted her with his secrets—some of them, anyway.

Why this abrupt and entirely nonsensical urge to now shut him out? To refuse the comfort of his embrace and the relief of his rescue?

"Let's go on a date, Rae."

She spun around. "What?" A snappish wind nearly drowned out her surprise.

"I'm tired of pretending I'm not crazy about you. Every other thing in my life might be a murky mess, but how I feel about you . . . I'm sure about that." He was yelling to be heard.

But even if he'd only whispered, she would've recognized his sincerity just by the look on his face. Even as he blinked raindrops from his lashes, an earnest light shone from his eyes.

Bear McKinley wanted *her*. The very hope of her heart for so many years, playing out right in front of her as a storm swirled and shook the scaffolding.

And all she could do was stand there. Shake her head. Deep breaths. Four seconds in, four seconds hold . . . she couldn't. "I can't, Bear."

"But—"

She scrambled across the platform, dropped to her knees, and lowered herself over the edge. Her feet slid against the wet rung at first contact.

"Raegan, please."

She held tight and hurried down.

"At least be careful," Bear called after her.

Finally, her feet landed on soggy ground. She heard Bear climbing down behind her. She couldn't drive in this, she knew that.

Bear's apartment.

She pulled the ring of keys from her pocket and made a run for it.

"Raegan?"

A soft voice pulled her from sleep. And the smell of coffee. And pastry. And . . . lavender?

Sara.

A weight settled on the bed beside her. But wait, not her own bed. Raegan forced her eyes all the way open, fatigue clinging to her bones as she pushed her way to a sitting position. She'd slept in Bear's apartment? That explained the scent of coffee. Had she been here all night?

But no sunshine streamed through curtains shielding the room's sole window.

"I grabbed a couple scones from Coffee Coffee downstairs right before it closed. Feel like a late-night snack?"

Definitely not morning.

Raegan looked over to the woman sitting beside her. Sara seemed as comfortable as could be, legs stretched out on the bed in front of her, a paper bag with the Coffee Coffee logo on her lap. "Bear called you, didn't he?" Raegan asked.

Sara nodded, reaching into the bag. "He's kind of funny when he's agitated, isn't he? Sputters, can't finish his sentences."

Her blurry mind tried to come into focus. She'd left Bear at the scaffolding, had escaped to his apartment. He hadn't followed. Or if he had, he'd been kind enough to leave her be. Soaked through from the rain, she'd wanted to hop in the shower, but the jagged lightning brightening the room in millisecond flickers had kept her from doing so.

She'd dodged the living room where her easel and paints and canvas would only remind her of Mr. Hill's visit earlier tonight. She'd ended up in the bedroom—a room she'd purposely avoided previously when playing pretend artist in the apartment. It had seemed too . . . intimate. After all, this *was* Bear's place. And at one point, this had been his bedroom. His bed.

But she'd been too overcome with emotion to think through her actions, curling up under the covers and letting sleep be her escape.

She allowed herself to look around the space now, though—beige walls, folding closet doors, ceiling fan. A small lamp on the bedside table was just enough to make out the emptiness of the room. Other than the furniture, little remained to tell of Bear's former presence here.

But she could feel it all the same. She shouldn't be here.

"What did Bear tell you?"

"That you were caught up in the rainstorm. That your chalk work on the mural was ruined." Sara used a napkin to pull a scone from the bag. "Oh yes, and he asked you out."

Had he told Sara the part where Raegan made a complete fool of herself? That she'd turned tail and run—literally? "I'm an idiot."

"You're not." Sara handed her the scone.

"Do you know what I would've given a few years ago for Bear McKinley to ask me on a date? Heck, a few days ago." And nothing had changed. She still wanted it. Possibly more than just about anything.

Except for having Mom back. She'd probably never want anything more than she wanted that. Unbidden tears flooded her eyes. *God, I feel like such a fool.*

And she couldn't help but think that was how God must see her. Hadn't she just a few days ago wished He'd finally show some inkling that the desires of her heart mattered to Him? What if Bear showing up on the scaffolding tonight and telling her how he felt was some answer to prayer and she'd gone running in the opposite direction? *A complete and utter fool.*

"What's wrong with me, Sara?" The scone dropped from her fingers into the napkin on her lap. "It's like I'm sabotaging my own life. My old art teacher starts talking about open doors and my future and I instantly begin shriveling up inside. Bear says the very thing I've been wanting to hear and I just . . . leave? Who does that?"

Sara closed the Coffee Coffee bag and set it aside. "Someone who's scared."

She wouldn't deny it. Couldn't. "But I don't know what I'm scared of." Tears trailed down her cheeks. "I don't know."

Sara reached her arm behind Raegan, pulling her close. "You don't have to know right now."

"But I w-want to know." Her voice broke. "I want to know why I keep running from the things I want and pushing away the people I love the most." Dad. Beckett. Bear.

The people she loved most. She'd just included Bear in that list. The impact of it squeezed her heart.

She *did* love him. She loved Bear.

And not like before. He wasn't just the handsome town mystery now. He wasn't just her cousin's best friend or the guy her siblings teased her about or the man who blew everyone away with his noble aspirations.

She was crying into Sara's shoulder now. No more holding back. And Sara didn't say a word. She simply held Raegan with one arm around her, the other brushing her hair from her face.

Raegan cried until her lungs squeezed and her well of tears emptied. She didn't know how much time passed, how long Sara waited. "I'm sorry."

Sara's voice was pure comfort. "There's not a thing to be sorry about."

She sniffled, raising her head. "Am I just a basket case? Is this . . . is this part of the panic disorder thing? Or am I just incredibly emotionally immature?"

Sara smoothed Raegan's hair from her forehead. "Emotionally immature people would rarely ever think to even use the term 'emotionally immature.'" She gave Raegan a gentle smile. "And you're not a basket case."

Raegan straightened on the bed, her rumpled clothes still damp in places. She really should've gone home, changed. She must look terrible, especially considering the tears still escaping one at a time down her cheeks. "Then what *is* wrong with me?"

Sara shifted on the bed, easing away from Raegan so she could turn to face her, legs crossed. "Raegan, I met you less than three weeks ago. We've only spoken a few times. Not nearly enough for me to make some grand pronouncement about the inner workings of your mind and heart. But I can tell you this: Fear is a self-protective instinct. So I don't think the question is just 'What are you scared of?' It's 'What are you protecting yourself from?'"

"What if I don't know?" She used the edge of the bedsheet to wipe her eyes.

"I think maybe deep down you do know. But perhaps allowing that *knowing* to surface is another thing you're protecting yourself from. Because once you know, once you face it, you'll have to decide what to do about it."

Raegan released an exhale, ragged and tired. "I can see why you and Mom were friends. You're a lot like her." At Sara's thin smile, she added, "I'm not just saying it to deflect the attention away from me and my current pathetic state."

"Well, if your mom were here, I think she'd say that her daughter and the word 'pathetic' don't belong in the same sentence."

If Mom were here . . .

Everything would be different.

"Maybe I'm protecting myself from loss." It came out a near question.

Sara watched her intently, quietly.

"If I stay in one place, if I don't step through the open doors, I can't lose what's on either side. If I don't tell my family about the panic attacks and about you and about . . . all of it, I can't lose whatever good opinion they might have of me now."

But she also couldn't gain. She couldn't grow as an artist. She couldn't truly connect to Dad and her siblings. She'd lashed out at Beckett the other night, expecting him to see her and understand her, but how could he when she only ever let him—any of them—in so far?

"And Bear?" Sara finally broke her silence.

"Maybe that's why I fell for him in the first place. Because all along . . . I knew he'd be leaving." Maybe her subconscious had known what her heart hadn't—that he was the safest man she could possibly fall for at the time. Because it could never go anywhere. Oh sure, there'd be the inevitable hurt when he left. But it'd be nothing compared to the true heartache of loving deeply and then losing harshly.

Like how she'd lost Mom.

"You cushioned your own fall," Sara said.

Raegan could only stare at the end of the bed, the blanket sliding off one edge, the wrinkled sheet pulled free and exposing the corner of the mattress.

"He's a good man, Rae."

"I know," she whispered.

"You know what the positive thing about fear is?"

"There's a positive thing?"

"It means you recognize the risk in front of you and there's a piece of you—however large or small—that wants to take it. If you didn't, you wouldn't feel fear. You'd simply feel resignation. Or nothing at all."

Raegan lifted her head. "I'd feel numb." She *knew* numb. She'd invited it into her life years ago—after Mom's death, after that horrible panic attack in the blizzard, the accident. Every day in the past decade that she'd pushed down the urge to reach for a paintbrush, it'd grown in scope.

And with every pretend *I'm fine* it'd claimed another room in her heart. Numb was the dogged dust that made even happy moments—holidays with family, milestones, good memories—just a little less shiny.

She met Sara's eyes. "I don't want to be numb anymore."

As if Bear wasn't already frustrated with himself enough . . . now both kids were mad at him. So mad, they refused to budge from the car.

"Guys, I know you wanted to go to the library—"

"'Cause there's a magic show," Erin huffed for at least the tenth time since he'd marched them out to the car this morning, insisting they accompany him out to the ranch.

"But I have to work. I made a commitment." Planks for the new flooring in the cabins would arrive on Thursday, which meant he only had two days to pull up the old boards in all four cabins.

"Seth would've taken us." Jamie's arms were folded tight across his chest. "He said he would."

Because Seth was a nice guy who didn't know the half of what Bear was dealing with at the moment. And Bear couldn't very well explain to the kids why he no longer felt comfortable leaving them in someone else's care for too long. He'd started questioning whether that was really Rio on the phone yesterday. But Rio or not, it *was* someone—and the fact that whoever it was refused to identify himself, that Chief Ross had confirmed the call was untraceable—it left too sour a taste in Bear's mouth.

It was one thing to leave the kids at the house when multiple adults were around. But he just didn't feel good about sending them into town without him.

Thus, their current standoff.

He hated making them miss something fun. Although he had a feeling Jamie was less interested in the magic show than his new little friend Elise. According to Jamie, she was due for a surgery soon.

"Look, you can stay in the car as long as you want. But if you get bored"—he held up the backpack he'd loaded with entertainment—"I've got books, puzzles, even a portable DVD player. Lots of snacks, too. Your choice."

He turned and moved toward the first cabin. Should he worry about them? The windows were open. He had the keys. He had the snacks. They weren't going anywhere.

Within minutes, he was at work in the cabin, ripping a rotten floorboard free, the stuffy air as cloistering as the state of his mind. It wasn't even that warm outside today, not after last night's rain. But in here, trapped heat buried him like one too many quilts on a bed.

Still better than running into Raegan back at the house, though. *Now who's avoiding whom?*

Whatever. He needed to get this done. He was lucky to even have this job. Sara never had brought up the background check again, though she'd had him sign a W-4.

Minutes rolled over each other, and eventually he heard the clank of a car door. Did that mean Jamie and Erin had finally given up their ground?

Ears tuned, he dug the end of his hammer underneath another board and wrenched it loose, waiting for one or hopefully both of them to appear in the doorway.

"So this is where you've been working."

Bear dropped his hammer as his gaze jerked up. Apparently the kids had a firmer stubborn streak than he realized. "Uh, hi, Mr. Walk—Case."

"Some reason there's two mournful-looking kids sitting in the car?"

"They're mad at me. I wouldn't take them to the magic show at the library."

The corner of Case's mouth quirked up. "Sounds about right. Well, I've got the morning off. I could—"

"That's all right. But thanks anyway."

Curiosity fanned to life in Case's eyes, but he doused it just that quick, instead giving the cabin a once-over. "This place is a pit."

"You should've seen it before I put a week of work into it." Bear tossed a freed floorboard aside and scooted on his knees to where another stuck up at a crooked angle.

"Sara actually thinks she can have a horse camp up and running yet this summer?" Case shook his head as he crossed the room and lowered to sit on the stepstool Bear had used yesterday to replace lightbulbs in the overhead lights. The cabins might be rustic and nowhere near ready for use, but at least the electricity was on. Later this week, an HVAC guy was coming out to install window air conditioners. That would improve his working conditions.

"I think she's just planning on a test run. Only local kids and families. I doubt she'll even charge anyone." Bear wedged in his hammer. "She's probably back at the house. You could ask her yourself." He didn't dare turn to see the expression that suggestion drew.

"Didn't come here to see her. Came out to talk to you."

That's what he'd been worried about. He stifled a sigh, hooked his hammer through a loop on his belt, and turned. "About?"

Case didn't beat around the bush. "I want to know what you know about my daughter that I don't."

"Case—"

"Son, I joke about prying into my kids' lives all the time. And usually it's just that—a joke. But you charged out of the house last night like a desperate man. You implied to Beck that she was in trouble. You can't fault me for being concerned."

"Why don't you just talk to Rae?"

"She's still sleeping. She never sleeps this late."

Just how long had she stayed at his apartment last night? Bear had sat in his car at the curb for at least half an hour after she'd left him, waiting until Sara arrived. Even then, he'd lingered, half hoping Raegan might come to the window and motion him inside.

Silly, he supposed, considering the way she'd practically run away from him. But why?

"Bear—"

"Can't do it, Mr. Walker." He slipped into formality. Couldn't help it. Case was treating him like a witness in an investigation. He respected the heck out of the man. But Case needed to talk *to* Raegan . . . not about her with someone else.

Then again, could Bear really blame Case for seeking answers where he thought he could? Raegan had kept a massive piece of herself hidden for years. She'd shouldered her burden alone and, yes, knowing that tore at Bear. But it *had* been her choice.

He wished he would've picked up on it. Wished he hadn't been just as distracted as everyone else by her vibrant style and nonchalant ways. He'd settled for the surface she presented.

But it *was* the surface she presented. To Bear, to her family.

Yet, Case Walker was a smart man. He might not know every detail of his adult daughter's life, but he knew enough to recognize something was wrong. For all Bear knew, Case had tried talking to Raegan in the past and had gotten nowhere.

So, no, he couldn't blame Case at all for coming to him.

But he also couldn't spill secrets or struggles that weren't his to share. Could he?

"She's more like her mother than she realizes," Case said now, his voice cotton soft and distant. "I'd try to get Flora to talk about things sometimes. Times when I could tell she was upset and I didn't know why. It was like . . . like those boards you're trying to rip loose. Sticking out all crooked, enough that you know something's wrong but just too stubborn to give way."

"Did you just call your wife stubborn, Mr. Walker?"

Case chuckled, regarded him for a moment, and stood. "Look, I knew this was a fool's errand. Inappropriate. I could hear Flora's voice in my head waxing eloquent about boundaries the whole drive out. But it's hard, sometimes, knowing how to be a parent to an adult."

Bear rose. "From what I can see, sir, you're just about the best there is. If I'd had a dad like you . . ." He swallowed lest his voice quaver. But his mind finished the thought anyway.

If he'd had a dad like Case or a mom like the woman he'd heard described so many times, he might not be a man constantly trying to outrun his past. If he'd had a family like the Walkers, he might not feel such an unrelenting shame hounding his heels. If he had siblings like Logan and Kate and Beckett and Rae—

No, not like Raegan. He could never think of Raegan as a sister. Not since kissing her.

Why'd it taken him so long to do that, anyway? *Idiot.* If he'd known how perfect it was going to be—

Case cleared his throat. Had the man just read his thoughts?

If he had, he didn't seem inclined to tease. "I'm sorry you had a tough childhood, Bear. And it pains me to think Jamie and Erin have experienced much the same. But I admire the way you've stepped into their lives." He clamped on hand on Bear's shoulder. "And for the record, you're the kind of man I'd be proud to have as a son."

So earnest were Case's words, they left Bear speechless. Speechless and overcome with déjà vu. This was what it'd felt like when John and Elizabeth had welcomed him into their home. Such unconditional acceptance. Love. Even respect.

Was he pitiful for needing this so much? Craving the

care and kindness of someone older and wiser? A parental figure? Did it make him less of a man?

Case still watched him, and all Bear could do was nod in gratefulness and then watch as Case crossed the cabin once more. But he stopped in the doorway. "I know you spoke with Chief Ross and that's wise. But if there's anything I can do, just say the word. Anytime."

Bear nodded a second time and Case left, leaving Bear alone in the silence of the cabin with only one thought to fill the hollow: He'd never get a second chance at his own childhood. But Jamie and Erin—they weren't so old. It could be different for them. He could help.

He might've called Rosa in an angry frenzy last week. Made some threat he knew he couldn't keep—not long-term anyway. However messy their lives, Rio and Rosa were Jamie and Erin's parents.

But that didn't mean Bear couldn't be involved. It didn't mean he couldn't be the presence John and, these days, Case had become in his life. He didn't know how it would work. But somehow, some way—

His phone trilled in his pocket. A text message. He pulled it free.

Sorry about last night. If you ask me out again, I'll say yes.

Bear grinned to the empty room. *Well, now, Raegan Walker.* There was a turn for the positive.

In that case, I'm asking . . .

He didn't have to wait more than three seconds for her reply.

In that case, I'm accepting.

Floorboards forgotten, he whipped off his tool belt,

let it drop with a plunk, and raced out of the cabin. "Case?"

Raegan's dad stood at the open window of Bear's rental car, chatting with the kids. "Coming out to make a truce with your niece and nephew?"

Stubborn kids. Bear's smile only widened. "Actually, turns out there is something you can do for me."

"I can't believe I forgot about Firefly Night." Raegan let Bear pull her along the sidewalk amid a chorus of laughter and squeals from kids of all ages, most carrying jars and chasing after the lightning bugs that flickered along the riverbank. A cool breeze hummed over the surface of the Blaine River, its water shimmering under the golden glow of lamplight and a hazy pink dusk.

Tonight couldn't possibly be more perfect.

And she couldn't possibly be more grateful for those hours spent with Sara last night. For the tears and the understanding—all of it like a healing salve for wounds she was only now beginning to recognize for what they were.

She'd been telling herself for years it was the panic attacks that had shaped her life into what it was—not a bad life, certainly, but a stagnant one. But that was only halfway true.

"I read this C.S. Lewis quote once," Sara had said while they still sat on Bear's bed, finally eating the scones she'd brought. *"He said he never expected grief to feel so much like fear. I wonder, Raegan, if perhaps you've never fully processed the loss of your mom."*

The words had foraged for a foothold in Raegan's mind. *"I still miss her, of course. But it's been ten years."*

"Grief is no respecter of time. And it thrives on isola-tion. The more you ignore it, the more it hangs around. The less you talk about it, the less inclined it is to loosen its grip."

Raegan glanced at Bear face's—clean-shaven for once, the skin of his cheeks and chin and jaw just a twinge lighter than the rest of his bronzed features. He would understand grief. He'd lost Annie.

Maybe someday Raegan would ask about her. But not tonight. Tonight there were no yesterdays and no tomorrows. Tonight there was only this present moment. Just Raegan and Bear . . . and, well, half the town.

"You aren't sorry I let the kids come along for part one of our date? I promise there won't be such a crowd for part two." Bear released her hand to slip his arm around her instead.

"There's a part two?"

Bear had refused to tell her earlier what he had planned for the night, but when he'd driven into town and she'd seen the swarm of families spread all the way from the square to the riverfront, she'd remembered—Firefly Night. When all the kids captured as many lightning bugs as they could and everyone gathered on the Archway Bridge . . .

And at eight-thirty exactly, with the sun low in the sky and anticipation brushing through the crowd, the mayor would give the signal. They'd free the fireflies all at once. And for a few breathtaking moments . . . magic.

Bear pulled her closer. "This wasn't even part of the plan originally. But Kit was at the house earlier and I heard her and Beckett talking about this firefly thing and I knew we couldn't have you missing out on one of your classic hometown events."

The hem of Raegan's coral sundress swished above her knees, and her white flip-flops slapped against the cement. Good thing she'd grabbed a sweater before leaving the house—it was always several degrees cooler around the river than anywhere else in town.

Somewhere up ahead, Jamie and Erin raced around with Seth and Ava. She didn't miss the way Bear kept his eyes trained on them, even as they strolled the sidewalk, unhurried.

"Speaking of Beckett, I think I owe him an apology."

Bear glanced at her. "You're not alone. I about bit his head off last night when I realized you were out in the storm. What did you do?"

"Got mad at him for researching you."

Bear stopped, mouth gaping as his arm dropped from her back. "Say what?"

"Yeahhhh." She drew out the word. "He might have done some Googling. Found an article about you and prison."

"Wait, are you saying you knew about . . . all of it before I told you?"

Was he upset? "Not really. Not much anyway. I refused to read the article. It's still crumpled up behind the desk in my bedroom."

Bear just stood there in the middle of the sidewalk, his eyes traveling her face and his lips slowly spreading. "You're something else, you know that?"

"Is that a good thing?"

His gaze deepened and his voice lowered. "I'd show you just how good if we didn't have an audience."

Warmth started in her middle and spread in both directions. Maybe she didn't need that sweater, after all.

"Wait—crumpled up behind your desk?"

"I was trying to make a basket in the trash can. Totally airballed it."

He laughed and then, apparently no longer caring about the crowd, leaned in to kiss her cheek, lingering long enough for her to close her eyes and put one hand to his chest. "We could skip the fireflies, you know." Her voice came out a mere whisper.

"Impatient, are we?"

"I'm just saying, any more of this and the rumors about us will be flying."

"The rumors about us have always been flying." He kissed her forehead, then backed away. He laced his fingers through hers and started walking again.

"Hey, Bear?"

She waited until he dipped his gaze to her once more.

"I hope you know everything you told me the other night . . . none of it changes the way I see you. It fills in the blanks a little, but that's it. Even if you'd done the things you were convicted of, it wouldn't change who you are today."

He squeezed her hand. "It's hard, though, when the label follows you around. Every job application, every interview. I think it's why I loved the fact that no one in Maple Valley knew for so many years. I could just be Bear McKinley, the new guy. Not Bear McKinley, the convict."

A string of kids raced past them, hands covering their jars. "To me you were always 'Bear McKinley, the guy I wish would hurry up and notice me.'"

He laughed. "Don't think for a second I didn't notice you. Why do you think I hung out at your house so much?"

They'd nearly reached the Archway Bridge. "Because Seth lived there at the time. And because there was always an unending supply of snacks."

Gosh, she loved Bear's smile.

"Okay, but those weren't the only reasons."

The crowd of townspeople filtered around them as they stopped at the foot of the bridge. Up ahead, Seth had Erin sitting on his shoulders now and Jamie held a jar glimmering with trapped fireflies.

"So is there a story to this whole Firefly Night thing?" Bear asked.

Raegan shrugged. "You'd think so. But if there is, I've never heard it. Just another wacky little Maple Valley tradition."

At the peak of the curved bridge, Mayor Milt stood on a box and held his megaphone aloft. His metallic voice called out instructions while the gathering teemed onto and around the bridge. "Remember to hold your jars as high in the air as you can—away from other people's faces. We don't need people getting poked in the eye by bugs. Point your jars toward the river."

He started counting down and the townspeople joined in. "Three. Two. One—"

For one uncanny moment, an awed quiet fell over the riverbank as thousands of beads of yellow-green light floated free, bobbing over the water, their reflections like moonlit snow. The distant buzz of cicadas, a toad's croaking, the gurgle of moving ripples—all a perfect backdrop as the trail of lights gradually spread and slowed and disappeared.

"Well, that wasn't wacky," Bear whispered.

"Not wacky at all."

A second later, applause broke out. Bear turned to her. "Someone should paint that."

"Got any someones in mind?"

Bear reached for her hand again, sent Seth a quick nod—he must be taking the kids back to Dad's—and then steered Raegan around a cluster of people. "I know you're busy with your mural, but after? You do have all those empty canvases waiting in my apartment, after all."

"Actually they're not all empty anymore."

243

He glanced at her with a question in his eyes.

"Last night after Sara left, I stayed behind. Couldn't help it. Just started painting and couldn't stop." And for the first time since lugging that easel up the steps to Bear's apartment, since ordering oils and picking out new brushes, she'd felt what she'd used to feel.

She'd felt . . . everything. An exhilarating melding of joy and desire and curiosity and adventure. Working on the mural had tugged on her creativity. But last night, all alone in that little apartment, she'd come alive.

It'd been all she could do not to hide away there again today. But she'd needed to get back to work on the mural. Thankfully, she'd been able to find someone to cover her shift at the pool this afternoon. She'd spent all day redoing the chalk work the rain had washed away the previous evening.

"Can I see what you painted?"

Grass tickled her feet as Bear pulled her away from the crowd. "Not just yet. But eventually, sure." They crossed the street that bordered the river and started down a parallel sidewalk. "So, what's part two?"

"Patience is a virtue, Raegan."

"Don't talk to me about patience. I've been waiting over five years for this date." He wasn't leading her back to the car, so wherever they were headed must be within walking distance. Up ahead, Coffee Coffee's striped awning flapped in the breeze. He wouldn't be taking her there, though. His apartment? No, he would've seen her painting from last night and asked her about it already.

The scaffolding that climbed the front of the Hay & Feed Store came into view. She could picture him planning a candlelit dinner atop the platform, but he'd said they wouldn't have an audience. And yet, he did seem to be leading her in that direction—

Her breath caught as realization dawned.

"You figured it out." He sounded more impressed than disappointed.

"No, I didn't. I have no idea where we're going or what we're doing."

"Liar." He sighed. But he was smiling, and yes, he tugged her straight to the building and rounded its corner, where a cracked-open window awaited. "I talked to your dad."

"Bear McKinley." She said his name through a wonder-filled exhale.

"He said when he took your mom here on their first date, they tried the front and back door and two other windows before they got to this one. We got a head start." He wedged his fingers under the window's base and hefted it up. "After you."

"You realize we're breaking into a building with half of Maple Valley milling around." Although at least on this side of the structure, they were removed from most prying eyes.

"Yes, but I've made nice with the local police chief. Besides, I've already been convicted of much worse crimes. This is small potatoes." He still gripped the window, waiting for Raegan to climb in. "I think this is the first time I've ever been able to joke about that."

Raegan stepped up to the window, the scent of Bear's aftershave enough to quicken her senses. "Obviously I'm a good influence on you."

"Obviously. Now, in you go."

She toppled in, blinking to adjust to the darkness. Bear climbed in behind her, snapped on a flashlight he must've stored here earlier. He reached for her hand and led her farther into the building, around a corner, into what used to be the store's main room . . .

And Raegan lost her breath. Dozens, maybe hundreds, of candles—all shapes and sizes, scattered over every surface—the floor, hollowed built-ins, a counter that ran along one wall. "How did you . . . ?" She couldn't even finish the question, she was so in awe.

"Kate, Colton, and Megan from the coffee shop. Couldn't have done it without them. Meg kept an eye on the place until we arrived."

"I didn't even notice her."

"That's because when you were climbing in one window, she was climbing out another." Bear stood just behind her, speaking over her shoulder. "I know how much you miss her, Rae. Maybe it's cheesy, but—"

"No. It's not. Bear, I . . . this is . . ." It was beautiful. And thoughtful. And a thousand other things she didn't know how to put into words. All she knew was that this right here was everything she hadn't known she was waiting for.

A man who could see into the depths of her loss and find a lingering beauty. Who could pull something special from something painful. And give her a memory to forever soothe her soul.

When she turned to face Bear, he was reaching into his pocket.

"Apparently your parents spent their whole first date playing cards." He held up a fresh deck, plastic packaging still in place. "How do you feel about Rummy?"

She threw her arms around him. "Very, very, *very* good."

14

"You're falling asleep."

Raegan's eyes snapped open at the sound of Bear's voice. Half the candles had burned down to nothing in the past hours, but just enough flickering light remained to highlight the amusement on Bear's face. "Am not."

"It's been your turn for two minutes. Your eyes were closed, your head bobbing. I was just waiting for the drool." Only Bear could smirk so charmingly.

"I don't drool. And I wasn't nodding off." Her flip-flops lay discarded beside her, her bare feet tucked under her crossed legs and the fanned skirt of her dress. She glanced at her cards, but the numbers didn't register. What time was it, anyway? "I was thinking. Strategizing."

"It's Rummy. Not a whole lot of strategy to it."

"I'm trying to decide whether to draw or take the top card on the discard pile—or take the whole discard pile. That's a big decision for this late at night."

Bear reached for a Twizzler from the half-empty bag between them. "This early in the morning, you mean."

"It's after midnight?"

"Rae, it's gotta be like two, at least."

"We've been playing Rummy for five hours?"

"Pretending to play Rummy."

She mirrored his grin. He had a point. They'd spent more time talking and laughing than shuffling and dealing cards. Hadn't even bothered keeping score. They'd talked about her mural, her worries about finishing in time and not being able to figure out what was still missing from her design. They'd talked about his ten months in Brazil, his work at Sara's ranch, all the things he'd learned about Jamie and Erin in the past two weeks.

Like how, despite the instability of her childhood so far, Erin could already read at a first-grade level. Like how Jamie definitely had a cute little crush on Elise. How both kids seemed so very hungry for affection and attention.

"Part of me is so angry at Rio and Rosa for the way they've raised Jamie and Erin," Bear had said. *"But then I remember . . . they're just doing what their own parents modeled for them. I know Rosa loves the kids. I saw it that night she asked me to take them. And Rio . . ."*

His fingers had curled his cards as a memory took hold of his distant expression.

"I went to see them right after I got out of prison. First time I ever met Jamie. He was four and sitting on Rio's lap. I was angry at Rio then, too. I thought in making the sacrifice I did, it'd prompt him into changing, making different choices. But even through my frustration, I saw the way he held Jamie, the love in his eyes." He'd laid his cards facedown on the floor. *"Maybe love isn't always enough."*

She hadn't known what to say. Hadn't known how to stop herself from taking his words and turning them toward herself. She loved Bear, but it might not be enough to keep him here.

So she'd done the only thing she could think to do. Cut off the worrisome thought by leaning over the pile of cards to cup Bear's cheeks and kiss him until her doubts had no choice but to flee.

Only when she broke away did she finally find words. "*Perfect love casts out fear.*"

She'd scooted closer to Bear during that kiss until her knees touched his and the cards scattered. His face was only a breath away. "*What?*"

"*It's a verse my mom used to say all the time.*" Especially after the cancer came back. "*I know you're scared for your family, Bear. You're scared they'll fall too far and you'll go tumbling with them. But you can't be their safety net.*"

"*So what am I supposed to do?*"

"*Make peace with your own imperfect love. Understand that you can't fix everything. Give yourself some grace and your fears to God. Put your faith in His perfect love.*"

She hadn't known where the words came from, only that she needed them as much as Bear. Because as surely as her love for this man had only grown tonight, so did her own fears.

That eventually this romantic bubble might pop. That Bear would return to Atlanta or maybe even Brazil. That there were still things he hadn't told her about his past, about Annie.

That even though she'd taken a series of big steps in recent weeks—the mural, the counseling, this date—she might one day reach the end of her bravery. If she couldn't finish the mural, if she couldn't tell her family about the panic attacks, if she couldn't leave Maple Valley . . .

It was Bear who'd cut off her thoughts then with another kiss. And another . . .

And that was the other reason their game of Rummy had stretched until it was pointless. The talking, the laughing, *and* the kisses.

"Should we call it a night?" Bear asked now. "Before you *do* start drooling?" He rose to his feet and held out his hand.

"I told you, I don't drool."

He only laughed and tugged her to her feet. "Come on. Help me blow out the rest of the candles. We don't want to burn this place down."

They padded in a circle around the room, blowing out each candle until darkness cloaked the space. The shadows and the quiet, other than a humming wind, might have been eerie if not for Bear's hand enfolding hers. Soon they'd erased any sign of their presence in the old store, climbed out the window they'd come in, and settled into Bear's rental car.

A peaceful silence owned the drive home. Raegan had to fight to keep her eyes open. If only tonight didn't have to end. If only those things she'd said about love and fear and faith were as easy to live out in everyday life as they were to say during a hushed, middle-of-the-night conversation.

Bear parked the car behind a lineup of vehicles in Dad's driveway. Such a crowd he had living here now. What would it feel like when it thinned out? When it was only Raegan's and Dad's cars left in the driveway?

"What are you thinking about, Rae?" Bear turned off his headlights.

"How this house was meant to be full." Did he hear the hint of sadness in her tone? She didn't want their date to end this way. She forced a grin. "And how I really hope someone remembered to leave the doors unlocked. Since you drove, I didn't bring my keys."

Sure enough, minutes later, they stood in the back-

All This Time

yard, having tried every door. No luck. Bear turned to her. "Soooo . . . do we just ring the doorbell?"

"Are you kidding? Get drilled by my dad—or worse, Beckett—about what exactly we were doing out so late?"

"I see your point. Except we're adults, not teenagers out past curfew. And it's not as if we were doing anything inappropriate." His lips spread. "Then again, a couple of those kisses—"

"Bear!"

"So how are we going to get in?"

"Simple." She walked around the corner of the house, flip-flops squeaking in dewy grass, and pointed. "Scale the lattice, heft ourselves onto the porch roof, and go in my bedroom window."

"You don't think this is just a little excessive? What if you can't get your window open? Also, you're wearing a dress."

She laughed. "I figured out how to open my window from the outside forever ago. Beckett thinks he's the only one who ever snuck in and out his window as a kid. Not so."

Before Bear could protest, she started climbing the lattice, praying nobody from inside picked that moment to look out the front windows. Bear was right, of course. This *was* excessive. Obviously she could just wake up someone inside the house and ask to be let in. No biggie. But then she'd be opening herself up to a lifetime of teasing. No thanks.

In less than a minute, she'd lifted herself onto the porch roof, Bear right behind her, and padded on hands and knees to her window.

Her window opened with ease. Except she'd forgotten the distance from her window to the floor. She tumbled into her bedroom with a light squeal, laughing as she righted herself and stood.

251

Only to see Logan standing in her doorway, arms folded. *Wait . . . Logan?*

She heard Bear scramble in behind her.

Her oldest brother lifted his eyebrows. "Morning, Rae. Bear."

Bear should be happy.

No, he should be jumping up and down with glee. Still damp from the shower he'd hopped in and out of after too-few hours of sleep, he stared at his phone—the email from John staring right back. He read it a second time.

> Bear, you've finally been cleared of all the vandalism. It was a few local teenagers. Apparently it started out as a result of boredom. Escalated into stealing our furniture when they realized they might be able to make a quick buck.
>
> Point is, we've got some church leaders down here who are feeling awfully sorry about the way they treated you. I spoke with the mission board yesterday. They got your application and they assured me you're under serious consideration. The goal is to open the clinic by the end of November. Will you have your EMT certification by then?
>
> Elizabeth sends a hug . . . and I do too. – John

Bear dropped onto the futon. Footsteps pounded overhead. Had Logan already spilled the beans on how he'd found them in the wee hours of the morning? Tumbling in Raegan's bedroom? Bear was still surprised Logan had let him leave the room without a drawn-out explanation. Hopefully he hadn't interrogated Raegan.

Unlike Raegan, Bear had actually known Logan was coming to town. A surprise Raegan would discover soon enough, and he looked forward to being a part of it.

He tapped the *Reply* button on his phone. Paused.

John wanted him back. The mission board considered him a credible candidate. He could be back in Brazil by Christmas. Finally fulfilling his promise to Annie.

He should be furiously typing a reply—one filled with all the joy John's email should've prompted.

Should've. But didn't.

And he knew exactly why. His reason had a face he'd memorized by candlelight during a first date that had been so much more than a date. It was the culmination of five and a half years of waiting and wishing. It was a bend in the road that changed everything.

It was as if, for so long, the lights in every chamber of his heart had dimmed, perhaps without his even knowing . . . but then that one kiss on Friday night had lit the first bulb. And with last night, all the rest had flickered to life. No, not flickered—flashed. Until his heart was so bright, he could feel it heating every inch of his mind and body and soul.

In the wee hours of the morning, as he'd driven Raegan back to the house, he'd realized for the first time he was grateful he'd been forced to leave Brazil. If he'd stayed, he would've missed out on so much—getting to know Jamie and Erin, falling in love with Raegan.

Love. That's what this was, wasn't it? Something deep and something wide. Strong roots that wove two hearts together while branches grew and stretched and reached toward a lifetime of possibilities.

He'd never felt this with Annie.

Annie. He dropped his phone, then flopped onto his back. *Brazil is what I've been praying for, God. Since the day Annie died, it's the only thing that's ever seemed to make sense. But now . . .*

Was he just that fickle? He'd made a *promise*. A vow.

Was he honestly lying here considering going back on it? After all Annie had given?

Dear, sweet Annie. Annie who had seen him as more than the kid from the wrong side of the tracks. Who'd studied with him for emergency medicine tests. Who'd introduced him to church . . . even better, to a God who—she insisted—had a plan for him. Who'd taken him home to her family and proudly introduced him as "someone who's going to save lives."

How many times over the years had he wished he could forget those words? The cruel irony was simply too much.

He'd made a promise. He'd. Made. A. Promise.

But that was so many years ago. And he hadn't known then that he'd meet Raegan Walker. That she'd turn out to be . . . everything.

"Bear?" Case Walker's voice boomed from the top of the basement stairs.

Uh-oh, had Case heard about the bedroom window incident? Despite his mental turmoil, just the thought of Raegan climbing up the lattice wearing that wrinkled dress made him nearly shake with silent laughter. "Yeah?" he called up.

"Sam Ross is here to see you."

Bear jumped off the bed. The police chief? Did that mean he had news about Rio?

Bear bounded up the steps, the front door already open to reveal not only Sam Ross, but another man with him on the porch. Bear stepped outside, and Sam didn't waste any time with the introductions.

"Bear, this is Detective Tate Rollins." Sam pulled off his ball cap. "From Atlanta."

Bear's attention jumped to the other man. He looked pure military, from his crew cut to his bulk to the strict crease in his slacks.

"I made some calls after you came to see me the other day. Ended up talking to Rollins here. He's got some questions for you."

And he couldn't have asked them over the phone? Dread trickled through him. *Rio* . . . "Wow, uh, okay."

The detective whipped his sunglasses away from his head. "I need to know the last time you talked to your brother, Mr. McKinley."

The trickle gave way to a river. "It's been years. I went to see him right after . . ." *He's a detective. He's looking for Rio. Obviously he already knows the bare facts.* He met Rollins' eyes. "After I was released from prison. That was almost seven years ago. Kept in touch with his wife—Rosa—now and again, but not Rio."

Skepticism curled in the detective's voice. "You haven't talked to him once since?"

Bear only shook his head. *A lie?* After all, there'd been that phone call, that voice he could've sworn was Rio's . . .

But he didn't know it for a fact. And something sharp and protective held him back from saying more. Why, though? If a detective was searching for Rio, then it confirmed everything Bear had feared for weeks now—that something even more serious than Rio's usual on-again, off-again criminal activity was at play.

"And yet, you're caring for your brother's kids," Rollins prodded.

"Yes, at the request of my sister-in-law. Look, I want to know where Rio is too. And I want to know why his wife hasn't answered a single call of mine in a week. I want to know why she told me Rio's in jail if he isn't."

The detective's eyes narrowed. "That's what she told you? And you don't know where she is either?"

The accusation in Rollins' voice was unmistakable. "I already told Sam all of this," Bear answered. "No, I don't know where Rosa is. She seemed to believe someone was threatening Rio. She was going to go to her father—who happens to be Luis Inez. He's—"

"I know all about Inez." Rollins turned to Sam. Nodded. A signal.

Sam sighed. "I really don't think this is necessary."

He didn't think *what* was necessary?

But Detective Rollins only replaced his sunglasses. Sam turned to Bear. "Could you come down to the office, Bear? Just for questioning."

"Questioning about what?" He slammed his attention into the detective. "Do you think I know more than I'm saying? That I'm actually pretending to have no idea where my brother is? Or that I have something to do with his current whereabouts?"

Rollins's eyebrows shot up above his glasses. "You said it, not me."

His pulse hammered. "Sam, this is ridiculous."

Chagrined agreement huddled in Sam's expression, but he didn't back down. "Shouldn't take more than an hour. Please. Don't make this more awkward than it already is."

Detective Rollins was already moving down the porch steps to Sam's waiting car. A bird whistled somewhere, a happy tune that would've felt just right thirty minutes ago, when Bear had first woken up to vibrant memories of last night's date. For those few perfect moments before John's email, nothing else had existed.

Did it have to fall apart so quickly?

"Why would I have even come to you, Sam, if I knew something more? If I had anything to do with . . . anything?"

"This feels as off to me as it does to you, trust me. About spit out my coffee when he came waltzing in to the department, claiming to be from Atlanta. But I checked him out, Bear. He's legit, and apparently he's been looking into your brother's whereabouts longer than you. May be that *he* has information you want. You're not being accused of anything."

Not yet. "I'm not wearing shoes." Or socks, for that matter. "And I need to make sure someone can keep an eye on the kids."

A car door clanked. Sam nodded. "Do whatever you need to. Drive yourself in. I'll have coffee waiting."

Bear didn't bother to say he didn't drink the stuff. Didn't say anything. Just turned, resigned and worried.

"Bear?"

He turned back to the police chief. "I'm going to show up."

"I know. It's just . . ." Sam combed his fingers through his hair and shook his head. "Rollins and another officer I spoke to in Atlanta both felt very strongly about getting child protective services involved."

Bear's empty stomach groaned, his jaw tightening. "But Jamie and Erin . . . they're doing just fine."

Sam toed the porch's floorboard. "Rollins told me in cases like this, it's protocol to call CPS. I expect you'll be hearing from a Georgia caseworker soon."

"Fine. They can call. I'll talk to anyone I need to." He swallowed the anxiety rising up his throat. "But they're not going to . . . take the kids away, are they?"

Sam didn't have an answer.

"It's not like he was arrested, Rae."

Logan lugged four buckets of paint—two in each hand—by their metal handles. He hefted them into his trunk alongside the other five they'd already loaded after Raegan signed for the order at the hardware store.

She stood at the side of the car, hands hidden in the oversized pockets of her overalls. Not the height of fashion, but perfect for keeping spare chip brushes easily at hand as she painted. Because today was the day she'd put color to brick and bring her mural to life.

If she could force herself to focus. "I wasn't thinking about—"

"You were." Her brother's cheeky grin might be subtle—Logan had never been as obvious as Beckett—but it wasn't invisible. She supposed she deserved it, though. He *had* seen Bear climbing in her bedroom window last night—well, this morning—and after an initial exaggerated, teasing questioning, he hadn't brought it up since. Surely Beckett, or even Kate, would've told everyone else by now and she'd have never heard the end of it.

"You're not a mind reader, Logan."

The breeze skimmed over his hair. Logan had the rest of the family's inky brown eyes and dark hair. He had Dad's quiet strength and Mom's sense of humor. "Not reading your mind, I'm reading your face. It's been pinched with worry for the last forty-five minutes."

That was the other thing Logan had—a keen perception that reminded Raegan of Sara.

And he was right, she was worried. Had been ever since she'd come down from her bedroom to find Bear in the middle of the living room, explaining to Dad that he had to run into town—to the police department. He'd tried to appear nonchalant, but she'd recognized the tick in his jaw, his too-straight posture.

Bear had spared her only a brief glance before heading out. One that promised they'd talk later. She'd been tempted to jog after him, but then Logan's daughter,

Charlie, had bounced up to her for a hug, followed immediately by Amelia, Logan's wife.

She still couldn't believe they were here—not when they were already planning to come for a visit next weekend. They'd all had the date mentally blocked off for months—what would've been Mom's sixtieth birthday. So why show up late last night? Was there some town happening this week she was forgetting?

A breeze whistled in, rattling a bronze street sign hanging from a vintage lamppost. Few cars dotted the curb along Main Avenue, odd for a weekday morning. And not a single person walked the town square's path. "Does Maple Valley feel a little ghost-towny today to you?"

Logan watched her now, one hand still raised to his open trunk. "If they were going to arrest Bear, they would've."

She reached up to close the trunk for him. "I was trying to change the subject, if you didn't notice." She rounded the car and opened the passenger-side door. "Let me try again: How is it you wound up in town so much earlier than planned?"

Logan met her eyes over the top of the car. "Missed everyone. Don't really like being the only Walker living out of state."

Might be part of the answer, but it wasn't the full answer. She knew Logan well enough to know that. But she also knew him well enough to know he wasn't one to be rushed or poked or prodded. He was like Bear in that way.

But unlike Bear, who tended to eventually spill his hidden thoughts in a rush of emotion, Logan would take his time, parse through whatever contemplations filled his patient mind until he was ready to reveal them. Gradually, evenly. It was both his most calming and endlessly frustrating trait.

She dropped into the passenger's seat, and seconds later, Logan pulled away from the curb.

"I can't believe I'm actually going to start painting today. I feel like I've been getting ready for this for months." Had it really only been two weeks?

"Why didn't you tell any of us you were painting again, Rae? Why'd you hide it away at Bear's? You know we would've all supported you, and we never would've had that stupid intervention."

"So you admit it was an intervention?"

"Raegan."

Logan was the only sibling who could say her name that way and not prompt a roll of her eyes. She could giggle with Kate and confess almost anything to Beckett.

But Logan . . . with just a word, a look, he made a person feel exposed. He had this way of seeing deeper, hearing the words that went unsaid.

"I wasn't ready. Just thinking about painting again . . . it felt like this quiet experiment. I didn't know where it was going. All I knew was, I felt this nudge in my spirit." She'd thought it might be God at the time. But she hadn't been sure. And she'd been even less sure about what might happen when she picked up a brush once more. What if her talent had leaked away in the years she'd ignored it?

Logan stopped at a red light—superfluous considering not one other vehicle was on the road. "I always wondered why you quit painting in the first place. I thought it might have something to do with Mom, but I wasn't around much back then. I feel bad about that sometimes."

"You were living your life." She reached into the cup holder for the travel mug she'd filled before leaving Dad's earlier. "You were pressing through your pain. I've always admired that about you." And she didn't tell him nearly enough. First he'd had to face Mom's death, then just two short years later, his wife Emma's.

But somehow Logan had carried on. He'd walked out his grief, and had eventually continued to pursue his passions, had even fallen in love again.

He might've gone numb for a season, but he hadn't stayed there. Not like Raegan.

"I think I quit painting because . . ." The light turned green, but Logan didn't press the gas. He only waited as she fumbled for words. "It made me feel too much. After Mom . . . didn't matter if they were good feelings or bad feelings, I didn't want any of them." Too much of either one and the panic set in.

Not just the physical panic, the emotional panic. The suffocating sense that nothing could ever be okay again. Even joy—the kind she so often felt when she painted— ushered in dread. She'd start on a high, but eventually sink to a low, certain something would creep in to steal her happiness . . .

Like death had stolen her mother.

And loss had stolen her security.

And grief, no matter how much she attempted to evade it, had stolen her peace.

"*Perfect love casts out fear.*" Her words to Bear echoed. An easy little line to recite, but how did a person truly grasp that perfect love?

"How did you do it, Logan? First Mom and then Emma."

"If you think I handled any of that well . . ." He shook his head, still idling at the stoplight. "I became a workaholic. I was basically an absentee father for a couple years. Even kind of lost my faith there for a while. I lived in a fog for years, Rae."

"But you found a way out. And it didn't take you a

decade. Not like me.”

He shifted in his seat to face her, the compassion in his gaze almost too much for her. Hadn’t she cried enough these past weeks? She squeezed her eyes closed before any more tears could break free.

“Everything changed when I realized I couldn’t hide anymore,” he said softly. “When I came home last year, I couldn’t fake it around Dad. When I got away from LA, I couldn’t hide in my work anymore. When I met Amelia, I couldn’t wear the mask, not with her.”

Raegan opened her eyes. The stoplight had gone from green to red again. “I’ve been pretending for a long time.” Pretending to be fine. Pretending to be content. Pretending there weren’t rivers of deep desire coursing through her—rivers she’d been too afraid to journey.

“Well, here’s the wonderful and unnerving thing about pretending, Rae. You can pretend all you want around people and you can do a good job of fooling them, even those you’re closest to. But you can’t fool God.” When the stoplight flickered again, he finally pressed the gas. “And if there’s anything I’ve learned in the past couple years, it’s that He’ll seek you out. As often as it takes. Not so that He can rip off your mask . . . but so that you can learn to see Him and love Him and trust Him, enough that eventually you’ll choose to take off your own mask.”

He steered the car toward the riverfront, the conviction in his voice settling around her like an embrace. And this time when she closed her eyes, it wasn’t to hold her tears at bay, but to hold this moment close.

Bear had seen more of her than anyone—but it hadn’t really been her choice. Not in the beginning when he’d witnessed that panic attack. And Sara—she’d provided an emotional triage and would continue to be a support system, Raegan knew. Thankfully, too, Raegan was on a slow road to revealing her heart, her secrets, to her family.

But maybe the person she most needed to get honest with was the One who'd seen through her pretense all along. The One waiting at the end of her pain and the beginning of her desires.

I haven't just been hiding from life, God. I've been hiding from You.

Perhaps grasping His perfect love started with simply opening up.

"Well, you wondered where everyone in Maple Valley is." Logan's voice tugged her back to the present. "I think we have our answer."

Her eyes snapped open. Logan had turned the car onto the road hugged by the river on one side and the string of waterfront businesses on the other. There at the end, the Hay & Feed building . . . and a crowd. An even bigger crowd than the day the scaffolding went up. "What in the world?"

She saw Dad with Charlie on his shoulders and Amelia at his side. Seth and Ava with Jamie and Erin between them. Kate and Colton. Meg from Coffee Coffee. Jenessa from the newspaper. There was Elise Linder holding her mom's hand and Mr. Hill, of course. Even Sunny from the hardware store, who she'd just seen minutes ago, had beat them here.

And draped across the scaffolding railing, a banner: *Good luck, Raegan!*

Logan slowed the vehicle as they neared the gathering. "I guess the word spread about you starting the mural for real today."

Not a speck of surprise in his voice. She stuffed her travel mug back in the cup holder between them. "You knew. You knew, and that's why you came home."

He only grinned as he scouted for a parking spot.

The thought of climbing the scaffolding, dipping a chip brush into a paint bucket, making that first stroke while everyone watched, it was enough to turn her palms clammy.

And Bear . . . Bear wasn't here. Was probably still sitting across from the police chief and that detective from Atlanta.

Despite it all, her heart trilled. *Lean into it.* It came from her soul, a divine whisper. *It's okay to feel this joy. When you're nervous, when so much is up in the air—especially then—it's good and right and okay to do the thing you were made for. It's how you'll find Me.*

The truth enveloped her. A creative God had blessed her with a creative spirit not to impress art critics or get her into college or even birth a career . . . but to connect with her.

And she'd missed out for too long.

Logan parked at the curb and cut the engine. "They're all here because they love you, Raegan, and they want to support you. But at the end of the day, it's just you and God and the gift He gave you. Let yourself enjoy it."

How did he do it? Read her so well? Know exactly what she needed to hear? "When did you get so discerning, big brother?"

"I think it comes with the territory, being the firstborn and all. Now let's get all that paint unloaded."

He opened his car door, and the cheers of the crowd rushed in.

15

*T*hree days.

It'd been three days since Bear had, for all intents and purposes, been hauled into the police department. Since he'd sat in a metal folding chair opposite Sam and Detective Rollins, facing a blitz of questions.

Every one of which placed him in the role of the accused. No matter what Sam said.

Bear pulled onto the gravel lane that led to the Walkers' house. After four hours of work at the ranch, sweat and grime covered every inch of him. Both his knees and his back ached after two days in a row of climbing over roofing tile, patching holes, and the sun had scorched the back of his neck.

But he'd take on a world of physical pain if it meant the loosening of his vise-grip-like angst. Seventy-two hours later and the weariness of that morning in the police station still hadn't worn off. Nor the humiliation. He'd done his best to put up a good front around the Walkers—even Raegan. Didn't stop the pulsing frustration or the implacable replays.

"Let me get this straight: You show up on your brother and sister-in-law's doorstep after not seeing them for years, and less than an hour later, you take off with

the kids?"

Yes, it sounded crazy, but it would've been crazier to leave Jamie and Erin behind, given Rosa's dire predictions.

"Rosa hasn't called in how long? You've got her kids. How long are you going to wait this out?"

Why did they think Bear had gone to the police in the first place? He didn't know what to do. Didn't know how long to wait.

"You said you weren't going to return Jamie and Erin?"

He'd been angry. Of course he didn't mean it. He'd only meant—

Rollins didn't let him finish. *"You show up in Atlanta in the same timeframe as your brother goes missing. You whisk your niece and nephew off to another state. Your sister-in-law subsequently goes incommunicado. Aren't you a bit worried about how this all looks?"*

"No!" He'd nearly snarled the word. *"I'm worried about Jamie and Erin's wellbeing and confused about Rio and Rosa's whereabouts and light years past baffled about why in the blazes you're wasting time questioning me."*

Rollins had returned to the kicker, the same question he'd asked a dozen times in a dozen different ways. *"And you seriously haven't talked to your brother—not once—since you left Atlanta six or seven years ago?"*

Three days later and Bear still didn't know if Rollins had believed a single one of his denials. He also didn't know anything new, for that matter.

Other than at least Jamie and Erin seemed fine. More than fine, really. Erin had bonded with Logan's daughter and Jamie constantly, happily, had his nose in a book. He'd asked to call Rosa last night but hadn't seemed upset when, again, she didn't answer.

He needed to take a cue from the kids. Get comfortable waiting. But that had never been his strong suit.

A rap on his car door window startled Bear from his mental unease. He didn't even remember parking in the driveway, cutting the engine. Beckett peered in the window, basketball under one arm, the other motioning for Bear to get out. Up ahead, Logan and Seth stood waiting underneath the hoop.

Bear released his sigh before lumbering from the car. One too many Walkers had seen him reach for Raegan's hand in recent days. Logan had been waiting in Raegan's room when they climbed in her window the other day, and Beckett had walked in on Bear kissing her goodnight last night. Barely a peck, perfectly tame, but still.

He gave the car door a tap with his heel and faced Raegan's brothers and cousin. He'd known this was coming, of course. Frankly, he was surprised it'd taken as long as it had.

Maybe he could still get out of it. "Hey, guys. Uh, thanks for keeping an eye on Jamie and Erin. Are they—"

Beckett bounced the basketball. "Inside with Ava and Amelia. Making cookies."

"Good, in that case—"

Another bounce. "Raegan's in town working on the mural."

Her usual spot these days. She was loving it—and he was loving watching her love it, even if it meant his time with her was limited. If not for Jamie and Erin, he would've headed into town straight from the ranch, grime and all.

"In that case, you might as well begin the interrogation."

But Beckett only shrugged innocently. "Who said anything about an interrogation?" He tossed the basketball at Bear. It smacked into his hands. "I, for one, merely want to play. We need a fourth. You have good timing."

"But if you just happen to dole out a few brotherly warnings in between possessions, I shouldn't think anything of it, right?" Bear followed him to the others.

"No warnings. But I might have a few questions." Beckett stopped at the edge of the driveway. "And I'm sure Logan and Seth do too."

The two men glanced at each other. "Actually, I don't," Seth said, turning to Bear. "I'm just relieved you've finally got your romantic act together, man."

Beckett frowned and looked to Logan. Logan only shrugged. "Sorry, Beck. I happen to think Bear's an okay guy."

Okay guy. He'd take it. "Thanks."

"Welcome." Logan took the basketball from Bear's hands and turned to the basket. He attempted a jump shot that bounced off the backboard.

Beckett grimaced. "I am the only one in this family who has any business playing sports."

Logan exchanged glances with Bear. "Unfortunately true."

"Hey, I'm offended. Your siblings might be athletically impaired. Your cousin isn't." Seth rounded to the front of the group. "And also, I think I just lied. Because I *do* have a question for you, Bear. I can't believe I haven't asked you before now. What's up with your name? *Bear?*"

"Not exactly the kind of question I was going for," Beckett muttered, dribbling the basketball.

Bear held out his palms face up. "Don't look at me, I didn't pick it."

"Yeah, but surely there's a story behind it. It's not exactly commonplace."

Oh, there was a story, all right. Bear just generally

didn't enjoy telling it. But maybe he could win points with Beckett by doing so. He looked as interested in Seth's question as Seth did.

"So apparently when I was born, I came out squawking. A nurse hands me to my dad. He smiles at me. I stop crying. Same thing happens later that day—I cry, Dad smiles, I calm." He clamped one hand over his opposite arm, mechanically squeezing the bicep his tattoo encircled. His name was a reminder there'd been a day when his father was interested in him. "One of the nurses makes a joke about my dad being like Davy Crockett—that legend about Davy Crockett being able to smile down a bear. And suddenly I've got a name."

Seth grinned. "Sweet."

Logan rubbed his chin. "Does Raegan know that story? I'm pretty sure she'd enjoy it."

"Are you kidding? She pried it from me, like, the second day she met me." They'd been strolling through the town square, and she'd gone on and on about the cuteness of it all while he just walked beside her, wondering if his mom or dad ever thought about that story now. Ever thought about him.

"So are we going to play or what?" Beckett dribbled the ball again. "I call Bear on my team."

Bear grinned but figured it was wise to hold back a reply. That was a truce if he'd ever heard one.

Logan shot Seth an apologetic look. "Sorry. They've got the athletic Walker and the giant. They're going to win."

Beckett whipped the ball to his brother. "We'll give you first possession, at least." He turned to Bear. "Maybe we should go easy on them."

He heard Seth's scoff and Logan's chuckle but addressed Beckett. "She means the world to me, Beck. I know I haven't been forthright about everything, but—"

"It's not me you need to be forthright with. Take it from someone who in the very recent past fell for a woman right when he was in the midst of grappling with his past and trying to figure out his future at the same time—it's not fair to string her along while you try to fit her into the puzzle that is your life. She's not just another piece."

"I know that." It was why he still hadn't responded to John's email. And he *wanted* to be forthright with Raegan. He needed to tell her the rest. He needed to tell her about Annie.

Maybe after this game, after cleaning up, after spending some time with Jamie and Erin, he could head into town. Pull her away from her painting for a bit. And they could just talk.

That is, if he could keep himself from kissing her senseless. He hadn't had nearly enough chances for that lately. He liked the Walkers, but there were just so many of them around these days.

Nope. No kissing until we talk.

Beckett groaned. "I really don't wanna know what that smile means."

Bear laughed as Beckett turned to guard Seth where he stood behind the crack in the driveway they always used as the boundary line. The next half an hour passed in a rumbling blur of enjoyment—the clatter of the backboard, the smack of the ball against the cement, panting breath and expended energy.

Only when Logan's wife appeared on the front porch, tempting them with cookies, did they abandon the game—Bear and Beckett so far ahead they'd eventually quit keeping score.

Beckett slapped Bear's back as he walked past him, and Bear caught Logan's eye. The older brother gave him a nod of approval. Seth came up beside him. "Think you just won more than that game, McKinley."

Bear grinned as he reached for his car keys and phone where he'd set them in the grass. The phone's display alerted him to a voicemail. Hmm, he didn't recognize the number. Rosa calling from a different phone? *Or Rio* . . .

He glanced at Seth. "Is it even fair to her? To Raegan? I feel like I'm inviting her into a mess."

"Man, you haven't invited her anywhere she didn't already want to go."

"Yeah, but to start dating when everything's so uncertain . . ." Never mind the fact that *dating* didn't feel nearly strong enough a word for the change in their relationship.

Seth plodded up the porch, reaching down to knead the muscle in his leg. "Sure, maybe it'd be easier to start out if you were both in this perfect, idyllic place in your lives. But part of being a couple is getting through the hard stuff. You've got a good testing ground, if nothing else." He pulled open the front door. "Come on, let's go sample cookies. We've earned it."

Bear followed his friend inside but stopped in the entryway to listen to his voicemail. Maybe this would be the miracle call he'd been waiting for. Maybe Rio had come home and Rosa had found a new place to live and . . .

But the voice on the other end wasn't Rosa's and it wasn't Rio's and it wasn't anything close to warm. "Hi. This is Marilyn Beach with the Georgia Division of Children and Family Services. I need to talk to you about the whereabouts of Jamie and Erin McKinley."

Bear's stomach clenched.

He'd known Raegan would come as soon as she heard. Didn't know who'd told her. Didn't know how much they'd said.

But he knew they were her pounding steps on the stairs and down the hallway.

Bear yanked open the top drawer of the dresser in Beckett's bedroom—the one Raegan's brother had cleared to make room for Jamie and Erin's clothes. He scooped up a pile of shirts and jeans, then realized he didn't know where he was going with them. He dropped the clothes back into the drawer and turned. Where was the duffel bag Rosa had packed nearly three weeks ago?

"Bear."

He didn't look at her, just stalked to the closet and flung open the door. He found the faded fabric bag on the closet floor. A lot of good that would do him. No chance all the new clothes he'd purchased for the kids would fit in this thing, not to mention the shoes, the books, the toys.

He could borrow an extra suitcase, but that'd be one more bag to check at the airport. If they were driving, it'd be different, but they didn't have a choice. They had to fly if they were going to make it back in time—

He froze, heart reeling. It couldn't be ending like this. That social worker in Georgia had it all wrong. So very wrong.

"Talk to me, Bear." Raegan's voice was as soft as her footsteps, padding over the carpet and coming to a stop beside him.

"I have to get Jamie and Erin back to Atlanta. I've got forty-eight hours."

Forty-eight hours until Marilyn Beach called the police and the police issued an arrest warrant. This couldn't be happening.

But he'd spent an hour arguing with the woman.

There was no swaying her. She couldn't get ahold of Rosa. She couldn't get ahold of Rio. And all she knew about Bear was that he had a criminal record. That he came from a family with the wrong reputation.

And she had a court order demanding he show up with the children by noon on Monday. *Make that* less than *forty-eight hours.*

Raegan leaned into his side, circling her arms around his waist. He let himself breathe in the smell of her and will her strength to rub off on him. She was all that was good and warm and right in his life. She fit into his heart as securely as she fit into his arms.

And he had to leave her.

"You could talk to Beckett," she said. "Even if he doesn't know anything about custody issues, he's probably got other lawyer friends who do and—"

"I love you, Raegan."

The whisper slipped from his lips before the words had even fully formed in his mind. He hadn't planned to say it. And somewhere in the farthest reaches of his mind peeled the faintest of alarm bells.

You don't tell a woman you love her when you're in the midst of a crisis. When you have to leave. When you honestly don't know when you're coming back.

But he couldn't bring himself to regret it. With his lips against her hair, he whispered it again. "I love you."

She tipped her head to meet his gaze, her eyes filled with wonder. "Bear McKinley."

He loved the way she said his name. Somewhere, somehow, he found a hushed, teasing tone. "That's all you have to say? I tell you I love you and I just get 'Bear McKinley'?"

She moved from his side to his front, stretching to wind her arms around his neck. "Bear McKinley," she said again. "I am pretty sure I've loved you since the day

I met you. I don't care how cliché it sounds. It's true."

"I'm okay with clichés."

She pressed a kiss to his lips. Another. And another.

And then he lost count as he surrendered to his desire, his need to forget everything else except the woman in his arms. He lifted her from her feet, crushing her to him, kissing her as if his next breath depended on it.

Abruptly, she pulled her head back, breathless. "Bear, I have an idea."

Really? She was capable of talking right now?

"A really good idea."

He trailed his lips along her cheeks toward her ear, making her shiver. "Shut the door in case your dad or brother happens to walk past?"

"I can go with you."

He stopped, loosened his hold on her just enough to let her feet touch the floor, her back pressed against the closet door. "What?"

"Take me with you to Atlanta."

"But you don't like new places." It was the closest his brain could come to forming a coherent thought. He should probably put more than a sliver of space between them. Catch his breath. *Think.*

But he couldn't make himself pull away.

"I don't like new places when I'm alone. If you're there, I'll be fine. I can help with the kids, support you however I can until this is all resolved and we can come home. I can just . . . be there for you. The way you're always there for everyone else. You could even show me where you grew up and—"

"No." *Now* he could pull away. Did. He reached down to pick up the duffel bag he'd dropped and returned to the dresser.

"But . . . why not?"

Was that hurt mixed in with the confusion in her

voice? He couldn't stand the thought of hurting her. But that was the very reason he couldn't let himself say yes. "It's not a good idea, Rae." He pulled a pile of clothes from the drawer.

"You just said you love me—"

"And I do. Like you wouldn't believe. But Atlanta is my old life. You're my new life. Mixing the two . . . it's just not a good idea," he said again.

"They're already mixed, Bear." Frustration laced her voice. "An old life or a new life, one life or two lives or three or however many—they're all *yours*. And you're a part of my life. The biggest part. The best."

"I don't even know how long I'll be down there. You've got the mural. You've got therapy." She'd had another appointment yesterday. She'd spent more than an hour last night telling him about it, thanking him again and again for being the one to nudge her into it.

Her eyes had glistened with tears. *"It's hard, but it's right, Bear. Even if I have cried more in the past week than in the past five years put together."*

He emptied the drawer and zipped the duffel bag. *Hard, but right.* "I don't want Beckett involved either."

"Please, Bear—"

"I just can't. Not again." He hung his head, vision blurring on the empty drawer, the duffel bag slipping from his fingers.

"What do you mean 'not again'?"

"I mean . . . Annie was my new life once." He heard Raegan's inhale, looked over to see her blink. He'd meant to tell her. Just not like this. "It was different than . . . than it is with you. I was just so grateful to her, to her family. They showed me this new way to live. They accepted me. I knew she had a crush on me and I wasn't sure I liked her the same way, but I dated her anyway." He closed the empty drawer and turned to her, forcing himself to go on. "We started making plans. She had a semester left of college. We were going to join her parents in Brazil."

Raegan didn't move. "Were you engaged?"

"Close." He hated this. Hated that he hadn't just been honest with Raegan from the start. Hated that he'd hid so much away and that now it'd come back to hurt the woman he loved. "I was saving for a ring."

And he would've proposed, too. Even knowing he didn't love her the way she loved him, he would've proposed and he would've married her and he would've gone to Brazil. Because everything he'd yearned for, for so long, he'd found with Annie and her parents. Because even as a young adult, he'd still been that little boy longing for a family bound by love and peace and commitment.

He would've married her because of what he'd have gotten out of it. *So selfish.* But even that wouldn't have been as bad as . . .

Raegan touched his arm. "Bear, what happened?"

He towed the words from gaping depths. "Rio. The warehouse. The arrest." That split-second decision in the back of the cop car. "When I confessed to Rio's crime, I chose my brother over her. I knew what I was doing. I knew it would ruin all our plans. She said she'd wait for me. She came to the trial. She visited me in prison, called, wrote letters. But it wasn't the same. Every time I saw her, she just looked . . . sick almost."

And the gaps between letters and calls grew wider. She didn't show up for a scheduled visit . . .

And then, John's letter.

"There was a car accident. She'd been on her way to Rio and Rosa's place. Because I asked her to check in on them." It was coming in spurts now—short, desperate utterances. "She had all these dreams, but one choice, *my* choice . . ."

Raegan's gasp filled in the gap where his choking words cut off. And then she was in his arms again—or was he in hers?—tears he couldn't contain trailing down his cheeks. "But Bear, you have to know . . ."

He shook his head against her shoulder. He had to know it wasn't his fault? He'd tried to believe it so many times. Accidents could happen anywhere, anytime.

But he couldn't escape the reality that behind it all was the way he'd hurt her when his old life had invaded his new. If not for him, she might have been in another country when that drunk driver on I-85 took to the road. She'd have been living out her dream, not tangled in his mess. If not for him. No second chances. "I can't do it again, Rae. I won't choose again. I need you here—safe, in a good place, with your family."

"But—"

He cut her off with a desperate, pleading kiss. When he finally felt her yield, he broke away with a ragged inhale. "You need to stay. I need to go. But I'll come back. I promise. Just wait for me, okay?"

She clung to him. "Always."

Raegan closed Beckett's bedroom door gently. Bear needed this time alone. Time to pull himself together before Jamie and Erin finished the Disney movie they were watching downstairs and he had to tell them they'd be leaving in the morning.

She squeezed her eyes closed, the force of Bear's pain still wending through her like a sharp, unstoppable gale.

It's not fair, God. He doesn't deserve this—this loss and hurt and guilt.

No, not just guilt. Shame—scathing and scarring. She'd caught glimpses of it before, but now he wore it as visibly as the tattoo on his arm. Wasn't it enough that the man had gone to prison for something he didn't do? That he'd left Brazil because of rumors and false accusations? Did he have to be drilled by the police and threatened by a social worker on top of it?

She slumped against the hallway wall, his crushing hurt becoming her own as a shudder wracked through her, clasping and then squeezing . . .

No. She swallowed the swell of anxiety. *Not now.*

"Raegan?" Dad rounded the corner.

Inhale four seconds. One. Two. Three. Four.

"Honey, are you okay?"

Five. Six. Seven.

"Please not now." Did the words eke past her lips? Was she talking to Dad or herself?

"Not now what?"

She gulped for air. *Slow down. Four seconds—hold.* She closed her eyes, counted around a wordless prayer, exhaled. The pressing eased. Another inhale.

"Rae—"

"Breathing exercise." *Hold. Exhale.* "Sara taught me."

No ringing in her ears. No blurring vision. It was working.

"Sara?" Dad nearly choked on the name.

Raegan met his eyes expecting riled confusion. But all she saw was concern. "I get panic attacks. Sara's helping me."

As she breathed and counted and waited for her hands to stop shaking, she watched the realization pass over Dad's face. The secret she'd kept. The fact that she had turned to the only woman he'd ever asked her to avoid. He'd want to know how long she'd been having the attacks, of course, and how many times she'd been to see Sara. He'd want to know Sara's diagnosis and if there was something he could do to help. He'd ask about medication and—

"Are you okay?" He touched her shoulder. "Right now, I mean?"

Her trembling ceased. "Yeah. I am." Thanks to the breathing exercise, to Sara's help, to a prayer that didn't need words.

It might not always be like this. Breathing exercises were a coping technique, not a cure, Sara said. Therapy was a marathon, not a sprint. And prayer didn't always mean sudden, miraculous healing.

Sara hadn't needed to add that last one.

But this moment, right now, it felt like a victory. Not only because she'd stared down the familiar dark well and found the strength to step back. But because she'd been honest with Dad. She'd refused to hide.

"How long?" he finally asked.

"Since before Mom died."

He closed his eyes for a long moment. "Why didn't you say anything?"

"Why have you never told me about Sara?"

He opened his eyes.

"Why didn't Beckett tell us for so many years why he stayed away from Maple Valley? Or Logan open up about how much he was really struggling back in LA? Kate still hardly ever talks about that thing with her college professor." And Bear—it'd taken him so long to let her all the way in. He still hadn't entirely, not really. Not when he was so intent on drawing a line between his life in Atlanta and his life here. "Why do any of us keep anything from the people we love most?"

Swelling music from the movie downstairs drifted upward. Dad opened his mouth and then closed it, the etched lines of his face seeming to deepen right in front of her eyes.

Finally, he took a step back. "Sara and your mother were best friends."

"I know."

"So naturally, I spent a lot of time with her as a teenager. Double dates, sometimes, but more often than not, it was just the three of us. Sara didn't really seem to mind being the third wheel."

The sound of a dresser drawer closing came from the other side of Beckett's bedroom door. Bear must've finally started packing again.

"Anyway, there was this dance in town the night before I had to leave for boot camp. Spent most of the time dancing with Flora, but Sara managed to corner me before we left. Next thing I know, she's saying all this stuff—that she knows I love Flora but that she loves me and—"

Raegan's jaw dropped—half surprise, half amusement. *This* was Dad's mysterious past with Sara?

"Then she kisses me."

She shouldn't laugh. She really shouldn't laugh.

"It's not funny, Rae. She kissed me in front of Flora, not to mention half of Maple Valley! That is not how I wanted my last night before shipping off to fight in a war to go."

"Did you and Mom fight? Did it ruin Sara and Mom's friendship? I'm waiting for the part of the story that would cause you to still be angry this many years later."

He folded his arms. "No, we didn't fight. You know your mother. She said obviously Sara had good taste and that she'd suspected it for a while. She felt bad for Sara, of all things. And yeah, they drifted apart and Flora regretted it for years. Completely unfair because it wasn't her fault."

Okay, that part of the story was unfortunate. But still, she couldn't hold back her grin. "And here I thought some huge scandal had happened."

"She kissed me!"

"Forty-some years ago."

"She wrote me letters, too. Do you know how much I got heckled in the barracks for getting letters from *two* girls back home?"

"Dad, you all but ordered the woman from your house." She was all-out giggling now. "Because of leftover high school romantic drama."

He dropped his arms like a last defense. Cracked a grin. Finally let out a laugh. "I guess it is a little comical."

"No, Dad, it's hilarious."

And then they were both laughing.

"I thought she'd, like, betrayed the U.S. during the war. Spied for Russia or China. Or at least broken your heart pre-Mom or something."

"I did kick her out of the house. Like a general ousting an enlisted man from an officer's club." He was laughing so hard a tear slipped down his cheek. "It's kind of horrible, really."

Raegan could barely speak through her laughter. "You should probably apologize." She let out a sigh, still bubbling with giggles. "Oh man, I really needed this, Dad."

He matched her exhale with one of his own, his chuckles subsiding as his gaze found her face. "I don't know why I couldn't tell you about Sara earlier or why you couldn't tell me about the panic attacks. But now that I know, you just tell me how I can support you and I'll do it." He laid his hands on her shoulders. "And if you don't need me to do anything, that's fine. Just know that I'm here for you and I love you and nothing will ever change that."

She stepped into her father's embrace, more thankful than ever for the man he was and consumed by the freedom of being fully seen and fully accepted. "I love you, Dad."

"Hey, Rae?"

Beckett's voice pulled her from the hug. Her brother glanced back and forth between them, but whatever he'd come to say must take precedence over the questions their obvious emotional state prompted because he didn't ask a one of them. Only hesitated, phone in hand.

"Is everything okay, Beck?"

"Just got a call from Meg at the coffee shop. She was closing up. Happened to check out the mural." He shifted his weight. "She says you need to come into town."

16

Raegan stared at the splattered brick, her careful brushstrokes—three days of intense work—obliterated by huge blobs of wayward color. Those paint cans she'd left uncovered atop the scaffolding now littered the ground in front of the building. Emptied. "Who would do this?"

Twilight doused the riverfront in shadows. Dad shook his head beside her. "I don't know. But we should probably call the police."

Was it the cool evening air or the vindictiveness on display in front of her that scattered goosebumps over her skin? "It's just paint. I know it's just paint." It could be covered up. But she'd already had to start over once—after that storm. She was on a tight timeline as it was. Less than five weeks until the art fair.

How many setbacks could one project handle?

And if someone in town was against this mural, why didn't they say so back before she'd ever started?

"Probably most of the shops along the street were already closed when this happened, but it wouldn't hurt to ask if anybody saw anything." Dad shook his head. "First time I've ever wished security cameras were a thing in Maple Valley."

A car door slammed behind them. Raegan turned.

Bear stalked across the road.

Shoot, he didn't have to come. She'd purposely not told him before leaving the house with Dad. He had enough to deal with. "Bear, you didn't need to—"

"Do you know who did it?"

She shrugged. "Bored teenagers?" Which would make this a case of meaningless vandalism. But that kind of thing just didn't happen in Maple Valley.

Except . . . there had been that incident in front of Baker's Antiques. The one poor Jamie had been pulled into.

"Left my phone in the car," Dad said. "Gonna go grab it so I can call the police."

She'd never seen Bear so eerily severe—fists flexing, rigid posture, eyes mere slits. "This is not happening again."

"Again? But—"

He wrenched his phone from his pocket, apparently not patient enough for Dad to retrieve his own.

But then, as if on cue, it rang.

Unbelievable. *Unidentified Number.* Of course. Bear whipped the phone to his ear. "Rio?" His gaze swerved to the ruined mural once again.

"You can't take them back to Atlanta."

All the air bolted from his lungs. Rio's voice. No question. "Where are you, Rio?"

"I don't want Jamie and Erin in Atlanta. Please, keep them with you."

Raegan and Case were both staring at him, questions playing over their faces. But he could barely make his mind fasten on Rio's words, on the possible implication . . .

Did Rio know he'd been planning to leave the next day. If so, how? "Believe me, I wish I could keep them here. But there's a court order. Maybe if both you and your wife hadn't gone AWOL—"

"You don't understand, Bear. There's more . . ."

An overpowering, aging muffler from the truck grumbling over the Archway Bridge muted Rio's voice. But wait . . .

Wait, he hadn't just heard the truck in the distance. He'd heard it through the phone, too. Which meant . . .

He spun on his heels, alarm mounting. *There!* A shadow under the bridge.

"Bear?"

He ignored Raegan's call as he burst into a run. The shadow didn't move. Bear's feet pounded over pavement that eventually gave way to grass that sloped down and then up again. Anger propelled him under the shade of the bridge to where Rio waited.

His brother. Just standing there. Gaping.

"It was you the whole time, wasn't it? The phone calls. The blue Taurus—"

"Blue Taurus? What are you talking—?"

Rio hadn't finished sputtering the questions before Bear sprang, both hands grabbing for his brother's collar. "Why the mural? What does Raegan have to do with any of this?"

Rio attempted to yank free, but Bear only held tighter. "That wasn't me—"

"We're going to the police now." He should call Rollins.

Rio pushed both hands against Bear's chest—just enough force to break away. "You don't know what's happening here, Bear. If you'd just let me explain—"

"Explain how you could abandon your wife and kids? Explain how nothing has changed in ten years? I have to get on a plane and deliver Jamie and Erin to a social worker's office by the day after tomorrow. I have no idea what's going to happen then. But maybe we can stop that if you turn yourself in. For once in your life, have the decency to put them first."

Rio just stared at him, eyes the same shade as his own burning with intensity. His shaved head, his cheeks and chin, were all shadowed by stubble. His wedding ring glinted in the slanting sun. "You think I don't care about Jamie and Erin?"

"If you did, you wouldn't be hiding under a bridge and making cryptic phone calls. If you did, you'd do the right thing."

"They're *my* kids, Bear. I decide what the right—"

Bear couldn't do it, couldn't hold back any longer. He lunged at his brother, all the force of all the warring emotions inside him spilling as they fell to the ground. Rio hit the dirt with a grunt but threw an elbow the moment he'd freed his arm. The impact on Bear's cheek was nowhere close to a deterrent. Dust clouded around him as they scuffled, flying fists and angry thrusts until Bear had Rio flat underneath him, his younger brother's angry panting and split lip only inches away, Bear's knuckles clenched and raised.

"Go ahead," Rio spat. "You've been waiting for a decade."

Bear's fist landed in the dirt beside Rio's head, the blunt contact breaking his skin and shooting pain up his arm. He heaved himself to his feet, lungs stinging.

Rio stared at him for a moment before slowly pulling himself up, his chest rising and falling. "Did you ever stop to think . . ." He winced, surely because of his bleeding lip. "That maybe what I'm doing, I'm doing for

Jamie and Erin? And Rosa. And you."

Bear's cheek throbbed. "Why would I think that? When have you ever—"

Rio whirled away, his shoes scuffing the dirt. When he turned back, genuine anguish bellowed from his expression. "So you're the only one who can do the right thing? The only one who can make a sacrifice?" Both palms clenched his almost-bald head. "Nobody but Bear McKinley can save the day?"

Bear finally caught his breath. "I don't understand."

"Of course you don't because you walked away. You played hero and it didn't work the way you wanted, so you left. I've never blamed you for that. Not once. I know it took me too long to see what I'd cost you. I know that."

"Not just me."

Rio stilled. "I know that, too."

Bear had to turn away, too much confusion rushing through him. Stifling air waved over him, the rusty smell of river water mixing with diesel fumes wafting from the bridge.

"I can't go to the police," Rio said slowly, evenly from behind him, "because my FBI contact went silent two months ago."

Bear turned. "*What?*"

"They're trying to smoke me out—Inez and his men. You mentioned a car. If you're being followed, then it means they gave up on using Rosa to find me and now they're using you. Maybe your girlfriend, too."

His girlfriend. If Rio knew about Raegan . . . "How long have you been in town?"

"Only a couple days. I just wanted to see the kids, see you, before . . ." Rio turned away.

"Before what?" Bear's pulse pounded.

"Of course, it's possible that mural doesn't have

anything to do with me. Might just be a message for you."

Bear tramped around his brother to face him. "Rio."

"Surely you know he's kept an eye on you." Rio touched his split lip.

Rosa's words came back to him. *"If they could find you in South America . . ."*

"When you confessed in my place, you didn't just incriminate yourself, Bear. You took a bunch of men with you. You shut down an entire warehouse."

"At least something good came of it." His tone was as dark as the dirt beneath their feet, the shadow of the bridge, the night sky. Too many jagged-edged pieces tried to cram together. *FBI . . . Inez . . . Raegan . . .*

Misery masked every other emotion on Rio's face. "Bear—"

A crack split through the night air.

A gunshot.

Raegan!

The blue Taurus. She'd known the moment she'd seen it.

Bear had just disappeared under the bridge. Dad was scrounging in his car for his phone. And the blue Taurus had pulled up.

Indecision had rooted her feet to the grass. Should she call for Bear? Would he even hear her with the river and the wind and a car motoring over the bridge? She reached into her back pocket, expecting to find her phone, but no. She'd left the house in too much of a hurry with Dad.

The Taurus's driver's-side door opened.

Dad. Had Bear mentioned the Taurus to Dad?

Would he look over and realize . . .

"Raegan Walker?"

The figure striding toward her knew her name. That fact didn't do a thing to aid her mental paralysis.

The man stopped in front of her. "I'm Detective Rollins. I spoke to your friend the other day."

For a moment, her apprehension ceased. Rollins. The one who'd questioned Bear. No, she didn't like the way he'd treated Bear, but at least he was law enforcement. At least he wasn't—

But no. The blue Taurus. Bear had said the detective had only come to town after Chief Ross called the Atlanta P.D. But Bear had spotted the Taurus multiple times before that.

Which meant . . . she didn't know what it meant. Only that whatever momentary solace had trickled in seconds ago now dried up completely.

And Rollins saw it all. His hand moved to his hip. "Just tell me where they are."

Fear climbed her throat. *Don't look at Dad. Don't look at the bridge.* A blast of wind knocked into her, rattling the metal scaffolding behind her. "Where who are?"

His fingers closed over the handle of a pistol. "I'd rather not make a big scene here."

"Like my ruined mural isn't enough of one already?" Her livid counter surprised even her.

"Trust me, you don't want to be in the middle of this."

Trust him? If not for that blue Taurus, she might have. She crossed her arms.

He lifted the pistol free of its holster.

"Raegan!"

Dad. No.

Rollins jerked at the sound of Dad's voice.

Strangling panic kept her from calling out. No breathing or counting, not even a prayer—

The shot sounded.

Leaden terror weighed Bear's every step even as he forced his mind to work, to process what he was seeing.

The blue Taurus. Raegan. Case.

Detective Rollins with his gun raised to the sky.

A warning shot. Thank God, only a warning shot.

The relief fled as quickly as it'd swept in. There was still a man with a gun standing in between Bear and the woman he loved. There was still an artillery of unanswered questions and hounding dread.

There was still Rio running behind him.

And Raegan—shaking, trying to breathe.

"Rollins!" He shouted through gritted teeth and winded lungs, stride widening. Almost there.

Rollins whirled, gun trained for the barest moment on Bear, and then, with a baleful sneer, behind him.

Bear came to a jarring stop, panting. Rio must've halted too because there were no steps sounding behind him. Nothing sounding at all, save a hissing squall that shook the scaffolding.

"All right, then," Rollins said. "We're all here."

Rio stepped up beside Bear. "This doesn't have anything to do with the rest of them."

"Except that now it does."

"Bear."

How he even heard Raegan's panicked whisper through the raging gale and the clattering metal, through his own distress, he didn't even know. He took a step forward.

Rollins instantly shifted his aim.

Raegan dropped to her knees. *Oh, Lord . . .* just as he'd feared. She was having an attack. Right now, while his two worlds collided.

"Bear, the scaffolding." Rio's voice was low. "I don't think it was only the mural they messed with."

His attention darted to the wavering structure and hooked on what Rio had seen. The guardrail, ready to topple—Raegan underneath.

Frantic, he tried to catch Case's eye. Tried to relay the warning. But Case's focus was trained solely on Raegan.

Rio stepped forward. Rollins shifted again. Somewhere behind them, a car door slammed.

"Go to her," Rio called.

"But—"

Rio took another step. "Just do it."

But Rollins, the gun . . .

Raegan. His brother.

Another thrust of the wind. Another clamor from the scaffolding.

He lunged toward Raegan.

Another gunshot.

17

*B*ear couldn't breathe. Why couldn't he breathe?

Fluorescent light strangled his vision and too many smells assaulted him at once—pungent disinfectant, stale coffee, someone's cologne.

"Drink it, Bear. You'll feel better."

Sam Ross. His cologne. His coffee. Or, no, apparently Bear's coffee, steaming from a Styrofoam cup in front of him. He willed his focus to scan his surroundings—a small, family waiting room in the Maple Valley hospital. Glass windows and a muted TV on one wall. Leather furniture and a lone table.

The table where he sat now, hunched and dazed, splatters of blood on his shirt and dirt under his fingernails and hazy images refusing to form a solid picture in his mind. *Rollins . . . Rio . . .*

Raegan. He breathed her name out loud.

The police chief scooted his chair up to the table across from Bear. "She's with a doc now. And her Dad. And Jimmy."

"Jimmy?" His trembling fingers closed around the Styrofoam.

"Another officer. She's okay—thanks to you and that knot on your head."

Knot on his head? Of its own accord, his right hand found the spot that he didn't even realize until now throbbed. He squeezed his eyes closed, trying to remember.

Rio had told him to go to Raegan. He'd sprung toward her. The gunshot.

And then?

Nothing. Blackness. Except . . .

He lifted the coffee cup, guzzled the thick, acrid drink, winced as coffee grounds scraped down his throat.

Scraping . . .

The scrape and clash of metal. There it was. The memory.

He'd charged toward Raegan, reaching her trembling form on the ground, no time to pull her away before the scaffolding's railing came toppling down. He'd covered her body with his own, his frantic gaze scouring for sight of his brother.

He'd seen the blood just before the impact.

His stomach lurched now, jerking his whole body.

"Oh, no." Ross ejected from his seat. "Garbage can. Now."

Someone thrust a plastic bin in front of Bear just in time for his first heave.

It was over thirty seconds later—his stomach empty and his throat scuffed raw. His head still pounded, but his gasping stilled.

"I'm sorry, Bear." Sam lifted the bin from Bear's hands, replaced it with a water bottle. "I had a feeling you were in shock. We can do this later. You should be the one in with an ER doc."

"Rio." He sputtered his brother's name. Now the picture in his head was too clear. Rio's sprawled body, the scarlet wound in his chest. Too many feet of grass in between them. Wait, how had his blood ended up on

Bear? His sight slid down his stained shirt. That was Rio's blood, wasn't it?

He swallowed a drink of water.

"You rode in the ambulance with him." Sam must have sensed his confusion. "The scaffolding knocked you out. You came to before the EMTs arrived, but you were pretty dazed."

Still was. "Is he . . . ?"

Sam stood behind his own chair, fingers gripping its back. "He was alive when he arrived here."

Was. His stomach clenched again.

"It's been about ten minutes since I got here. The doctor hasn't been out for an update yet."

Ten minutes. Had he been sitting here in this chair that long? Ten minutes that he could've been with Raegan. Or calling to check in on the kids. Rosa, someone needed to call Rosa. *Oh, God, please let her answer for once.*

He tried to stand, but the wooziness immediately forced him down. Another drink of water.

"We're taking care of things, Bear. I sent an officer to Case's house. Both Beckett and Kate are with the kids. We've called your sister-in-law. She's on her way."

On her way? Already? But how—?

FBI. Rollins. Inez.

Why couldn't he make his brain work? Why couldn't he piece any of this together?

Because of that picture of Rio's body in his mind. The image of Raegan, terrified, falling to her knees. The echo of the gunshot.

"I need to see Rio." This time when he stood, he refused to give in to the shock still wobbling his limbs. He finished off the water bottle, then dropped it onto the table.

"You can't. Not just yet. Who you need to see is a

doctor. Come on, I'll go with you."

"No—"

"You look like a zombie, your head is swelling, you can't hardly remember the past hour, and you just barfed into a garbage can. I'm insisting."

"Bear!" Raegan burst into the room. "There you are. I tried the main ER waiting room first and when I didn't see you—" She crashed into him, the impact enough to push him back into his chair. She landed on his lap, arms immediately circling his neck as she repeated his name too many times to count.

"Rae—"

"I'm sorry." She buried her face against his cheek. "I'm so sorry."

He could feel his heart stop. *Rio?*

"Of all the times to have a stupid panic attack. I tried to stop it, but it just . . . it wouldn't let go and . . ."

Not Rio.

With his hands on her arms, he held her back just far enough to look at her face. Other than the scrape on her chin, the pallid tone to her skin, she didn't appear hurt. But those tears in her eyes, the guilt in her voice . . . "You don't have a thing to apologize for. Not a single thing."

Whereas he—he'd brought this mess he didn't even understand into her world. The truth of it collided against him, thudding even harder than the aching pulse in his head.

Raegan brought her hands to his face, her fingers skimming over his swollen skin. She leaned forward to kiss his injuries, her soft lips attempting to soothe. "You need to see the doctor."

Sam harrumphed behind her. "That's what I've been trying to tell him."

Raegan blinked and pulled back as if just remembering they weren't alone, but she didn't move from his lap. "You could have a concussion."

"Do you know anything about Rio?"

She pushed a lock of his hair aside as she shook her head. "I'm sure Dr. Traeger will let us know what's happening the moment he can." With both palms on his cheeks, she looked into his eyes. "I'm so glad you're okay."

But he wasn't. He couldn't be. Not until he knew if his brother was going to live. And even then . . .

It was too much. The very thing he'd never wanted, the life he'd tried so hard to leave behind, had ambushed him here. It'd endangered Raegan, her father. And he hadn't known that in trying to outrun his own past, he'd apparently left Rio to deal with Lord knows what on his own.

Still. When Raegan leaned forward to kiss his lips, he was too selfish to stop her. He let himself cling to her.

While he still could.

Raegan had started to put the pieces together. Between Officer Jimmy's questions and then Chief Ross's and from the few utterances she'd heard from Bear, she could at least figure out the basics.

Raegan huddled into the jacket Dad had draped over her. He sat beside her now, but her focus was on Bear pacing the waiting room like a caged cat.

Rio, it seemed, had reneged on his criminal activities months or maybe even years ago. He'd become an informant for the police—or the FBI?—working undercover in an attempt to bring down someone named Inez. But when his main contact had gone silent and he started receiving threats, Rio went underground.

But Detective Rollins, who was apparently on Inez's payroll, had tracked him here.

It was as much as she could piece together in the minutes since she'd rushed into the room and thrown herself at Bear. Couldn't even bring herself to be embarrassed by that. In fact, if she had her way, she'd still be sitting on his lap, clutching him to her, just to convince herself again and again that he was okay.

She could still taste the horror of those seconds when Rollins had turned his gun on Bear. Even through the smog of her panic, a laser-sharp focus had lanced straight through her.

I can't lose him.

She wasn't Logan. She couldn't survive a second devastating loss. She wouldn't *want* to survive it.

Murky fear attempted to throttle her all over again.

But he's okay. He's right here in front of you.

Had it really only been a couple hours ago that they'd stood together in Beckett's bedroom? It'd felt like a blow when he'd declined her offer to come to Atlanta with him, but she'd told herself then that she had to acquiesce. Had to trust him when he said he'd come back. That was part of loving someone, wasn't it? Respecting their wishes even when you didn't understand the reasoning behind them.

Maybe she understood a little better now.

But everything had changed when Bear came charging across the street, drawing Rollins' aim. If he thought she was letting him go anywhere without her now—

"Bear McKinley?"

Her attention swung to the now-open door of the private waiting room. Dr. Traeger.

She was on her feet in a millisecond, leaving Dad's side and crossing the room in a few quick strides to reach

Bear. She grabbed his hand, but when his fingers didn't close around hers, she knotted her arm through his instead.

Dr. Traeger must've noticed the same white sheen to Bear's skin as she did. "Have you seen Dr. Lewis yet?"

"Tell me about Rio. Please."

Raegan squeezed his arm.

Dr. Traeger nodded, though the concern didn't leave his eyes. "The bullet hit his aorta. We've done our best to patch it but he needs a full repair and he needs it now. We're not equipped here. We're getting him ready to life-flight—"

Bear's muscles stiffened under her palm. "Where?"

"Iowa City. I've already spoken to the heart surgeon there."

"Can I—"

"There's not room to ride with. I'm very sorry about that."

"Can I at least see him?"

She could cry at the waver in Bear's voice, so miniscule she might be the only one to have heard it. But she *had* heard it and it was all she could do not to draw him into her arms.

Dr. Traeger shook his head slowly. "We truly don't have a minute to spare. I know that sounds dramatic. But we have to be ready when the helicopter lands."

Bear's nod couldn't mask his distress. She tightened her hold.

Dr. Traeger reached for the door.

But Bear found his voice once more. "Doctor?"

He turned.

"The chances?"

Dr. Traeger let out a breath, as if surrendering to a question he hadn't wanted to be asked. "It's bad. But if he can get into surgery within the next couple hours . . ."

Not an answer. But apparently it was as much as Bear was going to get.

As soon as Dr. Traeger left, the room fanned into action. Chief Ross said something about getting back to the station to question Rollins. Jimmy was on his phone with someone from Atlanta, apparently. Dad was asking Bear what he needed, if he should get the kids ready.

Bear raked his fingers through his hair. "Yeah, they need to come with. It might be scary for them, but . . . but it's their dad."

She didn't miss the tears he blinked away.

Chief Ross pulled on his jacket. "We'll get you a police escort, okay? It'll get you there faster and, well, considering everything, I think it's for the best."

Did he still think there was some kind of danger out there? That Inez might send another man? Or maybe he just had that many more questions for Bear.

She glanced up at his face. "Let's get you home first, Bear. We'll change fast and—"

"No."

She still held his arm. "I know you want to hurry, but the kids shouldn't see you in a blood-stained shirt." Blunt, perhaps, but he was in a daze.

Or . . . or he wasn't. Because his eyes were startlingly clear as he pulled away and faced her. "You can't come, Rae."

Dad cleared his throat behind her. Chief Ross nodded in front of her. Soft footsteps padded from the room.

"Bear—"

He shook his head. "I mean it."

"I'm not letting you go alone. If you're worried about me—"

"I am. But I'll worry less if you're here." The tenor of his voice had hardened and he turned away, facing the glass windows that stared into the hospital corridor.

"Bear, please. You shouldn't have to deal with this by yourself."

He spun from the windows to face her once more. "I can't handle having you caught in the middle of this anymore than you already have been. Okay? I've got a brother who might be dying. I can't be here for both of you at the same time. Can you understand that?"

"I can. I do." She willed her voice to stay steady despite the tossing storm inside and stepped toward him. "But who's going to look out for you? At some point, you have to learn to let other people help you."

She tried to touch his arm, but he backed away.

"Let other people help me? Rae, I've spent the better part of the past month letting other people help me and all it did was bring danger right to your doorstep. All while Rio was being hunted down by real-life bad guys." He panted the words ahead of an exhale as worn as his appearance.

His dark hurt was so palpable it thrummed in the air between them, fading out the bright overhead lights, a woman's voice over the hospital's PA system, air conditioning rattling through a nearby vent. Guilt spiked his pain—she could see it in every line in his face.

Comforting words ached to break free, but he didn't want them, did he? Wouldn't hear them if she tried.

"You need to stay. And I need to go."

It was the second time tonight he'd said those words. But this time, there was no kiss or embrace to punctuate them.

Worse, no promise to return.

18

Bear's gaze bore into the gravestone, Atlanta's heat swathing him in steamy, opaque air. So thick that if there were any chance of fleeing it, it'd be like stepping out of a heavy, damp bathrobe.

But there was no escaping it. Not now.

A thin figure in a navy blue uniform perched against a tree in the far corner of the cemetery. Police protection. It'd become his new normal in the week since the shooting. Did the officer wonder how much longer Bear would linger here?

Bear wondered himself. There was no peace to be had tracing with his eyes the letters etched in stone. The numbers underneath. Perspiration beaded on his forehead where the bruises were only beginning to fade.

"I thought I might find you here."

Bear almost jumped. It couldn't be—"John?"

The older man had stopped just feet behind Bear, skin even more sun-blotched than the last time Bear had seen him in Brazil, gray eyes swimming with compassion. "You didn't think we'd leave you to deal with this alone, did you?"

"We?"

"Elizabeth's in the car. She wasn't quite . . . ready."

John's focus settled on the stone behind Bear. If the words there unraveled Bear's emotion, what must it do to John?

Annie Beth Lane

Beloved dreamer, daughter, friend

"We met your sister-in-law," John offered. "She wasn't sure where you'd gone. But when she said you were on foot and when we realized how close to the cemetery the apartment was . . ." John's voice trailed off as he faced the grave.

Yes, the apartment. They'd been crammed into it for a week now. Rosa had found it during the first week he'd been in Iowa.

Before she'd solved the mystery of her husband's whereabouts, realized it was her own father endangering her family. She'd gone underground for the same reason as Rio—worry over her children. Rio had never been in jail, not recently. He'd concocted that lie himself, hoping to keep Rosa from looking for him, to keep her safe. But she'd put the pieces together quicker than Bear.

It was all still such a mess. But at least Inez had finally been arrested. Rollins was still behind bars, of course. And the FBI contact, the one Rio had been working with, had been found. That is, his body had been located.

But enough information had come out to clear up any lingering questions about Rio's part in it all. Rio had gone to law enforcement of his own accord more than a year ago, offering himself up as an informant. They'd known they couldn't just arrest Inez for a routine drug deal, throw shallow charges at him. All Inez would've had to do was whip out a fancy lawyer and not even Rio on the stand would've made a difference.

Instead, they'd set out to stop the whole operation,

cut Inez down at the knees. And it had started with Rio making nice with Inez, working his way into the man's inner circle, and figuring out who he had on the inside with the Atlanta P.D.

Rollins.

But six months into the undertaking, Inez had grown suspicious. The threats started. Rio's contact went silent.

"I can't believe you came all this way."

"Then you sorely underestimate our love for you, son."

Son. A sob caught in his throat. John clamped his hand around Bear's shoulder as he had so many times before, having to reach up to do so.

"How is he?"

"Alive. But weak. He's still not awake much." Rio had been transported from Iowa City to Atlanta just two days ago. Partially for health insurance reasons—such a mundane concern in a whirlwind of disorder.

But also because Georgia CPS had only allowed the briefest of extensions on that court order demanding Bear return the kids to its jurisdiction. Even with both parents now accounted for, it was still an open case. But Bear and Rosa had met with Marilyn Beach on Thursday. Things seemed to be smoothing over in that one area, at least.

And Jamie and Erin, after all they'd been through, were holding up. They'd been overjoyed to see Rosa, had been able to talk to Rio a couple times this week. They talked about Iowa constantly, and twice, Bear had let Jamie borrow his phone to call that friend of his back in Maple Valley—Elise. The young girl was due for a surgery of her own soon, wasn't she? Raegan would be nervous about it. She loved that little girl.

Raegan. Every thought eventually led back to her. And every time, his heart twisted.

Same way it twisted each day when, inevitably, one of the kids asked if he was staying.

John's hand was still warm on his shoulder. "From what you wrote—and what Rosa said at the house—it's a miracle your brother survived."

Yes. The surgeon in Iowa City had said so. The ICU doctor in Atlanta agreed. "He's got a long road to recovery, though." But just this morning when Bear had gone by the hospital to see him, Rio had been optimistic. Said he had the perfect incentive for recuperation.

"*I want to be in perfect health by the time Luis Inez's trial starts. Don't want to pass out on the witness stand or anything.*"

"*Rio—*"

"*I know it could be a year away. Might take them months just to settle on the charges, given his history. But no matter. That gives me plenty of time to get in shape. Wanna look good in case my picture ends up in the paper, too—the man who helped bring down notorious drug lord Luis Inez.*"

The security officer leaning in the doorway had snorted.

It was the most he'd heard his brother say since the shooting, the surgery. Bear had walked out of the hospital wearing his first full-fledged smile in days.

But he couldn't blink fast enough to stop his welling tears now. Rio had been given the miracle of another chance. But Annie . . .

The sorrow crashed in all over again. The shame. "It's my fault, John. Your daughter—"

"Bear, no."

He swiped the back of his hand over his eyes, sweat and tears mingling.

"I don't know how many more ways to tell you this, son. You can't keep living with this shame."

"I asked her to check in on Rio and Rosa. If not for me—"

"She's gone, Bear. I miss her everyday, but my Annie is gone from this earth and that's not going to change." His voice broke, but he pushed on. "You can blame yourself 'til kingdom come, replay every choice you've ever made, but it's not going to change anything other than to ruin your own life."

Maybe his life deserved to be ruined. He hadn't deserved Annie back then, nor John and Elizabeth's acceptance. He certainly didn't deserve Raegan or the life he'd begun to picture for himself these past weeks in Maple Valley.

He didn't even deserve his brother's love. He'd abandoned Rio as a teenager and then again as an adult. Like a hypocrite, he'd spent the past ten years resenting him— as if Rio's faults were so much more unforgivable than his own.

"So you're the only one who can do the right thing? The only one who can make a sacrifice?" Rio's words under the bridge came pummeling in. *"Did you ever stop to think that maybe what I'm doing, I'm doing for Jamie and Erin? And Rosa. And you."*

He'd given up on his brother. He'd walked away.

While Rio had done the thing Bear couldn't. He'd stayed. He'd put himself in danger to fight for a better life for his family.

"You've talked so many times, Bear, about the choice you made. And I know it eats at you." John came to stand in front of him, blocking Annie's grave. "But at some point, you have to make another choice—stay in this prison of unworthiness you've let erect itself in your soul or accept the grace that changes everything. It's your choice. You either believe God can redeem your past and your regrets and your pain . . . or you don't."

"What does that even mean?"

"I'll tell you what it doesn't mean. It doesn't mean all the hurt just instantly vanishes. But it does mean you stop carrying a load that was never yours to carry in the first place or holding yourself to a promise nobody ever asked you to make. It means instead of the gray walls of your guilt, you start focusing on the crack in the door filled with light. You move toward it—baby steps or otherwise. You get intentional about discovering the good God can bring from the bad."

Blessed cloud cover veiled the sun and ushered in a breeze. Bear gave up stopping his trail of tears. "But, John, I . . . I don't deserve . . ."

"None of us does, son. That's the point. But you can't cling to God's grace and your shame at the same time." John closed the gap between them, a father's love in his embrace. "Choose grace, Bear. For once. Choose grace."

The weight in his spirit crumbled as he let himself cry.

Raegan hadn't exactly meant to bring the swirl of conversation dancing over Dad's dining room table to such a sudden, skidding stop. But that was exactly what her abrupt announcement had done.

The tantalizing aromas from enough breakfast foods to feed a small army wafted from every corner of the table—a classic Walker tradition, made all the more meaningful today due to the reason they'd gathered. Everyone was here. Kate and Colton. Logan and Amelia and little Charlie, back from Chicago again. Beckett had brought Kit—an honorary and most likely soon-to-be-official member of the family. Dad was here, of course, and Seth and Ava.

A plate of Beckett's blueberry pancakes sat right next to a platter of Kate's French toast. They'd spent half the morning, as always, arguing about whose sugary, syrupy treat was best. Logan had only just left his position at the stove after an hour of taking individual omelet orders.

Normally Raegan would've prepared a fancy fruit arrangement of some sort—a colorful fruit salad or tropical fruit kebabs, perhaps. Once she'd even carved half the rind of a watermelon to look like a basket and shaped all the pieces of melon inside like little flowers.

Instead, today, she'd washed a bag of grapes and called her offering good. It was all she'd had in her. *"Sorry, guys. Any and all creativity I possess these days has gone into the mural."*

A convenient excuse and at least partially accurate. She'd spent every spare minute of the past week at the mural—first scrubbing and scraping away the textured blobs of paint from the vandalism. Rollins's doing. Because apparently he'd thought it would prompt Rio out of hiding. Or he'd just wanted to antagonize Bear.

Bear.

Bear, who wasn't coming back this time. He hadn't said it in so many words, in any of his sparse texts or short calls in the week since he'd left. But she heard it all the same.

"What did you say, Rae?" Kate asked the question from where she and Colton shared a piano bench at the far end of the table.

A reminder that everyone was staring at her, waiting.

Raegan took a breath, twisting her napkin in clammy hands. Why had she thought this was a good idea? "I said . . . I'm in therapy. I get panic attacks. Have for a long time. But now . . . I'm getting help." There, she'd said it. She picked up one of Dad's mini-quiches and stuffed it in her mouth.

The pattering of a light shower drifted in from the dining room's open patio doors, along with a gentle breeze and the earthy smell of rain. Fitting, the weather this day—Mom's birthday. She would've been sixty. Oh, how Mom had loved rainy days. She'd said they were perfect for curling up in front of the fireplace with a book or an old movie.

Maybe Raegan shouldn't have chosen this morning to open up to everyone all at once. Not when they'd intended to spend the time remembering their only missing family member.

Then again, maybe Mom was looking down right now and savoring this moment and the honesty that came with it.

"I go to counseling." Kate's husband looked at Raegan as he spoke. "Went once every two weeks like clockwork for almost a year. I go once a month now."

Everyone around the table knew Colton's story by now, the traumatic experience he'd had as a child, the blocked memories, the flashbacks.

Colton reached for the platter of Kate's French toast and helped himself to another slice. "It's been one of the best decisions I ever made."

A grateful warmth trekked through Raegan, even as discomfort held its grip. "I think it may end up being one of my best decisions, too."

Her gaze traveled the table, awaiting the responses she knew would come. Maybe not now—but eventually. Beckett would want to know what caused the panic attacks, all the facts, and would rack his brain for any instance of having personally contributed to them. Kate would hug her and cry and insist they sit on Raegan's bed and talk for hours. Quiet, gentle Logan would simply ask her if she was okay.

Dad met her eyes, a world of tenderness in his expression. "I'm glad we know now."

"Does Bear know?" Uncertainty tinged Seth's question.

"I'm going to guess he knew before most of us," Beckett answered without nearly as much tease in his voice as Raegan might have expected. Maybe none at all.

"Actually, Bear's probably the only reason anybody knows. He saw me have a panic attack and then proceeded to pester me until I agreed to talk to someone."

Seth grinned. "Sounds like Bear. Doesn't like anyone poking into his business but he'll heckle you about yours with ceaseless determination. Always with good intentions, of course."

Laughter coasted into awkward silence.

"You can talk about him, you know. I won't fall to pieces." There'd been too many tears already. First in her bedroom the night of the shooting. Then again in Sara's sunroom during this week's appointment.

When she'd apologized, when she'd tried to wave it off, Sara's light scold had interrupted. *"You don't have to pretend here, Raegan. If you're hurt, feel it. If you're angry, feel it. If you're miserable, feel it."*

"If I'm all those things and more?"

"Then I'm really glad my freezer's stocked with ice cream." Sara had waited until Raegan pushed out a lone laugh. *"Listen, I'm not encouraging you to wallow. That's not what this is. I'm encouraging you to be honest—not just with me or even yourself, but with God, too. He can handle it. Read the Psalms sometime. David was not one to hold back."*

"And then what? After I get honest, I mean."

"Then you let God start weaving the frayed pieces of

your heart back together in His way in His time. And you keep doing this—you keep talking." Sara had stood. *"Also, I wasn't kidding about that ice cream."*

Even if Bear never walked back into her life again, she'd never stop being grateful for his suggestion that she talk to Sara. Yes, she should've been candid with Dad and everyone else years ago. But even in her stubbornness, God had found a way to nudge her where she needed to be.

"Speaking of Bear," Dad piped in, "I had this thought of how we might spend part of today. That is, assuming the rain lets up."

"By the amount of food on the table, I figured the whole day would be spent eating." Logan grinned as he loaded Charlie's plate with a second pancake. "And recovering from a collective sugar coma."

"Which makes what I'm about to propose all the more fitting. A little physical activity will do us good after this feast." Dad glanced at Raegan. "I was talking to Sara Jaminski the other day—"

Raegan choked on her coffee. "What?"

"Don't look so surprised."

"Did you apologize?"

Kate's fork clinked on her plate. "Apologize for what?"

"For kicking her out of the house, of course." Beckett turned to Raegan. "Wait, so you know why he did that? And you haven't told us?"

"Uh, didn't previous conversation convey that I'm pretty good at keeping quiet about things?"

Logan just looked confused. "Dad kicked somebody out of the house?" He eyed his wife. "I think we might need to move back. We're missing too much."

Dad rapped on the table with his empty coffee mug. "People. Focus. You are all way too caffeinated."

Seth snorted. "*You* made the crazy-strong coffee."

Dad ignored the jibe. "Sara said that Bear called earlier this week to apologize for abandoning the work he was doing on her cabins. Apparently he feels horrible about it."

He would. Raegan returned to twisting her napkin. Bear felt horrible about too many things. If there was an opportunity to feel guilty about something, he took it. Did he even know how to operate without carrying the world on his shoulders?

"Anyway, I thought maybe we could head over to the ranch. If we all worked together for a few hours, we could make some nice progress. Bear already did the hard stuff. He replaced the floors and patched the roofs. I think it's mainly staining wood and cleaning at this point. Putting together new bunks. That kind of thing."

Wow, Dad really had talked to Sara.

"Although I understand if you need to work on the mural instead, Rae."

She shook her head. "I've had this date cleared on the calendar for weeks. No painting for me today." Mom would've liked this—the whole family working together to help someone else.

Besides, it was the one thing she could do for Bear. Even if he didn't know it.

"I'm in."

Moonlight angled in the window of Bear's apartment, dancing dust motes and shadows bumping into the stillness.

After a long day of working at the ranch and then dessert at Seth's restaurant, the rest of the family had dispersed—and Raegan had snuck away to work on the mural. A borrowed portable floodlight had allowed her to keep going after sundown, but when the wind picked up and shook the scaffolding, she'd finally decided to call it a night. Even if a slightly panicked piece of her had tried to insist she go on.

Less than a month now until the festival. After so many setbacks, her hopes of completing the project on time were dwindling. Would she be painting up until the day of? Like Kate with one of her writing deadlines?

The smell of oils mingled with the turpentine she'd used to clean her brushes. She'd only meant to stop by the apartment long enough to stash her mural supplies, but then she'd caught sight of the painting waiting at her easel, the one she'd started the night she'd run away from Bear in the storm. The night she and Sara had sat in this apartment and Raegan had poured out her heart through a river of tears.

So many tears. This morning at breakfast she'd had the thought that there'd been too many tears in recent weeks. But at least some of them had been healing tears.

Anyway, she'd found only the tiniest snatches of time to work on the painting since that night. But the second she'd spotted it tonight, a creativity that hadn't tired despite the late hour urged her to pick up her brushes once more.

Now, nearly four hours later, she stood in front of her easel, hands on her hips, a smile teasing her lips. This was good. It was really, really good.

The canvas presented a field of prairie grass and wildflowers, not all that different from the land that stretched behind J.J.'s Stables, rolling in brushes of gold. And in the middle of the picture stood a young girl in a fuchsia sundress, one arm lifted, the other holding a straw hat in place over flowing hair.

Wasn't just paint that splayed over the canvas. She'd used strips of fabric for the dress, real straw for the girl's hat, using paint to hold and weave in the textures. It'd been an experiment in mixed-media art. And it'd worked.

It'd be the perfect gift for Elise after her surgery next week. If the surgery was successful, she'd be able to see the painting. But even if it wasn't, the variety of textures would allow her to appreciate it in her own way.

"I thought you said no painting for you today."

"Dad?" She spun. She hadn't even heard the door. "It's the middle of the night. Shouldn't you be asleep?"

"It's only been a week since the shooting. Don't expect I'll be sleeping well for awhile. Not without all my kids safe under my roof."

She lifted her paintbrush. "Kate's not under your roof tonight." And Logan wouldn't be either after he headed home to Chicago tomorrow. One of these days Beckett would fly the coop, too.

And Raegan?

Not a clue. Mr. Hill still insisted that artist-genius friend of his could open amazing doors for her, but if she didn't manage to the finish the mural, the man might be wasting a trip.

Dad's attention had turned to her painting. "It's beautiful, Rae."

"It's for Elise. I shouldn't have stayed up so late working on it, though. It'll be morning in a couple hours and I haven't slept and the mural—"

"You'll finish the mural."

"You're a lot surer than I am." Should she warn Mayor Milt? Suggest he have some kind of backup plan if she didn't complete it on time?

"It's a father's job to have confidence in his children. Or, even better, to have confidence that God will help his children." He slipped his arm around Raegan. "It's also a father's job to be proud of his daughter. I couldn't possibly be prouder of you, Raegan. And if your mother were here . . ."

Maybe Raegan was wrong. Maybe there couldn't be too many tears. Maybe it was in the shades and swirls of emotion—the light and the dark, the joy and the grief—that lives entwined and hearts connected. No pretense. Just honesty.

And if honesty meant tears, she had plenty to offer.

"I don't think I'll ever stop missing her, Dad."

"Me neither."

She heard the hurt and the hope in his voice.

"But then, lucky for me, I've got a daughter who—though unique and very much her own person—looks exactly like her."

Raegan dabbed her brush in light blue paint. "Except for the pink hair and eyebrow ring."

And with a flourish, she leaned toward the painting and signed her name in the corner.

"Listen, Rae, about Bear—"

"He had to make a decision, Dad." And she didn't blame him. Missed him, loved him, couldn't imagine that changing. But she didn't blame him.

"I just want to make sure you remember . . ." Dad paused, squeezed her shoulder and glanced at the painting once more. "You have choices, too."

19

"Look at Mayor Milt. It's like he's completely forgotten the only reason Maple Valley is even hosting this thing is because of another town's disaster."

Raegan burst into laughter at Beckett's observation—an astute one, at that. Mayor Milt stood in the middle of the bustling town square, practically preening.

But he had good reason. The Annual Heritage Arts Festival couldn't have possibly come together more perfectly on such short notice. Tables and booths lined the square, with a lavish summer sun and pristine cerulean sky as a backdrop.

A mellow breeze wisped over Raegan's bare skin—the promise of a warm July day having coaxed her into yellow cotton shorts and a tank top. She'd packed a light sweater into the tote she carried over one shoulder just in case.

Beside her, Beckett tipped his sunglasses to the bridge of his nose. "Nervous?"

For the mural's unveiling? Maybe a little, but not nearly as much as she'd thought she might be. It helped that the town had watched the progress of her work these past weeks, their encouragement and approval spurring her on.

And that she'd finally figured out what was missing from her design.

But somewhere in this crowd of people, Mr. Hill strode around with the esteemed Forrester Carlisle Young. For a while, in all the craziness of the shooting and the aftermath of Bear leaving—was it really nearly a month ago already?—she'd almost forgotten about the renowned artist/professor/critic's plans to attend the festival.

Mr. Hill, though, had been eager to remind her. Again and again. Especially in more recent days. And it'd be a lie to say the thought of meeting Young didn't, at the very least, bring a few butterflies to life in her stomach.

"Part nervous," she answered Beckett. "Part starving." She reached into her tote, fingers feeling for the familiar plastic bag. Ah, she had remembered to pack the Twizzlers.

Beckett chuckled. "I should've known." He stopped in front of an abstract painting, splotches of color seeming to spill over the edges of the canvas. "Listen, Rae. It's taken me too long to say this, but—"

She already knew where he was going. "You really don't have to."

"I do. That night when I gave you that article about Bear . . . I don't think I really listened to what you were saying. Anything I've ever done to make you think I only see you as 'the little sister,' I'm really sorry for it."

"Beck—"

"I'm serious. I don't think you realize how many times in my life I've looked up to you." He glanced down at her. "Figuratively, that is."

"Well, you weren't all wrong that night." They started walking again. "Sara says we all tell ourselves stories—about who we are, about the people around us.

And they aren't always true. I think I too often told myself the story that I didn't measure up to the rest of you. That I was the odd one out."

"Pretty sure we've all told ourselves that particular story at one time or another. I know I have. Especially all those years when I refused to come home."

Raegan finished off a piece of licorice. *Home.* Lately she'd begun to expand her definition of the word. Try it on for size in a different way, even if just in her imagination. And, oh, the pictures her mind had painted.

Beckett had asked if she was nervous. *That*—those pictures and ideas swimming around in her brain—those made her nervous. But perhaps nervous was a good thing. It meant you weren't stagnant or stuck. It meant there just might be a leap of faith in front of you if only you were brave enough to take it.

"Hey, speaking of Sara, check it out."

Raegan followed Beckett's pointed finger. Well, now, would you look at that? Dad, ambling along the green, chatting as amicably as could be with one Sara Jaminski.

"Do we know how we feel about this?" Beckett asked.

"I know how I feel—entirely too overjoyed that now we can finally all get back at Dad for spending so much time prying into our love lives."

"Love lives? You actually think . . . ?"

"I think I invited Sara over for dinner a few nights ago and he didn't kick her out when she showed up. Soooo . . ." She tucked the bag of Twizzlers back in her tote as they rounded the corner and the Blaine River came into view. Almost time for the unveiling. "And now, as long as we're talking love lives, I have to ask: When are you going to hurry up and propose—"

"Tomorrow night. At the orchard. With lots of twinkle lights. But if you say a word to Kit or anyone else, I will break into your bedroom and steal every bag of licorice in the place."

"Beck!" She squealed his name, stopping in the middle of the sidewalk.

"Shut up," he hissed, his cheeks reddening. "She's right over there."

Over with the rest of Raegan's family, all gathered on the blocked-off road in front of her tarp-covered mural. Charlie was running circles around Logan while Amelia laughed. Kate and Colt stood with Seth and Ava. Kit, of course. And Dad and Sara were just now approaching.

Before Raegan could start forward again, a pair of skinny arms wrapped around her waist from behind. For a split second, she imagined they were Erin's arms or even Jamie's. Let herself imagine that Bear had come back and—

No. She shook away the fleeting thought and turned instead to see Elise's smiling face. Sunglasses covered her eyes—still sensitive to too much light after her surgery. Her *successful* surgery. No more finding her way in the dark.

Raegan held the girl to her. "Elise Linder, I thought you couldn't come today!"

"I begged Mom and Dad to come home from vacation early. They wanted me to see Mount Rushmore, but I just wanted to see your mural."

Tears pinched Raegan's eyes as they moved toward the crowd once more, Elise chattering about attending Sara's test run of the horse camp in a couple weeks. They joined the others as the crowd grew around them and Mayor Milt took his place on the platform up near the Hay & Feed Store. He'd wanted Raegan to do the honors—pull the rope to lower the tarp and display the mural. But she'd asked if someone else could do it.

Maybe it was silly, but she'd wanted to stand with

her family when the tarp came down. Wanted to gape at the immense blessing this project had become and catalog the whole experience in her heart—ups and downs, frustrations and joys, fear turned to hope, all of it.

And she wanted to treasure these fleeting moments with the people she loved here on the riverfront.

Because it might be a while before she returned.

A sunset in velvet shades of violet and blue gazed upon Bear's walk home. How long had it been since he'd felt this feeling? The simple delight of a simple accomplishment.

CPR refresher course—done.

Which meant he'd be ready for classes when they started in September. Late acceptance into Atlanta Tech had been just the most recent answer to prayer. Nothing near as miraculous as Rio's recovery, of course, but he was grateful all the same.

And since he'd withdrawn his application from the community center position in Brazil, it meant he had time to complete the full paramedic program at Atlanta Tech, rather than just EMT-basic. A second chance at the career that'd never gotten off the ground the first time around. He'd spoken to multiple people at both the college and the Georgia Office of EMS and Trauma about the felonies that would show up on his required background check. In another answer to prayer, it sounded like his record wouldn't ultimately be an issue.

It'd been such an odd mix of difficult and yet liberating to let go of the idea of Brazil. To come to terms with the truth John had laid out so clearly for him during the week he and Elizabeth had spent in Atlanta—that no one was holding Bear to that promise he'd made in prison. That God had never asked him to live out Annie's dream.

That had been his own idea, born out of a desperate, impossible desire to somehow right an unchangeable wrong.

Grace upon grace. It'd become the theme he clung to—when the past tried to pull him back, when his future felt uncertain. When he missed Raegan so much that even breathing felt like a strain on his tattered heart.

Bear stopped in front of the red-brick, two-story home he shared with Rio and Rosa and the kids as of a few weeks ago. Amazingly, it was the church down in Brazil that had made this living situation possible. John and Elizabeth had rallied the troops, taken a collection during a church service. They'd sent it along with an apology that it wasn't more.

But it had been exactly enough for the deposit and first month's rent on this house. White shutters, bright blue front door, towering oak in the front yard. It wasn't fancy or new, but it was nice. *Quaint,* that was the word for it. A word he'd never really thought fit anywhere other than in Maple Valley—certainly not a suburb of Atlanta.

Raegan would approve of this house. She'd like that it was old. She'd say it had character.

It wouldn't have been Bear's first choice to stay in Atlanta, even a suburb far from their childhood neighborhood. But with Rio's physical therapy and a slew of upcoming depositions, they had to stay in the area. At least for the foreseeable future.

Besides, something in Bear needed to stay. Not forever, but for now. Long enough to remember there *had* been happy times here, to find the beauty in the mess instead of chasing a shiny new life elsewhere. Long enough to make sure that if he ever did leave again, he wasn't running away.

And long enough to restore relationships he'd once thought lost for good. He wasn't sure if or when he'd feel ready to contact Dad or his mom and step-dad. He'd wait for God's direction on that. But this extended time with his brother—and with Jamie and Erin—meant more to him than he'd probably ever be able to express.

He'd come to understand and respect Rosa more and more, too. He'd caught glimpses of sorrow on her face now and then when she didn't think anyone was looking. She had her husband and kids back, but her father would eventually go on trial for decades' worth of criminal activity.

Bear nodded to the officer keeping watch on the house from an unmarked car at the curb. At some point, hopefully, the threat of retaliation from one of Inez's few men still on the streets might dissolve. But for now the extra measure of security provided peace of mind about his family's safety.

His family. Never had the words tasted so sweet. Messy and imperfect, but *his.*

Raegan understood, right? When he'd called weeks ago and told her all the reasons he needed to stay, she'd grasped the depth of his conviction, hadn't she?

"I'm not here to fix things or play hero or take over Rio and Rosa's roles as parents. I'm not trying to make up for anything. I'm just trying . . ." To listen, for once. Instead of making a hasty promise or rushing headlong into his own plan, to slow down and pray and do as John had said—look for the crack in the door filled with light.

The light kept leading him to the same place—right here with his family.

And though every day away from Raegan had been

its own kind of difficult, he was discovering there was freedom to be found in following the Spirit's leading. No longer was he obeying the hiss of his guilt or the bellows of his past. Only the whisper in his soul.

Stay. Be a brother to Rio. Be an uncle to Jamie and Erin. Be a friend to Rosa.

Raegan hadn't argued with him. In fact, she'd said very little at all. They hadn't talked since. He kept telling himself it was for the best. Believing it was another matter entirely.

Bear climbed the few cement stairs that led to the front door and let himself into the house. A blast of air conditioning budged into the heat of the July day—and Erin's shriek. "Uncle Bear's home!"

Like every time he returned to the house—usually from the job he'd landed with the same construction company he'd worked for post–high school—Erin launched herself into his arms.

"Oh no," he said the second he sniffed the acrid air. "Who burned what?"

As if he even had to ask. He finally understood all those takeout containers he'd seen in that apartment kitchen his first day back in the States. Cooking—not so much in Rosa's wheelhouse.

Jamie looked up from the couch, gangly legs sprawled on an oversized ottoman and a letter in his lap. From Elise, no doubt. Cute little pen pals, they'd become. Not that he'd dare use the word *cute* to Jamie's face. "I asked Mom if we could order pizza."

Smart kid. "What'd she say?"

"Only if we promise not to tell you she burned the fish."

Ew, fish. Maybe he should be grateful for Rosa's lack of cooking skills. He set Erin down. "I'll do my best not to give it away when I walk in the kitchen. Might have to hold my nose, though."

He was halfway through the dining room when Erin called after him. "Aren't you going to shower, Uncle Bear?"

Had he become that habitual? "Didn't work at the building site today. Not as dirty as usual."

He found Rosa in the kitchen, scraping a charred pan. "Don't say a word, Bear."

"Even if that word is *pizza*? Did you order yet? I'm starving."

"Not yet. Figured you'd need time to clean up first."

"Everybody's concerned about me cleaning up." He held his shirt up to his nose. "Do I smell or something?" Couldn't smell worse than this kitchen.

His petite sister-in-law grinned. Man, it was good to see her like this—none of the frantic alarm she'd worn that night she entrusted Jamie and Erin to him. No more circles under her eyes.

He grabbed a towel from the counter and reached for the pan now dripping on a drying rack. They'd developed an easy rhythm, everyone pitching in with chores, taking turns with meals. Bear and Rosa had coordinated their work schedules to cover caring for Rio and the kids.

And every day, Rio got a little better.

"You don't have to do that, Bear. I may not be able to cook without making a mess, but I'm perfectly capable of cleaning up said mess. Go on upstairs."

Fine, he would. But not to shower. He and Rio had cut off in the middle of a game of Scrabble this morning. Maybe they could finish before the pizza arrived.

He gave both kids high fives as he retraced his steps through the living room and angled onto the carpeted stairway. On the second floor, he trailed past Jamie's bedroom and then Erin's and on toward the bedroom at the end.

He knocked, then entered at Rio's beckoning.

His brother stood in the middle of the room, a five-pound weight in each hand and guilt on his face. "Now, look, before you lose it—"

"You just couldn't wait."

Rio curled his arms. "Two-point-five-pound weights, Bear? I didn't even know those were a thing. They've had me using baby weights for two weeks now. Ridiculous. I think I'm ready to move up."

If Rio had his way, he'd be ready to conquer a 5K. But darn it, was it so hard to listen to his physical therapist? "How'd you even get those in here?"

"It's very convenient having kids, big brother. They love sneaking things for you." He set down the weights. "Besides, I did a whoppin' ten reps. That's it. I don't think my heart's going to give out any time soon. That is, unless Rosa tries forcing fish down my throat one more time."

"Not her fault she saw that headline about heart-healthy food. She's just looking out for you."

"I was shot, Bear. I don't have high cholesterol or blocked arteries." Rio flopped onto the rocking chair in the corner. "And no, I don't want to play Scrabble. I want to go outside and shoot hoops. Throw a baseball around. Could even settle for a walk around the block."

Okay, someone had cabin fever. "The walk we can do."

Rio let out a dramatic sigh. "No. You just got home. You should relax. Go take a nap or something before supper."

"Since when do I take early-evening naps? Rosa wants me to clean up, you want me to nap. I'm not your third child, you know." Bickering with his brother. He'd forgotten how good that felt.

"Says the guy who's been monitoring how much I

sleep and move and eat for weeks."

Bear started for the door. "Fine, no Scrabble."

"Bear?"

He turned to his brother once more.

"Thank you. For everything. I know I've said it a hundred times—"

"Try a thousand."

Rio's eyes—clearer than he'd ever seen them before—shimmered with gratefulness. "I've meant it every time. You keep putting your life on hold. For me, for us."

One hand gripping the edge of the bedroom door, Bear shook his head. "My life isn't on hold, Rio. This *is* my life. And if you ask me, it's an awfully good one."

Lips pressed together, Rio nodded. And with a tap on the doorframe overhead, Bear left the room.

His own bedroom, the largest of the four, was at the other end of the hallway—the only one with an attached bathroom. He'd tried convincing Rosa and Rio to claim it, but they'd insisted he take it. He'd finally agreed, figuring if it made them feel better about the fact that he currently paid the larger half of the rent, then so be it.

But he stopped just outside his closed door. A sliver of light beckoned from underneath the door.

He pushed into the room. Stopped again.

His mystified gaze darted—purple bag at the foot of the bed, steam coming from under the bathroom door, humming coming from inside. *What in the world?*

And when the door opened, the biggest shock of all.

Raegan Walker.

Walking from *his* bathroom into *his* bedroom.

Wearing *his* T-shirt.

20

"Oh, hi, Bear."

Raegan held a towel to her wet hair, squeezing the ends and trying to convince herself that this—showing up so out of the blue—hadn't been the worst idea of her life. A little surprising, perhaps. Possibly bordering on intrusive. But not the worst.

Please don't let it be the worst.

"Oh. Hi. Bear." Bear folded his arms. And then unfolded them. And then did that thing he always did when his mind was racing—rubbed his palms on his scratchy cheeks. "You're . . . *here*. And that's all you have to say?"

She draped the towel over the bathroom doorknob. "No, it's not all I have to say. I was just giving you a chance to say 'hi,' too."

She watched his baffled gaze travel from her straggling hair down to her bare feet and back up again. "Sorry to borrow a shirt. Again. But the airline lost my luggage. I didn't even have a layover and they somehow lost it between Des Moines and Atlanta. All I've got is my carry-on"—she motioned to the bag on the bed—"which is full of paints but no clothes. Wouldn't have had to shower in the first place except this baby on the lap of the person seated next to me felt the need to spit up on me. Twice. Ruined my shirt."

She was talking too fast, wasn't she? Poor Bear looked like he could pass out.

No, poor Bear looked *great*. Every bewildered inch of him. "Maybe you should sit—"

"Maybe you should explain."

"I would've used that other bathroom down the hall, but Rio said it'd be better if I used this one and I figured I should listen to him. By the way, he's a complete carbon copy of you. And Jamie. Or, well, I mean, I guess Jamie's a carbon copy of him. And you."

"Rae—"

"And I know this is awkward—"

One dark eyebrow lifted. "I have a feeling it would've been a lot more awkward if I'd walked in ten minutes earlier."

No point in even trying to resist her blush. Probably going to be a lot more where that warmth came from if she managed to make it through all she'd come to say. And she might as well get to it, because Bear couldn't seem to do anything other than stand in the middle of the room and gape at her.

She crossed to the bed where her carry-on bag sat unzipped. She slid the envelope free. "At least I didn't put this in my suitcase." She moved to Bear and held it out.

"What's this?"

"Open it up."

All he had to do was glance inside to start shaking his head.

Predictable as ever. "Bear—"

"Can't take it."

"Sara asked me to deliver it. She said the deal was if the cabins were ready by July 1, you were due a bonus.

327

The cabins were ready." Thanks to literally every member of her family. They'd gone back multiple times since Mom's birthday. Not that Bear needed to know that.

"Yeah, but I didn't—"

She held up both palms. "If you want to argue, take it up with Sara." They stood close enough now she could smell that faint scent of spiced pine that always seemed to cling to him. She'd taken to wandering down to the basement back at Dad's, imagining she still smelled it even in Bear's absence.

Just like she'd walked past Beckett's room so many times, half expecting to see Jamie and Erin climbing on the bunk beds.

Was Bear honestly this surprised to see her? Did he truly not realize how completely and entirely he'd claimed her heart?

She'd finally begun to imagine a real future for her art. She could envision a life no longer constricted by the fear of panic attacks or constrained by grief. She could even picture making a home somewhere besides Maple Valley.

But she couldn't imagine any of it without Bear.

"Oh, guess what, I figured out what was missing from my mural design."

Bear stuffed the envelope in his pocket. "Huh?"

"The sunflowers. They weren't missing, they were just wrong. In my original design, they were all wrapped around the images of the town, kind of facing inward. But sunflowers follow the sun. They should've been facing out. Away from town."

Those gorgeous darker-than-chestnut eyes of his didn't leave her face.

"Oh, and I added fireflies in, too."

"What are you doing here, Raegan?" The timbre of his voice—soft and rich—had shifted from confusion to something else.

Something hopeful?

"I met this famous artist guy at the art festival. He likes my work—not just the mural, but a couple other pieces I've done, too. Both mixed-media."

"That's great—"

She hurried onward before she could lose her nerve. "He offered to get me into the Rhode Island School of Design, but I asked him if he knew of any art schools in Georgia instead, and it turns out he has a friend at the Art Institute of Atlanta and . . ." She took a breath. "I'm going to check it out and apply and hopefully start during the winter semester."

"Raegan." He stepped forward to lightly touch her arms.

"There's no point in arguing with me, Bear. I know all that stuff you said about not wanting your old life and new life to mix or how you couldn't make a choice between me and Rio or . . . or whatever. But the point is, you don't get to choose this time. Not when it comes to me. I'm taking it out of your hands. I'm staying, whether you like it or not."

By the time the last words pushed free, she was out of breath and out of bravery. Or maybe simply out of restraint. She threw her arms around Bear's waist and hid her face against his neck.

She didn't know how many seconds passed—too many or maybe none at all—before Bear's arms closed around her and his chest rumbled, something between a laugh and a gasp. And his voice, languid and soft against her hair. "Why in the world would I not like it?"

She looked up. "You're not going to tell me to go home?"

He answered her with a kiss that wiped away any speck of doubt about this whole crazy idea—and replaced it with all the assurance she'd ever need. And hope, so much hope. He kissed her until her knees went weak and she was pretty sure she was the one who needed to sit now and—

He broke away too abruptly. "Wait a second, you flew? By yourself?"

"I'm almost twenty-seven, Bear." She spoke between kisses on his cheek. "I'm perfectly capable."

He laughed and held her away. "But . . . the panic attacks. You said you never travel alone because . . ."

"I didn't before. I do now." Because now she had tools. She had exercises. She even had a medication Sara had prescribed. She wouldn't need it often, but it could help when she knew she was walking into situations that might trigger an attack. Sara had referred her to a therapist in Atlanta, too. She had that airline voucher Beckett had returned to her, too.

But more than anything, she had the kind of healing, honest, accepting love—a perfect love—that drove away her fears.

Bear pulled her close again. "Well, now I know why everyone was trying to get me to my room. Which reminds me, there's only one problem with all of this. We only have four bedrooms—and they're all full. Not like your dad's house."

She laughed with her forehead against his chin. "You've attempted to solve much larger problems than this, Bear McKinley. This one has a fairly obvious solution." She tipped her head to meet his gaze.

"Rather forward of you, Raegan Walker." The light danced in his eyes.

"Don't get any funny ideas. I'll require a change in marital status."

"Make that *really* forward."

He kissed her forehead, her nose, her lips. And then, to the tune of her oh-so-very happy sigh, he whispered in her ear. "Welcome home, Raegan Walker."

Epilogue

New Year's Eve

"Showing up late to Seth's wedding and my wedding?" Kate shrugged. "Fine. But showing up late to his own wedding?"

The brassy swing of a Glenn Miller tune lilted over the speakers in the barn-turned-community-center at the Valley Orchard. What had to be thousands of white twinkle lights were draped around ceiling beams and strung over every doorway and window.

And outside the windows, snowfall glistened under moonlight.

Raegan met Bear's gaze across the wedding party table. Everyone had abandoned their assigned seats forever ago, but too many family members had crowded around before she could claim the chair next to Bear.

So for the past half an hour, she'd settled for watching her handsome husband fidget with the bow tie that was clearly coming far too close to strangling him to death.

Beckett, his arms around Kit sitting in his lap, rolled his eyes. "I wasn't late for any one of those—especially not today's. I wasn't early, I can grant you that. But I wasn't even a second late."

"Beck, you barely beat me down the aisle." Kit's

331

honey-blond hair spilled from an updo long since undone by hours of dancing.

Beckett stood, keeping hold of Kit lest she topple off his lap. "You all exaggerate way too much and obviously it's a bad influence on my wife. So I'm taking her away—to the dance floor."

Kate stood, as well, holding her hand out toward Colton. "Come on, you. I'm not so huge yet that I can't dance."

She might not be huge, but she was definitely showing. Raegan hadn't done nearly a good enough job hiding her gasp when she'd first seen her sister after getting into town just before Christmas. Might not have been so surprising if she'd seen Kate at Thanksgiving.

But she and Bear had used that holiday for a different trip. A late honeymoon to South America to see the church Bear had helped build. From there, they'd gone on to a resort in Costa Rica with views Raegan could spend a lifetime painting. That bonus from Sara had come in awfully handy.

Kate pulled Colton toward the dance floor now, waving at Seth and Ava, who hadn't left the floor since the music began.

Logan leaned over at Raegan's side. "You look content, Rae."

She turned to her brother. His tie was crooked—of course—and his eyes filled with knowing. "Content is the perfect word."

And it fit like it never had ever before. Before, contentment had been a costume. Something she dressed up in to convince everyone she was fine.

I'm fine. I'm fine. I'm fine.

But she'd blazed past *fine* months ago and now, life was fuller and richer in a way she couldn't have described if she tried. She might come close to capturing the feeling in a painting. Like Logan could in a speech or a song.

But surely even her most vibrant colors on her largest canvas couldn't convey the full depth of her joy.

No, life hadn't suddenly become something only ever easy and light. There were still the hard days. The moments of missing Mom. Adjustments to living in Atlanta, being away from her family. Even a hefty dose of nerves about starting school in a couple weeks.

Plus, Luiz Inez's trial hadn't even started yet. That would bring extra stress to their household.

But the security of Bear's arms . . .

The peace of knowing she was right where she was supposed to be . . .

The faithfulness of God, who'd loved her all this time . . .

It all added up to contentment. Pure and sturdy and unbreakable.

"Well." Logan leaned back in his chair. "I should find my wife and daughter. Amelia's probably letting Charlie have a third piece of cake." He stood and tousled Raegan's unruly hair before strolling away.

She followed her brother's movements, grinned when he found his girls exactly where he'd known he would. Amelia reached up to straighten his tie and Charlie smeared frosting-covered fingers over his jacket when he swung her into his arms.

"Finally, I can sit by my wife."

Five months married to Bear McKinley and just the sound of his voice was still enough to turn her thoughts to mush. "Are you here to ask me to dance?"

"Better." His whisper against her cheek sent goose-bumps over her arms. "Let's get out of here."

"What? It's not even eleven. This thing's going to go 'til at least midnight."

"And we'll be back by the time it's the new year. Promise. Got something to show you."

"But—"

He pulled her to her feet and immediately tugged her to his side. "No arguments, Mrs. McKinley."

Cheeky man. He knew she was incapable of arguing when he called her that.

He nabbed her coat from a rack as they passed, but she stopped him before he could nudge her outside. "Bear." She pointed to where Dad and Sara Jaminski swayed on the dance floor. "He looks so happy."

As if he'd heard her, Dad's eyes caught hers. He winked.

She winked back.

And then let Bear tow her into the winter cold. He helped her into her coat as snowfall dusted every surface in sight—Bear's eyelashes, best of all. Could he really be even handsomer today than the day they'd married in that sweltering courthouse in Atlanta?

And how could he read her mind so completely perfectly? "Do you regret it at all?" he asked. "Eloping? Not getting any of this?" He swept his hand behind him—toward the music-filled reception.

"Are you kidding? I can appreciate a pretty event as much as anyone, but I wanted you and you alone."

He wrapped his arms around her, walking her backward toward their car in the lot while showering her cheeks with kisses. "Guess it's a good thing that's what you got, then."

She giggled until he reached behind her to open her car door, and minutes later, the warmth of the heater spread over her as Bear steered them toward town. "You going to give me any kind of clue as to where we're going?"

"And spoil the surprise?"

But it wasn't hard to figure it out, not when he bypassed Main Avenue and turned instead onto the road that traced the ice-glazed river. A blanket of snow covered its sloping banks and glittered under lamplight. Did he think the mural would look that much different at night? They'd already come by to see it days ago.

Still, he parked across the street and rounded the car to open her door. She thought he might lead her toward the old building. Maybe he meant to sneak them inside again.

But no, he simply held her hand and turned her until she faced the brick structure. "Well?"

"Well what? Are you waiting for me to critique my own mural or something?"

He chuckled. "No. I just want to know what you think of your Christmas present."

"My . . . Christmas present?"

"I know it's a little late, but with the excitement of the wedding and family constantly around, I had a hard time finding the right moment. Plus, it wasn't even finalized until a few days ago."

She turned to him. "I don't understand."

He reached into his pocket and came up with a crinkled envelope. He pulled out a folded paper and handed it to her. Her attention hooked first on the word at the top: *Deed*. And then lower, squeezed in typewriter font between a jumble of legalese: *Raegan Walker McKinley*.

She looked from the paper to the building to Bear. "You *bought* the Hay & Feed Store?"

"For such a crazy-low amount you wouldn't even believe it. My old apartment finally sold, so I used that money. Despite your masterpiece of a mural, Mayor Milt is convinced no business is ever going to move in. So . . . it's yours."

"I . . . you . . . *why?*"

"I think with some renovation it'd make an amazing art studio."

An art studio. He wanted to give her an art studio. "But we don't live here."

"Not now we don't. But that's fine. We don't have the money to fix it up yet anyway." He plucked the paper from her hands, refolded it, placed the envelope in his pocket. "But we both know we'll end up back in Maple Valley eventually, right? After we're done with school? Jamie and Erin talk about Iowa so much, I doubt it'd take all that much to convince Rio and Rosa to make a change, too. When it's time, the building will be waiting for you."

She couldn't even feel the cold anymore. Nor could she see through her tears. "Bear McKinley."

"I will never get tired of hearing you say my name."

Under the glow of the streetlamp and the swirling snow, she circled her arms around his neck. "Guess it's a good thing I'll never get tired of saying it." She kissed his warm lips and then proved her own point. "Bear McKinley. Bear McKinley. Bear McKinley."

And she laughed.

THE END

Acknowledgments

No, I don't want to do it! I don't want to admit this Walker series is over. And if I write the *Acknowledgements* page, that'll mean it's over . . . so, no, I won't do it!

Sorry. I'll stop being stubborn now.

But seriously, I love this fictional family probably more than is reasonable . . . and writing this final book in the series heightened every emotion I've ever felt for them. Not because I think they're the greatest characters ever written, but because writing about them changed me. Time and again, God used the Walkers to whisper to my heart the things I needed to hear. And I'll never stop being grateful to Him.

I'm also so thankful to the friends and family who a) don't think I'm crazy for my irrational character love or b) if they do, don't tell me and c) helped me along the way as this last Walker book took shape:

Mom and Dad—You are the best ever and that is all there is to it and I don't even know what more to say other than *I love you* and *thank you* and I think it might be that box of Reece's Puffs that helped me finally write the final scenes.

My siblings, Grandma and Grandpa, and my extended family—I will never stop being grateful for your love, encouragement and prayers.

Charlene Patterson—This story absolutely would not be what it is without your editing expertise. Thank you so much.

Jenny Zemanek—This cover! This cover! I adore it, and I'm grateful to you for visually capturing the heart of this story.

Susan May Warren, Rachel Hauck, Beth Vogt—I think I emailed all three of you at various points throughout this story asking for help and you always came through. Thank you. And Courtney Walsh, all those voxes where you let me go on and on about how this story was taking me soooo long to write . . . you are awesome, that is all.

My coworkers at Hope Ministries—You guys always indulge my author-y anecdotes, and I love getting to hang out with you every M-F. Thanks bunches for all your support! Thanks, especially, to Terri Simmons for being such an awesome proofreader.

Readers—Every time I write a book, I feel like I'm putting my heart into your hands and it honestly scares me half to death. But at the same time, it's turned out to be one of the most rewarding things in my life. That you're willing to take the time to read these books and, in many cases, write reviews, send reader emails, interact with me on social media—it just means the world. Thank you for allowing me to be vulnerable through my characters . . . thank you for joining me on the journey . . . and just . . . *thank you.*

About the Author

MELISSA TAGG is a former reporter, current nonprofit grant writer and total Iowa girl. She's the author of the Walker Family series, the Where Love Begins series, and the Enchanted Christmas novella collection. Her books have made both the Publisher's Weekly Top Ten and Amazon.com bestselling lists. When she's not writing, she can be found hanging out with the coolest family ever, watching old movies, and daydreaming about her next book. Melissa loves connecting with readers at www.melissatagg.com.

You Might Also Enjoy

FREE prequel e-novella
Three Little Words

A charming story of romance between polar opposites in this exciting introduction to Melissa Tagg's series about the charismatic Walker family and the endearing town of Maple Valley!

Walker Family Book One
From the Start

Kate Walker writes romance movie scripts for a living, but she stopped believing in "true love" long ago. Could a new friendship with former NFL player Colton Greene restore her faith?

Walker Family Book Two
Like Never Before

Widowed speechwriter and single dad Logan Walker never expected to inherit his hometown newspaper. But the change of pace, a town mystery, and working alongside scrappy reporter Amelia Bentley, might be exactly what he needs.

Walker Family Book Three
Keep Holding On

Beckett Walker hasn't stepped foot in Maple Valley in years. There's no getting past the painful memories—especially those involving his former best friend, Kit Danby—and there's every chance he'll be arrested as soon as he shows his face. Which is exactly what happens when he finally returns.

Other books by Melissa Tagg

Made To Last

Here to Stay

One Enchanted Christmas

One Enchanted Eve

"A Maple Valley Romance" in the *Right Where We Belong* collection

Coming in November 2017: *One Enchanted Noel*